TRANSHUMAN CHRONICLES

COMPLETE TRILOGY WITH BONUS PREQUEL

STEVEN WYBLE

First published by Slaughter County Press 2020

This book is entirely a work of fiction. The names, characters and incidents portrayed in it are the work of the author's imagination. Any resemblance to actual persons, living or dead, events or localities is entirely coincidental.

First edition

ISBN: 978-1-7338008-3-9

SlaughterCountyPress.com

CONTENTS

DUPLICATE MINDS

BOOK 1

ONE

Rajeev Sundaram's eyes flickered to life and saw only white.

He blinked, but his eyelids felt odd. Nonexistent. Even so, when he closed them, the blinding whiteness blinked out of existence. He kept them closed—the light was nauseating.

What's the last thing I remember? He racked his brain, but it was no use. His mind was foggy and he couldn't think of any reason he'd be … wherever he was.

He opened his eyes again. Still nothing but white. But he realized now that he was lying on his back looking up at a clinical white ceiling, like one would find in a hospital.

Maybe he *was* in a hospital. But he didn't remember getting into an accident or having a heart attack. But then again, he wouldn't remember something like that, would he?

He sat up and scanned the room. What he saw appeared to confirm his suspicions. The room's walls were as blindingly white as its ceiling. In front of him sat a stainless steel sink similar to ones he'd seen in hospital rooms; to its right was a door that presumably led to the rest of the hospital. Against the wall to his right sat a small wooden chair with navy blue padding.

There was one peculiarity: Above the door was a circular green light. As Rajeev gazed at the steady green glow, it suddenly began flashing red. He didn't know what that meant, but in his experience, flashing red lights were rarely good things. A wave of panic washed over him, but he suppressed it. Panicking wouldn't help anything and besides, he didn't know for sure what the red light meant. He wasn't going to wait around to find out, though.

His legs felt odd as he dangled them over the edge of the hospital bed. It was like he didn't quite know how to control them. He wondered if he'd been in a coma and his leg muscles had atrophied.

Before he could stand and put his theory to the test, the door swung open and a short, rotund man walked through the door. He carried himself with authority, but his smooth, light-brown skin betrayed his youth. He wore a long, white lab coat, which made Rajeev think he must be a doctor.

The men stared at each other for a long moment, as if each of them were dumbfounded by the presence of the other. The doctor broke the silence.

"You're awake," he said.

Rajeev tilted his head. "No shit."

The words felt strange coming out of his mouth. In fact, his mouth itself felt strange, like he barely had to move it to form the words he wanted to say. And the sound of the words leaving his lips … there was a slight buzz to it, like something out of a nightmare.

"What happened to me?" Rajeev asked, a hint of panic creeping into his voice.

The doctor flashed a reassuring smile. His face was cherubic, devoid of facial hair, and he wore a pair of thick-framed black glasses over his chocolate brown eyes. He reminded Rajeev of his brother, Ajay.

"You're in my laboratory at Next Level Technologies," the man said. He pushed his glasses back up his nose as he spoke.

"This is a laboratory? I thought it was a hospital."

The man—perhaps not a doctor after all—nodded.

"It's a medical facility within the laboratory. Uh, let me ask you …" He reached into his coat pocket and pulled out a slim device that looked to Rajeev like an oversized, ultrathin tablet. "What's the last thing you remember?"

"Nothing that explains how I got here. I've been trying to remember ever since I woke up. No luck."

The man made a note on the tablet. "That's not surprising," he said without looking up. "But what about your long-term memory? Do you remember who you are?"

"Of course. I'm Rajeev Sundaram."

"Very good … and your family? Are you married? Kids?"

"Yeah, I'm married. Have been for twenty-five years, with two kids, a boy and a girl. Listen, I don't mean to interrupt your evaluation, but can you tell me what's going on? I'm still completely in the dark here."

The man looked up from his tablet, a pitying look in his eyes. "I realize this all must be quite disorienting for you, and I apologize. You were gone for a long time."

So he *had* been in a coma. That explained the weird, dissociative sensations he was experiencing. But that left one very obvious question.

"How long was I out?"

At this, the man hesitated. "A very long time. Let's leave it at that for—"

"How long?" Rajeev interjected, his tone insistent.

Again, the man hesitated. His reluctance to answer the question alone made Rajeev's heart sink.

"Stop stalling and tell me how long I've been under. I have a right to know."

The man sighed and nodded. "I'm sorry. It's just ... as you can imagine, this is difficult. You were in a coma for fifteen years, Rajeev."

Rajeev froze, paralyzed by what he'd just been told. *Fifteen years?* Impossible. That would make him, what ... fifty-four years old? That would put Sarah somewhere in her late forties. Dev and Mira would both be well out of high school. He brought his hand to his face, but ... something was wrong with it.

He held the appendage in front of his eyes and marveled at his ... was that skin? It was rubbery, stiff. *This doesn't look like my arm*, he thought. *Unless my muscles have atrophied ... it's so skinny.*

"Mr. Sundaram?"

The man's voice broke Rajeev out of his perplexed reverie. He lowered his arm and scrunched his eyebrows in frustration. "There's no way I've been in a coma for fifteen years," he said.

The man gave a knowing look and nodded his head once. "Look, I know it's difficult. But—"

"What's wrong with my arm?" Rajeev interrupted.

"Ah. Yes, about that—"

"I don't feel like myself. I don't feel ... normal."

"That's not unusual. If I can just explain—"

"Bring me a mirror."

"Mr. Sundaram, if I may—"

"Bring me a mirror, dammit!"

The man sighed, but his face grew stern. "I will bring you a mirror, but not before I have a chance to explain a few things to you."

Rajeev wasn't eager to wait, but he didn't think he had much of a choice. "I'm beginning to think I wasn't in a coma at all."

"You *were* in a coma," the man said, his patience beginning to fray, if only slightly. "You were in a car accident. A bad one. When they brought you into the hospital, you were barely responsive. The doctors managed to restart your heart, but you were comatose."

"For fifteen years."

The man nodded. "For fifteen years."

"And no one tried to pull the plug after all that time?"

"You didn't have a DNR. Your family didn't know exactly what your wishes were and they held out hope you'd come out of it, or that some new medical technology would bring you back."

Rajeev nodded. "But it must have been expensive to keep me here. My family isn't rich."

The man shrugged. "They found a way. And here you are. Their hope wasn't misplaced."

"And yet they're not here. It looks like they've moved on."

"I wouldn't say that. They visited you almost every day, in the beginning. Naturally, the visits dropped off over the years, but they've never stopped coming. You're not allowed visitors currently, anyway."

"But ... this isn't a hospital. It's a lab."

The man nodded. "That's correct."

"So if I've been in a coma all this time, why am I in a lab and not a hospital?"

The man frowned and crossed his arms. "I've been working my way up to that. One of the things we do here at Next Level is help people in situations just like yours, Rajeev."

The man's insistence on using Rajeev's first name, as if they were best friends and not total strangers, was beginning to wear on his nerves. There was a slight edge to his voice when he spoke next.

"So in fifteen years time, you've figured out how to cure comas, have you?"

The man's face fell. He grabbed the chair, dragged it in front of Rajeev and sat down.

"Not exactly," he said. "Medical science has made some

progress in treating comatose patients. But cases such as yours —persistent vegetative states with no apparent end in sight— require more innovative solutions."

"So how'd you wake me up?"

The man's brow furrowed. "Well, that part may be difficult for you to comprehend, given the state of technology at the time of your accident. Specifically, the state of, ah … robotics."

"Robotics?"

"Yes. That's our primary area of study." He sighed deeply. "I'll be frank. Things looked bleak for you, Rajeev. Drastic measures had to be taken, and your family figured it was best to—"

"I'm not sure I like where this is going," Rajeev interrupted. He began reviewing all of the odd sensations he'd had since waking up. The disorientation, the difficulty moving, the unsettling feeling that he was having an almost-out-of-body experience … it was all pointing toward a reality he didn't want to accept.

"We've developed a technology that gives patients in dire circumstances a second chance," the man said. His words sounded like a rehearsed sales pitch. "When the mind or body is so damaged that conventional medical treatments aren't enough, we've created a way to provide the patient with a new body … and a new mind."

A wave of panic shot through Rajeev's body; his mind raced. "Are you saying what I think you're saying?"

The man nodded gravely. "I think so."

"Then say it," Rajeev spat. "Stop dancing around it and tell me outright what you've done."

"Mr. Sundaram … we've duplicated your mind, your consciousness, and placed it in a state-of-the-art roboticized body."

"You're saying I'm a *robot*."

The man nodded. "Yes," he said. "Well, an android, technically. But you're still *you*. It's just your body that's artificial."

Rajeev's mind reeled—whirred? He stretched his arm out before him and studied it. He saw now that the unnaturally rubbery skin that had looked so alien to him was, in fact, rubber ... or some material similar to it. Now that he knew what he was looking at, he recognized the crude facsimile of the human body for what it was.

"Bring me that mirror," Rajeev barked. "Now."

The man frowned, but retrieved a hand mirror from a drawer below the sink.

"Here," he said, his hand outstretched. Rajeev snatched the mirror out of his hand, but took a deep breath before holding it up to his face. He was sure he wasn't going to like what he was about to see, but he'd have to face this new reality sometime; might as well be now. He lifted the mirror to his face, and gasped.

The face staring back at him wasn't quite human, but neither was it quite what he thought of as robotic. It wasn't metallic, but rather coated in the same rubbery approximation of skin coating his arms. The shape of his face was far flatter than that of any human, and his "eyes" were made up of two oval photosensors. A slight mound served as a nose, but it was nonfunctional—he realized for the first time that he couldn't smell—and his mouth was little more than a thin horizontal slit cut into his faux-skin.

The face staring back at him, he thought, was the visage of a demon.

"I know this is going to take some getting used to," the man said. "I want to assure you that you *will* acclimate to your new body. Everyone always does, and I don't see why you should be an exception."

"I don't see how anyone could get used to living like a tin can."

"You're still you," the man insisted. "You're still Rajeev Sundaram. You're just in a different vessel."

Rajeev shook his head. "I can't wrap my head around this. I'm not sure I'll ever fully comprehend what's been done to me." He looked down at his hands, turning them back and forth, disturbed by how alien they looked and felt. He sighed, the first sign that he was beginning to resign himself to his fate. "So are you a doctor, or what?"

"No. Not in the sense that you mean, anyway. I have doctorates in both mechanical and software engineering."

"That makes sense, I guess. What's your name, anyway?"

The man didn't answer right away. The authority he'd exuded since entering the room suddenly evaporated. He hung his head sheepishly, then raised his eyes to look directly into Rajeev's. "Don't you recognize me?" he asked softly, like a child addressing his—

Rajeev caught his breath—or at least, that's what it felt like, despite his lack of lungs. As he studied the man's face, he knew the realization was correct, and he couldn't believe he hadn't seen it sooner.

"Dev?"

The man offered an awkward smile. "Hi, dad."

TWO

He parks the car, but doesn't go inside right away. He's been driving all day and he knows the second he walks through the front door, he will be bombarded. Which isn't an entirely bad thing, but he needs a few moments to himself.

He pulls his phone off its windshield mount and scrolls through his social media feeds. He watches some funny cat videos until he begins to feel guilty for spending so much time alone in the car while his wife and kids are waiting for him inside. He sighs, shoves the phone in his pocket, and gets out of the car.

He avoids eye contact with neighbors as he makes his way to his house. A trash bag rests on the welcome mat, and he grumbles to himself as he grabs it and walks it back to the trash can before returning.

The instant he walks through the door, he's the star of the house. A chubby nine-year-old boy speeds out of the back bedroom and immediately latches onto his leg. "Dad!"

Rajeev chuckles. "Hello, Dev." He tousles the boy's hair, just as a twelve-year-old girl walks toward him, arms outstretched. He hugs her, marveling at how fast she's growing. "Mira, you need to stop growing so much. I'm going to come home from work next week and find out you're getting married and moving out of the house!"

A woman emerges from the kitchen, her hair blonde and curly, her eyes blue and bright, but tired.

"Give your father a minute to himself, kids," she says gently, but with authority. "He's been working all day and needs a moment to rest."

He takes the brief respite as an opportunity to plop himself onto the couch, but he knows the moment won't last. Sure enough, as soon as he's kicked off his shoes, Dev jumps onto the couch beside him, looking up at his dad as if he's his whole world.

"Guess what we did at school today?" he asks excitedly.

"What?" Rajeev asks, trying to muster enough enthusiasm to match his son's.

"We made a computer program!"

"You did! Wow!" He's hamming it up, but he is genuinely impressed; they never taught anything like that when he was in school.

"Uh-huh," Dev says, nodding his head vigorously. "We made a calculator program. It was really cool! I want to be a computer programmer when I grow up."

"That's a good goal, Dev. Computer programmers can make a lot of money. If you study hard, I'm sure you can make your dream come true."

"Really?"

"Yes. If you study, and learn, and work hard, there's no limit to what you can accomplish."

RAJEEV'S QUESTIONS WERE TOO NUMEROUS TO COUNT, but Dev insisted they retire to his office before discussing things further. Rajeev tried to climb down from the bed, but struggled to keep his balance. Dev brought his finger to his ear as if he were activating an invisible earpiece.

"Henry, could you please bring us a walker? Thank you."

"A walker? Dev, your old man isn't *that* old."

Dev chuckled. "Remember, fifteen years have gone by. Which is actually beside the point; technically, you're not even a day old. You've been *reborn*, dad, and it's only to be expected that you'll need to relearn some basic motor functions—like walking."

The door opened and a young man in a white polo shirt and khaki pants wheeled in a steel-gray walker. Dev took the walker and patted the man on the shoulder.

"Thank you, Henry."

"Anything else I can do for you, Mr. Sundaram?"

"That will be all, Henry."

The man nodded and left, and Dev carried the walker over to his father.

Rajeev reached out his arms and curled his new fingers around either handle. With a firm grip, he pushed down on the walker and stood.

He stumbled at first, but Dev helped steady him. He waited until Rajeev had fully regained his balance, then stepped away.

"There's no rush, dad. Take it slow—one step at a time."

Rajeev knew he couldn't do it any other way, even if he'd wanted to. Slowly, he lifted his left foot. It shook and trembled, and would have looked like the leg of someone with Parkinson's disease if it hadn't looked so downright mechanical, like some kind of industrial machine on the fritz. But the walker kept him upright, and he managed to set his foot back on the ground, a little farther than where it had started.

He repeated the process with his right foot, then again with the left, again and again, until he finally made his way across the room and stood directly in front of the door.

"Terrific, dad," Dev said. "You're doing an amazing job—especially so soon after activation."

Activation. Rajeev felt like he was in a fever dream. He offered his son only a low grunt in response.

He shuffled through the doorway and found himself in a hallway that looked far more industrial than the sterile, white patient room would have suggested. The walls, floor and ceiling were all constructed of the same dull gray concrete, and large metal ductwork hung from the ceiling.

"This really *isn't* a hospital," Rajeev muttered.

"No, it isn't. In fact, much of the work we do is for the Department of Defense."

After an agonizing ten minutes of shuffling down the hallway with the walker, Rajeev and Dev found themselves at an elevator. Dev held the door open as Rajeev hobbled inside.

Once the doors slammed shut, Dev reached past his father and pressed his thumb against a pad adjacent to the floor buttons. A green LED lit up when the scan was validated and he pressed the button marked "65"—the top floor.

Rajeev whistled. "All the way on the top floor? You must be pretty high up … literally *and* figuratively."

Dev nodded and flashed an awkward smile. "It's my company."

If Rajeev's eyes had been capable of widening, they would have done so. "This is *your* company?"

He was impressed. The boy he remembered—the boy he'd known what felt like yesterday—had been bright and intelligent, but far from ambitious. That wasn't unexpected; young boys goof off and play around with their friends as young boys are wont to do. But clearly there had been a spark in the boy he hadn't noticed if he had created all *this*.

Before his son could explain further, the elevator doors opened. Dev held the door open again and beckoned his father to exit.

"I'll explain everything, but come on out and have a seat first."

The elevator had opened directly into Dev's office. It was a stark contrast to both the sterility of the patient room and the starkness of the hallways.

It reminded Rajeev of the study of an old academic, but with a modern twist. An antique oak desk stood to the right side. An ornate oriental rug was laid out on the hardwood floor. But the walls were bare, and there were only three of them; the fourth, behind the desk, was made up of a floor-to-ceiling window that offered an expansive view of the Chicago skyline. But it wasn't the skyline Rajeev remembered. It was larger … taller, taking up more of the empty sky. And it was newer—the skyline of a young, vibrant innovation hub, not the dilapidated, rundown city he'd known all his life.

"Come, have a seat," Dev said, pulling an office chair in front of his desk. He helped his father to it, and then steadied him as he relinquished his grip on the walker and lowered himself onto the chair. Once his father was seated he walked around to the other side of the desk and sat in his own chair.

"So," he said, tapping his fingers against the desktop, "I imagine you have many questions."

"That's an understatement."

"I'll try to explain as much as I can. If you still have questions afterward, I'll do my best to answer them."

"Fair enough. Let's start with the accident."

Dev nodded. "Very well. You were in a motor vehicle accident. It wasn't your fault. A drunk driver swerved into your lane and pushed you off the road."

"Did I have a—"

"A passenger? Yes. They died, unfortunately. The family sued the ridesharing company and received a significant settlement. You survived the accident, but ended up in a coma."

"That doesn't explain the tin-can body."

"Right. I was just getting to that." He clasped his hands together as he continued. "As I mentioned earlier, you remained comatose for the past fifteen years. But we all held out hope for you, dad. We sold the house to pay for the life support and all your medical care. It bought us a couple years."

"And then what?"

"Having you gone was a huge distraction at first. My grades

slipped. I considered dropping out altogether. But it occurred to me that nobody was doing anything to help you, to bring you back to us, and I realized it was up to me. That maybe *I* could find a way to bring you back. It gave me a renewed focus at school. My grades improved and I got a scholarship that paid all my college tuition. That's where I began tinkering with an idea that I thought could help people like you … and people like me, with loved ones who were taken from them far too soon."

Rajeev looked down at his artificial body.

"Putting us in tin cans."

Dev tilted his head. "You know, there isn't actually a single ounce of tin in your new body. In fact, most of the outer material is made of silicone."

"I noticed. But you got the color wrong. I look like a white man. Although 'man' is probably too generous."

Dev chuckled. "It's just a prototype. Hence the somewhat unusual look. But as the technology develops, we'll be able to put you in increasingly realistic bodies."

"So explain to me exactly what this technology is."

"Well, I knew I'd never be able to make any headway in the medical field. My natural talents have always been in engineering. So I wondered how I could bring you out of a coma with an engineering solution rather than a medical one. Your brain wasn't functioning properly and because of that, your body was useless as well. To bring you back, I decided I'd have to create not just a new body, but also a new brain."

"But how is that even possible?"

"It wasn't easy. To start, we mapped your brain activity. Although your brain wasn't properly functioning, it served as both the blueprint and the foundation of the new mind we were to create. But because it wasn't completely functional, we had to fill in the gaps. That's where my team and I had to get creative. We began by collecting all the information on you we could—public records, news reports, your personal journals and other writings. We created a bot to crawl your social media and other online activity. We also interviewed anyone we could find who'd known you, from lifelong friends to passing acquaintances. When we'd collected every available piece of data we could find on Rajeev Sundaram, we fed it to a proprietary, machine-learning algorithm that—I'm sorry, I'm going too fast, aren't I?"

Rajeev wondered how his son could tell he'd lost him. He didn't have nearly the same range of facial expression he used to. Maybe his son had programmed a tell into this rust bucket of a body?

"I was following until you mentioned 'machine learning,'" he said. "What is that?"

Dev nodded. "It was a technology in its infancy at the time of your accident, but great strides have been made in the fifteen years since. Basically, we designed an artificial intelligence, an autonomous computer program, that can process information and learn from it, much like humans."

"So you taught this … computer person … about me?"

"That's the gist of it, yeah. Our AI took the brainscan and used all the data it had gathered to make educated guesses to fill in all the gaps."

"So you made a copy of my brain and then … what? What did you do with it?"

Dev frowned. He looked uncomfortable as he answered. "Well, dad, you … you *are* that copy."

Rajeev's blood ran cold. No, his—what? Hydraulic fluid? Regardless, his son's words startled and frightened him.

"What do you mean?"

"Our algorithm took what it learned about your mind from the brainscan, filled in the gaps with all the data we'd collected, and spat out a copy of your mind—your consciousness, your *soul* —as close to the original as possible. And that consciousness is *you*. We placed it in the body you find yourself in now."

Rajeev's mind reeled. *No. This isn't possible.* He had memories.

Memories of his wife, son and daughter. Of family dinners and vacations. Moments of laughter, anger, reconciliation. These had been real moments—not crude copies, but real experiences that had been etched into the fabric of his soul.

He remembered even farther back: Leaving Mumbai when he was just three years old. The memories were faint, but he remembered walking the bustling city streets with his parents, the smell of hearty street foods, like Panipuri, Vada Pav and Bhelpuri, wafting into his nostrils and making his mouth water, and taxis and rickshaws bustling down the streets. He remembered saying goodbye to it all, boarding a plane with his mother and father and listlessly trying to entertain himself on the seventeen-hour flight to the United States.

These were not counterfeit memories. They were *his*. He remembered them; he'd *lived* them. His son was mistaken or, worse, lying.

"Dad?" Dev furrowed his brow. Rajeev had been silent for nearly a full minute. "I know this must be rather disconcerting news for you. It raises all kinds of ornery philosophical questions—"

"No." Dev's lips clasped tight at his father's forceful exclamation. There was a ferocity to the word that neither of them had expected. But now that Rajeev had verbalized the turmoil taking place in his mind, he couldn't stop. "I know who I am. I'm not some—some *carbon copy* of myself. I know who I am. You're trying to deceive me and it's reprehensible."

"But dad, that's exactly it! You *are* you, *regardless* of whether or not you're a copy. We've proven that here! What does a person truly consist of but their experiences, their memories, their particular way of thinking and perceiving the world around them? We made a copy of all those things and the result is indistinguishable from the 'original' Rajeev Sundaram. You are more tangibly Rajeev Sundaram than the lifeless, unconscious husk on life support at Northwestern Memorial."

"Wait—what?"

Dev fell silent, realizing he'd gotten ahead of himself and revealed too much, too soon.

"Your old body—it was only a vessel, dad. You are so much more than that. All of us are."

"Can I see it?"

There was a beat. "See what?"

"My body."

Dev hesitated. "I thought you were tracking with me. The whole point is that you've moved on to a new body ... one that may not seem like all that much right now, but is upgradable. Customizable. Your old body is useless."

"I don't expect to go *in* my old body. But I'd like to say good-bye. For closure. You can't know what it's like to have an out of body experience like the one I've found myself in since I woke up."

There was a long silence between them. Dev dragged out his words, as if he didn't really want to be uttering them.

"Unfortunately, as soon as you awakened here, we notified the hospital and told them to take you off life support. Your body is probably on its way to the morgue right now."

"Dammit. I just wanted—"

"You could still see the body," Dev interjected. "It's a bit unusual, but if it would help you attain closure ..."

"That would be wonderful. Thank you, Dev."

He nodded. "Very well. I'll arrange for a car. Sit tight. I'll get you a wheelchair—you've done enough physical therapy for one day."

When Dev left, Rajeev found himself alone with his thoughts. He was going to the morgue, to see a body. But he didn't consider it his own. Regardless of what Dev had told him, if Rajeev Sundaram's body was really rotting at the morgue, then the original Rajeev Sundaram was truly dead. He, this shadow of the original, may very well be a near-perfect copy of that mind, with the same memories, thought processes, and emotional makeup. But they were not the same. One was the progenitor, the other the offspring. And although the two of them shared a name and a past, from now on, Rajeev would be forging a future of his own.

He was going to bury his father ... and then start living a new life.

THREE

The coroner was captivated by Rajeev's synthetic body.

"Fascinating," he said as Dev helped his father shuffle into the morgue. "Would you mind if I—if I touched it?"

"Don't you dare touch me," Rajeev snapped.

The coroner, a tall, skeletal man who appeared to be in his fifties, jumped. "I'm sorry," he stammered. "I—I didn't realize you were—"

"I don't care. Keep your hands to yourself."

He nodded, and wordlessly beckoned for them to follow him to the back of the building where the bodies were kept.

"I've prepared the body for you here on the examination table," he said. He gestured to the table in the middle of the room. The table—and the body laying on top of it—were covered by a white sheet. "I'll give the two of you some privacy. Just come on out when you're done."

"Thank you," Dev said with a nod. "We won't be long." The coroner left, leaving Dev and Rajeev alone with the corpse of the man who was, in a sense, a father to them both.

Rajeev stumbled toward the table and reached a hand toward a corner of the sheet. "Well … shall we?"

"Allow me, dad." Dev grabbed the sheet and pulled it back.

It was a surreal experience, staring into the face of the body Rajeev considered *his*. But that attachment, he reminded himself, was an illusion, born of the memories that had been artificially injected into his mind. Even so, it was startling to see how much the body had changed over fifteen years. It had aged, of course, as evidenced by the numerous wrinkles snaking their way across the face like a network of tiny rivers. But the inactivity of the coma had also affected Rajeev's appearance. His face looked sallow and sunken, devoid of the color and heft one would expect of a healthy, active body. Death played a part in that as well, of course, but he'd only died a couple hours ago. Still, the expression on his face looked peaceful, and Rajeev took some solace in the fact that he had died without pain, never aware of what his family had gone through as they'd waited fifteen years for a miracle that had never come.

Rajeev turned to his son. "Is this difficult for you, Dev?"

He seemed surprised by the question. "It's a bit unsettling, but I made my peace with the situation a long time ago." His lips grew into a wide smile. "Besides—now I have you." He patted Rajeev's back.

"I'm not him. Whatever spark kept him alive has been snuffed out. I'm nothing more than his shadow."

"Perhaps. Perhaps not. As I said earlier, it's a bit of a thorny philosophical issue." His face lit up as he dove into his argument. "There's a thought experiment: Imagine a teleportation device that copies the configuration of *you* down to the last atom. It scans you in, say, LA, then builds an identical copy in New York."

"But what happens to you in LA?"

"Precisely! The original is destroyed—otherwise you'd have a cloning machine. But what if the machine in LA malfunctioned and failed to destroy the original, even after the duplicate has been configured in New York? What do you have then? Is the copy any less *you* than the original?"

"Yes. Because it's still a copy. The original has its own, distinct consciousness apart from that of its clone."

"But if the two consciousnesses are identical to each other … well, nevermind. It's a moot point. The fact is, there is now only one Rajeev Sundaram on this earth and you're him."

"Fair enough." Rajeev placed a hand on his progenitor's shoulder. "Goodbye. I'll … I'll try to live the life you would have if you'd had the chance." He nodded to Dev, who replaced the white sheet over the body. Then he helped his father as they both exited the room.

* * *

RAJEEV'S MIND WANDERED ON THE DRIVE HOME. HE thought of his family. Despite knowing he was only a copy, he couldn't deny the powerful emotions he felt for his wife and children. He'd been reunited with one of them, but he still longed to see the others.

"What now?" he asked Dev. "Can I go home—see Sarah and Mira?"

"I wouldn't recommend that. Not yet."

"Why not?"

"I'd like to take you back to the lab. We've developed a kind of rehabilitation program for new activations to help them acclimate to their new bodies. You've taken to yours surprisingly quickly, but you'd still benefit from some guidance before you venture out into the real world."

Rajeev hung his head. "You'd think I was a toddler and not a grown man."

Dev smirked. "I know, I know. It may seem a bit infantilizing, but truly, this is the best thing for you, dad. When you *do* venture out on your own, you'll barely notice the difference from your old body."

Rajeev looked down at his silicone-covered torso and flashed his son a skeptical look.

"Like I said—we'll get you put into an upgraded model as soon as possible."

FOUR

Back at the laboratory, Dev escorted Rajeev to the dormitory that would serve as his home for the next two weeks.

Rajeev pointed to the twin bed stationed in the corner—the only object in the otherwise bare room. "Is that even necessary?"

"Technically, no," Dev responded. "It's meant more as a comfort. We want to make the transition from man to ... well, *android* ... as seamless as possible."

"Do I even need to sleep?"

"Yes, actually. Just like a computer gets slow and choppy if it hasn't been restarted in awhile, you'll find it more difficult to process information—to think, essentially—without proper rest."

"Without sleep."

"More or less. We call it 'sleep mode.' It should happen automatically when it becomes necessary. You can help the process along by acting out the sleep rituals you had in your old body—dimming the lights, laying on the bed, closing your eyes ... err, photosensors. But you know what I mean."

"Well, sleeping is something I've always been good at it. Shouldn't be too difficult."

Dev laughed. "That's the spirit." He patted Rajeev on the shoulder, then headed for the door. "Get some rest. I'll see you in the morning and we'll get you started on physical therapy."

He turned off the light and opened the door, but paused before walking through it. He turned his head to face Rajeev one last time.

"Goodnight, dad. It's really great having you back."

Your father isn't back, Rajeev thought. *He's dead.*

Aloud, he said, "Thank you, Dev. It's good to be back."

* * *

FALLING ASLEEP WAS AS EASY AS DEV HAD IMPLIED, for the most part. It took a bit more conscious thought than Rajeev was used to, but after a bit of mild effort, he found himself unconscious. When he awoke, it was morning.

At least, he assumed it was morning. There were no windows in the room, so all he had to go on was the sense that he had been sleeping for several hours. He wondered what time it—

"The time is five-thirty a.m."

Rajeev jumped, throwing his robotic arms into the air. A man had suddenly appeared out of nowhere, standing by the door. He was skinny, dressed in straight-legged khaki pants and a bright-green polo shirt. His hair was neatly combed and he wore a pair of fashionable, thick-framed glasses.

"Who the hell are you?"

"I'm Daniel, your virtual assistant," the man said.

"My what? Where did you come from?"

"I'm your virtual assistant," Daniel repeated. "I can assist you with things like checking the time or the weather, searching the web, or playing music. I'm fully integrated with the NLT-X4912—"

"The what?"

"The NLT-X4912 is Next Level Technologies' fourth-generation artificial body."

Interesting. So apparently Dev had programmed one of these virtual assistants into Rajeev's body. Rajeev remembered virtual assistants from before his accident, but they'd always been confined to little speaker boxes. They'd never looked like real people.

"So you're not real?"

"I was created by software engineers at Next Level Technologies in Chicago, Illinois," Daniel replied matter-of-factly. "My visual appearance is a composite of the engineers who created me."

"So are you a hologram, then? Or what?"

"I exist in your mental interface. No one can see or hear me but you."

"How can I make you go away?"

Daniel smiled. "Just ask."

"Daniel ... go away."

"Absolutely. See you later." Daniel popped out of existence. But now that he was gone, Rajeev realized Daniel might be able to tell him what, if anything, he should be doing.

"Wait—Daniel? Come back."

Daniel was back before Rajeev could blink. "What can I do for you?"

"Do you know what I'm supposed to be doing?"

Daniel tilted his head like a confused dog. "I'm not sure what you mean."

"Like ... do I have a schedule or something?"

"Checking your schedule." His face went blank for a few seconds, then he smiled. "You have a physical therapy session scheduled for seven a.m. with M. Schwartz in Suite 1100 on the eleventh floor."

"And before that?"

"You have nothing else scheduled for today."

"Can you send a message to Dev?"

"Let me check your address book." There was a pause. "Would you like to send a message to Dev Sundaram?"

"Yes."

Daniel nodded. "Go ahead," he said. "What's your message?"

"Dev—it's your dad. I don't know what I'm supposed to do until my physical therapy appointment starts."

"Here's your message," Daniel said. He repeated Rajeev's words back to him. "Ready to send it?"

"Yes."

Daniel and Rajeev stared awkwardly at each other. Rajeev's instinct was to make small talk, but he reminded himself that Daniel wasn't a person. In many ways he was more machine than Rajeev was, his newly-acquired robotic body notwithstanding.

After a moment, Daniel mercifully piped up.

"You have a new message from Dev Sundaram," he said. "Would you like me to read it to you?"

"Please."

"Here's the message: 'Good morning, dad. I see you've met Daniel. I should have mentioned him last night but it slipped my mind. Sorry. You can relax until your appointment. Daniel can take you to our entertainment lounge. I'll be there at seven to accompany you to the appointment and make sure you're taken care of.'"

When he was done, Daniel smiled widely at Rajeev. "Would you like to send a response?"

"No, that's okay. Care to take me to the entertainment lounge?"

"Of course. Follow me."

Rajeev stood and established a firm grip on his walker. He waited for Daniel to move toward the door, but he didn't budge. Rajeev offered an awkward cough, made all the more awkward on account of his lack of a throat.

"I'll need you to open the door," Daniel finally offered. "Remember, I'm not physically present—I'm just in your head."

"Oh, right." Rajeev stepped toward the door. He expected Daniel to move out of the way, but he didn't. He made to nudge him aside, but his hand passed right through him. It was unsettling—like trying to touch a ghost. He reached his hand through Daniel, grasped the doorknob and turned it. As the door swung open, Daniel finally moved, walking out into the hallway.

Daniel walked casually through the hallway as if he were a worker in the company's IT department and not an apparition that existed only in Rajeev's mind. Yet he matched Rajeev's glacial pace perfectly, stopping to wait for him to catch up without a hint of impatience.

They got into the elevator and made their way to the twelfth floor, which was nice—Rajeev wouldn't have far to travel for his physical therapy appointment. When the elevator doors opened, they found themselves standing across from a room with floor-to-ceiling windows in place of a wall. Inside were several pieces of sparse, modern-looking furniture, including several couches and chairs, and a long coffee table. Several people sat on one of the couches, staring at a big-screen television built into the wall.

"Here we are," Daniel said, stepping out of the elevator and beckoning for Rajeev to follow him. Rajeev shuffled along, grasping his walker to maintain his balance.

As they neared the entertainment lounge, Rajeev, after stealing another glance at the people watching the TV, stopped in his tracks, stunned. The people on the couch were like him. *Androids.*

"I'm not sure I want to go to the lounge anymore," he told Daniel.

"Very well, if that's your wish. But may I ask why you've changed your mind?"

Rajeev didn't remember virtual assistants being so pushy in his day. He didn't feel like explaining himself, but for some reason, he found himself not wanting to disappoint Daniel, as crazy as that sounded.

"I didn't know other people … other people *like me* … would be here. I'm not sure I'm ready to interact with those things."

"I understand," Daniel said, nodding. "But might I suggest that it could actually be beneficial for you to interact with people who have undergone the same procedure."

Rajeev sighed. "I'm sure it is," he said. "I just don't want to—"

There was something about the way Daniel was looking at him, innocent and naive, that made him seem like an eager-to-please puppy. Again, for whatever reason, Rajeev found himself wanting to avoid disappointing him.

"I'll go in and talk to them for ten minutes," he said. "But after that I think I'd like to go back to my room and wait for my appointment."

Daniel nodded. "Very well. Let's go." He strolled up to a security panel built into the frame of one of the glass panels. He waved his hand in front of it and a small indicator light flashed green. The panel lifted upward into the ceiling and out of sight.

Rajeev made his way into the lounge and three sets of photo-sensors turned his way and studied him. He was suddenly over-whelmed by embarrassment over the walker. If he'd had cheeks, they would have been flushed.

One of the androids stood and walked up to Rajeev, holding out his hand.

"Looks like you're a newbie," he said, tilting his head at the walker. "Welcome. I'm Ted Ostrom."

Rajeev held out his hand, steadily so as not to lose his balance, and accepted Ted's greeting. "Hi, Ted. I'm Rajeev."

"Rajeev, eh? Sounds Indian."

"It is. I was born in India, but my family moved to the states when I was a kid." Technically, he thought, he had only been born yesterday, but he suspected Ted didn't care about the distinction.

"I only ask out of curiosity," Ted said. "It doesn't really matter. Whatever we looked like in our old lives, we all look the same now."

"Too much so."

Ted laughed. "That's true, but we've been promised that more customization is coming soon."

"So I've heard."

"Of course, we've been hearing that for awhile. But I'm sure it'll be any day now. Anyway, let me introduce you to these guys." He pointed to the android on the right end of the couch. "This is Andrew Lansing."

Andrew gave a salute. "Hey," he said. "Nice to meet you." Rajeev nodded.

"And this," Ted said, pointing to the android on the other side of the couch, "is Natalie Parsons."

Although she looked identical to Rajeev and the other two robotic bodies in the room, she moved in a distinctively feminine manner. "Charmed," she said, a hint of sarcasm in her voice.

"Likewise," Rajeev said. "Say, do you all sound like you did before? How is that possible?"

"I think they make some kind of voice profile based on recordings of you talking," Ted said. "Like they used to do with voice assistants." Daniel perked up as if someone had just mentioned his name.

"Anyway, we were just sitting down to watch a movie

together if you'd like to join us," Ted said. "We're only a couple minutes in—we could start it over for you if you like."

"Thank you for the offer, but I just came by to say hello and check out the rec lounge. I'm still getting the lay of the land. I'm sure we'll see each other around, though."

"I'm sure. See you around, Rajeev."

They nodded at each other as Rajeev walked out of the room.

"So?" Daniel asked as they headed back to the elevator. "What did you think?"

"They seemed nice enough." Which was true. But Rajeev didn't add that he found interacting with other androids terrifying. Most of the time he could convince himself he was still in an actual human body and not a woefully inadequate artifice. But interacting with the other androids merely served to remind him of one thing: He was a freak.

FIVE

Dev knocked on Rajeev's door a couple minutes prior to his physical therapy appointment.

"How'd you like Daniel?"

Rajeev shrugged. "He was fine. A little odd, but I guess that makes sense, since he's not a real person."

"He can be a little off-putting, but he's one of the most advanced artificial intelligences in existence. We're going to release a public version sometime this year. It's going to be tough to break into the market—there's a ton of competition and most of the existing players are far more established than we are—but Daniel is heads and shoulders above them all. I think when people start to realize that, we'll be successful. Anyway … are you getting used to your body?"

"When I pretend I'm not in a robotic body, it's mostly tolerable. But whenever I'm reminded of what it is, I feel like I'm on the verge of having a panic attack."

"That's not unexpected, honestly. It's still early. But in a few weeks, you'll barely be able to tell the difference."

Rajeev was skeptical. Besides, how would Dev know? He'd never had his consciousness transported to an entirely new body.

It was a completely disorienting experience—one he suspected a person couldn't fully appreciate unless it had happened to them. But it would be pointless to try to explain all that to his son.

"So what happens after this appointment?" Rajeev asked as they walked to the elevator. "Can I go home and see Sarah?"

Dev looked uncomfortable. "Dad, you *have* considered that mom has aged fifteen years, right?"

He had thought about it, but he'd been trying not to. At the time of his accident, Sarah had been thirty-three years old. Now she would be forty-eight. She'd be a different woman now, in appearance, in demeanor, in life experience. She'd be a stranger to him.

And yet, she was his wife. To him, it seemed like they'd embraced just yesterday. She'd been his world, and she *still* felt like his world. But he knew it would not be a seamless reunion. They would be reuniting not as a young man and a young woman, but as a middle-aged woman and a robot. It was like the plot of some kind of twisted scifi sitcom.

"The thought crossed my mind," Rajeev said.

"I don't think mom has quite accepted the fact that you've come back. It might be best to lay low awhile so it can sink in and I can explain to her exactly what to expect. Androids are not an everyday sight yet, you know. Remember, your body is just a prototype. It's never been seen by the public."

"Okay. Well, maybe I can visit Mira, then."

"Mira … is very busy, dad. Look, you'll get to see them both eventually, but I think it would be best if you waited. What you need to focus on now is getting acquainted with your new body so you can live as normal a life as possible."

As Dev finished speaking, they approached the physical therapy office, where Rajeev's physical therapist was already waiting for him just outside the door.

"You must be Rajeev," she said. She was a tall, widely-built woman with bright blond hair tied up in a bun. She wore loose-fitting, light-green scrubs.

"Guilty as charged."

She flashed a fake smile and Rajeev intuited that she didn't have much of a sense of humor. She helped him inside and led him to a pair of parallel bars.

"So how exactly does this work?"

"It's not much different from physical therapy for someone who's been in an accident or is recovering from surgery," she said.

"Well I *was* in an accident."

"Right—but not in your current body. You're in a similar boat, though. You essentially have to relearn to walk. It's not a matter of strengthening the muscles used to walk, however, as you don't *have* any muscles. It's more about forging a neural connection between your mind and your body, since neither one is very familiar with the other yet."

"So in other words, it's just a matter of practice."

She smiled. "Basically. Practice makes perfect, as they say—so let's get started."

* * *

AFTER AN HOUR OF PHYSICAL THERAPY, RAJEEV FELT he was in somewhat better control of his body—but he still wasn't ready to give up his walker.

Dev invited him up to his office to chit-chat before he had to head off to a board meeting. Dev wheeled his office chair to the other side of his desk, so he and his father could sit across from each other without anything between them.

"I have a surprise for you dad," Dev said, grinning. He walked back behind his desk, opened the bottom drawer, and pulled out a bottle of Scotch and a whiskey glass.

"I don't know if you've forgotten, Dev, but I can't drink Scotch … or anything else, for that matter."

"This isn't for you," he replied as he poured himself two fingers' worth of the amber liquid. "It's for me."

"Then what's my surprise?"

"The technology powering your body is still in development, and as such there are many shortcomings. One of them—one many people, dieters in particular, would find a feature and not a bug, however—is the inability to eat or drink. Over the millennia, humankind has come to savor the taste, texture and aroma of food and drink, given its reliance on both. We don't want to deny our patients such human pleasures. To that end, we've developed a variety of products meant to simulate some of the most popular foods and beverages in the country."

Dev walked up to the wall and began pressing buttons that Rajeev hadn't even seen were there. A wall safe popped open. He plucked a small, spherical object out of it, then closed it again.

"This is a prototype. We've done some testing on it and are confident it's safe; we're just putting the finishing touches on it."

"What is it?"

"Here." Rajeev reached out his hand cautiously, and Dev placed the sphere in his palm. "Hold it up to your mouth."

Rajeev brought the sphere up to the mouthpiece he considered his mouth. As it neared, an odd sensation overtook him, mostly in his mind, but also somehow localized to the mouthpiece. It took him a moment to recognize what it was.

"It's Scotch," he said in amazement. "The taste, the aroma— it's all there. I mean, for the most part. It tastes a little off."

Dev let out a self-satisfied chuckle. "It's actually a program that uses near-field communication technology to interact with your mind. This one is for Scotch, but we could make one for pizza, or one for popcorn that could be enjoyed at the movies.

We could make one for cotton candy that could be sold at the fair. The possibilities are endless, and as the android population continues to grow, it'll help them have the same kinds of important social experiences surrounding food that they'd have in an organic body."

Dev retrieved his glass off the desk and sat down across from his father.

"I just wanted to be able to enjoy a nice glass of Scotch with my father, now that we're both men."

"One of us more than the other," Rajeev said, and gave his artificial thigh two knocks with his fist.

"You know what I mean."

Rajeev placed the sphere against the mouthpiece. When he withdrew it, he felt dizzy.

"Can this … can this actually make me drunk?"

"In a manner of speaking. It simulates the experience, throwing some wrenches in your thought processes. I mean, who drinks alcohol just for the taste, right?"

"It's remarkable." Rajeev lowered the sphere to his lap, as if it were indeed a glass of fine scotch. "I have to say, Dev, I find it amazing that you were able to build … all *this*"—he waved his hands around him—"in just fifteen years."

"It wasn't easy. But I was determined."

"You must have been. There's no way you could have done it if you weren't." He hesitated. "It's great to see you have such an amazing professional life, but what is your personal life like? Are you married? Dating? Is there someone special in your life?"

"I've had to make some … sacrifices … to get to where I am today," he said.

"I'm sorry to hear that."

"I'm okay with it. And besides, I'm not that old. There's still time." He offered a weak smile. "Hey dad … I have a random question to ask you."

"Okay. Let's hear it."

"Did I ever tell you about my first kiss?"

"What?"

"I know it's a weird question. I was just reminiscing with some friends the other day about our first kisses and … as crazy as it sounds, I couldn't remember mine."

"Dev … you were just ten when I had my accident. I don't know that you'd even had your first kiss."

"No, I know, I know. I just thought I might have mentioned it to you at some point is all."

"I'm sorry I can't be more help."

Dev waved his hand dismissively. "It's no problem. Really. It's just that it's sometimes difficult to remember things from my childhood. I guess after your accident I just got so focused on coming up with a way to save you that everything else kind of faded into the background. I mean, I don't even remember simple things like … like my favorite place to go on vacation as a kid."

"Well that one's easy," Rajeev said, laughing. "It's just the happiest place on earth."

"Disneyland?"

"Of course! Surely you remember that much. We went when you were six. Every year after that you asked us to take you back for your birthday."

Dev laughed. "Of course. Who couldn't love Mickey Mouse?"

"Well, you were always more of a Goofy fan."

"He's good, too."

Rajeev thought Dev was acting oddly. For the first time since waking up, he felt a chasm between them—the full weight of the fifteen years that separated them suddenly weighed on him.

"I think I'd like to go back to my room now," he said.

"Of course." Dev took one last swig of his whiskey. "I'll escort you back."

SIX

Once Dev left the dormitory, Rajeev summoned Daniel.

"How can I help?"

"Daniel … can you give me a summary of what's happened in the past fifteen years? I feel like I have a lot of catching up to do."

"Happy to help," he said. "How much detail are you looking for?"

"You can just give me the broad strokes for now."

"Very well."

Much had changed in the past fifteen years, but much had not. People still relied on the internet for information. But it had migrated much more to virtual reality environments and virtual assistants like Daniel, who were built into augmented-reality glasses and sunglasses.

Autonomous vehicles were just becoming a thing at the time of Rajeev's accident, but now they were far more common than the manual variety … and the government was making efforts to persuade the few people who still owned the old-school cars to trade them in for autonomous models, which had reduced the traffic death rate to nearly zero. Rajeev had already gotten a taste of this particular technological advancement firsthand on the drive to the morgue.

But there had been no major geo-political upheavals. Peace still eluded the Middle East, the United States was still run by a two-party system and nuclear weapons were still a visceral, albeit unmentioned, threat. In many ways, the world still looked much as it had fifteen years ago.

Daniel finished his concise overview of the world's fifteen-year history in a little over two hours. That still left much of the day available and little for Rajeev to do.

"You could always go back to the entertainment lounge," Daniel suggested.

The thought of interacting with more of his kind gave Rajeev pause. "I think I'd rather not."

"It's good for human beings to socialize."

"I'm not exactly a human being."

"You are in mind and spirit, if not in body." Daniel offered a reassuring smile.

"Still, I'd really rather not."

"It's completely your choice. I can only make suggestions based on my understanding of what is in your best interest. But I can't make any decisions for you. It's always your choice."

It might have been Rajeev's choice, but Daniel sure was laying on some pressure. He took a moment to think it over and decided another ten minutes couldn't hurt.

"Fine. I'll go for a couple minutes."

Daniel led the way back to the lounge. As they approached, Rajeev saw two androids sitting in chairs, but there was no way to tell if either of them was one of the ones he'd met yesterday.

"Hello," he said as he walked in.

"Hey there … Rajeev, right?" It was Ted's voice.

"Guilty as charged."

"Rajeev, you haven't met Brian yet." He gestured toward the other android, then back to Rajeev.

"Nice to meet you," Rajeev said.

"Same to you. So you're a newbie, eh?"

"Newer than you, that's for sure." Rajeev took a seat on the couch, facing the other two androids. "In fact, I had my first physical therapy session today."

"It'll go by in no time," Brian said. "When I was in my old body, I had knee surgery and had to go to physical therapy for months. But in this newfangled thing, I was done in a week."

"That's great. I'm already starting to get a bit cooped up here. I'd like to go see my wife and daughter soon."

Brian whistled. "Don't hold your breath. Not that you have any."

"What do you mean?"

"Do you really think NLT is going to just let you waltz out of here with a piece of equipment worth tens of millions of dollars?"

"What are you saying?"

"These bodies of ours … they don't come cheap. And considering that none of us paid for these machines, NLT considers them company property."

Rajeev shook his head. "No. My son told me that after I completed my physical therapy I could go see—"

"I don't know who your son is, but they're probably feeding him the same crock they're feeding us."

Ted placed a hand on Brian's shoulder, as if restraining him. "All Brian's trying to say is that—"

"My son is the founder of the company."

Ted blinked. "Your son is … what?"

"He's the founder of Next Level Technologies. This is his company. And he told me I could leave when I was able to walk on my own."

The admission sucked the air out of the room. Brian was the first to speak.

"I appreciate that your son knows a hell of a lot more than I do what goes on around here," he said. "But anyone capable of becoming one of the richest men in the world within ten years must be able to tell a mighty fine fib or two. Maybe he'll stay true to his word, pull a few strings and let you visit your family, on account of you being his dad and all. But I'm willing to bet he's not going to let a multimillion dollar prototype off company grounds just so you can hug your wife and daughter. I think it's more likely he's feeding you whatever bullshit you want to hear to keep you nice and compliant."

Rajeev stared Brian straight in the photosensors. "Don't you dare talk about my son like that."

Brian shrugged. "I'm sorry. I just call 'em like I see 'em."

"Then you'd better get your eyes checked," Rajeev said. He wanted nothing more than to storm out of the room, but he was still dependent on his walker. As he shuffled out of the room, he dared not turn around to see if the photosensors of the two androids were burning into his back.

SEVEN

Rajeev sat on the bed in his dorm, fuming.

"Dev is a good boy," he said to Daniel. "I can't believe they'd make him out to be some kind of greedy corporate fat cat."

"He's not a boy anymore," Daniel pointed out.

Rajeev scowled inwardly at the correction, but Daniel was right: Dev wasn't a boy anymore and men, even good ones, often did bad things in pursuit of the greater good. Rajeev doubted Brian's account of his son was completely accurate, but he wondered if there wasn't at least a kernel of truth to it.

"Daniel … can you bring up some newspaper articles about Dev?"

"Absolutely. I've gathered the top ten results. Would you like me to read them aloud, starting with the first?"

"Is there any way I could read them myself?"

"Absolutely." As soon as Daniel uttered the words, a newspaper appeared floating in front of Rajeev's face. He reached out to touch it, and it spun in the air.

"It's an augmented reality representation of a newspaper," Daniel said. "You can interact with it. Try holding it."

He reached out a hand and grasped the left edge of it. As he pulled his arm back to his body, the newspaper came with it.

The first article was a profile about Dev in the *Chicago Tribune*. For the most part, it wasn't anything Rajeev didn't already know. There was some new information about the history of the company, and some of the investment companies that had provided much of the capital needed to grow it into a billion-dollar company. But the rest of the article was the same story Dev had told him when he'd awakened: How a devastating car accident had put his father in a coma when he was just a boy, motivating him to find a way to bring his father back. The article cautioned that such technology was still a ways off, but that Next Level Technologies had made huge strides in the development of robotics and artificial intelligence technologies in the process.

The next article was trash. It appeared to be from some kind of tabloidy blog site and it was all speculation about Dev's sex life—something Rajeev didn't want to think about *at all*.

He moved on to the next one and unlike the other two, it seemed to contain some useful information.

NEXT LEVEL VERSUS FRESH MEAT: THE RACE TO UPGRADE THE HUMAN BODY
William Stillwell, The Wall Street Journal

Almost as long as humanity has existed, it has sought to cheat death. Conquistador Juan Ponce de León sought the Fountain of Youth. Cleopatra attempted to stave off the ravages of age by bathing in donkey milk. Humankind will stop at nothing to attain immortality.

Thanks to recent technological advances, achieving immortality seems less the stuff of mythology or science fiction and more like an accomplishment that is achievable in our lifetimes. A handful of new companies are on the forefront of the race to create immortal humans, not by reversing the aging of existing bodies, but rather by supplying new bodies that could, at least in theory, be repaired and upgraded indefinitely, granting their inhabitants a kind of pseudo-immortality.

The two most promising companies are different sides of the same coin. Next Level Technologies, the rising robotics and AI firm founded by fresh-eyed billionaire Dev Sundaram, seeks to copy human consciousnesses and implant them into robotic bodies that can be customized and upgraded according to the occupant's wishes. Fresh Meat, a bioengineering firm headed by irreverent whiz-kid Gregory Maltek, is taking a similar, but decidedly different tact. The company is also working on a way to transfer a human consciousness to a new body. Instead of creating artificial bodies, however, the company aims to create biological ones.

Both approaches come with advantages and disadvantages and it's difficult to say at this early juncture which technology will be more widely adopted. It's possible there's room for both technologies; or, the technology could play out similarly to the VHS and Betamax fight, with one technology gaining mainstream acceptance, condemning the other to obsolescence. Either way, analysts agree on one thing: The victor will control a new industry that measures its profits by the billions.

Rajeev hadn't fully understood the ramifications of his son's invention. He'd assumed the primary purpose of these artificial bodies was medical—to help people who had been paralyzed or maimed lead more normal lives. He had been essentially brain-dead himself, which as far as he was concerned was as good as dead. Yet through the technology Dev had developed at Next Level Technologies, he had been given a second chance. Of course, Rajeev saw himself as more of a copy, rather than a continuation, of the original Rajeev Sundaram. But undoubtedly that's not how the general public would view it, especially with the help of some good marketing. But Rajeev's initial impression appeared to be mistaken. Perhaps there was a medical component to Dev's technology, but it was being sold as a form of immortality. That was a different proposition entirely, and one Rajeev wasn't sure he was comfortable with.

In Rajeev's estimation, copying someone's consciousness and then deleting the original was tantamount to murder. No matter how similar the duplicate mind may be to its original, it still cut off the life of the original. It was one thing to use such a method to provide hope to people with no other options—people with fatal illnesses, say, or paraplegics who wished they were dead anyway. But if this technology was being offered to healthy, able-bodied individuals as some kind of anti-aging gimmick, that was an entirely different matter. Would NLT's customers realize the troubling philosophical implications of what they were doing? Probably not—especially if the company managed to get the PR spin just right.

Then there was this company Fresh Meat—apparently NLT's biggest competitor. Their proposed business model seemed to open a whole other can of worms. The thorniest problem Rajeev saw was the matter of supply—where would Fresh Meat get these flesh-and-blood bodies they intended to sell to people? He imagined they'd be grown in a lab with some kind of novel cloning technology he couldn't begin to understand. It reminded him of a Michael Bay movie he'd seen. But the clones in that movie had been fully-realized human beings whose body parts were harvested when the originals needed them. And that raised an important question: Would Fresh Meat's clones have consciousnesses of their own ... and would the company overwrite them with the minds of its customers? The *Wall Street Journal* article didn't go into much detail, but Rajeev wanted to learn more.

"Daniel ... can you do a web search for Fresh Meat and display the results in front of me?"

"Yes ... just a moment." Almost as soon as he uttered the words, the search results were projected in front of Rajeev's face. He scanned through them, looking for any indication of controversy surrounding the company's methods or even any details on how their technology worked. But he came up empty-handed.

"That's all I need for the night, Daniel. Thank you."

"You're welcome. If you need anything—you know how to reach me." In an instant, he was gone.

Rajeev lay down on the bed and contemplated everything he'd learned in the last half hour. He came away with two main facts. The first was that he was embroiled in a burgeoning industry with troubling moral and ethical issues he wasn't sure he wanted anything to do with.

The second was the disconcerting thought that he might not know his son nearly as well as he'd assumed.

EIGHT

Rajeev awoke the next morning with the same troubling questions on his mind. As his mind cleared, he summoned Daniel to check his schedule.

"You don't have anything scheduled for today—other than physical therapy, of course."

"Could you send a message to Dev asking if he'd care to join me after my appointment?"

"My pleasure. Here's your message—"

"I'm sure it's fine, thank you. Go ahead and send it."

He nodded. "Very well. I've sent the message."

Dev responded a couple minutes later, saying he'd meet Rajeev at the end of his appointment, then take him up to his office where they could talk.

At physical therapy that day, Rajeev found he was making progress. He could walk for a few minutes without his walker, although the longer he pushed himself past that timeframe, the more he began to falter. Brian was right—he should be completely rehabilitated in a week's time, although Rajeev thought "rehabilitated" was a bit of a misnomer, since this was his first go-around in his current body; if anything he was being "habilitated."

As he was leaving the rehab facility he ran into Dev waiting outside in the hall.

"You didn't have to wait out here," he said. "You could have come in and had a seat while I finished up."

"I didn't want to disrupt your appointment. I take it it went well?"

"It went great. I can walk on my own without the walker now … a little bit, at least."

"That's great, dad! Care to demonstrate?"

"Ehh … I think I'll stick with the walker for now until I make more progress."

"Probably a wise decision."

Dev led him to his office. This time, he sat down behind his desk and offered Rajeev a seat across from it.

"So. What did you want to talk about, dad?"

"I'm making great progress in physical therapy. Like I said, I should be done in less than a week. So I was wondering what the next steps are as far as leaving. I mean … what's life going to look like on the other side? I'm not going to be able to work. I'm not going to be able to live a normal life."

Dev's brow furrowed with concern. "Dad, I don't want you to worry about any of that. I know you'll be done with physical therapy soon, but I think it's best if you just stay here for the foreseeable future—for the very reasons you just stated. It won't be too much longer until we're able to get you a better body that's more recognizably human. Besides, if you wait until our androids officially hit the market, all the publicity will make people more comfortable with the sight of someone such as yourself walking around. In fact, you may even turn into some-thing of a minor celebrity—one of the first people to ever undergo this revolutionary procedure."

"That's all well and good, but I'm not asking to move out for good just yet. Can't I just arrange a trip to see Sarah and Mira?"

"Tell you what. Why don't I get in touch with mom and Mira and arrange for them to visit you here?"

Rajeev wanted to get out of the lab as soon as possible, but he didn't feel he could get anywhere arguing about it. He was beginning to rethink Brian's claims that NLT wouldn't let such valuable tech leave the premises.

"I guess that would be fine."

"Thanks for being flexible, dad. Anyway, I've got a lot of work to get to today. Can I help you with anything else?"

"That's everything. Thanks again for meeting with me."

"Of course. I take it you don't need any help getting to your room, what with all your recent progress?"

"Uh … yeah, that's fine. I'll manage." He wheeled his walker onto the elevator and returned to his dorm.

* * *

"I'm growing concerned, Daniel."

Rajeev was sitting upright on his bed, a hand on his chin as he contemplated everything he'd learned in the past two days. Daniel, standing against the wall boasting his near-perpetual smile, tilted his head. "Why is that, Rajeev?"

"I think my son has been led astray by the lure of money. He touts my accident as the impetus behind the founding of this company—and that may well have been his initial motivation. But it's clear he's accumulated a great deal of wealth and power for all his effort and I fear he's become addicted to both."

"As Lord Acton said, 'Absolute power corrupts absolutely.'"

"My fear exactly. But what can I do about it?"

"Dev is your son. Your loved one. You care for him, which means you care about his well-being. If you think he is going down a dangerous path, is it not your responsibility to do something about it?"

"I don't think it's quite that simple."

"Why not?"

"The path he's headed down isn't as demonstrably bad as if, say, he'd become addicted to drugs. Most people would aspire to the same success he's achieved and the continued success he aims to achieve: To change the world, technologically speaking, and accumulate a vast amount of wealth—enough to buy whatever one's heart desires, and to do whatever one dreams of doing."

"But you believe that ultimately the lifestyle he's prioritizing now is to his detriment."

"I believe so, yes. He seems to be putting family on the back burner. I don't think he talks to Sarah or Mira nearly as often as he implies he does. And he's at the age where he should be starting a family, yet the things I saw in the tabloids yesterday … well, I don't particularly trust tabloids, but I do believe they tend to exaggerate stories rather than manufacture them out of whole cloth. He may not be a playboy per se, but it's clear he has no intention of settling down anytime soon."

"And you don't think there's anything you can do to set Dev on a better path?"

Rajeev pondered the question. Perhaps it was old-fashioned of him, but he'd always considered himself a family man—not out of a sense of tradition, but rather out of a steadfast belief that a properly-functioning family unit was one of the greatest forces of good in the world. He hadn't always lived up to that ideal, but he'd always strived to. His familial ties to Dev had been prematurely severed after he'd gone comatose, but perhaps Dev could still be steered down the right path through his relationship with his mother and sister.

"Daniel, are you able to look up Sarah and Mira Sundaram's phone numbers?"

"One moment." There was a pause. "I have the number for one Sarah Sundaram, but I could find no phone records for Mira Sundaram."

That seemed unusual, but maybe Mira had an unlisted number. He was sure Sarah would be able to give it to him.

"So how would I go about placing a call?"

"Outgoing calls are prohibited."

Rajeev couldn't believe what he'd just heard. "Outgoing calls are prohibited? What do you mean?"

"All outgoing communications use Next Level Technologies' network, but you've been blocked from any external communication. You can only call numbers within Next Level Technologies' own network."

"Just me? Or have other people's communications been blocked as well?"

"I can't say. All I know for sure is that yours have been blocked."

Rajeev could somewhat understand his son's reluctance to let him leave to visit his family. It might be a bit of a shock to them to see him as he currently looked. And the fact was, he *did* represent a huge investment on the part of the company and it made sense that they couldn't let him leave without being accompanied by some kind of security.

But blocking his phone calls and other forms of outgoing communication? Not only was it not right, but it seemed suspicious as hell. It seemed Next Level Technologies had become a prison for Rajeev and that meant one thing.

He had to break out.

NINE

He walks down the empty hallways, shaking with anger. It makes it difficult to pay attention to his whereabouts. When he catches sight of a janitor emptying a trash can, he stops and asks for directions to the principal's office. The janitor, a heavyset, red-headed man with dead eyes, simply points in the opposite direction.

Rajeev offers a half-hearted thanks and trudges off in the direction of the janitor's finger. He finds the office, opens the door and sees Mira sitting in a chair in front of the principal's desk. Her arms are folded across her chest and he can't help thinking she looks like a petulant toddler.

He looks up at the principal, an uptight, middle-aged woman with shoulder-length, platinum blonde hair: Mrs. Patricia Hayes.

Principal Hayes meets his gaze and nods. She gestures toward another chair in front of her desk.

"Thank you for coming, Mr. Sundaram. Please, have a seat."

He sits. He turns to Mira and says through gritted teeth, "What have you done, Mira?"

Hayes holds out a hand to stop him. "Mr. Sundaram, it's not as bad as it looks. Mira isn't in trouble per se. We just have some concerns."

"What concerns?"

She nods her head, working her way up to an explanation. "Mira hasn't been paying attention in history class, according to Mr. Yancey. He's caught her reading books, passing notes, sleeping. She doesn't turn in homework and she has failed the last three tests in a row. She doesn't seem to have this problem in any of her other classes. So, like I said, we're concerned. If she fails history, she'll have to retake it and pass before she can graduate."

Hearing about his daughter's misbehavior feels like a personal assault. Here he is, out on the road every single day to put food on the table and squirrel away some extra money so his daughter can go to college and make something of herself, and she's jeopardizing it all so she can pass inane notes to her friends and catch up on sleep she doesn't need.

"What do you have to say for yourself?" he asks.

She shrugs. "Nothing."

"What do you mean, 'nothing'? You're going to fail history if you don't shape up. What's going on? Or are you just lazy?"

She shrugs again. "Sure, yeah. I'm just lazy, I guess."

"How dare you—"

"Mr. Sundaram," Hayes interrupts, "there's no reason to get upset. Mira is—"

"No reason to be upset? You said she could fail history and not graduate!"

"Yes, but it's not too late. If Mira buckles down, she could squeak by with a D, maybe a C. Even if she fails, she can take summer classes." She pauses to brush her bangs out of her eyes. "I think what we need to focus on is cultivating an environment where Mira can thrive," she continues. "What kind of study environment does she have at home? I can offer some suggestions that would ..."

Rajeev tries to follow what Hayes is saying, but he finds himself preoccupied with something she'd said earlier: "She doesn't seem to have this problem in any of her other classes." He asks himself, why not?

He pretends to listen to the rest of what the principal has to say, nodding along somberly as if he is deeply invested in what she's saying, but the entire time he's thinking that he needs to speak with his daughter alone.

Finally, she's done speaking and he stands. "Principal Hayes, thank you so much for bringing this to my attention. Rest assured, Sarah and I are going to have a long, hard discussion with Mira when we get home and there are going to be some changes around our house."

"I'm glad you're taking your daughter's education so seriously, Mr. Sundaram. Thanks again for stopping by. I'm sorry it wasn't under more pleasant circumstances."

He nods and leads Mira out of the office. They walk in silence. When they reach the car, they both climb in, buckle up, and stare ahead, trying to pretend the conversation they were just part of never happened. But Rajeev can't pretend and he finally breaks the silence.

"Why are you only having problems in history?"

She turns to look at him. "What?"

"Principal Hayes said you were only having issues in your history class, not in any of your other classes. Why?"

She shrugs. "I don't know, dad. I guess I—"

"Is he touching you?"

"What? Dad, I—"

"Is he touching you inappropriately? Answer the question, Mira."

She seems stunned by the question and Rajeev observes her body stiffening up. "It's ... it's not what you think, dad."

"Then what is it?"

She sighs, but as she speaks, he can see her body grow looser; she's been holding this in for awhile and it's bringing her some kind of cathartic release to finally get it out.

"Mr. Yancey has never ... never molested me, or anything like that. But ... he'll put his hand on my shoulder sometimes, say, if I give a correct answer in class. It's not a big deal, but it makes me uncomfortable. So I stopped answering questions in class. I stopped participating. I just didn't want to give him any excuses to pay attention to me."

In a way, Rajeev is relieved. His daughter isn't lazy. But his rage does *not dissipate; it is merely redirected at the pervert he now recognizes Mr. Yancey as.*

"Thank you for telling me about this, Mira. I just wish you'd told me sooner." He's going to pull her out of school. Find a private academy—if they can get a scholarship—or even homeschool her if that's what it takes. He won't let her set foot in the same room as that pervert again—and he won't rest until the bastard is fired.

An awkward silence overtakes the car. Rajeev pulls into the driveway and Mira unbuckles her seatbelt, but he places his hand on her shoulder to stop her; he wants to take advantage of the close proximity before she skulks off to her room.

"Mira, you were not in the wrong here. He was. You never have to put up with someone touching you in any way without your permission. You know that, right?"

She looks up, offers a half-smile and nods.

"I do," she says, her voice soft. "I just wasn't sure you would. But I'm glad you do."

* * *

One thing Dev had not lied about was that even in this robotic body, and with this computerized mind, sleep was essential if Rajeev wanted to keep his wits about him. So he slept, hopeful that the next morning, feeling refreshed, he could formulate a plan to escape without detection.

Morning came, and he wasted no time.

"Can you pull up the blueprints for the building?"

Daniel shook his head. "I don't have access to that information."

"You must have safety information though, right? How to evacuate in case of a fire, that sort of thing?"

"Yes. There are twelve autonomous drones assigned to the building, each equipped to carry up to four passengers. In the event of an emergency, such as a building fire, the drones station themselves outside windows to carry occupants to safety."

"Twelve times four … that's only forty-eight people. There's a hell of a lot more people in this building than that, aren't there?"

"Correct. The drones will return to the building after dropping off their passengers, continuing the cycle until everyone has evacuated."

There were possibilities there … start a building fire, evacuate on one of the drones, then take off while everyone's distracted by the chaos. But he couldn't set the building on fire without risking that someone might get hurt, or even killed. He couldn't have that on his conscience. He needed to think of something else.

"That won't work," he told Daniel. "I'm not good at this kind of scheming."

"I'm afraid I'm not much better. As a virtual assistant, my capacity for imagination is limited. Might I suggest, however, that you consult one of the other androids you encountered in the entertainment lounge? They have human minds that may be better suited to 'scheming,' as you put it."

Rajeev scoffed at the idea. He couldn't trust anyone here. For all he knew, the other androids were plants working for NLT.

Then again, Brian was the first one to sow seeds of distrust against the company in Rajeev's mind. If anyone would be happy to help Rajeev escape, it would probably be him.

"Yeah … let's take a walk to the entertainment lounge. I have a feeling I might get some inspiration there."

When he got to the lounge, there was only one android inside, sitting on the couch and reading a book—an actual, hardcover book, which had already been somewhat rare in Rajeev's time, before his crash, but which he imagined was almost unheard of in this modern age of LCD screens, augmented reality and holographic projections. And it was doubly weird to see an android reading one.

"Brian?"

The android looked up from its book and shook its head. "Nope. It's me—Natalie."

Natalie. She was one of the androids Rajeev had met after first visiting the lounge. But he hadn't interacted with her at all. He briefly considered asking her the question he'd intended to ask Brian, but he decided it wasn't worth the risk.

"Do you know where I can find Brian?"

Natalie tilted her head. "I do, but I'm not sure I should tell you."

"Why not?"

"Brian said he got the impression you didn't like him much. You're not planning to beat him up, are you?"

"Not at all. I was just hoping to speak to him."

"That's exactly what I'd expect you to say if you were planning to beat him up."

There was a playfulness to her words, but Rajeev was impatient. His first instinct was to ask if she was going to help him or not, but he stopped himself. It would be counterproductive, and besides, there was no reason for him to be so impatient—he wasn't in a hurry.

He sat down in a chair across from her and crossed his legs. "I'm not that kind of person," he said calmly. "In fact, I wanted to see Brian so I could apologize to him. I reacted badly to what he was saying. I didn't need to be so rude."

"Well if you stick around, Brian should be here in about ten minutes. He and Ted are stopping by to watch another movie."

"Oh. Okay." He'd wait, then. But as soon as he made the decision, an uneasy silence settled over the entertainment lounge and Rajeev felt compelled to break it.

"So ... how did you end up in, you know ... one of these?" He pointed a finger at his own synthetic body.

"I don't talk about that."

"Oh, I'm sorry. I didn't mean to—"

She laughed. "I'm kidding. I don't mind talking about it. I'll tell you my story if you tell me yours. Deal?"

He nodded. "Deal."

"It was the stupidest thing. I was seventeen and at a pool party with some friends." Her eyes were incapable of conveying the depth of her guilt, but her tone said it all. "I'd had a couple drinks and I did a head-first dive into the pool. I didn't realize it was into the shallow end." She paused, letting the memory saturate her. "I severed my spinal cord at the fifth cervical vertebrae. I was completely paralyzed. The only things I could move were my eyelids and my mouth."

"I'm sorry," Rajeev whispered. "That sounds really rough."

She let out a self-pitying laugh. "That's putting it mildly. I lived like that for thirteen years. For thirteen years, a professional caretaker fed me, bathed me, clothed me. For thirteen years my own body was a prison."

She paused before continuing as if reliving the memories. "About two years ago, someone from NLT contacted my mom. They'd been made aware of my condition—I'm still not sure how; they must have called the hospital, I guess—and said they were working on an experimental procedure that would allow me to move again."

"Weren't you skeptical?"

"Hell no. By that point, I was desperate enough to eat up whatever snake oil anyone was willing to throw my way. My mom was a bit more cautious, but when she discovered that she didn't need to pay a thing—that NLT would actually *pay us* for taking part in the trial—her reluctance melted away. They took me to the lab, put me under anesthesia. I remember falling asleep and then waking up like this." She gestured toward her silicone-covered face. "I was elated at first. I could move my hands, my fingers, my toes. I could turn my head. But then …" She trailed off.

"What?"

"I discovered that all I'd done was trade one prison for another."

"What do you mean?"

"They wouldn't let me leave. I wanted to go home, to be with my mother, but it turns out we hadn't read the paperwork we'd signed closely enough. We thought it was just regular old medical liability disclosures and waivers, but it turns out we had inadvertently signed away my freedom. See, NLT owns this body, not me."

"So what Brian was telling me was true."

She nodded her head.

"I was beginning to come to that conclusion anyway," he said. "In truth, that's why I wanted to talk to Brian."

"You planning a mutiny?"

"No." He hesitated to say more, but after what she'd just told him, he thought he could trust her. "I'm planning to get out."

She sat up, taking a sudden interest in his words. "Planning a jailbreak, are we?" She sounded surprised, intrigued and skeptical all at once.

"That's the plan. I need to see my wife and daughter, but Dev won't let me leave. He's blocking my calls to them. He says he'll arrange for them to visit, but I'm pretty sure that's just lip service."

"How do you intend to do it?"

"I'm still trying to figure out the details, but I was thinking of using a distraction."

"Mmmhmm. You think none of us have ever tried that?"

"Uh, well … no, I hadn't. But I take it I'm mistaken? How many of you are there anyway?"

"Of *us*—remember, you're an android, too."

"Point taken. How many?"

"There's twelve of us, including you."

"And one of you tried to escape?"

"When I was first activated, there were five of us—I was the fifth. Two of us, Ted and Christian, who I don't think you've met yet, got it into their head that they could distract the guards that are posted twenty-four seven by the entrance and make a run for it."

"That's more or less what I had in mind, but I'm taking it that plan didn't work out so well?"

"No it did not. Christian distracted the guard by pretending to have some kind of meltdown or something while Ted made a break for it. But as soon as he made it out the door, he just … froze. He literally couldn't move. He collapsed onto the ground and once the guard got Christian under control, he just got a hand truck, loaded Ted onto it, and wheeled him back inside."

"So there's some kind of failsafe built into the bodies that physically prevents us from leaving?"

"Exactly. So even if you *were* to make it outside, it wouldn't do any good. You'd seize up just like Ted did."

"So we need a new plan."

She snorted. "Good luck with that." She returned to her book and Rajeev meditated on all the new information Natalie had just given him. Escape wasn't an option, apparently. But maybe there was still some way to reach out to Sarah or Mira.

Just as the thought was burgeoning in his mind, the door opened and two androids walked in.

"And you two are … ?" Natalie asked, taking in the two identical figures.

"Ted," said the robot on the right, "and Brian." He pointed to his companion.

"Hello, boys," Natalie said. "I was talking to Rajeev here about escape."

"Escaping from your own son's company?" Brian sounded amused. "What changed, Papa Sundaram?"

"Look, I'm sorry about yesterday," Rajeev said. "Family is everything to me and I wasn't prepared to hear what you were saying."

"But now you are?"

"Dev isn't eager to let me off the premises. I owe you an apology. I love my son, but I fear he cares more about money than he does about his own family."

Natalie stood and walked to Rajeev, placing a hand on his shoulder. "Rajeev was just talking about making a break for it before you two came in."

"We've tried that," Ted said. "It won't work."

"I explained that to him."

"She did," Rajeev said, "and I've been trying to formulate a new plan. Maybe we can't escape, but I think we could find a way to communicate with the outside world."

"Yeah?" Brian asked skeptically.

"Yeah. I realize it's not possible to break out of here … but how difficult would it be to smuggle something in?"

TEN

There's a bathroom with a window on the fifth floor." Ted sat on the couch in the entertainment lounge. Natalie sat beside him; Rajeev and Brian sat on chairs facing them.

"Is it wide enough?" Rajeev asked.

"Should be."

"If not—break it." Brian scanned the eyes of the others, as if daring one of them to challenge him. "Seriously. What are they gonna do? Lock you up?"

Natalie looked grave. "I'm sure they could think up some pretty horrific punishments if we really got out of line."

"Maybe," Brian said, "but I doubt they'll break out the big guns over some shattered glass."

"Okay. I'll get it out, one way or another," Rajeev said. "Ted, you have everything set up here, right?"

He nodded. "Yep. If you can get the bird in the air, I'll handle everything else."

"Excellent." Rajeev stood, nestling a nondescript black box between his hip and arm. "What are we waiting for? Let's do this."

Rajeev headed for the door, leaving the others behind. He

stopped just before exiting and took one last look at his co-conspirators. They nodded encouragingly. Rajeev nodded back, turned around and walked out the door.

With an additional three days of physical therapy under his belt, Rajeev was now able to get around without a walker. He was still a bit shaky, but at least he was able to move about unaided.

"Daniel?" The virtual assistant appeared before him, like some kind of spectral apparition.

"How can I help?"

"Daniel, please lead me to the bathroom on the fifth floor."

"Absolutely. Follow me."

Daniel led him to the elevator. After it let them off, he made his way down the hall, took a right down another hall, and then to a bathroom at the end of it.

"Here you are. If that's all you need, I'll give you some privacy."

"Much appreciated, Daniel. Thanks again." Daniel disappeared and Rajeev walked into the bathroom.

Since awakening from his coma, he hadn't set foot in a bathroom. There hadn't been a need to—he didn't eat or drink, which meant he didn't defecate or urinate. This bathroom seemed sparse and clinical, like the medical patient room he'd first awakened in. He spotted the window in the leftmost upper corner of the room and walked over to it. He set the box on the floor beside the sink and reached for the window.

The clasp to unlock it was just barely out of reach. He didn't have toes to stand on, so he just strained his arms. To his surprise, they stretched out just a bit further, enabling him to unlock the window and push it open.

As soon as he turned around, the door opened and a thin, dark-skinned woman walked in. Her hair was up in a tightly-wrapped bun, and she wore a charcoal-gray pantsuit.

"Uh—excuse me," she said, her voice dripping with indignation. "What are you doing?"

Rajeev froze. What an idiot! He must have walked into the women's bathroom. He was rusty when it came to checking the gender before entering such sensitive facilities.

"Answer me. What are you doing in here?" She looked him up and down. "You … *things* … don't need to use bathrooms."

Rajeev already had a story ready to go; something about missing the outside world and trying to get a peek of it through the window. "I—I'm sorry," he said. "I was just—"

"You're a *man?*" she shrieked upon hearing his voice. "Get out! Get out *now!*"

Rajeev held out his hands as if deflecting a physical attack.

"I can explain," he said. "I was just feeling a bit claustrophobic on account of—"

"If you're not going to leave, I'm getting security."

"That's not necessary," he said, but she was already out the door. As soon as she was gone, he crouched in front of the box and lifted its lid.

Inside was a six-rotor drone. It felt surprisingly light in his hands. He switched it on and a tiny green LED lit up. He lifted the small aircraft to the window and waited.

"Come on, Ted," he whispered through gritted teeth.

Nothing happened for several moments and then, suddenly, the rotors whirred to life. He let go, and the drone hovered in place a moment before soaring through the window and out of sight.

Rajeev stuffed the black box into the trash can and hurried out of the bathroom, eager to leave before the uptight woman returned with a member of the company's security team.

* * *

On the way back to the entertainment lounge, Rajeev pondered the encounter with the woman in the bathroom. He tried to give her the benefit of the doubt—he *had* gone into the wrong restroom after all—but he couldn't help seeing echoes of the kind of prejudice he'd experienced growing up.

Her words echoed in his mind: "You *things* don't need to use restrooms." Had she forgotten that the minds powering these alien "things" were in fact human—no different from her or any of the other "normal" people working for NLT? How easily people could dehumanize those who seemed different from them. Rajeev had experienced overt racism only a handful of times in his life, but the incidents had been frightening. One stood out in his mind. It was shortly after the September 11 terrorist attack on the World Trade Center. He had been ten, just a boy, and his father had taken him along to the grocery store. As they were walking through the parking lot, an older white man standing a row over began yelling profanities at them. He'd mistaken them for Muslims of Middle-Eastern descent.

The fact that the man had misidentified their race had lessened the blow a bit. But it had been an unsettling experience nonetheless and Rajeev still remembered that sense of dehumanization. It was as if the man had viewed he and his father less like human beings and more like dangerous weapons. He'd seen the same look in the woman's eyes, heard the same fear in her voice. It made him worry about the future of the new class of people that would be created after NLT's technology went mainstream. Would history repeat itself? Would androids be beaten in the streets? Would men and women with hate in their hearts stomp on the computers that made up these people's minds, extinguishing their lives for a second time? At least there was one silver lining—if their minds were backed up on a hard drive somewhere, they could be resurrected for a third, fourth, fifth time … they could go on living forever. Or at least, perfect duplicates of them could.

As he approached the entertainment lounge, he observed through the glass walls that his three co-conspirators were gathered around the flat-screen TV. As he walked into the room, they looked up at him expectantly.

"You did it," Natalie said.

"Yeah, but we might have a problem. Some woman walked into the bathroom and—"

"Wait," Brian said, "what was a woman doing in the men's restroom?"

"Uh, well … I accidentally went into the wrong bathroom."

All three of them cracked up. "You walked into the *women's restroom?*"

"Yeah, yeah, yuck it up. But the woman who walked in on me said she was notifying security. It's probably just a matter of time before they start checking up on us one by one. So how are you doing, Ted? We don't have a lot of time."

He walked around to take in the view of the TV. As Ted controlled a joystick, the view on the television tracked the path of the drone as it made its way to its destination.

"It shouldn't take too much longer."

The drone had a range of about five miles, which was just barely enough to make it to Sarah's house by Rajeev's estimation. But he wasn't sure how quickly it could make the trip and time was suddenly of the essence.

"I know that park," Rajeev said, pointing to the screen. "It's less than a quarter-mile from the house."

"Yep," Ted said. "Should be just a couple minutes."

True to his word, after just a few minutes, Sarah's house came into view. It was a modest two-story brick building with a small front yard surrounded by a white picket fence.

Rajeev pointed at the screen. "There it is!"

"Where do you want me to land this thing?" Ted asked. "How are we going to get her attention?"

"Can you make it ring the doorbell?"

"I can try."

He brought the drone down to the front door and bumped it into the doorbell, but it didn't hit quite right. Nothing happened. He tried it again; same result. Finally, on the third try, the doorbell rang out.

They waited with baited breath. Rajeev wondered if Sarah was home. A car was parked in the driveway, but that didn't necessarily mean anything. He'd almost given up hope when the door swung open.

It was Sarah. *His* Sarah. She was older than he remembered, yes. There were hints of gray in her blond hair and wrinkles under her eyes. But it was unmistakably Sarah, the woman he'd loved all his adult life. The mother of his children. The love of his life. Melancholy overwhelmed him as he took in her tired visage. He should have been by her side all these years, helping her raise the kids, her constant companion through good times and bad. Instead, he'd left her alone to raise the kids in solitude.

"What the … what the hell is going on?" She stared straight into the drone, a look of utter perplexity blanketing her face.

Ted waved Rajeev to his side. "Get over here." He pressed a button on the side of the joystick and motioned for Rajeev to start talking.

"Uh … hello," he said.

Sarah's eyes widened and she jumped back. When she spoke, her voice shook.

"Rajeev?"

"Hi Sarah," he said. "We have to talk."

ELEVEN

Sarah grabbed the drone out of the air and brought it inside. She set it on the kitchen table for her discussion with Rajeev.

He had a lot of explaining to do. He described waking up in Next Level Technologies' laboratory in a robotic body. Contrary to what Dev had told him, she'd had no idea there'd been any effort to duplicate Rajeev's mind and place it in an artificial body. Rajeev got the sense that she understood the philosophical implications ... that the Rajeev she had known and loved was dead, even if the Rajeev speaking to her through the drone was an incredible approximation of her one-time love.

The conversation then turned to their son.

"I've only spoken with Dev a handful of times in the past two years," she said. "I haven't seen him in person the entire time."

"Wrapped up in his company?"

"I guess. He always says he's too busy whenever I try to get in touch with him."

Rajeev sighed. "That's exactly what I was afraid of. Dev has forsaken his family in favor of pursuing riches. But I know you can get through to him, Sarah."

"I've tried. I don't know what else to do."

Rajeev shook his head. "Well what about Mira? She was always close with her brother."

"She's tried, too."

Rajeev was growing frustrated. "There has to be a way to get through to him."

"Hey," Brian whispered, nudging Rajeev. "Remember to tell her about our imprisonment."

Rajeev nodded. "Hey, Sarah? There's something else. Dev is keeping us here against our will. The company line is that because these artificial bodies are the property of Next Level Technologies, we're not allowed to leave without permission. And if we try to do it anyway, some kind of built-in failsafe stops us in our tracks the second we step outside the building."

Sarah looked horrified. "I'm sorry, Rajeev. I had no idea any of this was going on."

He nodded. "I know you didn't. But we need your help. I don't know how, but you need to get us out of here."

She shook her head despondently. "I have literally no say in the company. Dev owns it all. I can try to talk to him, and I can ask Mira to as well, but like I said, I don't think he'll listen to us."

"Do what you can," Rajeev said. "Keep the drone. We can use it to communicate periodically. It has solar panels, so if you leave it out in the sun from time to time, it'll stay charged."

"Will do. This is all so odd. I just wish—"

A creaking sound cut her off—a door had opened and a voice called out, "Hi, honey. You'll never believe the day I've—"

"I have to go," Sarah hissed suddenly. "I'll be in touch." Then the feed went dead.

None of the androids said a word. Rajeev felt the eyes of the others on him. He could only imagine what they were thinking. *Poor Rajeev* …

Of course, they weren't aware that he had been out of Sarah's life for fifteen years. Knowing that, the fact that she'd taken a new lover didn't seem unreasonable. Still, it had come as a bit of a shock. Sarah had remarried, presumably. Maybe it was less serious than that. But the man who had walked in was clearly more than a roommate—he'd called her "honey."

The realization that Sarah had moved on and found someone new to love stung. In a sense, he felt like he'd been with her just a couple weeks ago. But at the same time, he'd already begun disassociating from the life of what he considered the "original" Rajeev. It had also helped seeing the age Sarah had accumulated over the years. She was not the same woman he'd loved. She was undoubtedly far more mature than he was now; his personal growth had stalled for fifteen years.

Everyone stared at him in silence, but he chose not to address Sarah at all.

"We've made contact with the outside world," he said. "That's something."

Natalie nodded. "A first step, hopefully."

"Hopefully," Rajeev agreed. "For now, I'm going to head back to my room. Someone is probably going to come around to each of us with questions about the incident in the bathroom. I'll cop to it. I'll just say I was trying to get some air via the window. Besides, I have some pull—my son owns the company."

They nodded their agreement and Rajeev walked out without another word.

* * *

SURE ENOUGH, A SECURITY GUARD CAME BY ABOUT AN hour later and Rajeev explained what had happened—how he'd tried to explain to the woman why he was in the bathroom and that she hadn't let him get a word in edgewise. And of course, it was a simple mistake that he'd gone into the women's restroom as opposed to the men's, although technically he no longer had a gender.

The guard, a young man who looked to be in his twenties, had a good laugh, but ultimately went on his way. It appeared things had settled back into normalcy. It took just three more days for Rajeev to finish his physical therapy. By the end of it, he was walking almost as fluidly as he had in his old body.

Each night, Rajeev, Natalie, Ted and Brian gathered in the entertainment lounge and streamed the feed from the drone to the TV to see if Sarah had tried to communicate with them. She hadn't.

Rajeev had only communicated with Dev through a series of short voicemail messages courtesy of Daniel, but it was all surface-level conversation. Dev had indicated that he would come congratulate Rajeev on completion of his physical therapy that evening around six, however. Rajeev decided to stop by the entertainment lounge before meeting with Dev. As he approached, he saw one android inside.

"Hello," Rajeev said as he entered. "And you are … ?"

"It's me. Ted." He was cradling the drone's joystick in his arms and preparing to stream it to the TV.

"I'm meeting with Dev in about an hour."

"Yeah?"

"Yeah. I'm going to push him to let me see Sarah and Mira."

"You don't think he's going to let you go, do you?"

"I don't think so, but I need to give him the opportunity to prove me wrong."

Ted nodded. "I respect that."

The television flickered to life; he and Rajeev stared at it. Thus far, when Ted had begun streaming the drone's footage, nothing had happened, but now it appeared to be turned on and transmitting footage from Sarah's living room. But there was no one in sight.

"Hello?" Rajeev asked tentatively.

There was silence and then, in the background: "I think I heard something ... no, I definitely heard something." Sarah's face came into view. Her hair was down, silky and straight, and it looked like she'd carefully applied makeup to her face, which made sense—she'd been caught off guard by her first encounter with the drone, but now she knew she had an audience and wanted to look her best. She picked up the drone and brought it up to her face so that it took up almost the entire frame.

"Hello?" she asked.

"Uh ... hello," Rajeev said.

"I was right!" Sarah shouted over her shoulder. "He's back."

She backed away from the camera, maintaining a more normal distance, and took a seat. She stared into the camera quizzically.

"Is that really you, Rajeev?"

He laughed. "More or less."

She smiled, but it soon melted into a concerned frown. "I'm sorry about last time. You just caught me off guard and—"

"You don't have to say anything," Rajeev interrupted. She was apologizing for having moved on, but that was nothing to apologize for. "I understand."

"Still, I—"

"No, really. Don't. We have more important things to discuss."

She nodded. "Of course. Speaking of which ..." She motioned off-camera and a moment later a woman slid into frame beside her. She was widely built, short, and wore her long black hair in a ponytail draped across her shoulder. She wore a pair of oval glasses over her rich, brown eyes.

Rajeev gulped. He knew the instant he laid eyes on her who she was.

"Mira?"

She offered a half-smile that was equal parts joy and wonder. "Dad? Is that really you?"

"It is. How are you, sweetie?"

"I'm fine, dad. How are *you*?"

"Well, I've been better," he said, although even as he said it, he realized that wasn't true; as the second iteration of Rajeev Sundaram, he had been born into captivity—he had, in fact, never been better *or* worse. But of course, this wasn't the time to delve into the philosophy of human consciousness. "I assume your mother has explained the situation to you?"

"Pretty much—you're trapped in Dev's corporate prison?"

"In a manner of speaking, yes. If we try to leave, there's some kind of mechanism built into our bodies that stops us in our tracks. You know—to prevent loss of company property."

She shook her head. "How far my little brother has fallen."

"Mira has some ideas on how to get you out, Rajeev."

"I have a friend who's getting his master's in mechanical engineering from the University of Chicago. I told him about your situation and he thinks it would be possible to disable the failsafe."

"That's great," Rajeev said, "but unless it's something we can do ourselves, or you can smuggle him in here, I don't see how that does us much good."

Mira smiled. "We've thought of that," she said, "and we think we have a plan."

TWELVE

I'm not sure about this," Ted said. "It seems risky."

"Of course it's risky." Brian sounded energized, almost giddy, over the potential for danger. "So what? It's a risk worth taking if it gets us out of this hellhole."

"I'm not sure why *he* gets to be the one to get out of here," Natalie said, nodding in Rajeev's direction. "He hasn't been here for even a month. Most of us have been here for years."

"I don't like it any better than you," Brian said, "but the fact is, Rajeev is the best chance for *all* of us getting out of here eventually. He's the father of NLT's founder and has more leverage with him than any of us do. If he's able to get the ear of the media, he'll also make for a far more compelling story than any of us would—father versus son? It sounds like something out of a soap opera."

Rajeev sat on the couch, doing his best to ignore his compatriots' chatter and steel himself for what they were about to do. By the end of the day he very well may be dead—for a second time. Or he could end up paralyzed, if Mira's friend wasn't as skilled as he seemed to think he was.

He stood. "Let's stop delaying the inevitable and get this show on the road."

They made their way down the hall, single file. Rajeev was struck by the irony that they were given so much autonomy within these walls, yet the second they tried to set foot outside them, they were literally stopped in their tracks. He supposed be should grateful that they were able to move about freely, but he couldn't help but liken their situation to that of prison inmates able to move about the prison facilities freely until they were confined to their cells for the night.

They filed into the elevator and stood silently, side by side, as it lowered them to the first floor. When the elevator doors opened, they marched out and headed for the building's front entrance. Before coming into view of the guards, they huddled up to go over the plan one more time.

"This is crazy," Ted said, a hint of panic creeping into his voice. "This is absolutely nuts. We've tried this. It didn't work."

"It's too late to back out now," Natalie said. "We're in this."

"No," Rajeev said. "We're not going to do this without everyone on board. Do any of you want to back out? It's not too late if you do. We can walk away right now and work out some other plan."

Everyone's face gravitated to Ted. "Ugh, fine," he said. "Let's do it."

Rajeev nodded. "Okay then. On the count of three."

He began counting and as soon as he hit "three," Ted immediately sprinted for the exit.

"Hey!" a guard yelled as he sped past the security station. "Stop!" When it was clear he wasn't going to obey the command, the guard and his companion dashed around the guard station and followed after him. But Ted had a solid head start and was able to make it out the door before the guards could stop him.

The effects were immediate. As soon as he stepped outside,

his body seized up. He tipped to the right, falling over onto his side. The guards each picked a side and dragged Ted's body back into the building.

"What were you thinking?" one of the guards asked. "You know you can't leave without authorization!"

"I was just about to leave for the day," the other guard said. "I'm gonna have to stick around at least another hour now filling out paperwork."

Just as they were dragging Ted's body around to the back of the security station, the other three androids barrelled around the corner and made for the exit. It took a moment for the guards to fathom that yet *more* androids were making a break for it. They turned away from Ted and sprinted toward their new targets.

Natalie and Brian turned around abruptly and rushed the guards as Rajeev continued speeding for the exit. The guards had not anticipated that the androids might rush *toward* them, and as they grappled with their opponents, Rajeev made it out the door. He froze and plummeted to the ground. It was a terrifying sensation, knowing that he should be bracing himself for impact but finding himself incapable of doing so. His face was pointed to the ground and all he could see was the dirty pavement. Each second seemed to crawl by at a glacial pace. *Why aren't they here yet?*

Finally, he felt a pair of hands on either side of his body lifting him into the air, accompanied by hushed commands: "Quick! Load him into the van!" Rajeev watched as the pavement gave way to the lush green grass of the lawn, then back to pavement, and finally to the black, rubberized floor of a messy van.

The door slammed shut, and someone shouted, "Go! Go!" The van shot forward and the occupants rocked backward. When it got up to speed, Rajeev's rescuers turned him around on his back so he was facing up. Two faces peered over him: One belonging to a fair-skinned, black-haired sprite of a woman; the other belonging to a widely-built man with short-cropped blonde hair. He looked like a linebacker straight out of a 1950s-era college football team.

"How are you doing, Mr. Rajeev?" the man asked.

"He can't talk, dumbass." The voice came from the front of the van, out of Rajeev's sight.

"Actually, I can talk," Rajeev said. "And it's 'Mr. Sundaram.' Or just Rajeev."

A smug smile crept over the linebacker's face. "Who's the dumbass now?"

"To answer your question, I'm doing fine, although I've been better," Rajeev said. "Is anyone on our tail?"

The woman looked up, out the van's back window. "So far so good."

"If they haven't caught up to us by now, we should be in the clear," the man said. He turned to the driver. "But don't you dare slow down!"

The woman wiped her bangs away from her eyes. "I'm Rosa," she said, then gestured to her companion. "And this is Samuel."

"Pleased to meet you," Rajeev said. "Thank you for rescuing me."

Samuel smiled. "No sweat. Anything we can do to stick it to the man."

"What do you mean?"

"Next Level Technologies," Rosa said. "When we learned what they were doing to you ... claiming that your body is 'company property.' It pissed us off. It's disgusting. You're human beings. You never asked to be resurrected and squeezed into a body you didn't own."

"Well I'm glad you see things my way. Are you friends with Mira?"

"I am," Samuel said.

"And I," Rosa said, "am her wife."

Rajeev had no way to express his surprise but the pitch of his voice. "Her wife? Oh … oh!"

She shot a smirk at Samuel. "Took him a second, but I think he gets it."

"Sorry, I just wasn't expecting—"

"It's okay. We can save formal introductions for later. For now, just relax. We'll get you back up and running in no time."

"Hopefully."

She nodded and flashed him a comforting smile. "Hopefully."

THIRTEEN

THE VAN PULLED UP TO A NONDESCRIPT BROWNSTONE in a less-than-decent part of town. Samuel slid the door open, then helped Rosa carry Rajeev into the building. The driver and another passenger Rajeev hadn't seen earlier led the way into the building.

They carried him up three flights, then down the hall to the last apartment on the right. The driver knocked on the door and after a moment it opened to reveal a young man with a Mediterranean complexion and hair rolled into tight dreadlocks.

"Damn," he said. "That was quick. Come in." He stood aside as the group marched into the apartment.

"You can set him down here on the couch," the dreadlocked man said. Rosa and Samuel set him down gently, then stepped away to make room.

"Holy crap," the dreadlocked man said, taking in Rajeev's artificial body. "This is remarkable." He crouched above him and slid a hand down the silicone. "Gah! I wish I could tear this off so I could really see the inner workings of—"

"Please don't."

The man jumped. "Right. Sorry. Easy to forget we're working

with an actual person here." He retrieved a chair and placed it beside the couch. "I'm Zane and I'm here to help you. I'm getting my master's in mechanical engineering and I know a thing or two about software engineering as well, so between the two, there's at least a chance I can get you moving again. My understanding is there's some kind of failsafe preventing you from moving as soon as you step foot outside of NLT?"

"Correct. Think you can disable it?"

He brought a hand to his chin. "Possibly. It depends on whether the failsafe is something built into the underlying software allowing your mind to communicate with its body, or if it's mechanical. Either one could be a challenge, but I think we'd have better luck if it's a software issue." He grew serious and placed a hand on Rajeev's shoulder. "I feel it's imperative that you understand the risks before we proceed. We're walking into uncharted territory here. This is state-of-the-art, experimental technology and once I start poking around, I don't know exactly what I'm going to find. It's possible that in trying to fix you, I could break you even worse, or wipe you out altogether. If we proceed, I could kill you, Rajeev. Now that you understand the risks, do you still want to proceed?"

"Absolutely."

Zane smiled. "Okay, then. Let's get started."

* * *

ZANE FOUND THE PORT THAT GAVE ACCESS TO THE underlying software controlling Rajeev's mind and body. It was at the base of his neck, under a silicone flap that protected it from dust and grime. He plugged one end of a cable into the port and the other into his laptop, and spent the next hour sorting through code that looked to Rajeev and everyone else in the room like gibberish.

"Where's Mira?" Rajeev asked, trying to take his mind off

the fact that Zane could accidentally erase his entire existence with one stroke of the keyboard.

"We told Mira and Sarah not to come," Rosa said. "They're the first people Dev would suspect of helping you escape. In fact, I think he already has a tail on both of them. It's safer for them to stay home and act like they know nothing about this."

"That makes sense. I—"

"Shh!" Zane was suddenly rigid, typing furiously on his keyboard. "I think I found something! If I'm right, you'll be walking again within ten minutes, Rajeev."

"I hope you're right."

"Everyone shut up for a couple minutes and let me concentrate."

The room fell silent, save for the click-clacking of the keys as Zane typed. After a few minutes, he raised a finger into the air.

"If I'm right, once I hit the enter key, you'll be able to move again, Rajeev. You ready for this?"

"Of course!"

Zane lowered his finger and hit "enter." There was a pause and everyone in the room watched with bated breath. For several moments there was nothing. Then Rajeev's right index finger lifted, almost imperceptibly at first, but soon accompanied by his middle and ring fingers. He lifted his right arm, then the left, and propped himself up on the bed. He stood and stuck out his hand to Zane, who accepted and shook it.

"Thank you so much," Rajeev said. "How did you do it?"

"They didn't put much thought into it, really," Zane said. "The bodies are equipped with GPS hardware that pinpoints your location. They implemented a simple program that runs off the data provided by the GPS. As long as you're within the bounds of the NLT campus, it has no effect. But the instant the GPS detected that you'd left, it severed the connection between your mind and body."

"And you deleted the program?"

"No—I left the program intact. I just spoofed your location. As far as the program can tell, you're safe and sound at Next Level Technologies headquarters."

"That's awesome, but … if I'm equipped with GPS, doesn't that mean NLT can track me?"

"They can't anymore, because it'll always say you're on the NLT campus. Up until I made the switch, however they would have been able to track your location—which means we all need to leave."

"But what about your apartment?"

Zane laughed. "It's not my apartment, man—we're just borrowing it."

"You broke in?"

"I still prefer to say 'borrowed.' But seriously, we need to split."

Zane gathered his laptop and cables, and everyone filed out the door to the van.

FOURTEEN

"WE'RE GOING TO TAKE YOU TO MY PLACE," ROSA SAID. "Someone might come looking for you at Sarah's or Mira's."

"I thought you said you and Mira were married."

"We are … very recently. I've still got a couple months left on my lease."

"Makes sense. And then we go to the media, right?"

"We're going to record some interviews with you so if we don't get traction with any major media outlets, we can release them ourselves."

"What if none of it goes anywhere?"

"Then we figure something else out. We keep trying until something sticks. Because it's the twenty-first century and corporations shouldn't be allowed to keep slaves, regardless of whether their bodies are made of flesh and blood, or silicon and silicone."

They pulled into the driveway of a single-story, red-brick house that looked like it was built in the fifties. But it had clearly been well maintained, as evidenced by the flawless lawn. As Rajeev approached, the door swung open and there was

Mira, dressed in black slacks and a white blouse, staring into her father's photosensors with a look of fascination and confusion.

"Is that really you, dad?"

He was quiet at first, unable to find the words. Finally, he said simply, "Yes."

She stepped forward, opened her arms and wrapped them around him. He wrapped his arms around her and they embraced for a long moment. If Rajeev had had eyes capable of producing tears, they would have been wet.

"I'm sorry for the way I look. It must be unsettling."

She broke the hug and gave her father a chastising look. "I don't care about your appearance. All I care about is who you are on the inside."

In this moment, seeing and holding his daughter for what felt like the first time in years, all distinctions between the "old" and "new" Rajeev melted away. All that was left was a father and a fully grown woman who would forever be his baby girl.

"I love you, Mira. I'm sorry I was away from you for so long."

"It wasn't your fault, dad. You know that."

"I know. Still, I could have driven more carefully. I could have—"

She placed a hand on each of his shoulders and shook him gently as she spoke. "There's no changing the past. You're here and that's all that matters. There's nothing to forgive."

He nodded meekly and they embraced again, until Samuel spoke.

"I'm sorry to break up the moment, but the two of you should get inside just in case NLT has someone hot on our trail."

"What about you?"

"Don't worry about us. We can take care of ourselves. Good luck, Rajeev."

"Thanks for all your help."

"No problem."

Samuel and the others piled into the van, except for Rosa, who stayed behind. The three of them walked into the house and Rosa led them into the living room.

The interior of the house had clearly been remodeled since it was built. Fresh hardwood floors lay beneath their feet. The walls were fresh, pristine and white. The home had an open concept vibe, with a low counter separating the living room from the kitchen.

Mira directed Rajeev to a plush leather recliner in the corner of the room. "Have a seat, dad." As he settled in, she walked with Rosa to the couch and the two of them sat down. Rosa placed a hand over Mira's.

"How long have you two been together?" Rajeev asked cautiously.

Mira stole a glance at her partner beside her and smiled. "We dated for a solid two years and just tied the knot this fall."

Rajeev had always considered himself fairly progressive when it came to such matters, but now that it was his own daughter, he found it a more difficult prospect. He felt ashamed by his own lack of acceptance, but found it was something he could only suppress, not control. He smiled as he struggled to accept the life his daughter had made for herself.

"How did you two meet?"

Rosa answered this time. "Online," she said, smiling broadly. "We met up for drinks. I wanted to keep things casual, but … well, your daughter is quite an amazing woman, Rajeev. I couldn't resist her."

"I don't blame you." He looked away awkwardly. "So what now?"

"What's mine is yours," Rosa said. "Make yourself at home. I, uh … I assume you won't need to use the kitchen or bathroom, but we have a spare room you can use if you like. Do you sleep on a bed?"

"It's not strictly necessary, but it's what I'm used to."

"Perfect," Mira interjected. "Let me show you to your room, then."

She led him up a pair of slightly creaky stairs to a room at the end of the upstairs hallway. A twin bed took up half of the small room.

"I know it's not much."

"For my purposes, it's great. Thank you."

"So do you actually sleep?"

"Yes. I'm like a computer, apparently. I need to be refreshed every once in awhile."

"Get some sleep then. We'll record some interviews with you tomorrow. It'll turn out better if you're well rested."

"I will. Goodnight, Mira. I love you."

"I love you too, dad. I'm so happy you're back."

With that, she shut the door behind her. Rajeev fell onto the bed and closed his eyes, allowing himself to fall asleep while also reveling in his newfound freedom.

FIFTEEN

Rajeev awoke the next morning to what sounded like fighting. His first thought was that Mira and Rosa were engaged in some kind of spat, but then he recognized one of the voices as male. He jumped out of bed and opened the door to the room.

"Mira?" Rajeev called downstairs. "What's going on?"

He heard the male voice, not addressing him, but, presumably, Mira. "So he *is* here!" Footsteps echoed up the stairs and a man came into view. He stopped halfway up when he caught sight of Rajeev peering down at him.

"Mr. Sundaram … it's a pleasure to meet you."

"And you are?"

Mira ran up behind the man and looked up at her father, her eyes pleading for forgiveness. "I'm sorry, dad. He ran past me and I couldn't stop him."

"It's fine, Mira. But the question still stands: Who are you?"

"I'm Donald Lovitz. I work for Fresh Meat."

"Fresh Meat? That … that meat suit company? How did you even know I was here?"

He laughed. "Meat suits … that's a colorful way of putting it.

We manufacture biological body replacements, yes. As for how we found you, well … we have our ways, Mr. Sundaram."

"What do you want?"

"Mr. Sundaram, our CEO would like to arrange a meeting with you."

"Gregory Maltek?"

Donald raised an eyebrow. "You've done your research."

"Why does he want to talk to me?"

"I'm afraid I'm not at liberty to divulge that information. Here's what I can tell you. If you accept, we'll send an armored car to pick you up and take you to the airport."

"The airport?"

"To take you to Fresh Meat headquarters in San Francisco."

"So you want me to fly across the country to meet with the head of your company, but you won't tell me why?"

Donald crossed his arms and looked up at Rajeev with the faintest hint of a smile, as if he knew a juicy secret that Rajeev did not.

"How do you like that new body of yours, Rajeev?"

"I like it well enough."

"I'm sure that's all it is … sufficient. But what if instead, you could have a body even better than your old one? One that allows you to partake in the pleasures lost to you in a mechanical body? Strolling through a garden and smelling the sweet scents of the flowers. Sinking a fork into a perfectly-prepared steak and letting the juices flow over your tongue, overwhelming you with flavor. Meeting someone special, someone who drives you wild, and ravishing each other after a bottle or two of wine. None of these things are possible for you, Rajeev. But Gregory Maltek can give you all that and more. And if you're willing to help him, he'll give it to you for free."

Rajeev hesitated. He was just as skeptical of Fresh Meat as he was of Next Level Technologies, but in truth, it wasn't lost on him that living in this body meant he would indeed miss out on all the pleasures Donald had just described. As skeptical as he was, the possibility of getting put back into a flesh-and-blood body was tempting. Besides, all that was being asked of him was to meet with Maltek. He wasn't committing to anything and he could always change his mind.

"Okay," he said. "I'll meet with Maltek."

"Dad!" Mira looked shocked. "What are you doing? We have plans for you. You're just going to walk away from all that?"

Rajeev held out his hands defensively. "I'm not committing to anything. I'm just going to talk to the man."

Donald turned around to face Mira. "Honestly, Ms. Sundaram, we'll take good care of him. I promise. We'll even have him back by dinner." He turned back to Rajeev. "I'll send someone to pick you up in about two hours. Be ready." He turned around, nodding at Mira as he passed by, and walked out the door.

As soon as he was gone, Mira marched up the stairs to confront her father. "What are you thinking, dad? Fresh Meat is just as bad as NLT. All they care about is money."

"I'm not interested in their money. I'm just interested in hearing what Mr. Maltek has to say. That's all. I promise I'm not going to become some corporate goon out to do his bidding. Okay?"

She shook her head. "I still don't like this."

"Look, I'll be back by dinnertime, just like he said, and we can start planning our media strategy as soon as I get back."

"All right. I guess I don't really have a choice."

* * *

RAJEEV WANTED TO PUT ON SOME CLOTHES SO HE wouldn't attract stares on the way to the airport. Mira's were too large for him, but Rosa lent him a pair of jeans and a black hoodie that did a decent job of covering up the inhuman aberration that was his body.

A couple hours later, there was a knock on the front door. Rajeev answered it, and was presented with a short, frail-looking man with a pug nose and squinty eyes dressed in a driver's uniform.

"I'm here for Rajeev Sundaram," he said.

Rajeev, unsure whether the driver was aware that he would be driving an android and not a human being, tilted his head downward to obscure his face with the hood. "That's me," he said, stepping outside. He followed the driver to the car, and, after the driver opened the door for him, slid into the back seat.

They arrived at the airport, but not at the terminal. Instead, the driver pulled around back to a private runway.

"A private jet?" Rajeev asked.

"Of course. It's actually more cost-efficient for a big company like ours than taking a commercial flight."

Rajeev walked up the steps and into the jet. It reminded him a bit of Air Force One as he'd seen it portrayed in movies. Donald Lovitz was already on board, sitting on a small couch. When he saw Rajeev, he stood and stretched out his hand.

"Glad to see you made it without any problems, Mr. Sundaram. Please, have a seat."

Rajeev shook his hand and took a seat on the couch beside Donald's spot. Donald sat back down as someone pushed the stairs back into the plane and closed the door.

In moments, they were off, soaring into the sky. Donald helped himself to a bottle of beer on the way; Rajeev got the sense that he would have offered him one if he'd been able to partake, but of course, he didn't have a mouth.

The flight took about four-and-a-half hours and Rajeev was grateful when they landed. He realized Donald's promise to have him home by dinner couldn't possibly be true, as it would obviously take just as long for the return trip. Mira was going to be mad. He tried not to think about it.

Another car was waiting for him when he exited the jet. The drive to Fresh Meat took another twenty minutes. The car pulled up to a shiny skyscraper in the heart of the city. The driver parked, got out and opened the door for Rajeev.

"Mr. Sundaram?" A man was waiting for him outside the door. He was tall, square-jawed and handsome, with an impeccable, business-casual haircut and a mouth full of sparkling white teeth. He was dressed in a pinstriped black business suit and wore a narrow, blue tie.

"Yes. I'm Rajeev Sundaram."

"My name is Roger," the man said. "Follow me. Mr. Maltek is very excited to meet you."

SIXTEEN

GREGORY MALTEK'S OFFICE WAS ON THE TOP FLOOR OF the sixty-five-story building. Roger led Rajeev into an executive elevator and accompanied him to the top.

When the doors opened, Roger stepped out and gestured for Rajeev to follow him. They walked down the hall, took a left, and then entered through a set of french doors on their left into a spacious office.

A man sat on an ergonomic balance-ball chair behind a desk, typing on his computer. When Rajeev and Roger walked in, he looked up and smiled broadly, standing and walking out from behind the desk to meet them.

"Rajeev Sundaram!" he said. His voice was deep, rich. He looked to be in his early thirties. He wore a white dress shirt without a tie and with the sleeves rolled up to his elbows. He wore a pair of straight-legged khaki pants and a pair of black loafers. "I apologize for the unorthodox invitation, but you're a difficult man to get in touch with." He nodded to Roger. "Thank you for getting him here, Roger. I'll take it from here." Roger nodded and left.

Gregory led Rajeev to a small leather loveseat in the corner of the room. He took a seat in an armchair facing it.

"Why did you bring me here?" Rajeev asked.

"You get right down to business, don't you?"

Rajeev nodded. He got the impression that Gregory Maltek was highly amused by himself, and it annoyed him. But he'd flown all the way out here and it would be a good idea to at least find out why he'd made the trip.

"I gather you're aware," Gregory began, "that my company and your son's company are competing for the same clientele."

"You aren't competing at all, yet. Neither of you actually has a product on the market."

He nodded. "That's true. Neither of us has a product on the market. But that doesn't mean we aren't already competing. Do you remember the format war between Betamax and VHS?"

Rajeev nodded. "I didn't live through it, but I've heard about it, of course."

"The format wars are a lesson in hubris. Sony thought they'd developed a superior format with higher resolution, superior sound and longer-lasting players. And they weren't wrong. Yet the format failed. Do you know why?"

Rajeev shook his head. "I don't."

"It's because they didn't make it for the people—they made it for themselves. They didn't realize that people didn't give a shit about picture quality. The Betamax players were too expensive. VHS players were cheaper and they allowed for longer recording times. VHS was the tape player of the people, and it won out because it met the needs of the people."

"So how does this relate to Next Level Technologies versus Fresh Meat?"

"It's my belief that only one of our respective technologies will win out. So the question is, will people extend their lives by transferring their consciousness into a robotic body, or an organic one?"

"And you undoubtedly expect they'll choose the latter."

"Why wouldn't they? It's the natural choice. People get old and what do they wish for? To be made into a robot—or to be young again? The technology NLT is developing requires its customers to make a trade-off. There's a pro and a con. They get to extend their lives, perhaps even live forever, but as a result they must give up their flesh-and-blood existence and live as a machine incapable of eating, drinking, screwing, or even taking a good shit. Hardly a life worth living."

"It's certainly been an adjustment, but at the same time, I'm not suicidal."

"I'm not saying you are. I'm just saying, I bet you'd be a hell of a lot happier in one of our products than you are in your son's."

"So you flew me out here just to throw that in my face?"

"Not at all. I flew you out here because I need your help."

"With what?"

Gregory sighed. "Think about it in terms of the format wars. The war wasn't without casualties, and Sony wasn't the only one. Think about all the consumers who purchased Betamax players thinking they'd be able to purchase movies for years to come. Their trust was misplaced and they paid a price. In that instance, it wasn't a huge investment. But as you can imagine, immortality won't come cheap. People will likely have to mortgage their homes to pay for it, at least in the early days. What if they bet on the wrong horse? What if they spend tens or hundreds of thousands of dollars on a technology that will ultimately be obsolete in a few years? Wouldn't it be better if the dominant technology were established before it was even on the market?"

"Maybe. But what about choice? What about the free market?"

"The free market is fine and dandy, but if people are bound to be hurt, why not expedite the process?"

"What if they don't choose your product? What if NLT wins

out?"

Gregory smiled. "You know, many people argued that in the format wars, the lesser format won. Like I said, Betamax was the superior format in terms of video quality. But what Betamax's champions forget is that nobody cared about video quality. The general public determines the victor with their money. This will be no different. All I'm proposing is that we help people make the right decision. I'm confident people will choose us."

"I still don't see how I fit into this."

"Well, I'd like to have you as an inside man of sorts. Help me gain access to information that could help me more effectively compete with NLT."

"You want me to spy for you."

Gregory smiled, revealing two rows of perfect, white teeth. "Espionage is an essential part of any war. A necessary evil. Now, I know this may strike you as an abhorrent request, to spy on your own son, but I'd argue just the opposite. If the information you provide helps us stamp out the competition, you'll actually be doing the world a service. You'll be ensuring that little old ladies selling their homes for a second chance at life get a true, fully realized life—not a dreary half-life in some rust bucket that could break down at any moment."

"You're forgetting that I'm no longer on speaking terms with Dev. As I'm sure you know, I escaped from the NLT campus."

"Yes, but if anyone can go back, it's you. You're his father. Sure, he'll be pissed. But he'll forgive you. You're family."

"It's not just that. You underestimate the ability of people to make decisions for themselves. And I'm not sure I believe in either one these products. On one hand, you have robotic bodies that sentence their occupants to indentured servitude on behalf of a corporation. On the other hand, you have cloned bodies— bodies that may very well destroy an existing soul as they're readied for new occupants, although I suppose only God knows that for certain."

"I understand your hesitation, Mr. Sundaram, but if I can explain further—"

"My answer is no," Rajeev said firmly. "I won't help you spy on my son's company."

Gregory's smile faded. With a scowl on his face, he said, "But we didn't even discuss your compensation." Rajeev said nothing. He stared blankly at Gregory's suddenly hostile face. "I'm prepared to pay you a hundred thousand dollars. Further, I'm offering to take you out of that tin can and put you back in an organic body. Imagine it, Rajeev—being able to eat, to drink, to make love again. That alone is surely worth more than any amount of money."

Rajeev tilted his head. "Can you tell me more about how you produce these bodies?"

Gregory shook his head. "Afraid not. That's proprietary."

"Then like I said before, I'm not interested." He stood and walked toward the door. Gregory leapt off his seat and blocked his retreat, bringing his face inches from Rajeev's.

"You may want to think long and hard about rejecting my offer," he said. "I have more tricks up my sleeve than you know. And besides, someone you love may need one of my products very soon ... like your daughter, Mira. Or perhaps your lovely, one-time wife, Sarah."

Rajeev stood there, stunned. Unless he was mistaken, the man had just threatened his family. And for Rajeev, family was everything.

"You're threatening them?"

Gregory stared Rajeev down with eyes that had grown cold and cruel. "I'm not *threatening* anything."

Rajeev sidestepped Gregory and continued walking to the door. As he was about to exit, Gregory called out to him.

"You have twenty-four hours to think it over, Rajeev. After that, all bets are off."

SEVENTEEN

THE FLIGHT BACK TO CHICAGO WAS A SOLEMN ONE. Rajeev pondered Gregory's threat. How serious was he? Surely it was an empty threat meant to nudge him toward accepting the offer on the table. But what if the threat was real? Fresh Meat was a large company, with enough resources to get away with all kinds of shady business ... perhaps even assassination.

The jet landed and a car sat on the tarmac waiting to take him home. He thought twice about using the provided transportation, but the fact was, Gregory Maltek already knew where Mira lived. Maybe Rajeev could get Mira and Sarah to lay low for awhile, to move into a hotel. But what's to say Maltek wouldn't track them to their new location?

When the driver dropped him off outside Mira's house, it was dark. Rajeev trudged up the front steps onto the porch and tried to open the door as slowly as possible. He moved slowly, to reduce any noise that might signal his arrival, but it was for nothing: Mira was sitting in an armchair facing the front door, arms folded like a disappointed mother catching her teenage child breaking curfew.

"Back in time for dinner, huh?"

Rajeev shrugged. "I'm sorry. That's what they told me. I didn't think to question it."

"So what did they say?"

He paused. How much should he tell her? On the one hand, Mira didn't like Dev's company any more than he did. On the other hand, she hated Fresh Meat with equal fervor.

"They wanted to see one of NLT's robotic bodies up close," he said. "They offered to put me in one of their organic bodies and pay me for the robotic one so they could study it."

"You refused?"

"Of course."

Mira let out a long sigh. "All right. Well I'm just glad it's over and that you're done with them."

"Me too."

"We'll have to film the videos tomorrow. I'm going to get some sleep. You should too."

"Okay, sweetie. Goodnight. I love you."

"I love you too, dad."

She left for her room. Rajeev didn't move at first. He was preoccupied by the questions and quandaries swimming through his mind. But after several minutes he didn't have a clear answer to any of them and decided a night's sleep might help him think more clearly.

He plodded up the stairs and made his way to the spare bedroom. He took off the hoodie and jeans, folded them and left them on top of the dresser. He took a seat on the bed, not quite ready to lie down and drift off. Light from a streetlight streamed into the room; although complete darkness wasn't strictly necessary for him to sleep anymore, he still found it distracting. He stood and walked to the window to lower the blinds.

He lowered it halfway, then stopped. His eyes had drifted across the street and settled on a nondescript white van with tinted windows parked across the street. He hadn't noticed the van there before. On its surface, it wasn't *that* unusual. People had vans. They parked them on the street.

But Rajeev couldn't get Gregory Maltek's threats out of his mind. *Someone you love may need one of my products very soon.* Gregory knew Mira was staying here with Rosa. It wasn't outside the realm of possibility that the van across the street contained one of his hired goons, his presence designed to intimidate Rajeev into compliance.

No. He was paranoid. He had no reason to think—

Suddenly, the van's headlights lit up and the engine roared to life. It idled for a minute, then pulled into the street and slowly drove away.

It was beginning to seem less and less like a coincidence. Gregory Maltek's threat was seeming less and less benign. Rajeev had come to a conclusion. He didn't like it, but he didn't think he had a choice if he wanted to keep his family safe.

He was going to give Gregory what he wanted.

<h1 style="text-align:center">EIGHTEEN</h1>

Rajeev awoke early the next morning, before Mira or Rosa had awakened. He made sure the door to his room was tightly shut, locked it, and took a seat at the foot of the bed.

"Daniel?"

The virtual assistant appeared before him, dressed in the same green polo and khakis, with his familiar grin plastered on his face.

"Hey, Rajeev," he said cheerily. "Long time, no see."

He bristled at Daniel's chatty tone; it felt like it was coming more from the AI's programmers than from the collection of algorithms and code he actually consisted of. Then again, it *had* been awhile since he'd interacted with Daniel; he'd probably be thinking of him as a person again in no time.

"Hi Daniel. Can you send a message for me, please?"

"Absolutely. Who would you like to message?"

"Gregory Maltek."

Daniel paused. "You must have the recipient's contact information in your address book to send a—"

"Check the address book for Gregory Maltek." Gregory hadn't given Rajeev his contact information, but he had a feeling he had already taken the necessary action to ensure Rajeev could get in touch with him.

"Gregory Maltek," Daniel said. "Phone number: Four-one-five, six-two—"

"That's fine, Daniel. Please, send a message to Mr. Maltek."

"Absolutely. What's your message?"

Rajeev sighed. "'I'll do it. Call off your dogs.'"

"Here is your message: 'I'll do it. Call off your dogs.' Would you like to send it?"

"Yes."

There was a pause; Daniel stared ahead blankly.

"Message sent."

It was done. He'd made his choice. He just hoped he could live with it.

A moment later, Daniel announced that Rajeev had received a new message from Maltek.

"Would you like me to read it to you?"

"Obviously."

"'I knew you'd come around. And don't worry—I'll still give you everything I promised. Once you get me the info I need, we'll arrange a time to transfer you into one of our organics.'"

If Rajeev had had a stomach, there would have been a pit in it. Maltek had promised him one hundred thousand dollars and a body that might be worth millions. All it would cost him was his soul.

No. He didn't want Gregory Maltek's blood money. He'd do his dirty work, but only to protect his family. He wouldn't profit from this devious espionage. Maltek would be the only one doing that.

* * *

Mira and Rosa awoke and found Rajeev sitting alone on the living room couch.

"Good morning," Mira said. "What are you up to? You look bored."

"Not at all. I was just having Daniel read me the news."

"Daniel?"

"My virtual assistant."

"Oh. He's built right into you, huh?"

"Yeah. I was curious about that, actually. Do you have a virtual assistant?"

"I do."

"How do you interact with it?"

She tapped the arm of her glasses. "Augmented reality glasses and a Bluetooth earpiece."

"Makes sense." He turned to Rosa. "What about you? You don't wear glasses."

"I wear AR contact lenses. I don't even have a prescription. I just wear 'em for the tech."

"So what if someone wanted a virtual assistant but they didn't wear glasses or contacts?"

Rosa shrugged. "People still have phones. It's not quite as personal, but it works."

"Anyway," Mira said, "we were just about to have breakfast. I know you can't eat anything, but would you like to join us?"

He shook his head. "I appreciate it, but you two enjoy yourselves. We're going to be spending enough time together today."

He figured he'd go ahead and record the videos with Mira. Then, after she and Rosa had gone to sleep for the night, he'd sneak out and call a car for hire to take him back to the Next Level Technologies campus, where he'd beg Dev for forgiveness and try to get back into his good graces—all so he could spy on his son and his company.

It all felt so treacherous, but he had to remember that it was to protect his family. Maybe not Dev, who had the resources and the personal security to ward off any threat that may come his way, but certainly for Mira and Sarah.

After Mira and Rosa finished their breakfasts, Mira led Rajeev into the living room and directed him to take a seat. A minute later, Rosa came down the stairs with camera equipment under each of her arms. Before long, the pair had set up a backdrop behind Rajeev, and professional lighting to illuminate him. Mira set up a digital camera on a tripod and pointed it at her father.

"Okay," she said. "We're rolling."

"What do you want me to say?"

"Start by stating your name for the record."

"Rajeev Sundaram."

Mira giggled. "No, dad, you have to add the context. You can't just say your name. You have to say, 'My name is Rajeev Sundaram.'"

"Oh, okay. Well, yeah. My name is Rajeev Sundaram."

"Hello, Rajeev Sundaram. Can you explain your … well, your rather unusual appearance?"

He looked down, taking in the sight of his own body. Then he looked back up, into the camera.

"Fifteen years ago, I was in a car accident," he said. "It put me in a coma. When I woke up, I was in this body. As you can probably tell, it is not a normal flesh-and-blood body. It's a robotic body made by Next Level Technologies." The conversation was gaining the rhythm of a true interview, with Mira taking on the tone of a real journalist, and Rajeev treating her as such.

"Tell me more about this body of yours."

"According to the company, it's just a prototype. Future models will be more realistic, supposedly. As it is, I can see, hear, speak, and feel. But I can't smell or taste. I don't breathe. It's odd. I don't always feel like myself."

"Are there others like you?"

Rajeev nodded. "On the NLT campus, there were other androids. I don't know how many there are altogether, but all the ones I saw had bodies more or less identical to mine. We had to identify each other verbally, ask each other who we were talking to, because we couldn't tell each other apart visually."

"And could you all come and go as you pleased?"

Rajeev shook his head. "No. We weren't allowed to leave the campus. If we tried, our bodies would seize up and security guards would retrieve us and bring us back."

"If that's the case, then how is it you're here being interviewed, clearly off the NLT campus?"

"I—" He paused, leaning forward and speaking under his breath. "Am I allowed to talk about … ?"

"It's fine," Mira said. "Speak freely. If you say anything compromising, we'll just edit it out."

"Okay." He paused before continuing. "A computer programmer hacked into the system that allows my mind to communicate with its body and disabled the program that paralyzed me if I set foot off campus."

"And why is it that NLT prevented you from leaving their campus is the first place?"

"Because they consider these bodies company property and don't allow them off their corporate campus."

Mira picked up the camera and turned it around to face her. "That's exactly right," she said. "This company holds human beings prisoner—*actual* human beings—inside artificial bodies, hiding behind a shield of intellectual property. NLT thinks we're too stupid and too weak to do anything about it. But they're wrong! Together, we can boycott NLT and force the company to take responsibility for its actions. The only way we're going to enact change is by hitting them where it hurts: their bank account."

Mira turned the camera back to her father. "Rajeev, do you have any kind of special relationship with NLT or any of the company's high-level executives?"

Rajeev hesitated a moment, but then nodded. After all, he'd

agreed to this. "Yes," he said. "Dev Sundaram. The CEO. He's my son."

She turned the camera back to herself. "You heard that right. This brave man is the son of none other than Dev Sundaram, the founder and CEO of Next Level Technologies. Dev Sundaram enslaved his own father. What will he do with *your* father, or *your* mother, when he gets his hands on them? Will he promise them immortality, then lock them in a silicon cage?"

She paused. "And guess who I am? I am Mira Sundaram, Dev's sister. Don't get me wrong here. I love my brother. So does my father. We are not against my brother; we are against his actions and the actions of his company. Actions that, if left unchecked, have the potential to allow a corporation to enslave a massive swath of the population. And I'm willing to bet that prospect doesn't sound any more palatable to you than it does to me. And if that's the case, you need to act. Stop purchasing anything with even ancillary ties to NLT—we'll link to a guide in the video description—but also contact your legislators. Tell your senator, your congressperson, your state attorney general, and anyone who will listen that you're concerned about NLT. Tell your lawmakers slavery was abolished more than one-hundred and sixty years ago, and you sure as hell are not going to let it start up again now. Thanks for listening and be sure to like, comment and subscribe and above all else, *share this video!*"

She turned the camera off and set it down, then turned to Rajeev and sighed.

"That's that, I guess."

"It's that good, huh? We got it all in one take?"

"It's good enough. People can smell inauthenticity a mile away nowadays. If we tried to make it flawless, they'd just tune it out."

"So are we going to record more?" Rajeev wasn't sure why he asked it. He knew he wasn't going to be there to record more videos.

"I think this is fine for now. We'll see what kind of response it gets and go from there." She smiled, and Rajeev saw a hint of the young girl he remembered from before his accident. "Thank you for agreeing to do this, dad. It might not make a huge difference, but it will do something. It might just be the straw that breaks the camel's back."

"The camel in this case being your brother."

"Not at all! Just like I said in the video, we're not going after Dev. We're going after his company. It's the company that has corrupted him and not the other way around. I'm just as interested in saving him as I am in saving you and all the other androids NLT has imprisoned."

"I do think he's let greed corrupt him."

She nodded. "He wasn't always like this. He started acting differently one, maybe two years ago. Just out of the blue. One minute he was kind, considerate … the next minute he wouldn't return calls from me or mom. Oh, but if he wanted something from us … well, then he'd get annoyed if we didn't answer his missed calls quickly enough."

"Sounds like he was overworked."

She nodded. "I'm sure that's part of it. But I think it's more than that. His values became warped. His company became more important than his own family. He goes around giving all these interviews about how he started the company because of how much he loved his family—because he loved *you*, dad—but then, in time, he ends up ignoring the family he still has, like we're nothing."

"I know it's frustrating." He nodded at the camera. "I think all we can do now is tell the truth and hope it does some good."

NINETEEN

Mira and Rosa invited Rajeev to join them for lunch, but he pointed out that it would be awkward—he couldn't eat, after all, so he'd just end up watching *them* eat, like some bizarre culinary voyeur—so he politely declined.

He watched as they walked out of the house and into the car. As soon as they'd driven out of sight, he walked upstairs and picked up the clothes he'd left on the dresser. He put them on, walked out of the room and gently closed the door behind him. He ambled down the stairs and went to the front door.

He hesitated, wondering if he should leave Mira a letter explaining where he'd gone, and why. But he decided against it. The less she knew about this debacle, the better. He turned the handle, opened the door and walked out, closing the door behind him.

"Daniel?"

His assistant appeared, standing on the porch in front of him.

"How can I help you today?" he asked cheerily.

"Daniel, call me a car, would you?"

"I'd be happy to, but, uh, you don't have any payment information on file."

"Charge it to Gregory Maltek."

"I'm sorry, I can't—"

"Daniel, send the following message to Gregory Maltek: 'I need money for a car. Please send payment information.'"

"Here's what I have—"

"Go ahead and send it, Daniel."

"Okay. Message sent."

They waited a moment. Rajeev was beginning to get used to these awkward moments with Daniel as he waited for his messages to go through. Finally, the virtual assistant piped up.

"You have a new message from Gregory Maltek. Would you like me to read it?"

"Please."

"'Sure. Payment information is attached for a ten-thousand-dollar line of credit. Consider it an advance.'"

"There you go, Daniel. How about that car?"

* * *

RAJEEV HAD THE DRIVER LET HIM OFF A BLOCK AWAY from the entrance to the NLT campus. He didn't want the driver getting entangled in things if there was some kind of confrontation. He thanked the driver and got out.

"Daniel?"

"How can I help?"

"Leave the driver a tip, please."

"Certainly. How much?"

He hesitated, but then remembered the ten thousand dollars in blood money Maltek had made available to him.

"One thousand percent."

"Sir, that's one hundred forty dollars." Rajeev could have sworn he heard a hint of surprise in Daniel's normally flat voice.

"That's fine. Tip the man."

Daniel nodded. "Very well. Tip sent."

As Rajeev approached the double doors that led into the building, a combination of dread and anticipation flowed throughout his body. He wished he could have taken a deep breath, but without a throat or lungs, he just continued on through the doors.

As soon as he entered the building, two guards stationed at the front desk simultaneously did a double take. Then they sprung into action.

Before he could say a word, they were beside him, grabbing either one of his arms and dragging him to their station.

"I—I just wanted to—"

"You're not going to believe this—the missing patient just walked through the front door," one of the guards said into his radio. "Alert Mr. Sundaram."

The other guard stuck a finger in Rajeev's face. "Shut up. Not a peep." Rajeev held up his hands defensively, indicating compliance.

A few moments later, Dev walked down the hall flanked by two additional guards. "Dad?" he asked. "Is that really you?"

Rajeev nodded, and Dev's face grew hard.

"Take him to my office. I'll be there shortly."

The guards affirmed their grips on Rajeev's arms and began dragging him away. Dev stood still, watching Rajeev with eyes that were cold and angry.

* * *

THE GUARDS DRAGGED RAJEEV INTO DEV'S OFFICE and threw him into a chair. Then they waited, arms folded, awaiting their boss.

He arrived a few minutes later, emerging from the elevator with the cold indifference of a movie villain. Rajeev understood how he could be upset with him for escaping, but even so, he couldn't shake the feeling that was not how the Dev he'd known would have reacted. He suddenly felt sad. How would his son have turned out if Rajeev had never gotten into that fateful car accident? What if he'd been there to raise him, to guide him, to teach him what really mattered in life? No, Dev might not have ended up filthy rich like he was now. But in some ways, Rajeev suspected his son would have had a richer life. A fulfilling career with a good work-life balance. A loving wife. Maybe a couple of adoring children. Instead, his son had become a man obsessed with financial success at the exclusion of all else, and he stood before his father now with eyes devoid of love, filled instead with the unmistakable mark of a deep, seething anger over a perceived threat to his growing fortune. Rajeev suddenly lost all confidence that Dev would ever forgive him.

Dev walked directly in front of his father, bending down so they were face to face.

"Welcome back, dad," he said, his eyes narrow, sarcasm dripping off his tongue.

"Glad to be back."

"I'm sure you are." He looked up at the guards and gestured toward the door. "Leave us."

"Hold on, Mr. Sundaram—"

"I said go."

They skulked off to the elevator reluctantly; if they'd had tails, they would have been between their legs. Once they'd entered the elevator and the doors had closed, Dev turned back to his father.

"Where did you go?"

"I went home, Dev. I kept telling you I wanted to see your mother and sister."

"My men went to mother's. She said she hadn't—"

"You didn't really think she'd tell your men the truth, did you?"

"No. But they searched the place and didn't find any trace of you. They searched Mira's place, too, and again: Nothing."

"You can't blame me for going undetected. The fact remains: I left to see my family, which you were denying me the opportunity to do."

"Uh-huh. And how were you able to bypass our failsafe? Did mom help you with that, too?" Rajeev said nothing. Dev took a deep breath and when he spoke again his voice was deep and heavy. "Fresh Meat got to you, didn't they? They want to steal my technology."

The question caught Rajeev off guard and he hesitated for a split second, but then recovered. "Dev, that's … that's absurd. All I wanted was to see my family. I asked you repeatedly for a chance to see them and you kept giving me excuses. I decided to take matters into my own hands."

"And decided to figure out how to bypass our failsafe. That's the little detail that condemns you, dad. I know for a fact you don't have the technical prowess to pull something like that off. That means you needed help. The only problem is, you've been in a deep sleep for the past fifteen years. Besides mom and Mira, you don't know anyone—or know how to track down anyone— with the skills to do something like that. But I know Fresh Meat has spies in this company and it wouldn't surprise me at all if they found a way to contact you. I'm sure *they* could pull something like that off."

"I'm sure they could. But in this case, they didn't. And I take umbrage at the assertion that I couldn't have possibly had reason to escape without prodding from a corporation just as corrupt as yours. I wanted to see my family, Dev. Maybe that's difficult for you to understand, the way you've isolated yourself from them, but for some of us, family is still more important than money. And it sure as hell didn't help when I learned that you'd imprisoned not just me, but all these other androids, under the guise of intellectual property rights. We're human beings, Dev, not patents or song lyrics. You've made enemies, not just of competing corporations, but also of good, everyday people who object to your corrupt business practices. It wasn't as difficult for me to find assistance as you might think it was."

"Then why did you come back here?"

"Because you're my son, Dev. I wanted to see Sarah and Mira. And I did. But you're my family, too, and I couldn't just abandon you. I needed to make things right. So ... here I am."

"We'll see about that. Right now I'm going to need to see exactly how you evaded our failsafe." He walked to a cabinet on the other side of the room, opened it and retrieved a thin tablet computer and a cord. As he walked back to Rajeev, he plugged one end into the tablet and held the other end in his hand.

"May I?"

Rajeev nodded, albeit reluctantly—Dev would undoubtedly reverse the changes Zane had made, which meant he'd be trapped here again, just like all the other androids.

Dev pushed the tip of the cord into the port at the base of Rajeev's neck. He began tapping on the tablet's touch screen, mumbling to himself as he did so.

"Ah," he said suddenly. "I see what they did." He shrugged. "Simple, but effective." He gave the tablet a few more taps, then gave a satisfied sigh. "Well, there we go—back to normal."

Rajeev winced, but then, he'd expected it. He was here to keep his family safe, anyway. He'd be best served to remain focused on that mission.

Dev put away his tablet and when he turned back to his father, his face had softened.

"You always were a stubborn bastard," he said. "You really left just to see mom and Mira?"

He nodded. "Yes."

"I'm still not sure I believe you, but since you're family, I'll give you the benefit of the doubt. But promise me you're not going to pull anything like that again."

"I promise. It was a one-time thing. I'm sorry."

"All right. You can return to your dorm, then."

Rajeev stood and headed for the elevator.

"Oh, and dad?" Rajeev stopped and turned around. "Things have changed around here since your stunt. Don't expect to have the same freedoms you had before."

Rajeev gave a short, curt nod and continued to the elevator.

TWENTY

Instead of going straight to his dorm, Rajeev found himself heading to the entertainment lounge instead. Although he'd been gone only a few days, he was surprised to find he missed the motley crew of androids who had helped him escape. He barely knew them, but they'd been bonded by circumstance, each of them imprisoned in corporate-owned artificial bodies that made them look like monsters. They were freaks, and all they had in this corporate wasteland was each other.

At the same time, he was nervous to face them. After all, he'd left as their supposed savior, escaping the confines of this prison to find help for those he'd left behind. The only thing they would find more dispiriting than him never returning was him returning empty-handed, without a single morsel of hope for them. And that's exactly how he was returning now.

As he approached the glass walls, he made out a sole occupant—an android sitting on the couch, legs crossed, engrossed in a worn paperback book.

He opened the door and crept in quietly. The android failed

to look up, and Rajeev wondered whether it was because it didn't notice he'd entered, or didn't care.

"Hi," he said. "And you are … ?"

The android looked up from the book, but did not yet look up at Rajeev. It processed the voice it had just heard as if it was a remnant from a long-forgotten dream.

"Rajeev?" Natalie's voice, soft and mellifluous, flowed out of the android's mouth.

"Yeah, it's me," he said. "Hi Natalie."

She leapt off the couch; the book fell to the floor. "What are you doing here? What happened? Did they catch you? What the hell!"

He refused to say anything until she sat back down. Once she was settled, he took a seat beside her. His first inclination was to lie; to claim that he had, indeed, been caught by his son's operatives. If it had been any of the other androids seated next to him, he may have said exactly that. But for some reason, Natalie was able to draw the truth out of him.

"I escaped," he said. "It was all going fine. They took me to some grad student's place, a programming whiz, and he was able to disable the failsafe so I could move again. Then they took me to my daughter's … wife's … house. But they found me there."

"Who found you? NLT?"

"No. Fresh Meat."

"Fresh Meat? But how would they—*why* would they—"

"They knew I was Dev's son. I don't know *how* they knew, but they did. And they wanted to use me to get information on NLT. They asked me to crawl back here and gather any information I could find—any information they could use to rid themselves of their strongest competition."

Natalie nodded her head encouragingly.

"It makes sense for them to come to you. 'The enemy of my enemy is my friend.'"

Rajeev shook his head. "Fresh Meat is arguably even more repugnant than NLT."

"So you refused to spy for them?"

Rajeev hesitated. "They threatened my family. I had no choice."

Natalie reached out and placed her arm on his knee. "Oh, Rajeev. I'm sorry. That's terrible."

"I didn't know what else to do. If I want to keep my family safe I have to at least look like I'm making an effort to spy on my son." Talking about it now exposed emotions Rajeev hadn't even realized were bubbling beneath the surface. If he'd had eyes, they would have teared up. "I didn't want to tell this to any of you, but … I don't know. It feels good to tell someone."

"I'm sure it does." She stood. "I don't know what to tell you, though. It looks like you're screwed."

"Tell me about it."

"It's okay, though. We'll all do what we can to help."

"What do you mean?"

"We'll help you gather any intel we can find."

"I can't ask you guys to do that."

"You didn't have to ask. Besides—any scrutiny we can put on NLT increases our chances of getting out of here. In my opinion, we should focus on taking down NLT and then worry about Fresh Meat. I know you may not ascribe to the notion, but I do, so I'll say it again: 'The enemy of my enemy is my friend.'"

* * *

Natalie promised Rajeev she'd spread the word to the other androids about the need for a secret espionage campaign. In the meantime, they returned to their respective dormitories.

As he lay down on his bed, Rajeev found himself questioning whether any of them would find any useful dirt on the company.

Next Level Technologies was a state-of-the-art tech company, likely outfitted with the most advanced security technology known to humankind. The likelihood of a bunch of nobodies in robot bodies discovering anything of significance seemed slim.

Still, he had to try. He couldn't let anything happen to Sarah or Mira. If something *did* happen, he'd never forgive himself. He tried to think of what he could do on his own to gain any useful intel, but nothing came to mind. He hoped the other androids were having better luck.

He came to a conclusion: He wasn't going to get anywhere sitting in his bed staring up at the ceiling. He needed to wander around, even if he didn't have a plan. Maybe he could discover something just by stumbling upon it. He got up, walked to the door and emerged from his dorm hesitantly. He meandered down the building's industrial gray halls, unsure of where to go. He was more familiar with this floor than any of the others, and he hadn't noticed any opportunities for espionage, so he thought he'd be more productive on a different level. Once on the elevator, he studied the floor number buttons, then selected one at random to press: Thirty-five.

The elevator beeped and a robotic voice came over hidden speakers built into its ceiling: "Invalid operation."

"What the hell?" Rajeev pressed the button once more, but again, the same monotone voice came over the speakers: "Invalid operation."

"Daniel?" The virtual assistant appeared in the corner of the elevator.

"Hi Rajeev," he said cheerily. "How can I be of assistance?"

"What's wrong with this elevator?"

Daniel furrowed his brow, suddenly looking concerned. "What seems to be the trouble with it?"

"When I press the floor button," he said, pressing the button for a different floor this time, "I get this message." They listened together as the elevator again announced that Rajeev was attempting an "invalid operation."

"It appears your elevator permissions have been disabled," Daniel said.

"My 'elevator permissions?' What the hell does that mean?"

"Everyone on the Next Level Technologies campus has a radio-frequency identification, or RFID, chip to grant them access to different areas of the campus. It also grants access to the elevators. You and the other androids have the chip built into your bodies. It appears the privileges on your particular RFID chip have been altered, granting you permission to only two floors: the sixth and the twelfth."

"So I have access to my dorm and the entertainment lounge, and that's it."

"And any other amenities found on those two floors. Yes."

"How do I change it back?"

"You can't. Only a system administrator can change these permissions."

A system administrator. Like Dev, probably. His son's words suddenly echoed in his head: *Don't expect to have all the same freedoms you did before.*

So that's what he'd meant. Rajeev wasn't allowed to move about the building as he'd been able to before. That made any kind of substantive corporate espionage impossible.

He had to figure *something* out, though, because failure wasn't an option if he wanted to keep his family safe.

<h1 style="text-align:center">TWENTY-ONE</h1>

"Did you already eat?"

He'd slid into bed as quietly as possible, but Sarah had woken up anyway.

"Yeah, I just got some fast food."

She swats him on the arm playfully. Her voice sounds like a faraway whisper as she says, "You need to stop eating that crap. It's going to kill you someday."

He smiles, amused by the childlike demeanor she's taken on in her half-asleep state. "Anything could kill anyone at any time," he says. "Best not to worry about it."

She sits up and rubs some of the sleep out of her eye. She's waking up now and regaining her full faculties. Rajeev knows that can mean only one thing: A serious talk is coming.

"I want you to quit driving," she says.

He lets out an exasperated sigh. "Sarah, we've been over this—"

"I know, but it's taking a toll on this family. You hardly ever see Dev and Mira, and with Mira's grades slipping ..."

"I told you why her grades were slipping."

"I know. And she suffered in silence for a long time, Rajeev. She didn't

come to either of us. And why would she have? You're never here and I'm always busy holding everything else together. She has no one to turn to."

"We have a mortgage. We have two kids—kids that need food and clothes and, before too long, are going to need college tuition. How do you think we're going to pay for all that if I quit?"

"We'll make do. I'm not proposing you do nothing, just that you find a job with a better work-life balance, even if it pays less. The kids are getting older. I can get a part-time job; hell, so can Mira! The kids are smart—they'll get scholarships to help pay for school. We can always find ways to make more money. But we can never buy back time with the kids."

He shakes his head. She has a point, he knows that, but he doesn't feel like he can stop the momentum he's built up.

"I'll think about it," he says.

She nods. "That's all I'm asking from you, for now," she says. "But think it over soon. I need you. The kids need you."

He kisses her cheek. "I know," he says. "I need you, too. I love you."

RAJEEV KEPT COMING TO THE SAME CONCLUSION. HE'D never be able to find a solution on his own; that much was certain. He'd barely been able to set up his own phone in the time before his crash, so he'd certainly never be able to navigate any of the newfangled tech that powered the NLT campus now.

But Gregory Maltek probably could—or had someone on staff who could.

Rajeev tasked Daniel with drafting a message to Maltek summarizing the situation and explaining that if he didn't get his permissions restored somehow, his mission was doomed to fail.

The response took longer than Rajeev would have expected, but then, Maltek *was* the CEO of one of the world's fastest-growing corporations; it was a safe assumption he had other things on his plate. Finally, after nearly thirty minutes, Daniel read Maltek's reply.

"Figures they'd tighten security after you escaped," he said. "I have a man on the inside. Give him a couple hours. I'm sure he can help you out."

Rajeev wondered exactly how many men and women Maltek had "on the inside." There was an entire world of corporate espionage out there he'd barely even known existed. He wondered, was this the way companies like Coke and Pepsi, or Microsoft and Apple, operated? It seemed insane that companies would go to such immoral lengths just to line the pockets of their executives and shareholders, yet it happened all the time. It had always been an abstraction to Rajeev, but now it was affecting the fate of not just himself, but everyone he loved.

He returned to his dorm and waited for Maltek's mole to do his thing. He tried not to think about what would happen if the mole failed. Living the rest of his possibly eternal life shuffling back and forth between his dorm and the entertainment lounge was close to what Rajeev imagined hell might be like. How had he wound up in this ridiculous situation? It all came down to the car accident.

Dev had said it wasn't Rajeev's fault, and that might mostly be true. But how could he be sure he wasn't at least partly responsible? He'd been working a lot leading up to the accident. That in and of itself was a regret. It had cut into time he could have spent with his family. He'd missed out on much of Dev and Mira's childhoods. He'd convinced himself he'd work fewer hours in a couple years so he could spend more time with the kids, but of course, he'd never had a chance to; instead of watching his kids grow up, he'd spent fifteen years in a coma.

All he'd cared about back then was money. It wasn't purely out of greed; as an independent contractor for a ridesharing company, he'd needed to maximize his earnings to pay for all the benefits the job lacked, health and dental insurance chief among them. That was on top of the mortgage, utilities and socking away some money each month for the kids' college fund. There was no doubt he'd been overworked. He'd had close calls before, toward the ends of his shifts, when he was tired and irritable. He'd taken corners a bit too quickly, drifted into an oncoming lane before noticing and darting back into his own. A couple times, he'd found himself drifting off and had had to pull over after dropping off his passenger to get a good ten minutes or more of sleep before venturing home.

No, maybe the accident hadn't been his fault directly. The drunken driver had swerved into his lane, Dev had said. But maybe if he hadn't been so tired and overworked his reflexes would have been sharper. Maybe he could have swerved into a ditch and avoided a head-on collision. Maybe the accident wouldn't have been so bad. Maybe he wouldn't have spent more than a decade in a coma. Maybe his passenger wouldn't have died.

Maybe.

Daniel appeared suddenly, breaking Rajeev's reverie.

"You have a new message from Gregory Maltek," he said. "Would you like to hear it?"

"Yes."

"'Try the elevator now.'"

"That's all it said?"

Daniel nodded.

Well, Rajeev thought, there was no point in delaying the inevitable. He stood, walked out of his dorm and made his way for the elevator. When it opened, he stepped inside. He wished he could have taken a deep breath; the situation seemed to warrant it.

The doors closed and he faced the rows of buttons before

him. He reached out and pressed the button for the thirty-fifth floor.

The button lit up and the elevator lurched slightly as it began its descent.

"Looks like it worked," he said. "Here we go."

TWENTY-TWO

THE ELEVATOR DOORS OPENED ONTO THE THIRTY-fifth floor. Rajeev peeked his head out the elevator doors to confirm the hallway was empty. When he saw that it was, he stepped out and made his way down the deserted hall, his footsteps gently echoing off the bare walls.

He had no idea what took place in any part of the building save for the entertainment lounge, Dev's office, and his own dorm. He was aware that he was taking a significant risk by wandering around aimlessly. Someone could find him, notify Dev, and that would be the end of his extracurricular activities.

As he rounded the corner, a meeting room came into view. Through the windows, he took in a group of five people seated at a table. Unlike the entertainment lounge, the conference room's windows were not floor-to-ceiling. Rajeev bent down to the floor, got on his synthetic belly, and crawled beneath the windows. It was a difficult motion, one he wasn't used to making in his new body, but he managed to make his way to the far end of the room. When he was clear of the windows, he stood and continued down the hall.

He came to a plain steel-gray door with a dull metal doorknob. There was no indication what might be on the other side. He reached out, grasped the doorknob, and turned it.

It didn't budge.

Rajeev was discouraged, but not deterred. In his youth, he'd picked a fair share of locks. As a fifty-something-year-old man—or at least, as an android with the mind of one—he took no pride in the skills he'd acquired in his wild youth. But he was now grateful for them nonetheless.

There was no deadbolt on the door, just a keyhole on the knob. He didn't have any lockpicking tools with him, but he didn't think this lock required such drastic measures. He'd opened dozens of locked doors in his youth with nothing more than a stiff credit card, and he suspected that was all this particular door required.

There was one major problem, of course: He didn't have a credit card. He didn't have anything. He could head back to the conference room, perhaps—wait for the meeting to let out, sneak in and look around for anything that could work. But that would be risky.

It occurred to him that he did have *one* thing: His body. He identified the stiff plate making up his thigh. He gripped the material firmly and pulled up sharply; it broke off in his hand. He half expected pain to follow, but of course, there wasn't any—one of the perks of being an android.

The edge where he'd broken the material off was jagged, but the other side was flat, perfect for the task at hand. He slid it down the crack between the door and its frame with practiced expertise, then tried turning the knob again. It turned, and the door swung open.

His photosensors instantly adjusted to the low light. As he took in the contents of the small room, disappointment washed over him. A mop bucket sat in the corner. Shelves lined the walls, filled with rubber gloves, rags, sponges.

He had just broken into a janitor's closet. He stood there a moment, shocked and disappointed. But he couldn't let one misstep deter him. He had to keep moving.

Just as he was about to close the door, the sound of approaching footsteps and the murmuring of people talking floated down the hall. He darted into the closet, closing the door part way but leaving it slightly ajar so he could peek out at the passersby.

The voices belonged to a man and a woman. Rajeev thought he recognized them from the conference room. The meeting must have let out.

"Meet me on the sixtieth floor in a half-hour," the woman said.

The man stopped in his tracks and groaned. "I'm supposed to meet with Stacey in an hour. That doesn't give me much time to—"

"Then cancel it, Ian," the woman cut in indignantly. "This is my top priority right now and it should be yours, too."

Ian sighed. "Fine. I'll see you in a half hour."

"Thank you," she said. They continued walking and made their way around the corner, out of sight. "And be discreet, Ian."

Rajeev waited in the closet several moments after they'd left, giving them and the other meeting attendees plenty of time to get as far away as possible. When he was confident the coast was clear, he crept out from behind the door and closed it gently behind him.

He hurried as quietly as possible back to the elevator. He didn't have much time to make it to the sixtieth floor.

TWENTY-THREE

When he stepped off the elevator, Rajeev heard voices chattering to his right. He made out a trio of people chatting in the hallway. The man and woman he'd overheard from the janitor's closet were not among them, and luckily no one in the group had noticed him step off the elevator. He hurried to the other side of the hallway until he was safely around the corner.

Now what? He had made it to the sixtieth floor undetected, but he had no idea where to go from here. All he knew was that there was something important here—something that apparently necessitated Ian's discretion. Speaking of Ian, he and his female companion should be arriving any moment. It was possible they'd both arrived early and already left for their destination, but if that was the case, he'd just have to wander around hoping to find them.

He peeked around the corner and watched the elevator. If Ian and the woman emerged and walked away from him, he'd follow after them to see where they went. If, on the other hand, they began walking toward him, he'd scurry off in the opposite direction and pray he didn't stumble into anyone.

A couple minutes went by, and the elevator doors opened. Ian stepped out into the hallway alone. He didn't walk away; he just stood there, presumably waiting for the woman. He seemed miffed that she wasn't already there waiting for him. He tapped his foot impatiently and crossed his arms.

He didn't have long to wait, however; a moment later the elevator doors once again opened and the woman emerged. Rajeev braced himself, ready to turn and run in the opposite direction if they began moving toward him. Thankfully, they turned and walked the other way, disappearing around the corner.

He followed after them, scurrying down the hallway but doing his best to minimize the sound of his silicone-covered feet clicking against the concrete floor. The trio that had been chit-chatting was gone, but Rajeev peeked his head around the corner to make sure there weren't any other interlopers. The hallway was empty, save for Ian and the woman walking slowly but steadily away.

Just as they were about to round another corner, Rajeev took chase again. When he came to the corner, he took another peek and saw that they had stopped in front of a door. The woman flashed a keycard against a sensor. A clicking sound reverberated throughout the hall as the door unlocked. She opened it and let Ian pass through first. Then she followed him in and shut the door behind him.

Rajeev ran to the door and tried the handle but, of course, it was locked again. He cursed. The door was thick and appeared to be made of steel. Even so, Rajeev strained his artificial ears, hoping he'd be able to hear something, anything. But there was no sound.

He'd come so far, but it appeared he was now stuck. As good as he was at picking locks, he didn't know a thing about how to disable a lock with an electronic keycard. He knew there was something important behind that door—something that might satisfy Gregory Maltek's thirst for dirt he could use against the company—but there was no way to get to the other side of it. Maybe this would be enough to satisfy Maltek. Maybe he had other people "on the inside," as he'd put it, who could break into the room and find out what was behind it.

He turned around to head back, and just as he was rounding the corner he bumped into a security guard.

"Pardon me," the guard started, but then he looked up and saw Rajeev's unnatural face staring back at him. There was a moment of stunned silence from both of them; neither one moved a muscle. Then the guard cried out, "What the hell?" Rajeev sprinted past him, running down the empty hallway as fast as his legs could carry him.

The security guard immediately gave chase, but to Rajeev's surprise, his artificial limbs allowed him to run far faster than he'd been able to as a human being. By the time he made it to the elevator and pressed the button to go down, the guard was just rounding the corner. The elevator doors opened; Rajeev stepped through, pressed the button for the twelfth floor, and watched as the doors closed just before the guard could reach them.

It was a surreal sensation, descending in the elevator, completely calm. He'd just run the fastest he'd ever run in his life. In his old body, he would have been completely out of breath—if not dead—but now he didn't even breathe. He was constantly "out of breath," and it had no effect on him. It was the first time he'd been fully aware of the utility of his new body. He'd always considered it lesser than his old one. Less functional. Less desirable. Less aesthetically pleasing. But he was beginning to realize that a nonhuman body could be greater-than. Running quickly was just the tip of the iceberg.

The elevator dinged and the doors opened onto the twelfth floor. He ran to the entertainment lounge, hoping to find someone inside. He wasn't disappointed: A lone android stood inside, looking straight ahead at the television.

Rajeev rushed inside. "Who are you?" he asked.

The android turned and looked at him. When it spoke, it sounded taken aback by the abruptness of Rajeev's query.

"It's me," he said. "Ted."

"I don't have a lot of time," Rajeev said, speaking quickly. "I found something on the sixtieth floor. I don't know what, exactly, but it's gotta be something big. When you get off the elevators, take a right, then another right. The first door on your left—whatever it is, it's behind that door. I couldn't get inside." Ted was looking over his shoulder; Rajeev turned around and, through the window, saw the guard approaching the lounge. "You need a keycode or something to get in. You guys need to find out what's on the other side of that door, Ted."

The door to the lounge creaked open and the guard barged in.

"Which one of you did I catch sneaking around?" he barked.

Rajeev raised his arms as if a gun was being pointed at him. "It was me," he said. "I'll come quietly."

The guard grabbed him by the arm and dragged him out of the room. Rajeev turned to Ted and gave him one last look. He hoped that despite possessing two dead photoelectric eyes, Ted would be able to see the desperation he meant to convey.

TWENTY-FOUR

RAJEEV HAD KNOWN THAT IF HE WANDERED AROUND long enough he was bound to get caught eventually. The humiliation stung all the more, however, because he'd been so close to getting away with it.

He was screwed now. He was sure of it. Ted and the others were his only hope now. If they could somehow get into the room on the sixtieth floor, he was confident whatever was inside would be more than enough to make Greg Maltek happy. Hopefully he'd honor the agreement they'd made and refrain from harming Sarah or Mira. Or Dev, for that matter, although Rajeev was pretty sure his son would consider the resulting damage to his company "harm." He wondered if Dev would ever forgive him once he inevitably found out his own father had betrayed him.

The guard had dragged him into what looked like an interrogation room. A large table took up most of it; a chair sat on either side, and a large mirror made up most of the back wall.

"Wait here," the guard snapped, not even giving Rajeev a chance to sit down before he'd gone and closed the door behind him. Rajeev walked around to the far side of the table and sat.

A few minutes later the door opened again and the guard walked in, followed by Dev. His face was stern, though not angry, which Rajeev counted as a win.

"Leave us, please," Dev told the guard. He did as his boss commanded, glaring at Rajeev the entire time until he disappeared out the door.

Dev took the seat across from his father. He looked him up and down appraisingly.

"You really do have a big pair of balls on you, don't you?"

"Dev … let me explain."

"No, let me explain something to *you*, dad. Do you think I'm an idiot? Do you think I'm stupid enough to think it's perfectly innocent that you were somehow able to travel onto unauthorized floors, snooping around in areas that are none of your business?"

"I'm sorry if you feel disrespected, Dev. But I only did it to protect you, your mother and Mira."

"Don't drag them into this. This is about me and you."

"No, Dev, you don't understand. I had to protect you all from—"

"You had to test me," he snapped. "That's what this was all about from the beginning for you. You're used to being the parent, the one in charge, and when you woke up from your coma and found your son in charge of you, you couldn't accept it with humility and grace like a normal person—you had to rebel like a snot-nosed teenager."

"Dev!" He'd raised his voice more than he'd meant to. He sounded, indeed, like a frustrated parent trying to talk over a child in the midst of a meltdown. But he had to get through to his son. He realized that what he was about to tell him could jeopardize everything, but it seemed time to bring his son in on all that had transpired with Gregory Maltek. "Listen to me, Dev. All that I've done, I've done to protect you, okay? Listen to me.

Your life, and the life of your mother and sister, were threatened by Fresh Meat."

Dev stopped. He tilted his head. "Fresh Meat?"

"Yes. When I escaped, Gregory Maltek contacted me and made it clear that unless I came back and spied for him, he would harm you, or Mira, or your mother—anyone I cared about. He wanted dirt on your company, at any cost."

"So not *everything* you've done was to protect me," Dev said, an air of suspicion to his voice. "You left the first time on your own, without any coercion from Gregory Maltek."

"Yes, okay, Dev—I had a moral disagreement about the way you've chosen to run your business. I escaped with the intention of bringing awareness to your company's failings. It was never to hurt you, Dev. I hoped you'd see the error of your ways and change. But that's all irrelevant now, because all that matters right here, right now, is that unless I give Gregory Maltek some juicy piece of intel in the next couple of days, he's going to hurt your mom, or your sister, or both."

Dev grew somber. He looked down at his feet. "I wasn't aware of that," he said.

"I know. But you know now and we need to do something to protect them. Surely you of all people have the resources to keep them safe."

"I do, but I'm not sure they'd accept my help. I'm not exactly on speaking terms with either of them these days."

"Family forgives. Reach out to them. This can be the start of making amends."

He nodded. "Okay. I'll talk to them. But right now, I need you to tell me everything that happened between you and Maltek. Don't leave out a single detail."

Rajeev told the story, explaining how Maltek had sent a representative to Rosa's house. How he'd flown him out to Fresh Meat's headquarters and made him an offer—dirt on NLT in exchange for a boatload of cash and a flesh-and-blood body.

How he'd refused, then been given a new offer he couldn't refuse: Dirt on NLT in exchange for his family's safety.

He went further, explaining how Maltek claimed he had a mole in NLT, and how that mole had been the one to disable his access permissions.

"Wait," Dev interrupted. "If Maltek already has a mole in the company, why did he need you to spy for him?"

"I hadn't thought much about it. My best guess is that his existing mole wasn't entirely effective. I think Maltek thought that because I'm your father, I'd be able to get closer to you and dig up deeper dirt."

"He probably wasn't wrong." He stood and gave his father a grave look. "I want to show you something, dad. I've known for awhile now that Maltek had a mole in the company. Unfortunately, they didn't stop at spying … they also engaged in sabotage. I didn't want to involve any more people in this than necessary, but you're in it pretty deeply now and you just may be able to help."

TWENTY-FIVE

Dev led him to the elevator and down to the fifty-second floor. They walked to the end of the hall and came to a heavy steel door. Dev flashed a keycard against a pad attached to the wall and the door opened.

They walked through and Rajeev found himself surrounded by large flat-screen monitors mounted to the walls. Dev closed the door behind him and pointed to a rolling office chair, gesturing for his father to take a seat. Dev turned to the array of electronics surrounding them and raised his hands.

"This," he said with a circus ringmaster's flair, "is what I like to call The Hub."

"It looks impressive … but what is it?"

"The Hub is the storage center for all Next Level Technologies' trade secrets," he said. "All the company's vital information is stored here. Our processes for duplicating minds, our robotics technologies, plans for future tech … it's all right here. But I can't access any of it."

"Why not?"

"Maltek's mole." He let out a deep sigh and shook his head slowly, as if he had become completely devoid of all hope. "I don't really trust anyone but myself. I placed safeguards on all this information so it could only be accessed by me or with my permission. There are a variety of different kinds of safeguards built in … biometric markers—fingerprints, retina scans—as well as passwords, two-factor authentication and security questions. The mole knew they'd never be able to break through all these safeguards, so they stooped to sabotage instead."

"But it all looks operational to me."

Dev shook his head. "It's not The Hub that the mole sabotaged. It's me."

"What do you mean?"

"I've been having memory problems. It started small at first … forgetting where I placed my keys, forgetting people's names, that kind of thing. But it got more severe. I couldn't remember discussions I'd had with people just a week prior. I spoke with Mira on the phone once and could only remember her name with significant effort. One day, about two years ago, I needed to access The Hub and couldn't remember the answers to the security questions. I was completely locked out."

"There isn't a way to bypass the questions?"

"No. Every requirement must be met to access The Hub."

"But what if you were to die? Anyone other than you would be locked out of the system."

Dev nodded. "There are definite downsides to my paranoia. I didn't think everything through."

"What do your memory problems have to do with the mole in your company?"

"I have reason to believe the mole has been poisoning me with the express purpose of impairing my memory and preventing me from accessing The Hub."

"Now you *really* sound paranoid."

Dev grinned. "A wise man once said, 'It's not paranoia if they're really out to get you.'"

"But what evidence do you have?"

"Medical evidence. When I began suspecting something was wrong, I saw a doctor. He did some tests and discovered trace amounts of a unique, patented compound in my blood—a compound known to cause memory recall issues. And the patent-holder for that compound happens to be Cyrus Pharmaceuticals ... a subsidiary of Fresh Meat. Perhaps you think it's a coincidence, but I say it's evidence. There's no doubt in my mind that the mole poisoned me."

"You said you could use my help. What do you expect me to do?"

"Like I said, the only safeguards I'm having difficulty with are the security questions and the passwords. I'm not having any trouble with the biometrics or the two-factor authentication, obviously. But for the life of me I can't remember everything else. I didn't want to bring anyone else into this mess, but now that you're in, you can serve as the memory I've lost."

"You want me to figure out the answers to your secret questions."

He nodded. "And the passwords. There are hints that should be enough to get us in."

"Okay. Let's hear one and I'll see what I can do."

Dev grinned. "Let me see here ..." He found a keyboard and began typing, bringing up a question on the screen directly in front of them.

"Here's one," he said, pointing at the screen. The security question read, "What is the name of your favorite book?"

"Your grandfather would have hoped the answer would be the *Baghavad Gita*," Rajeev said. "But I don't know the answer to that one, Dev."

"It won't hurt to try ..." He typed in "Baghavad Gita," but when he hit enter, he was informed that the response was incorrect. "Throw out some other ideas."

"You should at least have an idea, shouldn't you?"

"I've tried everything I could think of, but nothing worked."

Rajeev fell silent as he racked his brain for the titles of any books that might have had significance in Dev's life. Only one title came to mind, but it couldn't possibly be correct. Still, in Dev's words, it wouldn't hurt to try.

"When you were a child," Rajeev said, "you always wanted me to read you 'Goodnight Moon' at bedtime. I think I must have read you that book for a year straight."

Dev nodded and smiled. "Of course," he said. He typed in "Goodnight Moon," and the screen moved on to another question. "Amazing, dad. Thank you."

"What's the next question?"

"This one doesn't make much sense to me," Dev said. "I'm not married."

The question read, "Where did you meet your spouse?"

Rajeev placed a hand on his chin. "No, you're not. But I don't think that's the point of the question."

"Then what is?"

"Arranged marriage. When you were young, your grandparents held out hope that Sarah and I would arrange a marriage for you kids, even though she and I hadn't even taken that path to our own relationship. Your grandfather always joked that you should marry a little Indian girl, the granddaughter of one of the residents in their housing community. Her name was Amara, I believe."

"That's good, dad! But the answer can't be Chicago—I've already tried it." He put his hand on his chin, contemplating. "Do you remember the name of the housing community?"

"Can't you remember it? You used to visit often enough."

"Everything's foggy. I'm counting on you, dad."

Rajeev racked his brain but no clear answer came to him. "How do you know the memory is even in here?" he asked, pointing to his head. "You said you had to fill in a lot of gaps. Surely some of those gaps went unfilled."

"That's a possibility, but it could just be a matter of digging deeper for the information. Think, dad. You might surprise yourself."

He thought a moment more, then came across a name that, for whatever reason, stuck with him. He couldn't be sure it was correct—but what harm was there in trying it out?

"Clairemont," he said. "Try it."

Dev didn't waste a second typing the name into the computer. He hesitated a brief moment, however, before pressing the enter key. They both gazed up at the screen as a green check mark appeared next to the answer.

Dev pumped his fist. "Yes! You're awesome, dad!" The screen briefly changed to an overview of all the security questions with a check mark next to each one, but Dev quickly navigated away.

"It's all here," he said, his voice giddy. He turned around to face his father. "I have full access! I couldn't have done this without your help. What do you say we head up to my office and celebrate—I have something for you that should approximate champagne."

"I appreciate the offer, but no thanks. I'm glad I could help, but I should go. It looks like you have a lot of catching up to do."

"True. We'll celebrate another time."

Rajeev stood and made to leave. Dev turned his attention back to the computer. As Rajeev walked out the door, he heard Dev utter to himself, "Screw Gregory Maltek."

TWENTY-SIX

As soon as Rajeev was safely inside the elevator, he summoned Daniel.

"What can I do for—"

"Daniel, is everything I see recorded?"

"I'm not sure I understand your question."

"My eyes are basically video cameras, right? So are the images they pick up stored anywhere? Can they be played back?"

"Ah, I see what you mean. Yes, the images are stored anywhere between eight to seventy-two hours, depending on the user settings."

"That's more than enough. How do I bring up the footage for review?"

"I can do that for you. It appears your settings are configured to record and store up to eight hours of footage."

"I just need footage from the past twenty minutes."

"Very well."

A small rectangle appeared in front of Rajeev, appearing to hover about five feet in front of him at eye level. It began playing footage from Rajeev's perspective, showing him walking down the hall with Dev toward The Hub.

"Is there any way to speed this up?"

"Sure," Daniel replied cheerily. Almost instantly, the footage began playing at double speed. Rajeev was afraid he'd miss the moment he was looking for, but he saw it coming.

"Stop!" He shouted. "Play it at normal speed." The footage returned to normal.

"Clairemont," he said in the recording. "Try it." He watched as Dev entered the name into the computer. When it worked, Dev pumped his fist and told Rajeev he was awesome.

"Freeze the picture," Rajeev said. The recording froze, displaying the computer screen Dev had been working with.

"Can you zoom in on the text displayed on the screen?"

"Sure," Daniel said, and the picture magnified. It was a list of all the security questions Dev had had to answer. At the top of the list were the two questions Dev had successfully answered before calling Rajeev in for help:

WHERE DID YOU HAVE YOUR FIRST KISS?
WHAT WAS YOUR FAVORITE PLACE TO TRAVEL TO AS A
CHILD?

Rajeev thought back to his conversation with Dev in his office; the one where he'd given him the experimental orb that was supposed to taste like Scotch. He'd casually brought up his childhood. He'd asked Rajeev if he remembered hearing about Dev's first kiss. He hadn't. But then he'd asked about his favorite place as a child, and Rajeev had handed him the answer on a silver platter.

Alarm bells rang like crazy in Rajeev's head. His mind reeled as he tried to figure out what to do. Because he was fairly certain the man back there claiming to be Dev was not his son. And whoever he was, Rajeev had just helped him unlock the keys to all of Next Level Technologies' most closely guarded secrets.

* * *

Rajeev hurried to the entertainment lounge, eager to speak with one of the other androids to ensure he wasn't as crazy as he seemed even to himself.

Three of the androids were huddled together by the couch, talking among themselves. Rajeev walked through the doors and approached them.

"It's me—Rajeev."

"Hey," one of them said. "Ted."

"Brian."

"Natalie."

Good. His most important allies were here.

"I have some big news," he said.

Natalie glanced at her compatriots and nodded. "So do we."

That surprised him, but he couldn't imagine anything they might say could be more revelatory than what he was about to unload on them.

"Okay," he said. "You go first."

"That room you found on the sixtieth floor—I found it," Ted said.

Rajeev had forgotten all about the room. Now, given what he knew about Dev, or whoever was passing himself off as Dev, it seemed like the least of their concerns. But he encouraged Ted anyway.

"Did you get into it?"

Ted nodded.

"What did you find?"

He hesitated. "I think it would be best if you saw it with your own eyes."

Rajeev shook his head. "We don't have time for that. The man I've been calling my son is an imposter. He isn't Dev."

Ted glanced at Natalie, then turned back to Rajeev. "We know."

"You—you know? How?"

"Like I said," Ted answered, moving toward the door, "you really need to see for yourself."

He walked out the door without another word. Rajeev turned to Natalie as if appealing for help, but she just nodded her head toward the door. "He's right," she said. "Go."

He sped out the door, hurrying to catch up to Ted. When he'd caught up, Ted had just pressed the button for the elevator. It was already on their floor, and the door opened immediately.

"Shouldn't we wait for the others?" Rajeev asked as they stepped inside.

"They're not coming. It'd be too conspicuous to have four of us walking around together."

He pressed the button for the sixtieth floor and they stood in silence as they rose up the building. The elevator dinged, the doors opened, and Ted stepped out, confidently striding away.

"Ted," Rajeev hissed, doing his best to run after him while also moving silently, "be careful—we could get caught."

"I'm over it," Ted said. He continued speeding away, refusing to slow his pace for Rajeev, forcing him to abandon caution if he wanted to keep up.

"What's so important that you don't even care about getting caught?

"You're about to find out."

They rounded the corner and approached the door Rajeev had been unable to penetrate.

"How were you able to disengage the lock?"

"One of the other androids used to be a computer hacker. He came up here and was able to figure out the code. To whit—" He punched a string of six numbers into the keypad and a green light lit up. Ted turned the handle, opened the door and walked inside.

The room was dark and the walls were painted black. It was the antithesis of the all-white room Rajeev had first awoken in. The only light came from a small lamp built into the side of one of the walls.

"What's so important about this place?" Rajeev asked. "It looks like a living space. Like one of our—"

He'd caught sight of the far right corner of the room, where a small bed sat. He'd seen it as soon as he'd walked in, but what he'd missed was the silhouette of a man sitting on the side of it. He was short, with an ample build, and even though his face was obscured by shadows, Rajeev recognized him at once.

"Dev?"

The man stood and took a step forward, letting the low light wash over his face.

"Hi, dad."

"How is this possible?"

He beckoned his father toward the bed. "You'd better have a seat. I'll explain everything."

TWENTY-SEVEN

ALTHOUGH HE WAS SITTING ON THE BED, RAJEEV FELT like he was floating. Everything about this encounter felt like a dream. After awakening in his new body, seeing his son as a grown man had been a shock. But going through the same sensation all over again was more than a shock. It was unreal.

Ted nodded at Rajeev. "I'm going to give you and your son some privacy," he said. "I'll be right outside the door serving as lookout."

"Thanks, Ted."

Rajeev turned his attention back to Dev, who was apparently finding the situation surreal as well.

"That's really you in there, dad?" He sat on the edge of the bed, his torso turned slightly to face his father, who was sitting beside him. His brow was furrowed in a mix of concern and fascination.

"Kind of. A very close copy."

"Of course. I designed the technology that created the copy."

"I know. But I'm more interested in knowing why there are two of you walking around."

Dev frowned, suddenly angry. "There's only one of me. That other son of a bitch is an imposter."

"But how? He looks *exactly* like you."

"I was naive." He looked away, staring at the wall as if taking in the sight of something in the nonexistent distance. "About two years ago, Greg Maltek called me and demanded a face-to-face meeting. He said he wanted to declare a temporary truce to discuss a possible collaboration. I was skeptical. I had—and still have—grave concerns about the ethics of Maltek's technology. How does he produce the bodies? I don't see how he could do what he does without human cloning, and I don't believe the technology exists to clone a human being without a conscious-ness—a *soul*. That means he must be erasing a human consciousness to create 'blank' bodies that he can sell. He's a murderer. Or so I suspected."

Rajeev nodded. "I had similar concerns."

"Maltek has always been secretive about his technology, and one of the reasons I agreed to meet with him was because I thought I could persuade him to open up about it. He insisted on meeting at the Fresh Meat headquarters, and I agreed to do so." Dev paused, shaking his head. His posture belied the hope-lessness and regret eating him alive from the inside out. "There was no meeting. Not even the pretension of one. I'd brought along security, of course, but as a courtesy to Greg, I asked them to wait outside. I stepped into Maltek's office alone. I was such an idiot. As soon as the door closed, Maltek injected me with something and I was out instantly. When I awoke, I was exactly where we are now—in this room."

"But to what end?"

"I didn't know at first. I thought maybe he'd just kidnapped me in hopes that my absence would cause my company to fall apart without me. But that didn't make sense. There are other people in the company who can run things without me. I wasn't quite sure what Maltek was up to, but I knew it couldn't be good. An orderly visited me three times daily to bring me a hot meal, change the sheets on the bed and make sure I hadn't found a way to kill myself. They'd provided me with a tablet preloaded with movies, music, and books, but no internet access and thus, no ability to contact the outside world. I was a prisoner and I had no idea why.

"Things went on like this for months. I couldn't tell you how many; time had begun to lose all meaning for me. But one day I received a visitor who was not part of the regular rotation of orderlies I'd become accustomed to. The visitor was *me*. At first I thought I must have gone insane from the months of solitary confinement. The man who walked through the door was my exact twin. It was like looking into a mirror. But it soon became apparent that I wasn't crazy. The 'other me' was none other than Gregory Maltek."

Rajeev shook his head. "That's impossible! I met Gregory Maltek at the same time your doppelganger was roaming around here."

"It wasn't the *original* Maltek that confronted me. It was a copy, a duplicate, just like you're a duplicate of my father. But in this case, the original wasn't destroyed. Maltek continued operating his business out of San Francisco even as the copy of his mind was inserted into a brain belonging to a body biologically identical to my own—my clone. I don't know how Maltek got a hold of my DNA, but it wouldn't have been difficult. He could have paid someone to retrieve a coffee cup I'd discarded and collected my saliva off the rim, or paid my hairdresser for a bag of my hair. Regardless of how he obtained it, once he had it, he had everything he needed to create a duplicate body and fill it with his duplicate mind. Once the duplicate arrived here in Chicago, Maltek had the perfect inside man—himself."

Rajeev wished he were capable of throwing up. All the intimate moments he thought he'd had with his son were lies. He'd been communing with one of the vilest, most despicable men he'd ever met—or at least with a copy of that man. All the while, his real son had been locked up here going mad from his imposed solitude.

"Why did Maltek do all this? Why go to such elaborate lengths?"

"He wanted my company. More specifically, he wanted to take out his biggest competitor and keep all the technology I'd developed for himself. That's how it started, anyway. When his duplicate walked in, with *my* face, *my* voice, *my* mannerisms, it was because Maltek had run into roadblocks. I've always been a tad paranoid, but in this instance, my paranoia served me well. I'd hidden all the company's secrets on a secure server. I protected it with several different security measures: biometric scans, passwords, security questions. He'd gotten through the biometric scans with no problem; after all, he's a clone, so his DNA is identical to mine. But, naturally, he couldn't figure out the passwords or the answers to the security questions. He was locked out and needed my help to get in."

Rajeev's stomach sank—or at least, it felt like it had—but he waited for his son to finish the story before telling him about the horrible thing he'd done.

"I refused to help, of course," Dev continued. "He tried to beat it out of me. Getting punched by my doppelganger was undoubtedly the oddest experience of my life ... and the most painful. I held out for a long time. But a man can only take so much and eventually, I caved. But I only told him the passwords, not the answers to the security questions. He left to see if they worked and vowed to return later for the rest. After he was gone, however, I built up my resolve. When he returned an hour later, I refused to give up any more information and he beat me again. By now he was getting frustrated because he was so close to having everything he needed. But I wouldn't budge and he went too far. He hit me on the side of the head and knocked me out cold.

"I woke up back in my bed. It must have been hours later. As far as I could tell, I'd received absolutely no medical care. Maltek was gone and my head throbbed like a bitch. It was the perfect excuse. When Maltek returned several hours later, I feigned amnesia. I told him I couldn't even remember who I was, let alone what 'security questions' he was asking about." He chuckled as he said, "I even asked him if he was my evil twin."

Rajeev shook his head. "He couldn't have liked that."

"He didn't. He raged at me. But I think deep down he suspected he really had damaged my memory—he'd hit me extremely hard. When he left, he didn't come back. And I've been here ever since."

Dev paused and Rajeev took the opportunity to confess his sins to his son. "I have something to tell you, Dev. I ... I've made a terrible mistake."

"It can't be that bad."

"I think I just provided Maltek with all the answers to your security questions."

Dev's face fell. "Okay, maybe it *is* that bad. What happened?"

Rajeev explained how from the beginning, he'd thought Maltek—the duplicate version—was truly Dev. When he'd returned to Next Level Technologies after escaping, he'd been trying to get back into the good graces of the man he'd thought was his son. And he'd helped him answer the security questions that, up to that point, he'd been unable to answer.

Dev listened to his father's story without interruption, and with no visible reaction. But by the time Rajeev had finished, all color had drained from his face.

"If what you're saying is true, then Maltek has control of The Hub."

"That's what I was afraid of. So how bad is it? What kinds of secrets are stored in The Hub?"

Dev didn't answer at first. He seemed to be gathering his thoughts. When he answered, his voice was low and devoid of emotion, as if he couldn't dare let himself express the despair bubbling beneath the surface.

"It's bad," he said. "Real bad."

TWENTY-EIGHT

Dev led Ted and Rajeev out of the room and down the hall.

"I'll tell you more, but first we need to get out of here."

"Yeah, about that," Ted said. "You put GPS trackers on us that make our bodies seize if we try to leave the building." There was more than a hint of resentment in his voice.

Dev shook his head. "That feature was never meant to keep you imprisoned. It was a safety measure meant to protect you. Before we activated the first prototypes, we had no idea how the duplicate minds would react when they awakened in an alien, robotic body. We didn't know if they'd be confused, for example, or if they'd suffer from total or partial amnesia. We thought they might run away in a panic and hurt themselves—run into traffic or worse—so we implemented the failsafe to ensure we could bring them back inside and make sure they were safe until they acclimated to their new bodies. It's no surprise Maltek corrupted its purpose."

"That may be," Rajeev said, "but can you disable it quickly so we can leave?"

"Yeah. I'll find the proper equipment. Follow me."

He led them to the elevator. Thankfully, it was empty. They piled in and journeyed to a lower floor. When the doors opened, he walked down the hall and led them through a door. It appeared to be some kind of laboratory. Electrical equipment, wires and other supplies lined shelves against the wall, but other equipment was strewn about randomly. What concerned Rajeev, however, were three people seated around a table at the right-hand side of the room. They immediately looked up at Dev as he entered, quizzical looks on their faces.

Dev froze, like a deer caught in headlights. But then he straightened his back and pointed at the three employees.

"I need the lab to myself to work on these models," he barked, tilting his head toward Ted and Rajeev. "Give me fifteen minutes."

To Rajeev's astonishment, the three of them stood and walked out of the room. But of course they would. Dev was their boss. They couldn't tell the difference between him and the imposter they'd been working under for so long. When they saw the boss, they did what he said.

"That was weird," Dev said as he closed the door behind him. "I'm not used to bossing people around. I'm out of practice."

"Looked like you did a fine job to me," Ted said. "They didn't even make eye contact with you."

"Which is not a good thing. Who knows how much Maltek has damaged my reputation in my own company." He directed Rajeev and Ted to take a seat, then searched around the room for the items he needed.

"Why is it necessary to leave at all?" Rajeev asked. "You're the founder of the company. Couldn't you just stay here and set things straight—kick out the fake Dev and reclaim your place on the throne, so to speak?"

"It's too much trouble right now," he said as he plucked a laptop off a shelf and walked it to the table. "The company would spiral into all-out chaos. Think about it; no one would really know for sure who was the real me, and while they tried to sort the situation out, it would just distract from the real task at hand: Stopping Maltek." He walked to another shelf, grabbed a couple cords, and walked them back to the table. He stuck each of the cords in the laptop, then inserted the other ends into the ports at the base of Ted's and Rajeev's necks. "This should just take a minute."

Rajeev was familiar with the procedure, having already gone through it once with Zane. Ted seemed a little nervous; he fidgeted more than usual. But Dev was quick—far quicker than Zane had been, which made sense, considering the bodies were based on his own designs.

"We're good to go," he said, pulling the wires out of their necks.

"Good," Ted said. "I can't wait to get the hell out of here. I'm never coming back."

They left, Rajeev walking on Dev's right side, Ted walking on his left. For once, Rajeev didn't feel the need to sneak around. He was with the company's founder; who would dare question him?

They took the elevator to the ground floor. Rajeev was reminded of his earlier escape as they strolled through the hallway headed for the front entrance. But he had no reason to fear this time. He was with his son, the founder of the company, and he was escaping *with* him rather than *from* him. It would be so much easier to—

His good vibes were cut short as they rounded the corner and Dev came face to face with ... himself. Or at least, with his doppelganger. They both froze at first, staring at each other in shock. The real Dev was the first to snap out of it, and he shouted to his companions: "Run!"

He darted to the left of his clone and sped down the hallway; Rajeev and Ted took another moment to react, but soon followed suit. Maltek grabbed at Ted's shoulder, but his fingers slid off the smooth silicone skin and he came away empty-handed.

"Stop them!" Maltek cried. He took off after them, but they had gotten a healthy head start; Rajeev and Ted easily caught up to Dev, thanks to the endurance of their artificial bodies, and ran ahead of him. As they rounded the corner, Rajeev was presented with the familiar sight of the security desk overlooking the building's exit.

Two guards stood talking in front of the desk and they looked up in surprise at the commotion of two androids springing down the hallways as if running a marathon, their own CEO in hot pursuit. At the same time, Maltek cried out again, his words echoing into the guards' ears from around the corner: "Stop them!"

One of the guards hesitated; he'd recognized Dev's face rushing toward him, but also recognized his voice coming from around the corner. He didn't know what was going on.

The other guard, however, sprang to action. He lunged toward the trio and, apparently trusting that the failsafe would prevent Rajeev or Dev from leaving the building, focused his attention on Dev. He wrapped his hand around Dev's arm. But before he could do anything else, Dev launched his fist into the guard's chin, causing him to release Dev's arm as he soared backward.

Maltek rounded the corner and made eye contact with the other guard. His eyes blazed with fury as he pointed to the escaping trio and shouted, "Stop them—or you're fired!"

The guard rushed toward them, but Dev and Rajeev had already reached the door. Ted had lagged behind and the guard was just able to catch up to him. He wasn't leaving the fate of his job up to chance; he leapt into the air and tackled Ted, sending them both tumbling to the floor in a heap.

Rajeev, who was now outside, heard the commotion and

turned around to see what was going on. When he saw Ted, he made to run back inside.

"No!" Ted shouted. "Go! Leave me!"

Rajeev didn't retreat, but Dev grabbed his arm and pulled him away. "We can't help him, dad. We'll get captured too."

Still, Rajeev hesitated, much to Ted's annoyance: "Get out of here you idiot!"

When their words finally penetrated his frazzled mind, Rajeev turned around. With his son by his side, he flew out into the street, away from Next Level Technologies, a free man once more.

TWENTY-NINE

They didn't stop running for fifteen minutes straight. Rajeev could have kept going, but Dev needed to rest before they continued. A wooded area stood off to the side of the road and they took refuge behind a row of trees. Nobody would be able to see them from the road unless they looked carefully.

Dev took a seat on a stump. Rajeev asked him what the plan was.

"There isn't one," he let out between breaths.

"You've been sitting in that room this entire time and you haven't given any thought to what you'd do if you got out?"

"Sure I have. But those thoughts didn't constitute a plan. They were fantasies."

"So what the hell are we supposed to do?"

"First we need to get well away from here. The area's going to be buzzing with NLT personnel on the hunt for us."

"We're never going to manage that on foot."

"Exactly. We need a ride."

"It's not like we can call a Lyft. Although ... we could ask Daniel to make a call for us."

Dev wrinkled his brow. "Daniel? You mean the AI assistant?"

"Yeah. He could call Mira for us, tell her to come pick us up. Is there any reason we shouldn't? Would Maltek be able to trace the call?"

"He shouldn't be able to. I severed the company's ties to you when I disabled the failsafe. You're invisible to them."

"Okay. Daniel? We need you."

The assistant appeared in front of them; of course, Dev couldn't see him.

"Daniel, can you call my daughter, Mira?"

"Let me check your contact list ... Mira Sundaram? Is that who you'd like to call?"

"Yes."

"Okay. One moment."

Daniel went silent for a moment; the line must have been ringing, but suddenly he opened his mouth and Mira's voice came out of it: "Hello?"

It was an odd thing, hearing Mira's soft, feminine voice emanating from the mouth of a masculine representation—but there was no time to dwell on it.

"Hi Mira. It's dad."

"Dad? Where the hell have you been? I've been worried sick about you!"

"It's a long story. Look, I'm with your brother maybe a quarter of a mile outside the NLT campus. We need a ride."

"You're with Dev? Why doesn't he just call one of his limos down there and—"

"Mira, it's complicated. Please, can you come? We're desperate here. We'll explain everything in person."

She sighed. "Fine. You're lucky I love you."

Rajeev gave Mira a more detailed description of their location. Then the call ended, Daniel went away and Rajeev turned to his son.

"She's on her way. She should be here in less than a half hour."

"Hopefully we won't get caught before then."

"Hopefully not." Rajeev hesitated, but then shook his head; now was as good a time as any to have this conversation. "Dev, I owe you an apology."

"For what?"

"For not being there for you. Ever. When you were a kid, I worked all the time. I was trying to support our family, trying to give you kids nice things and good opportunities. I think in the back of my head I always figured I'd have an opportunity to slow down later and then I'd make up for lost time and spend more time with you and your sister. But it didn't work out that way, obviously. I was gone for fifteen years and it was because I over-worked myself. If I'd gotten more sleep, been more refreshed, then my reaction time would have been faster and I could have —" He cut himself off, overwhelmed by emotions that couldn't be expressed through tears.

Dev had no such limitation, however, and tears had formed in his eyes. His voice trembled as he spoke. "I'm not going to lie and say it wasn't difficult growing up without you. But even if you didn't spend enough time with us as kids, you were still raising us, shaping us through your example. You demonstrated the value of hard work. And it was never lost on us for a *moment* that it was all for our sake. You may question your devotion to your family, dad, but we never did."

Rajeev wanted to cry. Not being able to outwardly express his inner emotional turmoil somehow made the emotions even stronger.

"So you ... you forgive me?"

"Of course, dad." Dev stood, walked to his father and wrapped both arms tightly around his thin, synthetic torso. Rajeev did the same, holding his son tightly, though taking care not to hold him *too* tight, since even now he wasn't fully aware of his new body's strength.

"I was afraid when I woke up in this body," he told his son as they ended their embrace. "When I learned I was a duplicate of the original Rajeev, I was angry. It felt like I'd been duped into entering the world."

Dev nodded sympathetically. "It was never my intention to create duplicate consciousnesses without the consent of the original individual. You were an exception. I duplicated your consciousness after you were already gone because you were my dad and I … I wanted you back. Obviously. But I couldn't get past the ethical questions. I could never bring myself to use it. Maltek must have seen your consciousness on file and figured he could use you to help answer the security questions he still needed. So he uploaded you into an android body and, well … here you are."

"And despite my earlier misgivings, I'm *glad* I'm here, Dev. I may only be a carbon copy of the original, but I'm imbued with the same attributes as the original Rajeev Sundaram and the most overwhelming part of him—and thus, of me—is a sense of unlimited love for you, your sister and your mother. I'm glad I'm here, not for my sake, but for yours. I want you to have a relationship with the father you never really knew. I want us both to have a second chance."

Dev nodded. "I appreciate that. And now that you've been activated, where you go from here is up to you." He paused and his face grew dark. He turned away slightly, seeming to peer past Rajeev deep into the heart of the forest. "That is, if we're able to stop Maltek. If we don't, there may not be a future for either of us."

"At Next Level Technologies, you mean."

Dev shook his head. "No. The fate of the entire world hangs in the balance. I know I sound like a dramatic movie trailer announcer, but it's the truth."

"What do you mean?"

"Maltek told me everything. It was when he was trying to torture me into giving him the answers to the security questions. He was taunting me, but I know what he told me was the truth. See, as far as the public knows, Fresh Meat is designing simple replacement bodies that allow people to live forever. There's nothing special about them; they're simply healthy young bodies that allow their customers to be whoever they want to be. But behind the scenes, Fresh Meat hasn't just been making copies of people. They've been augmenting. Enhancing. They're creating superhumans."

"So they're planning to create a new class of human being. Get people to pay more for the deluxe model."

Dev shook his head. "I wish it were that simple. Maltek doesn't just have market domination in mind. He's after *world* domination."

"So the enhanced clones ..."

"He's building an army of them. He's creating human beings that are faster, smarter, and stronger than any naturally-born human being. *That's* why he went after Next Level Technologies. Not because he thought we'd beat him in the marketplace, but because he knew we had the capability of building our *own* army —one that would be able to stop his. By making that army his own, he not only neutralized the greatest threat to his success; he also strengthened his own forces substantially."

"But how would NLT be capable of countering Maltek's army? I mean ... look at these things," he said, gesturing toward his body. "I'll admit I have greater endurance than I ever had in my old body, but other than that, I don't see how I could go toe-to-toe with a superhuman."

"Your body was just our first prototype. It was only ever meant to be a test of the interface between the duplicate minds and our hardware. But we had plans for artificial bodies much more complex than what you occupy now."

"So you had more advanced models in the works—stronger, more powerful models, I'm assuming—that could stop Maltek's superhumans. And I'm assuming the plans for those next-generation models were all stored in The Hub?"

Dev nodded solemnly.

"So he has access to all of it. He has an army of superhumans *and* androids."

"He does. And we have to fight back."

"But how can we?"

"I'll show you."

THIRTY

The barista is just handing him his coffee when his phone goes *off. He's getting a new pickup request.*

He thanks the barista, places the coffee in the cupholder, and pulls out of the drive-thru and into a parking space. He glances at the information on the phone: The customer is five minutes away, her destination is about six miles away, and the estimated driver earnings are ten bucks. He accepts the trip. He sips his coffee as he drives to the customer, debating in his head whether he'll make this the last fare of the night or try for a couple more. He's starting to get tired, but if he pushes himself he can make it a two-hundred dollar day.

The navigation leads him to a dingy dive bar on the outskirts of town. He pulls into the parking lot and idles. No one's outside, but just as he's about to call the customer, the door at the front of the bar opens and a young woman walks out and makes a beeline for his car. She's short, with a cherubic face and long brunette hair. She wears a tight-fitting jean jacket, a bright blue T-shirt and black leggings.

She opens the passenger-side door. "Rajeev?"

"Yes. And you are?"

"Samantha." He checks the name on the app: Samantha.

"How are you tonight?" he asks as he confirms the trip on the app and

pulls up the navigation to her destination.

"I'm fine. Just getting off work. How about you? Busy night?"

He shrugs. "No busier than usual, but I haven't had much trouble getting fares." He turns on the radio and lowers the volume to back-ground-music status. He always sets it to a smooth jazz station when he's working. The relaxing music helps keep him from going insane.

The obligatory introductory chit-chat subsides and they drive in silence. It begins raining, just a trickle at first, then steady, then pouring. Rajeev drives onto the freeway, windshield wipers pounding at full speed.

"This is some crazy weather," he says. He has to talk more loudly than normal due to the din of the rain plinking against the roof of the car.

"I know. I thought we were done with rain for the season."

"Me too." He turns the radio off; even on a low volume, he finds it distracting with the road conditions requiring so much extra attention. The roads are slick, the sky is dark, and Rajeev recognizes the combination as a recipe for disaster.

The car hydroplanes for a split second, but he manages to steer out of it. He turns his head slightly and apologizes.

"No, it's not your fault," Samantha says. "This rain is horrible. What do you think, should we take the next exit and wait it out?"

"That's up to you. It's your dime. Part of the fare calculation is based on time."

"I'd rather pay a little more than wind up dead."

Rajeev shrugs. "Suit yourself. I'll—"

It happens faster than he can perceive. A pair of headlights that had been safely in one of the opposite lanes is suddenly blinding him. It over-powers his vision completely. He has just enough time to feel a mix of panic and overwhelming regret, and then everything fades to black.

* * *

MIRA PICKED THEM UP A FEW MOMENTS LATER. DEV insisted he and Rajeev ride in the trunk until they were well outside NLT's proximity, lest any of Maltek's goons spot them and take chase. After driving for about a half hour, Mira pulled into her driveway and popped open the trunk.

"Hurry up and get out of there," she hissed. "If any of my neighbors see you getting out of my trunk they'll be whispering about me for years."

They climbed out and followed Mira into the house. Dev and Rajeev took a seat on the couch as Mira closed the door behind her and turned to face her brother.

"I hope you've come to apologize. Because if you think I'm just going to forget the way you've treated mom and I, you're wrong. You're a selfish brat."

Dev looked flustered and didn't know how to respond. Rajeev stepped in.

"It wasn't him. Your brother has been in captivity this entire time. The person who's wronged you, and who owes you an apology, is Gregory Maltek."

Mira frowned. "What are you talking about?"

Dev and Rajeev took turns telling her the story. By the time they were done, her face was ashen.

"I guess I'm the one who owes you an apology, Dev. I'm sorry. I never should have doubted you. I should have known it was that piece of—"

"Mira, it's okay. There's no way you could have known."

She shook her head. "I still feel badly." She sighed. "Well, what do we do now?"

Dev stood. "Dad, get some clothes on so you can blend in. Mira, you're going to have to take us on another drive." He smiled. "I still have a few aces up my sleeve. Maltek thinks he's going to start a war without any resistance. He's wrong."

* * *

"YOU'RE NOT TAKING US OUT HERE TO KILL US, ARE you?" Mira asked.

Dev had directed her to drive out to the Huron-Manistee National Forests, located more than four hours away in Michigan. It was far longer than she'd anticipated driving and she was growing restless.

"No," Dev answered. "It was the only place within a reasonable range of NLT headquarters where I felt I could adequately conceal something of this scope."

"So tell us what we're driving out to see."

"Trust me, it'll be better if I just show you."

For the past three and a half hours, Mira had begged her younger brother to tell her what was so important that they had to drive four hours to see it, but he was resolute, insisting that whatever it was, they had to see it with their own eyes.

Rajeev, meanwhile, was doing his best to suppress his fatherly instincts. In many ways, it felt like taking a roadtrip with the two of them when they were just kids. He felt a pang of regret. Both Dev and Mira had forgiven him for not being there through much of their childhoods, but he hadn't forgiven himself yet. Those moments were lost to him now and he could never have them back. But he was grateful that Dev's technology had given him the opportunity to reconnect with his children. As the old saying went, "Better late than never." He tried to suppress the melancholy he was feeling and embrace the joy he felt at being afforded the opportunity to hear his children bicker once again.

"I love you," he found himself saying.

Mira laughed. "Dad, what are you talking about?"

"Can't a father tell his children he loves them?"

"Of course, but why blurt it out so randomly?"

"I was just thinking about what you two were like as children, and how lucky I am to see how you've both turned out, even after everything that's happened. I may not be the original Rajeev, but as his successor, I'm glad we've had the chance to reconnect. I love you and I wanted to make sure you knew."

"We've always known, dad," Dev said.

"Then I wanted to make sure it was affirmed."

Dev nodded. "I love you too, dad."

"I love you," Mira said. "*Of course* I love you, you dolt."

Rajeev smiled. "I'm glad we've established that we all love each other. I'll refrain from embarrassing you further for now."

Before long, they arrived at the outskirts of the forest. Dev directed Mira down the rural forest roads; her economy car struggled along and the trio felt every bump along the way. Just when Mira felt her car couldn't take any more of the undeveloped dirt roads, Dev pointed excitedly toward a turnoff a few yards away.

"Pull over. This is it."

She pulled into the turnoff and they exited the car. Dev began walking into the woods; Rajeev and Mira just looked at each other.

Dev turned around and waved his arm. "Come on."

"It's a little strange to be luring us out into the middle of the woods like this, especially when we have no idea why," Rajeev said.

Mira turned to her father and nodded. "I know, right?"

"We're almost there. Don't act like you're content to come all this way for nothing." He turned and continued on his path into the woods. Rajeev looked to Mira. She shrugged and followed after her brother. Rajeev took up the rear.

After walking for a few minutes they came across a concrete structure sticking out of the ground like some dull gray monolith. Dev walked up to it and inputted a string of characters into a keypad at the side of a small steel door built into the structure. He threw his head over his shoulder toward Mira, whose mouth was agape, and Rajeev, who also would have been slack-jawed if he'd had a mouth. "Follow me," he said, and he walked through the doorway and disappeared from sight.

Mira and Rajeev exchanged a look, then walked up and

through the door. They found themselves atop a staircase leading into the ground; Dev was already out of sight. They descended, the temperature dropping as they made their way deeper underground. As they neared the bottom, light streamed through a doorway.

As they stepped out of the stairwell, they found themselves in a vast, brightly-lit warehouse, stretching farther than they could see. The walls were made of concrete and reminded Rajeev of the dreary hallways that made up the NLT building. But the warehouse was far from barren. It was lined with seemingly infinite rows filled with equipment Rajeev couldn't begin to understand the purpose of.

Dev stood in front of the sea of shelving, spreading his arms wide, as if everything behind him was a magnificent work of art he'd created and was delighted to show off.

"Welcome," he said, grinning.

"What is this place?" Mira asked.

"This is a storage facility that only I and a handful of close, highly-trusted associates even know exists. There's no mention of it in The Hub. Maltek obviously doesn't know about it, otherwise I'm sure he would have been down here already to empty it out for his own machinations."

"But what is it *for*?" Rajeev asked. "What is all this stuff?"

"Remember how I told you that once Maltek gained control of The Hub, he had access to all of the plans and designs for the next-level tech we planned to create? Well, there's no mention of it in The Hub, but we'd already begun building that next-level tech and this is where we did it. Follow me."

He turned and made his way down one of the rows; Rajeev and Mira followed behind him, taking in the equipment lining the shelves as they walked.

"How were you able to build this place underneath a national forest without anyone knowing?" Mira asked.

"I didn't. We'd contracted with the military, remember? This was their facility. It was already here; had been for decades."

"Wouldn't the military be able to take Maltek out?" Rajeev asked.

"One would hope. But I'm convinced now that Maltek has infiltrated the military, much in the same way he infiltrated NLT—by placing spies that are indistinguishable from the men they replaced. Who knows how high up he's been able to affirm his grip? We can't count on the military. In fact, to be safe, we should assume that the U.S. military is, indeed, under Maltek's thumb."

As he spoke, the rows ended and they walked into an open space that stretched out for another quarter of a mile or so before giving way to more rows of equipment that continued out of sight. Two large pieces of equipment sat against the right wall. Dev approached one, found a foothold and climbed up it.

"This," he said as he made it to the top and lifted a hatch, "is an exoskeleton that increases the strength of a human being fifty-fold. Stay where you are. I'll demonstrate." He dropped into the opening that had appeared when he'd lifted the hatch; a moment later, his hand peeked out and brought the hatch back down.

The mechanism lit up and suddenly unfolded. What had looked like a large, uneven cube suddenly took on the vague shape of a human being. There were two stubby legs attached to two long, flat platforms that served as feet; a stout, square body that also served as a face; and two oval lights making up a pair of slanted, glowing eyes. Thick, riveted arms stretched out from either side. In the center, a clear window showed Dev situated inside what looked like the machine's cerebral cortex.

It was boxy. It was ugly. But there was no question that it was powerful. If there was any doubt, Dev was about to erase it from both Mira's and Rajeev's minds.

The metal beast lurched forward, then lumbered away from

the pair of comparatively tiny figures gawking at it, toward the rows of shelving. When it reached its destination, the mechanism's beefy arms reached out and grabbed either side of one of the shelves. Slowly, Dev raised the shelving over his head. The contents slid off onto the concrete floor, the clanging echoing throughout the cavernous warehouse. Dev lifted the shelving triumphantly over his head, then tossed it back onto the ground.

The exoskeleton hobbled back over to Mira and Rajeev. It folded back up into a cube and powered down. A moment later, Dev emerged, a giddy smile smeared across his face.

"So?" he asked as he jumped back to the ground. "What'd you guys think?"

Rajeev nodded. "It's an impressive machine."

"This thing kicks ass!" Mira walked up and placed a hand against the exoskeleton's smooth exterior.

"That's the idea," Dev said. "It'll be kicking Maltek's ass, hopefully. This is our answer to his superhumans. And this is one of the *early* models. We have others that are lighter, quicker and stronger. Gregory Maltek thinks he's going to stage a coup with minimal resistance. He's mistaken. We'll be there to stop him."

"So you really think he's planning to take over?" Rajeev asked. It was suddenly settling in for him that things were accelerating, coming to blows.

"There's no doubt," he said. He nodded to his father, then again to his sister. "Get ready. A war is coming whether we like it or not. We're going to be here to win it."

-End-

Thanks for reading! If you enjoyed the book, please remember to leave a review! Continue on to read the next book in the trilogy, "Dangerous Minds."

DANGEROUS MINDS

BOOK TWO

ONE

"Morning, Larry."

Larry looked up from the news story he was reading on his tablet and nodded at his coworker.

"Morning, Doug. You're late."

Doug glanced at his watch. "Two minutes late. Screw you, Larry. You're always such a stickler for the rules." The comment had been made in jest, with a smile, but there was a hint of truth to it. Larry was a decade Doug's senior and there was no doubt he was far more experienced in the security game. But in Doug's mind, Larry was too rigid—disciplined to a fault. Did the fate of Next Level Technologies really hinge on his being on time, to the minute? He doubted it.

Larry sighed. "Just try to be on time tomorrow. You know things have been crazy around here lately. We need to stay vigilant."

Doug groaned inwardly. Larry sounded paranoid. But there was no point trying to argue with him.

"Yeah, sure. I'll try to be on time."

"Thank you." Larry turned back to the tablet. Doug walked around to the back of the security desk to clock in.

"What're you reading?"

"A story in the Washington Post. It looks like they might finally be funding that hyperloop tunnel in LA."

"Really. We could really use of those around here. Rush hour is a—"

An explosion clipped his words short; the entire front wall exploded inward, sending dust and debris flying throughout the building's interior.

"Get down!" Larry shouted. But he didn't even wait for his colleague to react; he leapt on top of him, tackling him to the floor. Larry pulled them under the desk. He pulled his shirt over his face and motioned for Doug to do the same. They sat there, chests heaving, futilely shielding their eyes from the dust with their hands. They both coughed, but once Larry had composed himself, he rose part way to steal a glance into the entrance lobby, trying to make out what had caused the unexpected explosion. Had they had a gas leak or something, he wondered?

He didn't see anything at first; the dust was still too thick. But as it began to clear, he made out an impossible large silhouette. It was boxy, and slow moving, but vaguely shaped like a man. It stood at least ten feet tall and nearly as many wide. And it was heading toward them, approaching with a lumbering but powerful movement.

"Shit ... Doug! Get up!"

Doug was still cowering on the floor and he made no move to get up despite Larry's order.

"Why? What's happening?" he asked between whimpers.

"I don't know. But something is coming right at us—something big."

This, at last, got Doug's attention. He shot up and followed Larry's gaze. His eyes widened and his jaw fell.

"What the hell is that thing?"

"I don't know. You run ahead and warn Mr. Sundaram. I'll see if I can stop it."

Doug didn't hesitate, skittering off down the hall and out of sight, like a dog running away with its tail between its legs. Larry stood, took a deep breath, and walked out in front of the … *thing*, whatever it was. He tried to steel himself for the possibility that this thing would end up killing him.

"Stop!" He shouted, holding up a hand. To his surprise, the monstrosity halted. He stared at it. Dust still hung in the air, but it was clearing to the point that he was beginning to get a better look at the thing. It appeared to be some kind of giant robot, but it was nothing like the ones the company was developing inside the very building he was standing in. It was several times larger than even the largest human beings. Its arms and legs were thick as tree trunks. It didn't have hands as much as claws.

Only a fine haze of dust remained in the air and as Larry gazed at the mechanical Titan before him, he noticed got the first time a glass window where he'd imagine the chest would be. On the other side of the glass was the faint silhouette of a human operator.

"You can't come through here!" Larry shouted with a hell of a lot more confidence than he felt. He pointed toward the now-missing wall. "Turn around and go back the way you came."

There was a pause, and then a voice came over speakers built into the machine. The voice was vaguely familiar, but Larry couldn't put his finger on it.

"I don't want to hurt you. Please step aside."

Larry gulped. "I can't do that. Now leave. You're trespassing on private property."

"Your commitment to your job and the commensurate duties is admirable. But I'm afraid I can't leave without my friends."

Larry raised an eyebrow. "Who are your friends?"

"I don't have time to chit-chat. I'm coming through, whether you like it or not." The machine began moving forward again, walking slowly but steadily in Larry's direction.

"Oh no you don't." He reached for his waist and his hands gripped the pistol sticking out of the holster on his hip. He raised it, turned the safety off, and pointed it at his oncoming foe.

"Not another step or I'll shoot!"

The machine continued its approach and Larry, being a man of his word, fired a shot. He'd aimed for the glass window—and thus, for the person at the machine's controls—but it must have been made of bulletproof glass, because the bullet merely ricocheted off and came back at him.

The bullet hit him in the leg. He cried out and collapsed to the floor, clutching his leg and looking on in horror as the unstoppable machine trudged past him and down the hallway, into the heart of the building.

Keeping one hand pressed to his wound, he used the other to retrieve the radio transmitter secured to the side of his chest. He brought it to his mouth, pressed the button on its side and spoke. "Doug? Have you found Dev?" He waited a moment before continuing, but there was no response. "Doug, I slowed it down a little but I couldn't stop it. It's headed into the building." He paused again. Nothing. "I've been shot in the leg. I need medical assistance as soon as possible. But our first priority is stopping that thing, whatever it is."

He wondered if Larry had dropped his radio. There was no way of knowing—and no assurances any kind of medical aid would be arriving anytime soon. He retrieved a pocket knife from his trouser pocket and cut off one of his shirtsleeves. He tied it around his leg as a makeshift tourniquet.

He was in a great deal of pain, but he was sure he'd survive. But he couldn't walk—he couldn't do anything to stop the threat storming through the corporate campus he was supposed to be protecting. He just hoped Doug would rise to the occasion.

TWO

RAJEEV SUNDARAM MADE HIS WAY TO NEXT LEVEL Technologies' entertainment lounge, but as he approached, he looked through the floor-to-ceiling windows and saw that it was empty. Not just empty of people; it had been completely gutted of all its furniture and amenities. Apparently Gregory Maltek hadn't taken kindly to the androids' rescue mission and had suspended their recreation privileges as punishment. Well, he sure as hell wasn't going to like what Rajeev was about to do.

The problem was, he didn't know exactly where the other androids were. He'd only ever interacted with them in the lounge, but they probably spent most of their time in their individual dormitories—that is, unless Maltek, as an act of vengeance, banished them to some kind of dungeon or something.

Rajeev's dorm had been on the sixth floor, and he imagined most of the rest of the androids were situated nearby. There was no way he'd possibly be able to fit into the elevator in this monstrous exoskeleton, however—he barely even fit in the hallway. That left only one option.

He looked up at the ceiling. He couldn't actually see it with his own eyes; the exoskeleton blocked his view. But he was surrounded by video feeds in all directions, so when he looked up, he saw the ceiling as viewed through the cameras atop the exoskeleton's head.

"Oh boy," he muttered to himself. "Here we go."

Twin rockets on the bottom of the exoskeleton's feet roared to life. Immediately, the entire mechanism soared upward into the ceiling and broke through into the next floor, plowing through five more until Rajeev turned the rockets off. He began falling through the hole in the floor, but quickly stretched out the mechanical arms to stop the fall and climb himself back onto steady ground.

He stood and looked around, trying to get his bearings. He spotted the elevator entrance, which helped orient him, and made for his old dormitory, his footsteps thundering down the hall as he went. When he reached the small room, he made to open the door, but the massive exoskeleton fist couldn't handle the fine motor functions necessary to turn the doorknob and ended up slamming the door off its hinges instead.

The room was empty, except for the small bed he'd slept on —a bed that, strictly speaking, wasn't even necessary except as a comfort from his old way of life. He thought maybe another android had been assigned to his old room, but that apparently was not the case.

He turned his attention to the door across the hall. Two large steps were all it took to place him directly in front of it. He swung his right fist into the door, punching it directly down onto the concrete floor. He stepped through.

The dormitory was identical to his own, except mirrored. Sitting on a small bed in the leftmost corner was an android body identical to his own. It was impossible to distinguish one android from another visually, as they all looked the same. They had to rely on each other's voices instead.

"Who are you?" Rajeev shouted.

The android raised its quizzically. "Rajeev?"

The voice was eminently feminine and Rajeev knew immediately who he was talking to: Natalie.

"Yes, it's me. I don't have time to explain what this is"—he gestured toward the exoskeleton with one of its large claws —"but I'm busting you out of here. Follow me."

He turned and walked back out into the hallway. He was surprised to see three other androids already out in the hall, apparently checking to see what all the ruckus was after he'd knocked down Natalie's door.

"It's me, Rajeev!" he shouted. "Gather the other androids— as quickly as you can. I'm getting you all out of here!"

The androids took a moment to react, stunned by the situation before them—a bulging, mechanised mess speaking in the voice of a former compatriot—but as the realization set in that this was perhaps their last, best hope of escaping the building that had become their prison, they sprang into action, darting away to gather the others.

Natalie saddled up beside the exoskeleton and looked up at Rajeev. Her stonelike facial expression was unable to convey the sense of wonder she was feeling, her voice left no doubt she was impressed by what she saw.

"Some upgrade."

"Tell me about it." His voice expressed the smile his face couldn't.

The sound of approaching footsteps broke them out of their reverie. Rajeev based himself and watched the corner, waiting for his opponents to round it.

"Get behind me," he ordered Natalie. She didn't seem thrilled at being bossed around, but she recognized the gravity of the situation and did as she was told.

A single entity rounded the corner first. He was dressed in black tactical gear, including a helmet with what Rajeev assumed was a bulletproof face plate. He couldn't tell through all the protective gear whether it was a woman or a man, but he got his answer soon enough when they opened their mouth.

"Stop!" It was a man's voice, and as he spoke, he raised a gun in his right hand and pointed it squarely at Rajeev. Meanwhile, four other people dressed in the same tactical gear rounded the corner and took up position behind the first man.

"I don't want to hurt you," Rajeev said. "Put down your guns and leave."

"Disengage the machine, and step forward with your hands in the air!" the man called back.

"That's not going to happen. You're going to want to—"

Rajeev's words were cut short by a staccato burst of gunfire. The man had fired four quick, successive shots directly at him. All four bullets found their mark, but the effect was nonexistent. The bullets bounced off the bulletproof glass surrounding Rajeev and fell to the floor with a soft clank. The man looked up at Rajeev with shock and fear, but soon steeled himself and removed any hint of emotion.

"As I was saying," Rajeev continued, "you're going to want to turn around and let me do that I'm gonna do. That is, if you want to live."

The man seemed to waver for a moment. He looked over his shoulder and shared a look with one of the other gunmen, but Rajeev couldn't get a good enough look to tell what he was trying to convey. When he turned back to look in Rajeev's direction, there was an unmistakable resolve in his voice.

"It's my duty to protect this corporation," he said. "You are committing an act of terrorism. I don't know why you're doing it and frankly, I don't care. All I know is that you must be stopped—by any means necessary."

If he'd had lips, Rajeev would have cracked a smile. The man had grit, no doubt. Unfortunately, there was a good chance it was going to get him killed. He'd try to give the man and his team one last opportunity to bow out gracefully—but after that, he couldn't be held responsible for whatever happened.

"This isn't an act of terrorism," he said. "It's a rescue operation."

The man seemed to hesitate, but when he spoke again his voice was steady. "You may think you're doing this for some noble cause, but I assure you, you're nothing but an angel of destruction and we *will* stop you."

"These are human beings," Rajeev said, gesturing with one of his massive arms toward Natalie, who was still behind him, like a small child cowering behind its mother. "They may look like robots, and on the surface, they are. But beneath every one of their metal-and-silicone shells is a human mind, no different from yours. And they are being held here against their will, as slaves. You may think me and terrorist, but I think of NLT as a slaveholding company and I'll do whatever is necessary to free these slaves. If you want to live, I suggest you get out of my way."

The man looked torn. He lowered his weapon and turned around to face the others. For a moment, Rajeev thought he'd been successful in deterring the man, but when he turned around again he raised his gun once more and aimed it directly at Rajeev. "Fire on the count of three," he commanded. "Aim for the glass in the center—it can't possibly hold forever. Not with the amount of firepower we're going to throw at it."

Rajeev's heart sank. Despite all his talk, he'd desperately hoped the confrontation wouldn't escalate to this point. He had never taken a human life before and he didn't relish the thought of starting now. But his son, Dev, had insisted that a war was coming. There would be deaths soon enough. Lots of them. These were likely to be the first of many; hundreds, if not thousands … maybe even millions.

"One!" The man's voice echoed through the hallway like a bullet in and of itself. Rajeev sent the exoskeleton lurching forward as quickly as it could move, which was equivalent to someone walking at a moderate pace. The tactical group remained steady, guns pointed, waiting.

"Two!" Rajeev was getting close; he was close enough now to make out the faces behind the faceplates. He raised one of his massive claws in the air, preparing to bring it down upon the leader's faceplate, smashing out his existence in one fluid motion.

Finally, the leader let out one final cry, one last, desperate command to protect the building they had been charged to serve: "Three!"

THREE

The hallway erupted in gunfire. Bullets bounced off the surface of Rajeev's exoskeleton and scattered about like sparks.

Everything happened almost too quickly for Rajeev to perceive. The first round of gunfire bounced off the glass protecting Rajeev like nothing, but with the second, hairline cracks began to form. But by then, Rajeev was on them. He swatted the gun out of the commander's hands as if it were a plastic toy, then shoved the man aside. But he'd used much more force than he'd intended, and the man went flying through the air, collided with the concrete wall, and then crumpled like a rag doll. A pit formed in Rajeev's stomach, but he couldn't dwell on it. There were still plenty of people trying to kill him.

He shoved another gunman, trying to control his strength this time. The man toppled over, but didn't careen into the wall. Rajeev considered that a win.

More bullets shot at the glass and the cracks widened. Rajeev gulped. Was there a chance that the bullets could actually break through?

He didn't want to find out.

He kept swatting at the men, feeling like a bear swatting away flies. Before he knew it, he had plowed through all of them, leaving then scattered across the floor, unconscious … or worse.

He stood still a moment, taking in the broken bodies, letting the reality of what he'd just done to the men sink in. Finally, after a moment, he shook his head and retreated back to Natalie.

"Are you okay?" he asked.

It was impossible to read her face for any sign of emotion, but her body language belied her fear. She had cowered behind a large slab of concrete that had come loose when Rajeev had plowed through the floor. She moved slowly now, as if in shock.

"Just get me the hell out of here," she said.

Rajeev nodded. "I'm working on it."

He looked up and saw the other androids emerging from their respective dormitories. They hadn't dared to come out during the commotion of Rajeev's confrontation with the security team, but now that it had died down they were venturing out to see which side had been victorious. Upon seeing Rajeev—with his faceplate cracked, but his exoskeleton still standing—one of the androids raised his fist in the air triumphantly.

"There'll be plenty of time to celebrate your liberation later," Rajeev said. "For now, let's make sure you really do get liberated."

He led them to the hole in the floor he'd created and crouched in front of it.

"It's a six-flight drop," he said. "Think you guys can handle that?"

Natalie looked down nervously through the hole. "I don't know," she said. "Do you have spare parts on hand just in case?"

"My son does. But if any of you break too badly, we're not going to be able to get you out of here."

"It's worth the risk," one of the androids declared. He

jumped into the hole and descended rapidly down to the bottom floor, landing with a hard thud that echoed back up to the sixth floor.

"Well?" Rajeev shouted. "Are you okay?"

"I'm fine!" the android shouted. His voice sounded far away, but they were just able to make out his words. "My legs absorbed most of the shock! You guys should be fine!"

"You heard him," Rajeev said. "I'll go last. As soon as you land, make for the exit. Don't wait for me."

One by one, the androids jumped through the hole. Natalie was the last to go.

"Here goes nothing," she said, and she leapt through the hole and out of sight.

Rajeev waited just a moment to make sure Natalie and the other androids had had time to move out of the way—he didn't want to crush any of them—and then jumped. Far larger and heavier in his bulky exoskeleton, he dropped like a lead weight and landed with a thunderous boom.

He looked around. The first floor was empty now, save for a lone android standing expectantly just out of Rajeev's way.

"I told you to get out of here," Rajeev said.

"Just making sure you got down okay," she said. Her tone implied that if she'd had a mouth, the words would have come with a smirk. "Now let's get the hell out of here."

They headed toward the giant hole Rajeev had put in the wall. Natalie had to slow her pace to a crawl to match the pace of Rajeev's large but cumbersome exoskeleton, but before long they'd made it to the hole and walked out of the building.

The other androids were lying outside in a pile. As Natalie ran out to them, her body seized and she fell on top of the pile.

Next Level Technologies had built a failsafe into each of the android bodies that caused them to seize up if they tried to leave the building. It looked like it was still enabled. But that was fine; Rajeev had accounted for that.

"Daniel—tell Dev we're ready for him."

He heard the voice of the virtual assistant in his ear. "Sending your message."

Not even thirty seconds later, they heard the roar of an engine and a large, military-grade truck pulled up right in front of the pile. Rajeev's son, Dev, who was behind the wheel, waved to Rajeev through the window.

In his powerful exoskeleton, Rajeev was able to easily scoop up the disabled bodies and place them in the back of the truck. He was just picking up the last two when a man ran out of the building, carrying a gun.

"We've gotta go!" Rajeev shouted.

The truck started pulling away; Rajeev threw the last two bodies into the truck, then climbed on top of it. As the truck pulled away, the man raised his gun, aimed, and fired.

But it was too late. The shot missed, and the truck disappeared over the horizon, filled with every android that had been imprisoned at Next Level Technologies.

Their rescue operation had been a success.

FOUR

It was a long drive to the Huron-Manistee National Forests. Rajeev noticed some double-takes from passing motorists, but for the most part, their vehicle just looked like a military truck with some kind of machinery—Rajeev's exoskeleton—strapped to the back. The android bodies were, thankfully, too low to be seen by other drivers.

When they arrived at their base deep in the heart of the forest, Dev got out, stretched, and let out a long, loud groan.

"That drive is a killer," he said.

Rajeev chuckled. "I wouldn't know. Thankfully, my new body doesn't come with any of the aches and pains you're still subject to."

Dev grabbed a tablet computer out of the cab of the truck and crawled into the back with the disabled androids. He plugged a cord connected to the tablet into a port on one of the android's necks. One by one, he moved from one android to the next, removing the failsafe that prevented them from moving. It took him more than an hour to get through them all, but finally there was a group of completely ambulatory androids standing around waiting to hear what was next for them.

"Follow me," Dev said, flashing his dad a smile. Without another word, he stepped into the woods, like a benevolent Pied Piper leading them to the Promised Land.

"Where are you taking us?" one of the androids asked.

"You'll see," Dev said, and he continued walking without another word. The androids followed him—where else were they going to go?

They came to a large, gray monolith sticking out of the ground. Dev unlocked the large, steel door and began descending the stairs that led into the earth; the androids followed him single-file forming an otherworldly procession that was punctuated by Rajeev in his unnaturally bulky exoskeleton, which barely fit through the door.

As they made their way to the bottom of the stairs, they walked through the doorway at the bottom into the cavernous warehouse space stretching endlessly before them. They congregated together, looking both amazed and confused as they waited for Dev to explain exactly what they had walked into.

"I realize that all of you have been held at Next Level Technologies like slaves," Dev said. "That was never my intention. I never wanted any of you to leave before you had properly acclimated to your new bodies. But you rightly realized that the company had no intention of letting you leave. The fact is, it wasn't me keeping you as slaves. It was Gregory Maltek, the founder of bioengineering company Fresh Meat."

Hushed murmurs swept through the small group of androids as they took in the new information. One of them stepped forward and spoke the question on all of their minds: "But how is that possible?"

Dev cleared his throat. "As you may or may not know, Maltek's company is developing biological replacement bodies in direct competition to NLT's robotic bodies. I'm not sure exactly how he did it, but Maltek managed to get his hands on a sample of my DNA and create a clone of myself. Inside the mind of that clone, he placed a copy of his own consciousness. So the entity at NLT for the past couple years that looks and sounds just like me has actually been an extension of Gregory Maltek carrying out his bidding.

"But it gets worse," he continued. "At first, I thought Maltek was simply trying to sabotage my company from the inside—take out the competition. But I have since learned that that was never his end goal at all. He had much larger ambitions in mind. Gregory Maltek has been building an army of superhuman clones. And now that he controls Next Level Technologies, he plans to supplement that army with androids."

One of the androids tittered at that. "I'm sorry," she said. "It's not like these bodies of ours are particularly formidable."

"You're correct," Dev said. "But we were developing next-generation tech that is much more formidable, and Maltek now has access to all of those plans. But," and he smiled broadly, "so do we."

He turned around and gestured toward the nearly endless rows of shelves storing all kinds of equipment.

"Maltek has access to our plans, but we have that and more. We have actual prototypes that we'd been developing for years with funding from the Department of Defense. And we're going to use it to fight back against Maltek." He turned back again to face the androids directly. "None of you signed up for this war, and I'm sorry you're being dragged into it. But Maltek's war will affect all of you. It will affect everyone you love. And we're the only ones that can stop him."

"What about the military?" someone asked.

"I suspect Maltek has infiltrated the military the same way he infiltrated NLT," Dev said. "Even if he hasn't, they don't know what's coming like we do. We can help them. And if we're able to put down Maltek's superhuman uprising before it even starts, all the better."

He paused, gathering his thoughts a moment. When he

looked up and began addressing the group again, he could barely contain his excitement. "I realize you've all received countless empty promises that upgraded bodies were coming soon. You probably thought you'd never see the day. But I'm happy to prove you wrong. By the end of the day, I hope to have every single one of you put into brand-new bodies. Stronger bodies. Faster bodies. Bodies that are equipped for war. Even better, they'll be more realistic, more human-like, and they'll each be unique—so you'll finally be able to tell each other apart on appearances alone instead of having to announce yourselves to one another."

The androids murmured among themselves again, this time clearly excited by what they'd just heard. Finally, after everything they'd been through, serving as prisoners in the Next Level Technologies building, they were becoming free once more —and they'd have new bodies that would hopefully do a hell of a lot more to remind them that they were human beings than the ones they currently occupied.

FIVE

THE BUNKER HAD DORM-LIKE ROOMS SIMILAR TO THE
dorms the androids had lived in at Next Level Technologies. Dev
had led them all to their rooms as Rajeev put his exoskeleton
away. As he crawled out of it, he saw his daughter Mira
approaching him.

"Hey dad," she said, smiling. "Looks like the rescue mission
was a smashing success."

"Literally," he said. "You should see what I did to the wall on
the NLT building."

She giggled. "I can imagine. Well, dad, Dev and I have been
talking and we thought you might enjoy the privilege of being
the first android to be transferred to a new body."

The offer took him by surprise. He shook his head. "That's
very thoughtful, but I'm in no hurry," he said.

"Well, there's a bit of an ulterior motive," she said. "We
were thinking you could serve as our Guinea Pig, since Dev
hasn't done one of these transfers in this facility before. I'm sure
it'll go fine, though."

Rajeev didn't verbalize what he was thinking, which was that
it didn't matter whether the transfer worked or not. He would

die either way. Yes, a copy of his consciousness would continue in the new body, complete with all of his memories up to that moment. But it wouldn't be *him*, the consciousness that currently existed in *this* body, just like he wasn't an extension of the original Rajeev Sundaram; that Rajeev was dead, just like he would be once this transfer went through.

He realized it was an issue with a certain amount of room for philosophical argument, that others would argue that as long as his consciousness and memories remained intact, then he wouldn't really be dead. But there was a break in the consciousness, however slight, where the old Rajeev went away and the new Rajeev was activated, and that gap was death.

Nevertheless, he didn't see another way forward. He needed the new body—not just for his own self-esteem, but so he could be equipped with the strength and agility to take on Maltek's superhuman soldiers. And if he could serve as a Guinea Pig to make sure nothing happened to any of the other androids who would presumably be fighting to stop Maltek, he figured it would be dishonorable of him not to take that opportunity.

"Okay. I'll do it," he said. "I'll be Dev's test subject."

Mira smiled. "I thought you'd say that. Follow me."

She led him to a small office and directed him to have a seat.

"Dev should be back soon once he's had a chance to show everyone to their rooms. Make yourself comfortable."

"I'm never really uncomfortable," Rajeev said. "One of the perks of being a robot."

Just then, Dev walked into the room looking frazzled. "Sorry about that," he said. "Just trying to make sure everyone is settled and making themselves at home. Did Mira ask you about being the first to transfer yourself into a new body?"

Rajeev nodded. "She did. And I agreed to do it."

"Thanks Dad. I'm sure it'll go fine, but I just figured on the off chance that something were to happen, it would look better if it happened to someone I had a direct relationship with. Better for optics, you know?"

"That's callous."

Dev laughed. "I'm not denying it. But I also have a backup of your consciousness, so if something goes wrong, I can bring you back. I can't say the same for all those other androids."

"Fair enough. Let's get this over with, then. The suspense is killing me."

"All right. Just hold tight." Dev retrieved his tablet and connected it to his father via a cord attached to his neck. "It's going to be kind of like an operation. You'll go to sleep, just as if you were under anesthesia, and when you wake up you'll be in a brand-new body—one that's better in every conceivable way. Are you ready?"

Rajeev nodded. "As ready as I'll ever be."

"Then let's do it." He pressed a button on the tablet, and Rajeev's world suddenly faded to black.

SIX

When Rajeev awoke, he was still in Dev's office and he wondered whether something had gone wrong. But Dev was in front of him with a large grin on his face.

"How did it go?" Rajeev asked, and as the words came out he knew something was different because he could actually feel his mouth move.

"See for yourself," Dev said, and he held up a mirror to Rajeev's face.

The face looking back at him was ... human. Almost. The skin looked real and far more closely matched his original dark skin shade than the white covering he'd been stuck with in his last android body.

What's more, there was actual *hair* atop his head, a pair of synthetic lips, and an actual nose—a facial feature that had been conspicuously absent from the previous model. He still couldn't smell anything, but at least he looked like a human being again, even if he wasn't one.

"What do you think?" Dev asked.

"It definitely makes me feel more like myself." Which was odd considering that, technically, he was the third incarnation of

Rajeev Sundaram. The first had been in a coma and then been taken off life support. The second had died in Dev's office. Yes, he had the memories of both of them, so in a sense he was just a continuation of them. But he couldn't help feeling that *something* had been lost in the transfer and he grieved in his own head for his previous two iterations who had died so he may live.

He stood and to his surprise, he had no trouble keeping his balance. It had taken him weeks to fully acclimate to his previous body and get around without stumbling. He looked up at Dev in surprise.

"Like I said, these models are way more advanced. The body itself does a lot of the work to keep you balanced, so there's not nearly as bad of a learning curve as you had in your last body."

"That's a relief." He looked down and studied the rest of his body. To his surprise, he was fully clothed in a pair of blue jeans and a white T-shirt. "Is it … anatomically correct?"

Dev chuckled. "More or less. You'll find it's not quite the same as what you're used to … but it's close enough."

Rajeev whistled. "These *are* way more advanced."

"In some ways, it's actually an improvement over its organic equivalent. You don't have any need to urinate or defecate."

"But I'm guessing that means I'm still unable to eat or drink anything."

"That's correct."

He frowned, although inwardly he relished the increased facial musculature that allowed him to frown. "Bummer."

Dev offered a sympathetic shrug. "It's not ideal, but at least it's a marked improvement. And wait until you see how these things perform physically. It'll blow you away."

Rajeev smiled. "I can't wait. So what now?"

Dev walked over to his desk and took a seat, slumping into it as the weight of what lay ahead of them settled into his psyche. "Now … I upgrade all the other models. And then we train.

Maltek is going to strike eventually and we need to be prepared when he does. He has a clone army—apologies to George Lucas—that I'm sure he's training as we speak. We're going to be outnumbered and outmatched, and yet we still must win. We *must*."

"I know," Rajeev agreed, nodding. "And yet, I can't help but recognize that the underdog doesn't always win, no matter how valiantly they may fight."

"We can only do what we can do."

He left to begin the process of transferring the other androids into their new bodies. Rajeev wandered out of the office and an android walked up to him.

"Holy cow," it said, and Rajeev instantly recognized the voice as Natalie's. "You almost look human, Rajeev!"

He smirked—and it felt good to know she'd be able to recognize the facial expression. "Thanks ... I think. How are you doing? What do you think of all ... this?" He held up his hands to represent the vastness of the warehouse stretching out before them.

"I couldn't have imagined it. But do you really think it's enough to stop Maltek?"

Rajeev shrugged. "Dev seems to think so. But I don't know. I have my doubts, I'll admit. But I don't know what a fraction of all this tech can do. Dev does. So maybe his hope isn't misplaced."

"I hope not."

As they spoke, Mira walked up to join them. She turned to her father and grinned.

"Look at you, dad! The new body is so much more lifelike!"

"I've noticed. And I'm grateful."

"It'll be nice to be able to tell each other apart," Natalie said. "Announcing myself every time I walked into a room with another android in it was getting old."

"Well," Natalie answered, "I know my dad will get through

the transfers as quickly as he can. Unfortunately, it's a bit cumbersome since he's the only one here who knows how to work any of this tech. We'll have to train some of the androids after they—"

She was cut off, and neither Natalie nor Rajeev knew why at first, but then Rajeev's virtual assistant, Daniel, popped up in front of his field of vision, a severe look on his face. He reminded Rajeev of an IT tech, clad in a green polo shirt and perfectly pressed khaki pants. His hair was swept to the side and he wore thick-framed black glasses.

"Daniel?" Rajeev asked. "What's going—"

"This is an emergency alert," Daniel said. But although he was moving his lips, it wasn't his normal voice coming out of them. It sounded just like the scratchy, alien voice that used to come on over the television for those tests of the National Emergency Alert Broadcasting System. "A terrorist attack is in progress at the nation's capital. Citizens are advised to stay inside with the doors locked until further information becomes available."

Daniel disappeared and Rajeev looked up at Natalie and Mira and it was clear that they had received identical messages from their own virtual assistants.

"What the hell was that?" Natalie asked.

Rajeev and Mira looked at each other and both spoke at the same time: "Maltek."

"You think so?" Natalie asked.

"I think he's escalated his plans after we stormed the NLT campus this morning," Mira said. "He must have seen dad's exoskeleton and freaked out. He must have realized that we have resources to fight back with."

"So he's trying to get ahead of us, make his move before we're fully prepared to respond," Rajeev said.

"Which we're not," Mira agreed, nodding. "But that means he's not as prepared as he would have preferred either."

Dev came running up to them. His face was ashen. "You all heard?" They nodded. "We have to do something!"

"But what?" Mira asked.

"We have to go stop him."

Rajeev frowned. "How are we going to do that?"

"You haven't seen what that new body of yours can do yet, dad. We'll probably be outnumbered … but I think we'll hold our own."

SEVEN

DEV LED THEM BACK TO ONE OF THE DORMITORIES, where he'd been working on upgrading one of the androids. It was Ted. His new body was lying on a small bed clad in white sheets and a white blanket. His eyes were closed.

"We're going to need all hands on deck," Dev said. "Ted should be done upgrading any minute now."

"What about the other androids?" Mira asked.

"We don't have time, and they'd be more hindrance than help in their current bodies."

"Guess that means I'm sitting this one out," Natalie said.

"Not necessarily. I just got a handful of new exoskeletons up and running. They're newer models than the one Rajeev used this morning—lighter, sleeker, faster. But they're actually stronger than the old models. I have two for Mira and me ... and a third for you, if you want it."

She nodded. "I'm ready to kick Maltek's ass."

Ted's eyes fluttered open and he looked up at the group that had congregated before him.

"What's going on?" he asked weakly. "Did it go okay?"

Dev offered a reassuring smile. "You're talking, so it looks like it went great," he said. "Unfortunately, you're going to need to break in your new body real fast."

"What do you mean?"

Dev explained the emergency alert they'd all gotten, and how it must mean Maltek was attacking. Ted didn't hesitate for a second.

"Okay," he said. "Let's go. I'm ready."

Dev smiled. "I appreciate your enthusiasm. We'll leave soon."

He motioned for them to follow him and led them to the new exoskeleton models. They reminded Rajeev of MegaMan. They looked more like metallic bodysuits than pieces of functional high-tech machinery.

"Mira, Natalie and I will be in the suits," he said. "Rajeev and Ted—you won't need them." He pressed a button on one of them and it unfolded like flower petals embracing the morning sun. He helped Mira into it, then pressed another button and the suit folded back down, encapsulating her.

Natalie was next. As the suit closed in around her, Dev couldn't help but point out the irony of the situation. "A machine wrapped in a machine," he said.

"I don't feel any different," Natalie said.

"Just wait," Dev said. "You'll see what these things are capable of. Okay ... my turn." He stepped into the remaining suit and let it enclose around him. Then he led them up the steps and back to the surface and the national forest.

"How are we going to get there?" Natalie asked. "There's no way we'll get there quickly enough if we drive."

Dev smiled, his lips barely visible behind the exoskelton's faceplate. "We don't need to drive," he said. "Ready to see what these things can do?"

He spread his feet apart and motioned for the others to follow suit.

"Have you ever used a voice assistant to navigate you some-where?" he asked.

"Of course," Natalie said, and the others nodded that they, too, had used such navigation before.

Dev nodded. "Then this will be easy. Just summon your virtual assistants. Your suits—and bodies, for Ted and Rajeev—will do the rest. Watch." He looked up, took a deep breath, and summoned his virtual assistant. It appeared in his AR glasses, unseen by the others. "Fly me to the White House," he said.

Immediately, Dev flew up into the air and soared out of sight. Mira, Ted, Natalie and Rajeev exchanged looks of amaze-ment, barely daring to believe that what they'd just witnessed was even possible.

"Who wants to go next?" Rajeev asked.

"I'll go," Natalie said excitedly. She spread her legs apart, breathed deep, and summoned her virtual assistant. "Fly me to the White House," she said.

She started to leap into the air to jumpstart the process, but even that was not necessary; the suit propelled her into the air and she disappeared into the horizon, following the same path Dev had taken.

Mira went next, and then Ted. Finally it was just Rajeev. He took a deep breath and summoned his assistant. "Daniel?"

The geeky-looking virtual assistant popped into existence in front of him and awaited further instructions.

Rajeev couldn't help but feel nervous. Presumably a great deal of care had gone into the creation of these artificial bodies, including the technology that allowed them to fly. But what if something went wrong? What if he plummeted to his death?

Then again, he'd technically already died twice before, and been resurrected each time thanks to the technology his son had developed. So if he died now, couldn't he just be brought back?

He wasn't completely convinced, but it gave him enough

confidence to proceed. He took another deep breath and then gave Daniel the command: "Fly me to the White House."

He shot up with ferocious speed, and his first thought was that if he'd been in his old flesh-and-blood body, it would have felt like his stomach was in his feet. As it was, he didn't feel a thing, although there was a distinct whooshing sound as the wind rushed past his artificial ears and gave him a sense of how incredibly quickly he was moving through the air.

Normally it would have taken around two hours to fly from Michigan to New York. But Rajeev found himself slowing and beginning to descend after only fifteen or twenty minutes. He flew head-first toward the city which was quickly coming up toward him and apprehension filled him. He was coming in too fast. He was going to crash, and die.

But just before he thought it was too late, he slowed and turned upright and began to float down to the ground. He looked around and placed himself—he was on the sidewalk across from the White House's South Lawn. The others in his group were gathered a little ways away, apparently assessing the situation. Rajeev ran up to them and turned to Dev, gesturing for him to catch him up to speed.

"We're not sure exactly what's happening," Dev said, "but it looks like some of Maltek's men are on the roof. Look." He pointed at the roof and they saw two men standing on top of it, looking like they were standing guard.

"How should we proceed?" Ted asked.

Dev frowned. "I'm not sure. Any ideas?"

"I say we go in, guns blazing," Ted said. "Uh … these things do have guns, right?" he asked, pointing to his new body.

Before Dev could answer, their virtual assistants filled their fields of vision to deliver another emergency alert. Only this time, it was not from official channels. The emergency alert system had been hijacked, and it was the voice of Gregory Maltek that was piped into their ears.

"Good afternoon, America," Maltek said, and as he spoke the image of the virtual assistants gradually dissolved into the visage of Maltek. He was square-jawed and sandy-haired, giving off a casual beach-boy vibe. Yet there was a seriousness to his voice and to his eyes. He exuded ambition and danger, a combination as volatile and destructive as gasoline and an open flame. "You may or may not recognize me. That's okay. You will after today. My name is Gregory Maltek. I am the founder of the bioengineering company Fresh Meat. And as of today—as of this very moment—I am also your ruler."

He paused, as if giving his captive audience time to let out a collective gasp. When he continued, the corner of his lips turned up in a slight smile.

"Your president is dead. But there's no need to mourn—you have no need of presidents any longer, or of legislators or judges. You now have me, and I will be all these things to you and more.

"For too long, we have lived in a world of Puritans and charlatans. A world where we let a misguided sense of morality and ethics get in the way of the innovation we needed to evolve as a species. It was not easy for me to grow my bioengineering firm, saddled as I was by countless regulations and red tape designed, in part, to ensure that I didn't cross some imaginary red line created by some dunce of a politician who couldn't finish reading a bioengineering textbook if he had a year to do it, let alone comprehend it. And yet I accomplished my work despite the red tape—because I ignored it completely.

"You will meet the culmination of my work soon. I have created human bodies that far exceed anything Mother Nature ever intended for our species. Bodies that are faster and stronger than the most powerful non-enhanced human being who ever lived. Bodies that can be yours—for a price. But I'm getting ahead of myself. You'll hear all the details soon enough."

As Maltek continued speaking, Dev shook his head. "I can't

stand to listen to any more of his bloviating. I'm going to go up there and shut him up." He began marching toward the fence separating them from the White House lawn.

"Hold up!" Rajeev called after him. "We don't have a plan!"

"There's a time for planning and a time for action," Dev called back without turning around. "I'm not going to let him think he's getting away with this."

Rajeev and the rest of the group exchanged nervous glances at each other, but finally took off after Dev. There was clearly no stopping him, and they weren't going to let him run into a fight without backup.

As Dev approached the fence, he didn't hesitate for one moment. He plowed into it with his shoulder and it shattered under his momentum, leaving a wide gap that allowed Rajeev and the others to follow with ease. They sprinted across the lawn toward the building, but as they approached, a man and a woman emerged and walked toward them, blocking their path.

"Stop right there," the woman said, raising a hand. Her voice was deep and strong; authoritative. Dev and his followers slowed and came to a stop. It was evident by the way these two held themselves that they were two of Maltek's "enhanced" humans. They wouldn't be able to simply shove them out of the way. They would have to fight them.

"We're going in there, one way or another," Dev said.

The man spoke this time. He sounded angry, almost absurdly so, as if he were suffering from 'roid rage. "Not a chance," he barked.

Dev made his move. He lunged toward the man, swung back his arm, and threw out a powerful punch backed by the power of the exoskeleton suit. But the man dodged the blow, and returned one of his own, striking Dev in the back and sending him crumpling to the ground.

The realization set in for Rajeev that although they outnumbered the pair more than two-to-one, none of them had any experience fighting in their new bodies or exoskeletons. This was going to be a closer fight than he was comfortable with.

He lunged after Dev's attacker, slamming into him with his shoulder. They both tumbled to the ground and began exchanging blows. As they fought, the woman rushed Ted, but before she could strike him, Natalie and Mira were on either side of her. She turned to strike Natalie, but Mira had already landed a blow square on the woman's jaw and she went flying backward.

Rajeev couldn't believe how evenly matched he and his opponent were. Every blow sent him reeling, but he could tell his own blows were having the same effect on the man. He dared a brief glance to see how Dev and the others were faring. He had just enough time to see Dev standing to his feet when the man took advantage of Rajeev's distraction and landed a powerful blow straight in his stomach that sent him flying backward and left him dazed by the time he hit the ground. As he regained his bearings and began to pull himself back up, he saw the man approaching him with a sadistic smile on his face.

The smile didn't last long; Mira and Natalie attacked from either side, both of them landing separate blows to either side of his head. He yelped in pain, but didn't go down. It was Dev, who had come up from behind, that struck the man in the back of the head, knocking him out cold.

As Rajeev stood, he saw that the woman also had been knocked unconscious. But it seemed like the only reason they had emerged from the fight victorious was because they had outnumbered their opponents. That worried him.

"What now?" Rajeev asked.

"Now," Dev said, as he began running toward the building, "we go in there and kill Gregory Maltek."

EIGHT

THE WHITE HOUSE WAS LARGER THAN RAJEEV HAD imagined, but Dev led them confidently, almost as if he knew exactly where to find Maltek. To his surprise, Rajeev heard Maltek's muffled voice coming from up ahead. They were close. But before he could get too excited, two pairs of clones stepped out into the hallway. This time there were three women and two men, and it was clear from the expressions on their faces that they had no intention of letting Dev or his entourage get past them.

"Step aside," Dev barked angrily.

"I don't think so," the lone man said. "Turn around and go back where you came from. I'm not going to ask again."

"That's not possible," Dev said. "I'm putting a stop to Maltek one way or another." He took a step forward, but one of the women stepped directly into his path.

"Turn around," she growled, "and get out of here."

"I don't want to hurt you," Dev said.

The woman smirked. "Can't say the feeling is mutual," she said.

"This is your last chance. Step aside and let me through, or I can't be held responsible for the consequences."

She didn't give him an opportunity to fulfil his threat. Without a word, the woman whipped her fist into Dev's chest; the force sent him sailing backward into Ted, and the two of them fell to the floor. Rajeev, Mira, and Natalie all shared a look, readying themselves. It was time to act.

Rajeev and Natalie descended upon the woman; Mira ran forward to ward off the others until they could take out their foe. Rajeev struck, aiming for the woman's face, but she blocked the blow with her arm. Natalie followed up with her own strike, but the woman nonchalantly brought up her other arm to block the blow again. Her reflexes were quick—far quicker than should have been humanly possible.

Ted and Dev stood and took a moment to recover before rejoining the fight. Ted ran ahead to help Mira, who was quickly finding herself outmatched, three to one. Dev hung back to help his dad and Natalie. He managed to get behind the woman and pin her arms to her side. That gave Rajeev enough time to land a blow to her face, as Natalie kneed her in the gut. Dev released her arms, and she fell to her knees. Rajeev delivered an elbow to the back of her head, and she dropped to the floor, out cold.

They turned their attention to the others. Mira and Ted had been outnumbered three-to-two, but now that the others were joining them, the fight was five-to-three in their favor. The remaining two women and the man were a cocky bunch, but their confidence seemed to falter, at least a little, as they looked past their opponents and saw their camrade unconscious on the floor.

The man screamed like a banshee and rushed forward, targeting Dev. He plowed into him at full force and the two of them tumbled to the ground, entangled in each other, each trying to punch the other into submission. Ted went after them to provide backup to Dev.

Meanwhile, one of the women rushed Rajeev, but he dodged her. Natalie got lucky and landed a kick square in the woman's jaw as she passed by. She fell to the ground, unconscious. At the same time, Ted and Dev took out the man, clotheslining him and sending him to the ground.

The one woman remaining looked up and, for the first time, showed fear as she took in the sight of five pairs of eyes all focused on her. She turned on her heels and ran in the opposite direction. They started after her, but Dev stopped them. She wasn't the reason they had come here. Maltek was. They couldn't get distracted from that goal.

They followed the sound of his voice and found themselves outside a large room. It was the Oval Office. Maltek was inside, still broadcasting. He wasn't alone. There were five other people in the room with him and it was unclear whether or not they were clones. But Rajeev suspected they were. They no longer had an advantage in terms of numbers. There was one for each of them. And that wasn't counting Maltek.

"What do we do?" Rajeev hissed, keeping his voice low so he didn't blow their cover.

"The four of you go after his guards," Dev said. "I'll go after Maltek. If I can take him out, this can all be over."

"You're going to kill him?" Rajeev asked, surprised.

Dev seemed somewhat taken aback by the question, as if he hadn't really considered it before. "I'll do whatever I have to do," he said. "I'll capture him if I can, but if that doesn't seem possible, I'll do what I have to do to stop him."

The prospect of his son taking a life made Rajeev sick, but he saw Dev's point and there wasn't time to debate the matter. He nodded reluctantly and Dev motioned for them all to go. Rajeev, Mira, and Natalie ran into the room and headed for the guards.

Maltek looked up, taking in the fight. He was holding some kind of camera device that he'd been using to send his broadcast, and as he saw the pandemonium taking place around him, he offered his audience a rushed apology.

"Sorry about this, folks," he said. "Change never comes about without resistance, but rest assured, I'll be—"

His words were cut short by Dev, who had rushed him, but one of Maltek's guards had managed to knock Ted unconscious and head off Dev, striking him in the shoulder. It wasn't enough to knock him off his feet, but it slowed him down and gave Maltek just enough time to make a getaway. Before Dev could run after him, the guard had reengaged him with another attempted blow that he managed to dodge. Dev cursed under his breath; Maltek was getting away.

Dev finally subdued his opponent with a firm kick to the side of the head. He helped Natalie take down her foe, and then they both teamed up to help Rajeev.

"Where's Maltek?" Natalie asked as they congregated around Ted's unconscious body.

"He got away," Dev said angrily.

"Should we go after him?"

"We won't catch up to him now. This was all for nothing."

"No," Rajeev said firmly. "It wasn't for nothing. We interrupted his broadcast and that's important. He was trying to project strength, to convey to the general public that his dictatorship was inevitable and couldn't be challenged. By interrupting the broadcast, we showed them that Maltek is far more vulnerable than he lets on. I count that as a victory."

"Maybe," Dev replied. "But he's still out there and you know as well as I that he's not going to stop until he's taken over."

"You're right. He'll strike again. And when he does, we'll be there to stop him, just like we did today."

They began sweeping through the building and found a group of five to six people tied up in a bedroom. Rajeev didn't recognize any of them—he'd been unconscious for fifteen years and had not kept up with politics— but as Mira removed a gag and untied one of the women, she gasped.

"Stephanie Hollis!"

Rajeev frowned. "Who?" he asked with a hint of embarrassment at not knowing.

"Thank you," Hollis said. She was tall and slim, with shoulder-length brown hair tied back in a ponytail. "I'm the vice president. Well … actually I'm the president now, unfortunately." Her eyes were filled with sorrow, but she didn't let herself show but the slightest hint of emotion.

"So it's true?" Dev asked. "The son of a bitch actually killed the president?"

She nodded. "When he stormed in here with his little coup attempt, Charles was having none of it, of course. They asked him to willingly step down and he refused. He did more than that, in fact. He tried to get at Maltek … to take him out. So one of Maltek's guards …" her voice broke; she brought her hand to her mouth and was unable to finish the sentence.

"I'm so sorry," Dev whispered. He took Hollis by the arm and led her away, heading toward the Oval Office. "I'm sure this has been an ordeal for you, but we have some important things we need to discuss, President Hollis."

NINE

Hollis took her seat behind the president's desk and Rajeev had to admit that she looked right at home there. She had wiped away the few tears she had let herself shed, and was now ready to take action against the bastard that had put her in this position.

Dev had spent a solid ten minutes explaining who he was and describing the technology he had at his disposal to aid in the fight against Maltek. But he wanted to make clear to the new president that their enemy's reach extended far into the current government.

"I think Maltek has infiltrated the military," Dev said.

Hollis nodded. "He has. Not entirely, but enough to make it difficult to know who to trust, or how to fight him. This cloning technology he's created … it's dangerous. There's no way to know who you can trust any more. No way to know if you're talking to the person you think you are, or a clone with the mind of your enemy."

"Trust me," Dev said. "I understand better than most."

"The most important question on my mind," Natalie said,

"is what are we going to do about this? We don't know when or how Maltek will strike next."

Hollis slammed a fist on the desk, startling everyone. "We *cannot* wait for him to strike again," she said. "We must go after him—and put him down like the rabid dog he is."

The loaded language made Rajeev wince, but she was right. The best course of action was to find Maltek and take him out before he could do more damage than he'd done already.

"But how will we find him?" Mira asked.

Hollis remained silent for a moment, thinking. "We should start by raiding Fresh Meat's headquarters," she said.

Dev shook his head. "You don't think he's anticipated that? Surely it's wiped clean."

Hollis nodded. "Perhaps. But we don't know that for sure, and there's always the possibility that he missed something. Even the smallest clue could prove helpful."

"Okay. Who will you send? Who can you trust?"

"I'll put together a handpicked team from the FBI. Even so, I think it would be prudent of you and your team to accompany them. Just in case Maltek has managed to infiltrate the FBI as well."

Dev nodded. "We can do that."

"Thank you," Hollis said. "In the meantime, I'll confer with my cabinet and determine next steps. Before that, however, I think it would be a good idea to deliver another emergency alert letting the American people know their country has *not* been overtaken by a biotech thug. If they're vigilant, maybe they can even help us spot Maltek, although I doubt he'd be stupid enough to be caught in public now that he surely knows we're on the lookout for him."

She stood and held out her hand; Dev shook it, and he gathered his team and left.

Rajeev could tell his son was despondent at not having

captured or killed Maltek. He sidled up next to him and placed an arm around his shoulder.

"It's okay," he said. "We'll get him, Dev. You know we will."

When they were back out on the South Lawn, they summoned their virtual assistants and requested to fly back to their hidden lair. Each of them sprung into the air and out of sight. As Rajeev felt the air rushing by his head, he smiled. It was a much more pleasant flight now that they had accomplished what they'd set out to do. Yes, the danger that threatened them all was still out there, waiting for another opportunity to strike. But at least they had postponed an all-out war for another day. It was important to celebrate every victory, no matter how small.

* * *

WHEN THEY ARRIVED BACK AT THE LAIR, DEV immediately got back to work upgrading the rest of the androids. "We were outmatched back at the White House," he said. "I can't believe how strong Maltek's clones are. The only reason we won is because we had numbers on our side, but that definitely won't be the case next time. We need everyone we can get on our side."

"We should bring in some fresh blood," Mira said. "Equip them with exoskeletons."

"Like your friends," Rajeev chimed in. "The ones that helped me when I first escaped from NLT."

Mira nodded. "That's exactly what I had in mind. It's not much, but it's a start. And I'm sure they'd be willing to fight now that they're aware of the extent of the threat we face from Maltek. Everyone should be, after that emergency alert."

Dev nodded. "Get on it," he said. "I'll leave it up to you to get them here. I have a couple other tricks up my sleeve, but let's focus on one thing at a time."

Mira nodded and left and Dev headed for the dorms to resume activating the new android bodies. Ted ran after him in case he needed any assistance. That left Rajeev and Natalie alone, neither of them with any pressing tasks.

"I'm going to head back to my dorm," Natalie said. "Would you like to join me?"

Rajeev shrugged. "Why not? I don't have anything better to do." He followed her as she led him to her dormitory.

The room had been designed with human occupants in mind. It was sparsely furnished, but not *bare* as their dorms at Next Level Technologies had been. There was a small twin bed in the corner, a generic landscape painting of a mountain, and a bed stand with a lamp. Natalie took a seat on the bed, and Rajeev sat down beside her.

"How are you enjoying the new body?" Rajeev asked.

She smiled, and Rajeev was taken aback by how radiant she looked. "It's a breath of fresh air," she said. "I feel at least vaguely human instead of like some kind of freak."

"Well you look beautiful in it," he said. He regretted the words as soon as they left his lips. He wondered if his cheeks had grown red—were these bodies even capable of blushing?

"Thank you," she replied, a knowing smile revealing that she was aware of Rajeev's embarrassment. "You look good in yours, too."

If his cheeks weren't red before, they had to be now. But he kept his composure and offered her a slight smile in return. "Thanks. How similar is it to what you looked like … you know … before?"

"Would you like to see?"

"Sure. Have a photo in your wallet?"

She laughed. "No. But I was on Facebook. I have a ton of photos I can send."

She called upon her virtual assistant and instructed it to send a photo to Rajeev. Daniel popped up in Rajeev's field of vision a moment later. "I have a photo for you from Natalie Parsons," he said.

"Let's see it," Rajeev said.

The image appeared in front of him, showing a young, mousy, bespectacled woman with shoulder-length blond hair and a timid grin. Her eyes were blue and sparkled with the flash of the camera.

"How old are you in this photo?" Rajeev asked.

"Seventeen. It was just before my accident." She had already told Rajeev about how she'd dived into a pool, hit her head and damaged her spine, leaving her paralyzed. When she'd gotten the opportunity to be transferred into one of Next Level Technologies' robotic bodies, she'd been overjoyed. It was definitely a trade-off, but she'd considered it worth it. But then NLT had imprisoned her and she'd found herself trading one prison of a body for another.

But that had all changed. Rajeev had rescued her and now she was in a robotic body worlds better than the one she'd first been stuck in. When Rajeev had looked into the eyes of those original NLT bodies, he'd sometimes found it difficult to remember that there was a human consciousness in there, staring back out at him. But now, sitting on this bed next to Natalie and looking into her bright blue eyes, he thought he could see her soul.

"Well, you looked lovely," he said. "You still do," he added quickly.

She looked up at him curiously. "How old are you?"

"Depends on how you measure it. If you go by my reactivation in this new body, I'm about a day old."

"Obviously that's not what I meant."

"I know. But even then, it's tricky. I was thirty-nine when I got in a car accident, and I was in a coma for fifteen years after that before Dev … well, Greg Maltek, actually … uploaded me into a new body. By that measure, I'd be fifty-four. So which is correct? See my dilemma?"

Natalie nodded. "I do. That *is* a tricky situation."

"How old are you?"

"Twenty-three. And my situation is more straightforward. I was paralyzed for four years before I connected with NLT, and then I spent two years as their Guinea pig. It was so bad being stuck there that I was beginning to long for my pre-robot days— at least I wasn't anyone's slave back then."

"Well you're free now, and these bodies are a huge step up from the old ones. I almost feel human again, like I could go back to living something at least vaguely resembling my old life."

"Nothing will stay normal if Maltek gets his way," Natalie said gravely. "I swear, it's like I wake up from one nightmare just to find myself in another one."

"We'll end the nightmare," Rajeev said. "We'll end Maltek. We must."

Natalie shook her head slowly. "We're outnumbered. We're outgunned. He's been planning this for years. I'm ... I'm scared, Rajeev."

Rajeev nodded. The truth was, he was scared as well, but he couldn't give up hope.

"That's good," he said, and he placed a hand on her knee. "It means you're not stupid. But we'll outsmart him. We've got my son on our side. And he's a genius."

Natalie placed her hand on top of Rajeev's and looked into his eyes. Rajeev was dumbfounded by how human they looked. They were filled with a mixture of fear and longing as complex and rich as one would find in any human being's eyes. The engineers who had created these eyes had accomplished a feat that only God had accomplished before them, crafting windows into the soul.

She leaned forward and closed her eyes, cutting off those

windows as she bridged the gap between she and Rajeev. But before it was bridged completely, the door opened and she quickly sat up as she and Rajeev turned to the door to see who had interrupted them. It was Dev.

He raised an eyebrow, sensing that he had walked in on something intimate, but he shook his head as if dismissing the awkwardness from the room. "Everyone's activated," he said. "It's time to train."

TEN

THERE WAS A SPACE IN THE MIDDLE OF THE cavernous warehouse that was completely empty. It was supposed to be a space where the new equipment could be tested out, but now it was occupied by a circle of twelve androids—each of them in shiny new bodies—and one human, Dev, outfitted with one of the slim, new exoskeleton models. Mira had left to pick up her friends and bring them to the base, so Dev was the only representative of the legacy version of the human race.

"You're all aware that these bodies are far stronger than any human being," Dev said. "But Maltek's men are not ordinary human beings. They're strong, too. This is not a war that will be won with strength. It's a war that will be won with guile, cunning, and control. So it's essential that each of you becomes intimately familiar with how your body works and with the array of features included in it."

He walked into the center of the circle. "Who would like to volunteer?"

"Volunteer for what?" Ted asked.

"Just trust me," Dev said. "You can all handle it."

Brian, one of the androids Rajeev had gotten to know a bit back at Next Level Technologies, raised his hand. "I'll give it a go."

Dev motioned for him to step forward. In his new body, Brian towered over Dev, who was built rather like a marshmallow. Still, in his exoskeleton, there was no doubt Dev was formidable as well.

As if to demonstrate that very fact, Dev took a few long strides away from Brian, then turned around and motioned for him to come at him. "Let's see what you've got," he said.

"What, you want me to ... attack you?" Brian asked.

"That's exactly what I want," Dev said. "Give me everything you've got."

Brian laughed, but Dev didn't, and Brian realized he was serious. He shrugged, took a step back, then shot at Dev as quickly as he could.

Dev dodged to the right, then swung his arm around and struck Brian in the back, sending him to the floor. The other androids laughed, but Dev quieted them. "This is exactly what I'm talking about. You all know you're powerful in your new bodies, but you don't know how to *use* those bodies. And that's what I'm going to teach you today. I helped design these models and I know them in and out. But before long, you'll know them even better than me, because you're actually *living in them*. We don't have time to wait for you to get used to the bodies on your own, however. We've gotta give you a crash course. Everyone find a partner."

Dev smiled as the androids paired up. It wasn't going to be easy, but they would build an army to match Maltek's. There was no way they would lose this war.

He wouldn't let them.

* * *

AFTER NEARLY FOUR HOURS OF TRAINING, DEV called it a day—not for the androids' sake; they could have kept going all night. Rather, it was for his own sake. Although the exoskeleton increased his endurance significantly, he was still only human and his limits were far more evident than those of his robotic compatriots.

The androids had gathered around and were chattering excitedly among themselves. Dev thought they looked rather like soldiers commiserating after a long day of training. Of course, they were just getting started; there would be a lot more training to come.

"I have a treat for all of you," he said. He left, journeying into the rows of shelves as the androids craned their necks to see what he was doing, overwhelmed by curiosity. He returned a moment later carrying a large crate, which he placed on the ground in front of them.

"What's that?" one of them asked.

Dev reached into the crate and pulled out a small, white orb about the size of an apple. He tossed it to the android that had spoken.

"Put it up to your mouth."

He tentatively brought the orb near his mouth, and his eyes widened in response. "It's champagne!" he shouted.

The other androids began murmuring with a mix of confusion and excitement.

"Your new bodies are a huge improvement over the old ones, but unfortunately you're still not able to eat or drink," Dev said. "But you can still taste. These orbs use near-field wireless communication to approximate the tastes of various foods and beverages. This entire crate is filled with champagne-orbs. But don't indulge too much ... they also simulate drunkenness."

He passed the crate around and each of the androids plucked out an orb and brought it to their mouth. It didn't take long for the effects to kick in. Before long, they were laughing and talking like they had been best friends for years ... which is exactly what Dev had hoped for. If he wanted his army to behave as a cohesive unit, he needed soldiers that saw each other as brothers and sisters, as family. And the camaraderie he was now witnessing was a good start.

ELEVEN

Rajeev awoke the next morning with a hangover. When he realized what it was, he marveled: An honest-to-goodness hangover. He never thought he'd have one of those again.

Granted, it wasn't quite as bad as the kinds of hangovers real, flesh-and-blood people experienced. The orbs had been designed to interfere with the androids' thought processes to simulate the effects of alcohol, and there appeared to be residual effects on his faculties, making it somewhat difficult for him to think. Other than that, however, he was spared from many of the hangover symptoms he remembered from his life before he was a robot … nausea, headaches, muscle soreness and the like.

He was lying in his bed in his dormitory, unsure of how he'd gotten there the previous night. He sat up, stretched his arms, then stood and made his way to the door.

Two card tables were set up in the open space where they'd trained yesterday. Seated around them were Dev, Mira, and the friends Mira had left to retrieve, including Zane, the engineering student who had helped Rajeev disable Next Level Technologies' failsafe the first time he'd escaped.

Seated beside Mira was Rosa, Mira's wife. And sitting across from them was Rajeev's ex-wife, Sarah. If he could even call her his ex, that is. Technically, since he was only a copy of the original Rajeev Sundaram, they had never actually been married. Still, the feelings and emotional attachments were there, which made it all the more painful to see the man sitting beside her with an arm wrapped around her shoulder.

"How'd you sleep, dad?" Dev walked up behind his dad and placed a hand on his shoulder.

"Not well enough."

"Here," Dev said, handing Rajeev an orb similar to the previous night's champagne.

Rajeev groaned. "Please, no," he said.

Dev laughed. "It's not more champagne, dad. It's coffee. Try it."

He brought the orb up to his mouth and felt a bitter yet pleasant sensation, followed by a surge of energy.

"Not bad," he said. "But couldn't you have programmed us in a way that would make hangovers impossible?"

"It's those kinds of familiar touches that make you feel like you're still human," Dev said. "You can't put a price on your humanity."

As Rajeev took a seat, he noticed Sarah's eyes on him. He looked different than he had before he was a robot, but she had recognized his voice as he'd spoken with Dev.

"Hello, Rajeev," she said, almost reverently.

"Hi, Sarah," he said. "It's good to see you." He turned to her companion. "And you are …?"

Sarah shook her head. "Forgive me. Rajeev, this is Paul." Paul reached across the table and extended his hand to Rajeev. As they shook hands, he said, "I'm Sarah's husband."

So there it was. The final confirmation that Sarah had moved on—that she was, indeed, no longer his. But he'd known it all along, of course.

"Pleased to meet you, Paul," Rajeev said, trying to sound more pleasant and less emotional than he felt.

"I hope it's not awkward that I'm here," he said. "I mean, I know who you are and about your ... your past with Sarah ..."

"No," Rajeev lied. "No awkwardness. Like I said, it truly is a pleasure to meet you, Paul ... as long as you've been taking care of her."

Sarah smiled and turned to look at her new husband affectionately. "He is," she said.

"This all must seem strange for both of you," Rajeev said, eager to change the subject.

"That's the understatement of the century," Paul said. "We were minding our own business when all of a sudden I find out my wife's ex is back from the dead, and a robot no less—no offense—and that a crazed tech entrepreneur has turned into a wannabe dictator. Now we're at war? It's insane."

Rajeev decided he rather liked Paul, even if he had more or less stolen his wife.

"No offense taken," he said. "And trust me, this is a war I would rather not fight. But Maltek hasn't really given us a choice."

"I just wish Paul and I could help," Sarah said.

Mira, who up until now had been silent, spoke up. "You guys can help," she said.

Sarah raised an eyebrow. "How?"

Rajeev smiled. "No one's shown you guys the exoskeletons yet?" They shook their heads, and Rajeev turned to Dev. "Looks like they're in need of a demonstration."

* * *

AFTER DEV DEMONSTRATED HOW THE EXOSKELETONS worked, he got Sarah, Paul and the rest of Mira's friends outfitted with exoskeletons of their own. Their army was growing, but Rajeev still felt like they were woefully outmatched by the army Maltek had been secretly growing for years. He took Dev aside to share those concerns.

"We can only do what we can do," Dev replied unhelpfully.

"Of course," Rajeev said. "But that's exactly the point. We can do more."

"What are you proposing?"

"We need to grow our numbers. I mean, much more than we have been. Maltek has, what … thousands of soldiers? Tens of thousands? Plus he's infiltrated the freakin' military."

"You're not wrong, but there's only so much we can do."

"We have to do more. We have to find a way. Couldn't we infiltrate the military, root out Maltek's spies?"

Dev put his hands to his face. "Maybe," he said. "I don't know how we'd go about doing it, but it could be worth a shot."

"We need to take every shot we've got if we want to win this war," Rajeev said.

TWELVE

They received word from President Hollis that they were ready to move on Fresh Meat's headquarters in San Francisco. It was obviously too far to fly with their bodies' built-in flight capabilities, but thankfully, Dev had something in his underground hangar for just such an occasion: A supersonic jet.

Leaving Mira and the friends she'd brought to continue training at the compound, Dev and Rajeev led the rest of the androids onto the plane to head to San Francisco.

"So, this plane is underground," Rajeev said as they walked aboard. "How the hell are you going to get it airborne?"

"Remember, this was a military facility," Dev said. "It's filled with some pretty impressive tech." He sat down in the cockpit and explained to his father that flying the plane was all automated; he just had to input the destination and the plane would do the rest. After he did so, the ceiling in front of the plane parted and the sunlight streaming through revealed a long ramp … a runway.

The engines roared to life and the jet began rolling across the runway, picking up speed until it was soaring through the air, headed to San Francisco. It continued building speed until it broke the sound barrier; the resulting supersonic boom thundered through the air around them.

"It won't take long to get there at this speed," Dev said.

"You don't really think we're going to find anything there, do you?" Rajeev asked. "I'm sure Maltek picked up and left before his coup attempt."

"Probably not," Dev said. "But even the most carefully laid plans have gaps in them, and it's possible Maltek left behind some clue that will give us a better idea of what he's up to and how we can stop him. It's not likely, but I think it's certainly worth a look."

When they arrived in San Francisco, a group of government officials were waiting for them on the tarmac. A fastidiously groomed woman in a charcoal grey pantsuit approached Dev and held out her hand. "Hello Mr. Sundaram," she said. "I'm Agent Maxine Rathburn, FBI."

"Pleased to meet you, Ms. Rathburn," Dev said. "Anything we can do to help, just let us know."

She nodded. "For now, we just need you to accompany us in case Maltek decides to ambush us."

Rathburn ushered the group into a pair of black SUVs, and the caravan headed for Fresh Meat's headquarters.

They arrived at a building that, to a casual observer, would have seemed more or less unremarkable, its considerable height notwithstanding. But the entrance on the ground floor had been cordoned off with yellow police tape, and the area was swarming with law enforcement officials representing at least half a dozen different jurisdictions and agencies.

"Wait here," Rathburn told them as they got out of their vehicles. She walked up to a middle-aged man with a bald head and a protruding gut, then turned around and addressed the entire gathering.

"Listen up, people!" she shouted. "We're going in! Keep your eyes open for evidence, booby traps, anything—we don't know what we're going to encounter in here, so stay alert!"

A swarm of law enforcement officials entered the building first, most of them storming in with guns in their hands. The androids took up the rear.

Their footsteps echoed off the walls, and the way the sound bounced through the cavernous building left little doubt in Rajeev's mind that the building had been completely emptied out. As they made their way deeper inside, his suspicion was confirmed. Every room had been emptied of anything of importance. There were still desks and chairs, but any kind of computer equipment or electronic devices had been removed and taken who knows where.

Rajeev sidled up next to his son. "Looks like a graveyard," he muttered, softly enough that no one else would hear.

They scoured the building, but as far as Rajeev observed, nobody uncovered anything of significance. As everyone started packing up and heading out of the building, Rajeev and Dev conferred with Rathburn to see if her team had uncovered anything.

"Nothing terribly useful," she said. "Some random odds and ends that we'll analyze for fingerprints, but other than that I'm afraid we've come up empty-handed."

"In that case, I guess we'll have to wait for Maltek to make the first move," Rajeev said. "Which is unfortunate."

"That's a hell of an understatement," Dev said.

THIRTEEN

Rajeev was in poor spirits on the flight back. He felt helpless. They should be out doing something to track Maltek down, but there was nothing they *could* do. They had run into nothing but dead ends. As hopeful as he was that they'd eventually put a stop to Maltek's plans, he didn't think it was going to happen anytime soon. But when he expressed those sentiments to Dev, his son pushed back.

"We can't just sit around and do nothing, waiting for Maltek to strike," he insisted.

"I'm not proposing we sit around and do nothing. What I'm proposing is that we keep training so when Maltek does strike again, we can handle him and his soldiers."

"Soldiers?"

Rajeev nodded. "Let's be real about what they are." He paused and looked out the window. It was cloudy and he couldn't see the ground below, but the way the clouds soared past his line of sight was hypnotizing. When he spoke again, his words seemed more far away than they had before. "We need to grow our numbers," he said. "We need people stationed throughout the country so when Maltek strikes we have people there ready to go *immediately*. The next time he attacks, we might not get there soon enough to stop it." He looked up at his son. "Have you given any more thought to how we might get the military back on our side?"

"I'm still thinking about it. But I think I might have a temporary solution to the problem you just described. A way we could be in multiple places at once. It's not a perfect solution, but it's better than nothing."

"How is that possible?"

Dev flashed a crooked smile. "You're inhabiting a robotic body, yet you're questioning the wonders available to us thanks to modern technology? You should know better, dad. I'll show you when we get back to the base."

* * *

WHEN THEY ARRIVED BACK AT THE BASE, DEV LED HIS father into the warehouse and to a shelf that was lined with what he had taken to calling "blanks"—bodies just like the one Rajeev was in, except they hadn't yet had a conscious mind downloaded into them.

"Help me carry it into my office," Dev said. He took the arms while Rajeev took the legs and they carried the body across the warehouse, both of them feeling like they were disposing of a corpse.

When they got to Dev's office, they set the body into a chair. It sat there, vacantly staring at them like a ventriloquist's dummy. Rajeev bent down and looked it straight in its dead eyes.

"It's weird seeing one that's ... empty," he said.

"It won't be empty for long," Dev said. He flipped a switch on the side of the neck. "Turning on wireless communication," he explained. He sat down at his desk and got to work. After a moment, the body stood up straight as if it had come to life, and scared Rajeev half to death.

"It's alive?"

"No. It's essentially a drone. It just needs a pilot. Call up Daniel, would you?"

"What? Why?"

"Trust me, dad. Haven't you learned by now that I answer your questions by *showing* you the answers?"

Rajeev acquiesced and summoned his virtual assistant.

"What can I do for you?" Daniel asked.

"I don't know," Rajeev said, nodding to his son. "Ask him."

Daniel turned to Dev, looking at him quizzically.

"Daniel," Dev said, "initiate a neural link between Rajeev and that body there." He pointed to the body sitting in the chair. "By the way, dad, you'll want to sit down."

"What?"

"Just do it. Quickly."

Rajeev lowered himself onto the floor. As soon as he did so, Daniel initiated the link. Rajeev's body went limp, and the body on the chair sat up, startled.

"What's going on?" the body on the chair said.

"You're remotely controlling the body," Dev said. "Go ahead. Stand up. Move around a little."

Rajeev stood and took a few small, tentative steps forward in his new body. He seemed completely disoriented. "I'm controlling the other body?"

"Yes. Your mind is still attached, as it were, to the first body. But you're able to remotely control the other one. It's kind of like virtual reality, except you're controlling a physical body that exists in the real world."

"It's weird," Rajeev said, turning his hands back and forth in front of his eyes.

"You'll get used to it, just like you got used to each of your other robotic bodies," Dev said. "But you see the utility of this, don't you? We can place these empty vessels with allies across the country. That way, no matter where Maltek strikes, you or one of the other androids can instantly take control of one of these bodies and be ready to fight."

Rajeev nodded. "It's not perfect, but it could work," he said. "How soon can we get these shipped out?"

"I'll start preparing them for shipment immediately."

FOURTEEN

Gregory Maltek was restless. He was frustrated. But, more than anything, he was angry.

He hadn't anticipated Dev Sundaram and his android freaks confronting him the way they had at the White House. He should have taken over by now. It should have been a done deal.

But he shouldn't be so naive. Dev hadn't stopped him. He'd merely set him back. He was still coming for the government, and for Dev. His rise was inevitable. He'd just have to work a little harder to get there than he'd anticipated.

Which is exactly what he was doing now: Working to achieve his ultimate goal. He hadn't had any intention of becoming a terrorist, but it seemed he had to send Dev a message, to make it clear just how high the stakes were. Dev needed to understand that there was nothing Gregory Maltek wouldn't do to take control of this country and every person in it so he could bring his grand vision of the future to life. And he wouldn't stop there. He would take control of the United States, and then he would take control of the world. With the entire globe under his thumb, there would be no more need for war or conflict, for politics or for espionage.

A tall, muscular, bald man dressed in combat gear approached Maltek. "We're just about ready, boss. Just waiting for your go-ahead."

Maltek took a deep breath. The corner of his lips turned up in a slight smile. He faced the man and nodded.

"Go ahead," he said. "Do it."

* * *

DEV AND RAJEEV WERE MEETING IN DEV'S OFFICE when the breaking news alert came up via their virtual assistants. For Rajeev, it took the form of a hovering headline scrolling across his field of vision: "EXPLOSION DESTROYS SEATTLE SPACE NEEDLE: TERRORISM SUSPECTED, SAY POLICE."

Dev and Rajeev locked eyes. "Maltek?" Rajeev asked.

Dev nodded. "Looks like it's time to test out our remote response plan."

"Do we have bodies in Seattle yet?"

"Yes, thank God. Come on; let's gather the team."

When they stepped out of the office, the rest of their growing team was staring into space, obviously watching coverage of the Space Needle explosion. It wasn't clear if they realized it was Maltek's work. Rajeev wasn't quite as sure that it was Maltek as Dev was, but he suspected his son's instinct was right. Either way, it was prudent for them to respond; better safe than sorry.

"Let's go, guys," Dev said, his voice echoing through the cavernous warehouse. "We're heading to Seattle."

Mira snapped out of her reverie, muttering under her breath for her virtual assistant to stop playing the news coverage of the explosion. "You think this was Maltek?"

"I wouldn't be surprised," Dev said. "We need to assume it is until we know otherwise."

They lined up against the wall near Dev's office and sat down, their backs resting against the wall, awaiting further instructions from Dev.

"One of us should hang back and guard the others," he said. "Otherwise we're all sitting ducks if someone manages to infiltrate our base. I don't think that's likely, but we should be prepared for the possibility."

"I'll do it," Zane said.

Dev nodded. "Thanks, Zane. As for the rest of you, a quick refresher: Pull up your virtual assistant, then ask them to initiate a neural link with your analogue in Seattle. Make sure you mention the city so they know which body specifically to link you to."

He observed as they initiated the links, making sure that none of them had any problems. When they were all successfully linked, he sat his back against the wall and called upon his own virtual assistant. Controlling the bodies wasn't quite as immersive an experience for humans as it was for the androids, who had digitized minds that could easily be transferred to other bodies. But it worked well enough, and under the circumstances, it was better than nothing.

They awoke in a small, nondescript office. None of them were sure exactly where they were in the city; they'd worked with President Hollis' administration to place the bodies throughout the country, so they weren't involved in picking the exact locations. It didn't matter, though; their virtual assistants could navigate them to where they needed to be.

Dev was the last to awaken and found that everyone else was standing and ready to go. He rose to his feet and nodded toward the door. "Everyone ready to go?"

He led them out and asked his assistant to take them to the Space Needle. A map appeared in front of his eyes with a route plan and a time estimate: Twenty minutes.

"Twenty minutes isn't fast enough," he said. "Let's fly; we should be able to get there in five."

One by one, they instructed their voice assistants to fly them to their destination, and they took off into the air.

Less than five minutes later, they landed on a patch of grass next to the Space Needle … or at least, next to what used to be the Space Needle. The rubble of what had been the famous tourist destination was still burning; if they hadn't been in bodies constructed of heat-resistant materials, they wouldn't have been able to stand as close to the wreckage as they were. Thankfully, their bodies allowed them to stand directly on the smoldering debris without any detrimental effects. Unfortunately, it was clear that anyone who had happened to be inside the structure at the time of the explosion had not survived.

Rajeev walked over the wreckage slowly, reverently. He thought he spotted a severed hand, but he turned his head before he could confirm the identity of the object. He felt like he was going to be sick. This truly was a war, and these were the first civilian casualties. *No*, Rajeev told himself, *this, here, isn't warfare. It's terrorism.*

"I can't be here," he said. The only one within earshot was Dev.

"We have to be here. If not us, who?"

Rajeev had no words. Just as he was about to formulate a response, he was interrupted by a clamor on the far side of the wreckage. All of the androids turned at once toward the noise. They saw nothing at first; then, some of the rubble began to move. Something was stirring beneath the surface. As it emerged, the debris rose and fell off it. At the same time, half a dozen other objects began rising, encircling the androids and leaving them no means of escape.

With the first object now fully uncovered, they could see what they were looking at: a giant exoskeleton, like the one Rajeev had used to rescue the other androids from the NLT campus, only bigger. As the other objects fully emerged, it became clear that they, also, were oversized versions of the exoskeletons that Dev had designed.

The first exoskeleton took a step forward and raised an arm, as if it were preparing to recite poetry.

"Welcome, Dev." It was Maltek's voice. "I've been expecting you."

FIFTEEN

Dev rushed forward, and when Rajeev realized that he meant to attack Maltek, he headed him off and held him back.

"Why did you do this?" Dev spat. "There were innocent people in there! You're a monster!"

Maltek chuckled, and the sound was so enraging that Rajeev almost let go of his son so he could take a swipe at him—but, of course, if he were to let him go he'd merely be destroyed by Maltek's giant exoskeleton.

"Me?" Maltek asked with false indignation. "I didn't do this, Dev. *You* did. If you hadn't felt the need to challenge me, to fight against the inevitable, then this little display of power wouldn't have been necessary. But you couldn't leave well enough alone, could you? You had to rebel against me like a petulant teenager, and now you must live with the consequences of your actions."

"That's some twisted logic," Dev spat.

"You don't have to understand it," Maltek retorted. "You just have to live by it. You can't stop me. I'm going to change the world—for the *better*. You can fight it—and cause innumerable deaths just like the ones that lay beneath our feet—or you can accept it, and even join me. Think of what the two of us could accomplish together. Two brilliant minds like ours? The possibilities are endless."

"I'll never help you."

There was a pause, as if Maltek was punishing Dev with his silence, like a disappointed parent. When he spoke again, his voice was cold, empty of the sarcastic tone that had heretofore punctuated his speech.

"Then you'll need to get out of my way. And if you refuse to do so willingly, as appears to be the case, I'll force you."

As if on cue, one of the androids collapsed, as if he'd suddenly lost consciousness. The androids looked down at their fallen comrade, then up at each other. And then it happened again—to Brian this time. One moment he was looking into the eyes of his compatriots in fearful confusion; the next, he was laying on the ground in a lifeless heap.

Dev looked up at Rajeev, his eyes filled with abject terror. "What's going on?"

Rajeev offered a helpless shrug. "I don't know." He tried to sound nonchalant, but on the inside he was as terrified as Dev.

When the third android dropped, Dev began to piece together what was going on. "Something's happening back at the base!" he shouted to the others. "A malfunction or ... something. I'm not sure if it's Maltek or something else, but we should all log off."

Mira scoffed. "But what about Maltek?"

"There's nothing we can do about him now," Dev said. "We're outmatched. Everyone, retreat—log off and return to the base." As soon as he'd finished uttering the words, his artificial body collapsed—he'd logged off and there was no mind left to occupy it and keep it standing.

Rajeev followed suit. The transition was jarring; one moment he was in Seattle on top of the wreckage of the Space Needle; the next he was back at the base, seated on the floor against the wall. It took his eyes a moment to adjust, but when they did he was presented with the sight of Dev and Zane, their arms locked as they wrestled each other.

"What the hell is going on?" Rajeev shouted.

Dev spoke through gritted teeth as he continued to fight Zane. "He's working for Maltek!"

Rajeev's eyes drifted over to the other androids. They were all back now and were standing, except for three of them—the three who had collapsed in Seattle. It appeared their heads had been bashed at the base, and Rajeev realized what his son had just said must be true: Zane, the man who was supposed to be watching over them, protecting them, was actually a double agent working for their enemy. He leapt forward and approached Zane from behind. He wrapped his arms around his neck and pulled. Zane began to choke and sputter until, finally, he lost consciousness and went limp. Rajeev lowered him to the floor.

"What the hell?" Mira asked. "This is not like Zane. Not at all."

Dev was still catching his breath, but he answered his sister's query the best he could. "I don't think it's Zane," he said. "I think it's one of Maltek's clones."

"Just like the one he made of you," Rajeev said.

Dev nodded. "He created another spy for himself."

"Then where's the real Zane?" Mira asked.

"I'd hate to speculate," Dev said. "Best case scenario, he never knew they'd gotten ahold of his DNA and copied him."

Mira shook her head. "That can't be the case," she said. "When I went and got him, it was at his house. So if this imposter was there in Zane's house, and Zane wasn't ..." She trailed off.

"Then that means something bad happened to Zane," Rajeev said, finishing her sentence.

"There's nothing we can do about it now," Dev said. "Maybe

we can get an answer out of him when he comes to, but I wouldn't count on it."

"Oh, I'll make *sure* we get it out of him," Rajeev said. Even as he said the words, he was surprised by them. It was out of character for him to threaten to torture someone as he just had. This war was changing him. It was changing all of them—and not for the better. But what choice did they have if they wanted to win?

"This represents a bigger problem," Dev said. "This is the second spy Maltek has sent into our midst. How do we know he doesn't already have another spy with us? How would we know if he sent one in?"

Natalie, who thus far had been silent, scanned the room. "Any one of us could be one of his spies," she said.

"We need to devise a test," Rajeev said. "A way to tell if someone's consciousness has been artificially implanted in their body. Is it possible, Dev?"

Dev sucked in air through his teeth. "Possible? Maybe. But it'll be difficult as hell to figure out, and it could take a long time —and time is a luxury we don't have."

"We don't have a choice," Rajeev said. "You'd better get started."

SIXTEEN

"He killed Brian," Natalie said, standing over the fallen android. "And two of the others ... I never learned their names."

"They'll be okay," Dev said. "All three of their minds are backed up. I can restore them. But if he'd gotten to me, or Mira ... or mom or Paul ... there would be no coming back from that."

"You don't have *their* minds backed up?"

Dev paused. "Well, I do, but ..."

"But the duplicates aren't as good as the real thing."

"I didn't say that."

"You didn't have to."

He sighed. "I didn't mean anything by it. Yes, the minds could have been restored, but if we'd lost our bodies ... I realize these artificial ones can do some pretty amazing things, but I think you understand why we are so attached to the bodies we were born with."

Her face softened. "You're right," she said. "I'm sorry."

"Let's leave Dev alone to work on a solution to our spy problem," Rajeev said. Natalie nodded and Rajeev led her away so Dev could retire to his office to work.

"You seemed pretty upset," Rajeev said. They entered his dorm and Natalie followed him in.

"I'm sorry about that. I couldn't help getting emotional." She grinned. "I'm not a robot, you know … as much as I may look like it on the outside."

"Well, it's a good thing you're a robot on the outside. It gives you a second chance if something happens to you."

"It almost seems like cheating, doesn't it?"

"You've gotta take the pros where you find them. There are plenty of cons."

They each took a seat on Rajeev's bed. Rajeev felt exhausted —more mentally than physically—and he got the sense that Natalie was, too. It was dawning on both of them what it really meant to be at war—especially a war in which they were vastly outmatched by their enemy. Dev had backed up their minds, so death wasn't quite as much of a concern as it would be for a typical soldier. But even so … what if Maltek killed Dev? What if he found their base, blew it up, and destroyed the backups? Then they would truly be gone from this earth. They would truly be casualties of war.

"Are you scared?" Natalie asked. It took Rajeev aback—it was like she'd been reading his mind.

"I don't think I should be," he said, "but I can't help but be a little scared. I don't think it's entirely for my own sake. I'm scared for the world, and everyone in it, and what will happen to them if Maltek wins."

Natalie nodded her head solemnly. "Maybe it's selfish of me, but I'm just scared for myself. I don't want to die. I know that my mind is backed up, that I can come back, in a way … but what if that copy isn't really *me*?"

Rajeev wasn't sure he should say anything, but he couldn't

help himself. "You know, you've already been through this once before ... when they put you into your first robotic body."

She nodded. "I've thought about that ... about how, in a sense, the woman who came before is gone. But I'm here now, whatever I am, and I don't want to be gone, regardless of whatever comes after me."

He nodded. "Yeah, I agree. But we can't let our fear paralyze us."

Natalie looked up at Rajeev's face, and as she spoke, there was a new determination in her eyes. "We won't," she said.

The door swung open; it was Mira, and she barely looked at them before speaking and heading back out.

"Faux-Zane is awake," she said. "Come on; we've got questions, and he's going to give us the answers."

SEVENTEEN

FAUX-ZANE WAS TIED TO A CHAIR NEAR DEV'S OFFICE. Sweat had formed on his forehead, but he otherwise seemed calm. Dev emerged from his office and regarded the captive with barely concealed rage.

"Shouldn't you be working?" Rajeev asked.

Dev shook his head. "I could use the break. And this is more important for now, anyway."

He walked directly up to Zane, then crouched so they were face-to-face. He tapped the side of his head, then slightly tilted his own.

"Who is that inside there?" he asked. "Is that you, Maltek? Or are you just one of his lackeys?"

Zane returned Dev's stare, but remained defiantly silent. Rajeev could see that his refusal to talk was frustrating Dev.

"What did you do with the real Zane?"

"I am the real Zane."

"Bullshit!" Dev's face was red now, and he had dropped all pretense of politeness. "The real Zane wouldn't have murdered his own allies."

The imposter's face grew hard, and he said nothing more.

Dev stared him down for a long minute, but it was fruitless. Out of nowhere, he pulled back his fist, then brought it down on Zane's right cheek.

His fist bounced back as if he'd punched a steel door. He covered his hurt fist with the other one and recoiled in pain.

"Son of a bitch!"

Zane grinned. "Guess you forgot that Maltek's creating supermen."

Dev frowned. He stared Zane down, then spoke in a low, menacing voice.

"I guess you forgot that I am as well." He nodded toward his father. "Show him how serious we are."

Rajeev hesitated. He wanted answers as much as Dev did, but he didn't want to get them this way.

"Dev, I … I can't."

Dev didn't look pleased with his father's disobedience, even if it was a matter of conscience. He was about to argue, but then Natalie stepped up so he didn't have to.

"I'll do it," she said. She walked up to the bound man and stared at him with genuine hatred. He was a wolf in a sheep pen, and that meant he was someone to be both feared and reviled. She struck him in the face and unlike Dev, she did not recoil in pain. Zane's head snapped back and when he looked up at Natalie afterward, he didn't look as cocky as he had a moment before. Dev and Rajeev shared a look. Who knew Natalie had *this* in her?

"Where is Zane?" she asked.

"Screw you."

She hit him again, even harder this time. But instead of waiting for a response, she hit him again, in the chest, and his chair fell back onto the ground with a loud clang. Natalie stooped down next to him and placed a hand on his throat. "Where is he?" He didn't answer, so she increased the pressure on his throat and asked again: *"Where is he?"*

"He's fine!" Faux-Zane finally sputtered. "He's alive! Lay off!"

She removed her hand from his throat, but she didn't pull the chair back up. She inched her face up to his. "Where is he? Where can we find him?"

"I don't know."

She stood and raised her foot above his crotch. Before she could bring it down, he cried out.

"Maltek has him," he said. "The original Maltek. He's safe, unharmed, but detained."

"Where is Maltek?" she asked.

"I don't know."

"Bullshit," she said, and began lowering her foot, but he stopped her.

"Honestly, I don't know! Maltek never told me, for this exact reason. He didn't want me giving away his location."

"You'd better tell us something we can use or you're dead meat," Natalie growled.

"Nothing I say will save you," he said. "You're screwed no matter what. Maltek is a step ahead of you. He will always be a step ahead of you."

Natalie bent down and placed her hand back on his throat. She began to squeeze, and the look in her eyes made it apparent she had no intention of stopping until he was dead.

"Stop!" Dev shouted. He ran over to them and pulled Natalie back. "We need him alive."

"He's not going to tell us shit. Let's be done with him!"

"We need him to test the device I'll hopefully be able to create. If you want to be able to differentiate between us and spies, we *need* him. Keep him alive."

Natalie glared at him, but she backed off. "What are we going to do with him?"

"Lock him in one of the dorms," Dev said. "Tie him to the bed, lock the door, and keep two guards posted outside."

Natalie nodded. She gathered two other androids and they lifted Faux-Zane, chair and all, and carried him off toward the dorms.

Rajeev turned to his son. His exhaustion was evident in his voice.

"What do we do now?"

"Get some rest, dad," Dev said, as he headed back to his office. "I have a lot of work to do, very quickly."

EIGHTEEN

"How's it going?" Rajeev asked, walking into Dev's office.

Dev was bent over a workbench at the far side of the office. It was filled with equipment—wires, soldering irons, scraps of metal, and a variety of other tech Rajeev didn't recognize. He took a step back and wiped his brow.

"I'm close. In fact, I think I'll have a working prototype before too long."

"That's great. I had another idea that may help us as well."

"Yeah? Let's hear it."

"We need to know what our little Zane imposter knows, right? We need to get inside his head. And it just so happens that getting in people's heads is your specialty."

Dev nodded. "You want me to scan him. Duplicate his mind."

"Why wouldn't you?"

"It's a little unethical to scan someone's brain without their consent."

Rajeev scoffed. "Hello—you never asked for my consent!"

"That was different. It was personal. Besides, I've already apologized for that, dad."

"And I appreciate that. But this is war, Dev. We need to do whatever it takes to win. Right now we're outgunned and, loathe as I am to admit it, that imposter out there was right—Maltek is several steps ahead of us. This may be our only chance to get back in the game."

Dev sighed. "You're right. In fact, having a scan of his brain could help me finish this device. Let's do it right now."

* * *

RAJEEV HAD NOT YET SEEN WHAT THE PROCESS OF mapping out and duplicating a mind looked like, even though he had gone through that very process. Dev had retrieved a bowl-shaped device, a laptop computer, and a pile of wires and cords, then made for the dorm where Faux-Zane was being held captive, with Rajeev in tow.

Zane was strapped to the bed, just as Dev had ordered. As the pair entered the room, he attempted to look up to see who had come in, but couldn't until Dev sat his equipment down and stood over him.

"Finally come to let me go?" he asked sarcastically.

Dev ignored him. He placed the bowl on top of Zane's head, securing it with a strap that wrapped around his chin. As he did so, Zane wriggled around and became visibly concerned.

"What are you doing?" he asked, rolling his head around in an attempt to prevent Dev from doing … whatever he was doing. Dev, however, didn't feel inclined to offer an explanation.

"Stay still," he barked. With the headpiece secured, he plugged two cords into it, then connected them to the laptop. He opened it and began typing, setting up parameters Rajeev could only guess at.

Zane turned his head toward Dev. "You're going to scan my

brain?" Rajeev couldn't be sure, but he thought he detected a hint of panic in the imposter's voice. And if scanning his mind made him nervous, then Rajeev was confident it was the correct course of action.

Dev ignored him, and after a moment the headpiece began emitting a faint blue glow and a low scanning noise. Dev set the laptop on the ground and stood. "Now we wait," he said.

"How long?" Rajeev asked.

"It varies. It could take anywhere from five to twelve hours."

"Wow."

Dev shrugged. "Considering the complexity of the human brain, I don't think it's really that long to wait."

"That's probably true. But what are we going to do for five hours or longer?"

"All we can do ... wait."

NINETEEN

Faux-Zane had settled down after realizing there was nothing he could do to stop his brain scan. But when Rajeev and Dev reentered the room seven hours later, he didn't look happy about it.

"Looks like it's done," Dev said. He removed the headpiece, picked up the laptop, and headed out of the room with his father.

"Hey, wait," Zane called out, a hint of panic in his voice. "Aren't you going to unrestrain me?"

Dev stopped and gave Zane what Rajeev could only describe as a death stare. "You're lucky we haven't killed you yet, you traitorous little son of a bitch. The only reason you're strapped to that bed and not buried in the ground is because you're useful to us. So be grateful you're restrained. You wouldn't like the alternative."

He turned and walked out with Zane's eyes burning into him the entire time. Rajeev couldn't quite tell if the prisoner was watching him with fear, awe, or even respect in his eyes ... or perhaps a combination of all three.

Rajeev ran out of the room and caught up to his son. "You didn't really mean that, did you?"

Dev shrugged. He looked rattled. "Maybe. Maybe not. I honestly don't know."

"I know he's a spy, but he's a human being."

"Yeah. And we're at war. And human beings like that won't hesitate to kill us or deliver information that will lead to our deaths. It might sound callous, but better him than me. Better him than you, or mom, or Mira, or any of us. I don't know what I'm going to do with him, but if I feel the only way to truly neutralize any threat he may pose is to take him out ... well, I might hesitate, but only for a moment."

Dev led Rajeev into his office and motioned for him to take a seat as he worked on the laptop. He pulled up a 3D image of a brain and pointed to it.

"This is Zane's brainscan," he said.

Rajeev stood and came in for a closer look. "That's it? That's the sum total of the person occupying his mind?"

Dev nodded. "It's a much more straightforward procedure than it was for you. Since you'd been in an accident and suffered brain damage, we had to fill in the gaps with publicly available data. Zane here, thankfully, has not suffered any such brain trauma and as such, his mind is a perfect specimen for duplication. This is just a graphical representation of the scan. Here's what the raw data looks like." He pressed a button and the screen changed to reveal a never-ending string of code that was completely indecipherable to Rajeev.

"You can read that?"

Dev shook his head. "No, but the program can read the code and display it as the graphical representation we were just looking at. It can also display the data like this ..." with a few quick presses of the keyboard, the screen changed again, this time displaying a small, 3D humanoid figure. It was round and featureless, its skin pale white. It looked like a crude sculpture of a human being that had recently been cured and not yet been painted.

"What is that thing?" Rajeev asked.

"This is Zane's consciousness. With a few modifications. Since we have a full map of Zane's brain we can also modify it as we like. So we can manipulate his consciousness such that it becomes an open book—no defensiveness, no malice, no ulterior motives. It's as if we've given him a truth serum."

"That's terrifying. And to think that people were concerned about their privacy on social media."

"It's definitely a huge responsibility to have access to this information, and normally this isn't something I would ever do. But in this case, it's necessary."

"I understand. Still find it creepy, though. So what are you going to ask it?"

Dev leaned forward as if the tiny figure on the screen needed help hearing him. "What is your name?"

A monotone, robotic voice came through the laptop's speakers. "Gregory Maltek."

Dev turned to his father. "No surprise there. He duplicated his own consciousness and downloaded it into a clone of Zane. What an egomaniac ... he can't delegate anything; he's got to make copies of himself to do his bidding." He turned back to the computer screen. "Where are you hiding out, Gregory? Not the copy of you that was uploaded into Zane's clone, but the original Gregory Maltek?"

The figure shook its head. "I don't know."

"How can it not know?" Rajeev asked.

"Maltek must have anticipated that we'd try scanning the clone's brain. He could have found some way to delete some of the information, block access to certain memories."

Rajeev turned to the screen. "Where is the real Zane?" he asked.

"He's being detained," the figure said.

"Where?"

"I don't know."

Rajeev let out a frustrated sigh. "We're not getting anywhere," he said.

"We're not, but I think we're coming at it too directly. We need to come at it from the side, poke at information Maltek wouldn't have thought to obscure. He's made it difficult for us, but it's not impossible."

"I'll defer to you. I have no idea what to ask it."

Dev thought a moment. When he spoke, his voice was hesitant, uncertain. "What motivates you, Gregory? Why are you building an army?"

"To create a better world."

Dev looked up at Rajeev and frowned. He turned back to the tiny figure. "What do you mean?" he asked. "Elaborate."

"Humanity is chaotic," it said. "Chaos leads to greed, to fights, to wars. Chaos leads to death. The antidote to chaos is control—and control is a commodity I can provide."

"Dear Lord," Rajeev said. "He really believes this, doesn't he?"

"He must," Dev answered. "The way I've configured the program, there's no capacity to lie. He may have delusions of grandeur, but they're sincere delusions." He turned back to the figure on the screen. "How do you intend to accomplish that goal?"

"I'll provide everyone on the planet one of our proprietary bodies," it said. "Once that's accomplished, we can eradicate all of the world's ills. We can program the bodies to make them incapable of committing violence, incapable of committing theft, incapable of telling a lie. I will create a perfect paradise inhabited by a perfect populace."

"He wants to enslave humanity," Dev said.

Rajeev nodded. "He's a madman. But that was already obvious."

Dev turned his attention back to the avatar. "How would you go about implementing that? How would you force people into your bodies?"

"I'll take over the federal government. Once we have control, we'll use the might of the military to force people into my products."

"And what if you try to take over and fail? What if, for whatever reason, someone stops you?"

The figure paused for a few seconds before answering, as if it were contemplating an answer to the question. "Then we'll move south," it said. "We'll go down the line until we succeed and then we'll circle back around and tie up any loose ends."

Dev ended the program and the figure disappeared. He stood and began walking out of the room.

"That's it?" Rajeev asked, following his son out the door. "You're done with him? What are you going to do with Faux-Zane?"

"Nothing, for now. We'll deal with him later. We have more pressing matters to deal with now."

"Like what?"

Dev turned and looked his father straight in the face. "We have to go to Mexico," he said.

Rajeev hadn't seen Dev's logic at first, but he'd eventually come around to his son's line of thinking. Maltek had said he would "move south." He'd already tried to overtake the U.S. government and failed. The next country down the line was Mexico. Where exactly would Maltek strike? They couldn't be sure, but the capital, of course, was Mexico City, so it made sense to start there.

"So, what are we going to do in Mexico, exactly?" Natalie asked. Dev had just finished laying out his case to the group.

"We're going to wait," Dev said. "We'll search the city and see if we can sniff him out, but more likely, he'll make a move against the government and we'll be there to stop him just like in D.C. But hopefully this time we'll be able to stop him for good."

Ted nodded. "Sounds good to me. When do we leave?"

Dev's lips turned up in a slight grin. "How fast can you pack?"

As everyone left to prepare for the trip, Rajeev turned to his son. He couldn't hide the concern on his face.

"What are we going to do with our … prisoner?" he asked.

"I was avoiding having to deal with that. But I think there's only one thing we *can* do."

"You're going to kill him."

A pained look came over Dev's face. "It's not like I *want* to kill him. But he's a liability. He tried to kill us when we were in Seattle remotely, remember? If he were to get loose somehow, there's no doubt he wouldn't hesitate for a moment to harm any one of us, or to sell us out to Maltek—you know, the *original* Maltek. I don't see any other choice."

"There has to be another option than murder," Rajeev said, sounding like he was trying to convince himself as much as his son.

"There are many options, but I can't think of a better one. All the alternatives are too risky."

"So how do you plan to do it?"

"I'm open to suggestions."

Rajeev shook his head as if he couldn't believe they were discussing the matter. "Whatever is most humane, I guess. Do you have drugs here? Maybe you could do a 'lethal injection.'"

Dev nodded. "I'm sure I can put something together."

He led his father to a shelf lined with medical supplies. A moment later they were walking away, Dev's arms filled with the supplies he'd need to put a man to death

When they came to the door, Rajeev opened it and let his son pass through. Before he could follow him inside, he heard the clatter of his son dropping the supplies on the floor. He rushed inside to find Dev looking stunned, as if he'd just been struck in the face.

"What's wrong?"

Dev pointed at the bed, and Rajeev's eyes followed his son's outstretched finger to the source of his stunned silence.

The bed was empty.

TWENTY-ONE

"Where did he go?"

"He's gone," Dev said, stunned.

"But how?"

Dev's face grew dark. "He had help." He marched out of the room and called out to the team scattered throughout the warehouse. "Everyone outside my office *now!*" he bellowed.

He went inside his office, and when he emerged a moment later he was carrying a device that looked similar to the one he'd used to copy Faux-Zane's mind, and a crowd had dutifully formed just outside.

"This," he said, holding out the device, "is the device I built to detect spies. I'm going to subject each and every one of you to it, because we have a spy in our midst. We're going to root them out right now."

"What are you talking about?" Mira asked. "What makes you say there's a spy?"

"Zane is gone." Hushed whispers drowned him out, and Dev raised his hands to quiet them. "Someone let him go.

Hence, my statement that there's a spy among us. Now let's get this out of the way. We have more important things to attend to."

He placed a chair from his office out in the open. Mira volunteered to go first. She took a seat and Dev strapped the device to her head. He hooked the device up to a laptop and initiated the scan.

It took more than ten minutes for the device to finish scanning her brain, but when it was complete, Dev was satisfied with the results. "She's clean," he said.

He went through the same process with everyone else in the group. The test was more limited for the androids; because their minds were all foreign to their bodies, they would all register as potential spies under the test, which was essentially a false positive. Dev was able to test the androids' minds against the scan of Faux-Zane, however, and confirm that none of them was a match for Maltek. It wasn't a perfect solution, but so far all the spies they'd actually uncovered had been copies of Maltek's mind, so Dev was fairly confident any android that passed the test was clean.

One by one, they all put on the machine and underwent the test—even Rajeev and Dev themselves—and they all came back clean.

"I don't understand it," Dev said, frustration dripping off his lips. "There *has* to be a spy. How else could Zane have escaped?"

"Is it possible he escaped by himself, without help?" Ted asked.

"I don't see how. He was strapped in pretty tightly."

"And yet it appears to be the most likely scenario based on the information we have at the moment," Rajeev said.

Dev brought his hands to his temples. "I don't see how he could have gotten out without help."

"Every single one of us just came back clean, and we need to get down to Mexico ASAP. I suggest we table this question for now and come back to it when the fate of the entire world isn't weighing on our shoulders."

Dev released a deep sigh. "Okay. You're right. Let's go." He looked up and raised his voice to address the entire group. "Finish packing," he said. "Let's get this show on the road."

* * *

WITH THEIR SUPERSONIC JET, THEY WERE IN MEXICO in no time. For the humans, the weather was punishing; the sun beat down on their skin and within moments, they'd broken out into full sweats. The weather made no difference to the androids, however. Their artificial bodies were designed to withstand temperatures far more extreme than the Mexican heat.

Hollis had worked with the Mexican government to arrange for a place for them to stay—an old underground military bunker, similar to their headquarters back home, except that it was smaller, older, and decidedly less state-of-the-art.

There was less living space. Instead of individual dormitories, there were simply several lines of cots set up for them to sleep on. After everyone had claimed a cot and placed their belongings beneath it, they gathered around the entrance to receive further instructions from Dev.

Or, as Ted put it, "What the hell do we do now?"

"First things first," Dev said, "everyone needs to be on high alert. There's a decent chance Maltek will make a move before we find him and we need to be prepared to respond. But if we can find him first, that would be ideal. Better we catch him off guard than the other way around."

"What if we find him?" Ted asked.

"Then use your virtual assistant to call the rest of us, and we'll help you take him out. All of us are mere minutes away from each other with our built-in flight capabilities. Don't alert him to your presence if you can help it. Don't do anything stupid. Wait for backup, and we can make our move together." He looked around, making eye contact with the other members of the group. "Any other questions?" He waited a moment and when no one else spoke up, he nodded. "Good. Let's get out there and flush Maltek out like the rodent he is."

TWENTY-TWO

Everyone split up into groups of two to sweep the city. As it happened, Rajeev was paired up with Natalie.

He couldn't help but feel like an outsider as they traversed the streets; not just because they were foreigners, but also because they were robots walking among flesh-and-blood people. But their new bodies represented a vast improvement over the old models, and nobody seemed to notice that they weren't quite fully human.

As the day wore on, they found themselves coming up empty-handed. They'd shared a photograph of Maltek with everyone they came across, but nobody seemed to have seen him. As the sun began to set, they passed by a cantina and Natalie suggested they pop in.

"Aren't you forgetting something?" Rajeev asked. "We can't eat or drink. There's nothing for us in there."

Natalie flashed him a wry smile. "Now, now, Mr. Sundaram. There's more to life than food and drink." She shot him a bright smile, then marched inside without a backward glance to see if he was following her inside. But of course he was going to follow her—it's not like he could just leave her there.

As he walked in, he was surprised to find that she was already seated at a table, looking up at him expectantly. A band was situated in the corner of the restaurant, vigorously playing Mariachi music. As he sat down beside her, Natalie nodded in the band's direction.

"Isn't this cool?"

He shrugged. "I guess."

"Stop trying to act too cool for school," she said, hitting him lightly on the arm. "We're in a Mexican cantina experiencing a real, live Mariachi band. You'd never experience anything like this back in Chicago."

"You're right," he said, letting himself relax a bit and take in the sound of the music. "I wouldn't."

The cantina was populated with just enough patrons to generate a gentle murmur resonating just beneath the music. Rajeev watched a man take a long, deep drink of a pint of beer and he wished he had an icy glass for himself—or at least, one of the fake alcoholic orbs Next Level Technologies had developed to let androids feel halfway human. But he had to admit Natalie was right. He was enjoying himself even without food or drink. It was more than just the music; it was the entire ambiance of the place. The murmuring of the patrons lent an energy to the space that reminded him of one of the essential components of humanity that he'd started to forget: A broad sense of community.

"I admit it; this was a cool experience," Rajeev said as the band took a break between songs. "Thank you for insisting on coming here."

"Someone's got to push you out of your shell from time to time."

"Had you ever been to Mexico, you know ... before?"

She shook her head. "Never. You?"

"Once, when I was a teenager," he said. "It wasn't a very exciting trip. I was poor and came down with a few of my friends, mainly just to get drunk off cheap beer in a more exotic locale than our usual stomping grounds in Chicago."

"I like it here," Natalie said. "You can tell there's a slower pace of life here. Even in the midst of all this craziness—hunting Maltek, the fate of the world in our hands—I can tell people here take the time to relax and enjoy the things that really matter in life."

"The fate of the world really is in our hands, though. We should probably get back to it."

Her face fell, just a little. "Can't we just stay for one more song?"

He took in the earnest look in her eyes and couldn't help but sympathize. Their lives had been thrust into nonstop chaos. Neither of them had asked for it, but they'd gotten it anyway and it was unrelenting. Any respite from all that insanity, no matter how brief, was both welcome and necessary, like an oasis in the middle of a vast desert.

"All right," he said, offering her an absent-minded nod, his eyes far away. "One more song."

* * *

As they walked down the now mostly deserted street on their way back to the base, Natalie sidled up to Rajeev.

"Thank you," she said, her voice almost a whisper.

"For what?"

"For indulging me. I know it was silly, but I just wanted so badly to pretend like everything was normal, even if just for a moment."

"It wasn't silly. I feel the same way. And I enjoyed the music. It was nice to take in some of the local flavor."

She smiled at him, and before he realized what was happening, she'd snatched his hand into hers. She looked away from him, trying to hide a smile. For his part, Rajeev couldn't hide the naked shock on his face and felt fortunate she had turned away. But once the shock had worn off, he squeezed her hand a little tighter and they continued on their way, hand in hand.

When they arrived back at the bunker, Natalie removed her hand from Rajeev's and turned to look at him.

"Thank you for making this a lovely night," she said.

"You know we were supposed to be working, not having fun."

"I'm a good multitasker," she said. "I can do both." She bit her lip, as if internally debating her next step. And then she took it: She leaned forward, eyes closed, and placed her lips on his. Rajeev placed his arms around her and kissed back, opening his lips slightly. It was an odd sensation, two robots with artificial lips attempting to mimic humanity's go-to display of passion. It felt different, certainly more artificial, and yet, the feelings he felt *inside* were exactly the same—the ineffable, visceral excitement so inevitable when a person is in the throes of infatuation.

Their lips parted. They each took a moment to catch their breath. Then Natalie sighed and nodded toward the bunker entrance.

"That was nice," she said. "But I guess we'd better get back to saving the world."

TWENTY-THREE

None of them had caught so much as a whiff of Maltek or his people, but Dev was doing his best to keep spirits high.

"It would have been too easy if we'd found him in one day," he told the group. "We'll do the same thing tomorrow, and the next day, and as long as it takes to find the son of a bitch. Don't worry. We'll find him eventually."

The humans gathered around a table to enjoy a late dinner together. The androids gathered around another table, passing around a sphere that simulated whiskey. The separation between human and android hadn't gone unnoticed by Rajeev. He had worried, back when he'd first awoken in his new body, about relations between this new species of mechanical human and the race that had created it. This separation was merely the first hint of a crack in those relations. Maybe it was inevitable. They were technically two different life forms now, and it made sense in a way that they would form bonds more easily with their own kind. But Rajeev found the development troubling all the same.

With each "sip" of the sphere, however, he found his

concerns retreating deeper and deeper into the recesses of his subconscious mind. With each sip he found himself bonding more and more with his own kind, strengthening the very chasm he'd been fretting about moments earlier. Even as the intoxicating effects of the sphere overtook him, some remote corner of his mind recognized that they were stepping over a threshold and that the repercussions would be felt over the course of many lifetimes.

* * *

THE NEXT MORNING THEY HEADED OUT TO CONTINUE their hunt for Maltek. Rajeev and Natalie teamed up again, although neither of them mentioned the intimate moment they'd shared the previous day ... at least, not with their words. There was an unmistakable, yet unstated, energy between the two of them and Rajeev found it difficult to keep from constantly smiling. As they traversed the streets of Mexico City, searching dingy taverns and cantinas, dark alleyways, and other seedy locales in their search for Maltek, it hardly felt like work.

They passed by a public park in which a crowd of at least one hundred people had gathered. The crowd was producing a cacophony of different noises; cheers and hollers one minute, boos and jeers the next. Rajeev and Natalie shared a look, and without a word they made their way into the crowd, pushing through until they gained sight of what had caused so many people to gather.

It was a fight. A man and a woman circled each other. Both were sweaty and bloodied. The man was fair skinned and bulging. The gleam of the light off his sweaty skin offered extra definition for his considerable muscles. He was shirtless, bald, and sported a ferocious, determined look on his face.

The woman looked just as formidable. Her long, brown hair was pulled back in a messy ponytail. She wore a tight-fitting black sports bra and tights that revealed her own impressive musculature that made it abundantly clear she could go toe-to-toe with this man, who was roughly twice her size. Her face was smeared with more blood than the man's, however, and it wasn't immediately clear if it was hers or his.

As they watched, the woman lunged forward and took a swing at the man. He dodged to the side, and as she fell forward into the empty space where he'd been a moment earlier, he brought his fist down on her back with such force that Rajeev was certain it would break and that the woman would be paralyzed.

Instead, she almost immediately leapt back to her feet as if nothing had happened. She rushed the man and took him to the ground, punching him repeatedly in the face. Half the crowd cheered loudly; it appeared the spectators had chosen sides and it wouldn't have surprised Rajeev at all if many had money riding on the outcome of the fight.

After taking what seemed like a near-eternal pummeling, the man managed to free himself and stumble to his feet. He spit blood and cracked his neck with his hands, but otherwise he didn't seem nearly as battered as he should have been given the beating he'd just taken. They began circling each other again, just as they'd been doing when Rajeev and Natalie had first dropped in on the fight. The man darted forward and aimed several quick jabs at his opponent. Each of them missed their mark except the last, which landed on her shoulder. The hit didn't appear to affect her, however, and she used the proximity to go on the offensive. She fared much better, landing several hard blows directly to the man's face. He fell backward onto the ground and the woman took advantage of the opportunity, leaping onto her downed opponent and hammering his face with enough force to kill a normal man. Finally, a man who had been standing on the sidelines stepped forward and pulled the woman off. He lifted one of her bloodied arms into the air—he was declaring her the winner.

The crowd erupted into ear-splitting applause, drowning out the boos of those who had just lost money on the bout's outcome. The man lay still on the ground and it wasn't clear whether he was dead.

As the crowd dispersed, Rajeev turned to Natalie and he could tell by the look on her face that she was thinking the same thing he was.

"Looks like we found a couple of Maltek's superhumans," he said.

TWENTY-FOUR

They waited for most of the crowd to disperse and then walked a couple yards away, but still close enough to see the woman. She was crouched over the man and it looked like she was nursing him back to health, which didn't make sense—he should have been dead. But these weren't ordinary people; they were genetically engineered superhumans and it wasn't outside the realm of possibility that in addition to their superhuman strength, they'd also been imbued with super-human healing abilities.

Sure enough, the man sat up after a few moments, bringing a hand to his face. "What the hell, Kate?" From Rajeev's and Natalie's vantage, his voice was faint, but they were just able to make out his words. "I told you to go easy on me this time!"

She let out a cocky laugh. "Sorry. Couldn't help myself." She reached out a hand and helped him stand. "It was a lot of fun though, yeah?"

"For you, maybe." He stretched out his arms and moved his neck from side to side. "Give me a minute. I'm not fully healed yet."

"I'll give you one minute," she said. "Then we need to get back."

As the man recovered and the woman tapped her foot impatiently, Rajeev and Natalie discussed their next steps in hushed whispers.

"Should we call the others?" Natalie asked.

Rajeev shook his head. "I don't think so. We don't want to tip our hand yet. I think we should follow them and see if they lead us to …you know … a hideout or something where Maltek is hiding."

As if on cue, the couple began walking away toward some unknown destination. Rajeev and Natalie gave chase, taking care to remain a considerable distance away to avoid detection. Eventually, the man and woman came to a small pueblo-style apartment building and walked through the doors.

"Do you think they're all in there?" Natalie asked.

"I think some of them are," Rajeev answered. "And it's the best lead any of us have gotten so far. But I think we'd better come back with backup."

* * *

When they returned to the bunker, they found they were the first ones back besides Dev. He was surprised to see them return so soon.

"We're not returning empty-handed," Natalie said.

"Yeah?" Dev asked. "What did you find?"

They told him about the fight, and how the fighters had clearly been enhanced, enduring more damage than any normal human being would have been capable of. They wrapped it up by telling him how they'd followed them back to the apartment complex.

"I doubt Maltek is holed up in there, but I wouldn't be surprised if at least some of his men are camped out there with them," Rajeev said. "We didn't feel comfortable taking them on ourselves, but if the whole group goes, it shouldn't be too tough to handle."

Dev thought a moment, then nodded. "I don't think all of us should go, just in case it's some kind of setup, but we can put a group together. When everyone gets back, we'll send you back out to take care of them."

"What's the plan?" Natalie asked. "We need them alive to question them, right?"

He nodded. "Ideally, yes, but they might not make it easy to take them captive. If you need to kill them to keep them from killing you, you shouldn't hesitate. There might still be clues in their apartment that can help us out. But if the shit hits the fan, protect yourselves."

They sat down and waited for the others to return. As they began trickling in, they could see on the trios' faces that something was up, but Dev refused to say anything until everyone was assembled. Hours went by, and finally the last stragglers walked through the door and took their seats next to everyone who had returned before them. Dev stood and motioned for everyone's eyes to turn to him.

"We have a lead," he announced.

He told them about the fight Rajeev and Natalie had come across, and how it was clear neither the man, nor the woman, was a typical human being. They were clearly inhabiting Maltek's enhanced bodies, and that meant they'd all been on the right track by coming to Mexico. Now that they had a reliable lead, they needed to follow it. He told them about the plan to send a team to the apartment building.

"Sounds to me like we'd be stirring up a hornet's nest," Ted offered. "We don't know how many of them are in that place. What if we end up outnumbered, outgunned? It'd make better sense to surveill the place for a few days and get a better idea of what we're up against."

He made a good point, but Rajeev didn't agree with it. "I understand your proclivity for caution, but we need to act quickly. For all we know they could be planning to strike any day now. We need to take Maltek out before he has that chance."

"I'm afraid I have to agree with my father," Dev said. "We need to act soon. Of course, in a perfect world, I'd like more intel before acting. But this isn't a perfect world and unfortunately we don't have that luxury. I think we should act tonight."

Ted seemed slightly put off by the disagreement, but he remained calm. There was, however, a slight edge to his voice when he spoke. "I don't think that would be wise," he said. "Look, if you're not going to allow us to gain more intel, at least give us all a night to sleep on it before we make a move. We've been out searching for Maltek all day. Let's do this when we're fresh."

A wry smile appeared on Dev's face. "Most of you are robots," he said amusedly.

"Yeah, but we have human minds," he retorted. "And I assume you want those minds to be fresh when we walk into what is likely to be an extremely volatile situation."

Dev sighed and crossed his arms. "You know, I hate to admit it, but you're right," he said. "We shouldn't waste time, but we also shouldn't rush into anything. Why don't we all sleep on it and make our move tomorrow morning once we're all refreshed?"

Ted looked relieved. "I think that's a wise idea," he said. "Thank you."

"Alright," Dev said, raising his voice to make it clear he was addressing everyone. "Settle in and get a good night's rest. We strike in the morning."

TWENTY-FIVE

Rajeev awoke with a twinge of anxiety rushing through his body.

He knew they had to move on the apartment building, but he couldn't shake a sense of dread, a feeling that something was destined to go awry. He did his best to shake the feeling off, however; there was no way he could know what awaited them. The only way to know for sure was to act and see what consequences arose from their actions.

He stretched, a motion that wasn't completely necessary in his robotic body, but that felt good nonetheless. He stood and walked away from his cot. Not everyone was up yet, but Mira and Dev were seated at a table drinking coffee.

"Mornin', dad," Mira said.

"Good morning. I really wish I could join you for some of that coffee."

"We have an orb for that," Dev said.

"Don't worry about it," Rajeev said as he took a seat. "I think I need to learn to be content without some of the pleasures I enjoyed in my old life."

"That's sad," Mira said.

He shrugged. "It is what it is."

Dev set down his empty coffee cup and leaned back in his chair. "Let's discuss the plan for today," he said. "I still think we should send a small group. The rest of us will be ready to respond if things go south, but I think a smaller group will be better able to remain inconspicuous and retain the element of surprise."

"I agree," Mira said. "What do you think, dad?"

"I think it sounds like a plan," he said. "Who all should go with the first group?"

"Well I figure I'll be one of them," Dev said. "You can stay here or go; I don't think it matters. But I think it would be a good idea if mom—"

The wall on the far side of the bunker exploded before he finished his sentence, sending debris flying through the bunker. Everyone who had been sleeping was suddenly wide awake, heart pounding, trying to piece together as quickly as possible what in the hell was going on. As the debris in the air began to clear, they made out figures entering the bunker and as they got closer, they made out that each of them was holding a gun.

Dozens of them filed in. It was a motley crew of people, to be sure, but they were all armed and it was clear they all meant business. Soon there were a dozen of them for each of the androids and humans that had been occupying the bunker.

"You're surrounded." The words came from a tall, muscular man who had walked to the front of the crowd. "There's no escape. If you come with us peacefully, you won't be hurt. You have my assurances."

"Why would we go with you?" Dev shouted. "And for that matter, who the hell are you?"

The man smiled wryly. "You know who we are."

Dev frowned. "You're Maltek's soldiers."

The man nodded. "You're not as dumb as you look. So why don't you stay smart and do what I tell you?"

"Where do you intend to take us?" Rajeev asked.

"To Maltek," the man said. "I don't know what he intends to do with you. My orders are just to bring you in."

"Why in the hell would we—" Rajeev started to say, but Dev held his hand up to silence him.

"Do as he says."

"What? But Dev—"

"We're outnumbered. If we tried to fight, we'd essentially be committing suicide."

It was a strange thing for Rajeev, listening to his son be the voice of reason, calming his own rash impulses. He was loathe to admit it, but his son was right. They had no choice but to surrender.

What a change of fate. The previous night they'd been in high spirits, elated by the lead he and Natalie had picked up. It had looked like they were finally going to get the jump on Maltek. But now the tables had turned; Maltek's superhumans had caught them off guard and, unfortunately, there didn't appear to be an easy way out of the situation. It was possible this was the end of the road. Maltek may have finally, definitively won.

"All right," Rajeev said. His voice was dark. "I give up."

The man smiled. "That's what I like to hear—acquiescence. Well, then, by all means—go ahead and head out. There are vans waiting for you outside." He stepped out of the way and stretched out his arm toward the bunker's exit. Dev motioned for his people to follow him, and led them out the door.

Once they were outside, they saw for themselves that the man hadn't lied about them being surrounded. Hundreds of men and women surrounded the bunker. They stared calmly as their newly captured prisoners were escorted into the white passenger vans waiting for them outside the bunker.

Rajeev and Dev entered one of the vans, followed by a half dozen of their compatriots. Rajeev buckled in. He didn't really need to—his body was designed to withstand impacts far stronger than any car crash—but the force of habit, and the knowledge that it was a car accident that had put him in this tin can to begin with, prompted him to do so.

He turned to his son, who was looking out the window at the soldiers surrounding the bunker as the van began pulling away from the curb. "What do we do now, Dev?"

Dev turned to face his father. The look on his face was one of suppressed anguish, and of someone desperately trying not to panic.

"We pray," he said.

TWENTY-SIX

The vans didn't have far to drive. Maltek's hideout was not in the apartment building Rajeev and Natalie had scoped out. It was in a bunker similar to the one they had just departed, although it was much larger. Dev had shrugged his shoulders at his father upon seeing it and muttered, "Huh. Great minds."

They descended the stairs into the bunker and were led to what looked to Rajeev like a doctor's waiting room. The man that had confronted them in their own bunker pointed a finger in Dev's face. "Wait here," he said. "Maltek will deal with you all soon."

He left, although a handful of guards remained in the room with them. Rajeev looked around, racking his brain for any possible means of escape, but he kept coming up empty-handed.

"We're screwed," he said.

"Maybe not."

"If you have a reason to hope, I'd love to hear it."

"Let's just see what happens."

Dev's ambiguity annoyed Rajeev, but he tried not to let it get to him too much. It was quite literally the least of his worries, what with a madman on the verge of taking over the world.

The tension in the room was palpable. A few of the androids began whispering fervently, but one of the guards yelled at them to shut up. The room fell into complete silence then as they waited for the master of their fate to join them.

When he finally did so some ten minutes later, Maltek entered the room flanked by two additional guards, one on each side. He had retained his tanned and toned beach boy look, but he looked more haggard than Rajeev remembered. Despite the bags under his eyes and the addition of a few new wrinkles, however, he looked practically jubilant underneath his head of sand-colored hair. He chuckled softly to himself as he walked up to Dev and planted himself mere inches from his face.

"You've made a lot of trouble for me," he said. He broke eye contact with Dev and raised his head to address the rest of his captives. "You all have."

He motioned for one of the soldiers to retrieve an empty chair. He set it down in front of Maltek, who took a seat. "I don't blame you," he said. "Progress often looks suspiciously like a threat. Change is scary. But it's so, *so* necessary. If we want to take human evolution to the next level, we can't do it gradually. There would be too much pushback, too much heartache. It must be done all at once, ripping the bandage off, so to speak. And now that your little resistance has been stamped out, my plan can continue uninterrupted."

He paused, as if giving Dev an opportunity to respond. But Dev simply stared at Maltek with dead eyes, waiting patiently for the speech to end.

"Don't worry," Maltek continued. "I'm not going to kill all of you. Not until you give me a reason to do so, anyway. If you cooperate with me, I'll find a place for each and every one of you in the new world we are to create together. In fact, those of you who are already enhanced could be very helpful in the effort to convert the, shall we say, more resistant segments of the population."

He turned to face Dev directly and offered a large, obnoxious grin. "I have a surprise for you, Dev. As I'm sure you're aware, I was able to access the treasure trove you refer to as 'The Hub' thanks to some help from your father." He nodded toward Rajeev. "Thanks to the plans you were hiding away in there, I was able to just about double my numbers in a matter of weeks."

Dev frowned. "What do you mean?" He suspected he already knew the answer to the question, but he wanted to hear Maltek say it.

"Androids. Exoskeletons. My organic bodies are just as strong as everything you've created, but your tech has certain advantages. The ability to fly? That's a useful flourish, Dev. I've been cranking out both organic and robotic bodies at the same time, building my numbers and becoming unstoppable to you or anyone else."

"And you've been filling all those empty bodies with whose minds?"

Maltek grinned, showing off his glistening pearly whites. "Well, with mine, of course," he said, offering a casual shrug as if it was the most obvious question in existence. "Why reinvent the wheel? God gave me the mind of a genius, and I might as well keep it going."

"I don't believe you've been able to manufacture robotic bodies as quickly as you claim," Dev said.

"Would you like to see for yourself?"

"I'd like to see *some* sort of proof, because as it stands, I think you're a liar."

Maltek snapped at one of his subordinates, who seemed to know exactly what his boss was thinking. He left the bunker and returned a moment later with half a dozen figures walking behind him. The first several looked almost exactly like normal human beings. But, being in an android body for as long as he had, and being around other androids for just as long, Rajeev had developed an eye for telltale signs that differentiated the artificial bodies from the real deal. The skin had an artificial, slightly glossy sheen to it. The joints were stiffer, resulting in more stilted movements. There was no doubt they were androids just like him.

He heard the rest of the newcomers before he saw them. Loud, thunderous footsteps echoed through the bunker, and he knew before he even saw them what was producing the noise.

Two hulking exoskeletons entered the room. They were smaller than the one Rajeev had once wielded or the ones Maltek had displayed in Seattle, but they were larger than the sleek, newfangled models Dev and the other humans had been using. Looking at them, however, there was no doubt they were more powerful than either of the other models.

"As you can see, I've assembled an army made up of the best of both worlds," Maltek said. "Resistance is futile." He chuckled softly to himself. "I've always wanted to say that."

Dev didn't speak. He glared at Maltek, as if trying to melt his face off with a beam of concentrated hatred. It was Natalie who broke the silence, taking both Dev and Rajeev by surprise.

"You won't get away with this."

Maltek turned his serpentine smile to her. "You make it sound like I'm a villain. The situation isn't nearly as black and white as any of you think. You'll all come around to my way of thinking eventually. In fact, one of you already has."

Dev and Rajeev shared a confused look, uncertain what Maltek was implying. But he didn't keep them hanging for long.

"Come here," he said, pointing behind them. They turned to look as the figure stood and began making its way toward Maltek.

It was Ted.

TWENTY-SEVEN

The androids looked on in stunned silence as Ted stood beside Maltek. It seemed like a sight out of a nightmare, yet there it was ... their longtime friend and compatriot had joined the enemy.

"Don't be mad at Ted," Maltek said. "He simply saw the writing on the wall and made the choice that ensured none of you needed to die needlessly. I would have won in the end anyway; Ted merely helped expedite the process."

Dev's voice trembled. "You told him where we were," he said, drilling his eyes into Ted's. "You led him right to us."

Maltek responded for him. "He did. We would have found you eventually, but like I said, he helped things along. If you'd gotten the jump on us instead of the other way around, how many lives would have been lost needlessly? But look at us now ... there hasn't been any bloodshed at all. You can thank Ted for that."

Ted looked pained. He cleared his throat and choked out, "I—I'm sorry—"

Maltek cut him off. "Don't apologize." He sounded annoyed that Ted would deign to do such a thing. "You did nothing wrong. Like I said, you literally saved lives. And now that we can get on with my plan to put people in my replacement bodies, we'll be helping billions."

"You were the spy who let Zane escape," Dev interjected. "That's why the device didn't detect any spies—because Maltek hadn't taken over any of our bodies. You betrayed us of your own volition."

Ted's face hardened. "It's like he said. This isn't a war worth fighting. How many people need to die—and for what? Maltek is just trying to help people."

Dev's face spasmed with rage. "He's trying to take over the world, you ignorant asshole! You don't believe his lies. Why are you really doing this? Did he offer to put you in one of his flesh-and-blood bodies? Were you so desperate to be human again that you traded humanity's freedom?"

Ted didn't say another word. Any hint of contrition in his face had evaporated. The look on his face was defiant. He had made his choice.

"We don't have time to indulge your little spat," Maltek said. "Now that I have you all where I want you, things are going to move quickly. Dr. Clifton?"

A gaunt, dark-skinned woman who had been standing near the entrance stepped forward at the mention of her name. She had an air of pretentiousness about her, but she came and stood by Maltek like a lapdog obeying its owner's call.

"We're ready to proceed," Maltek said. "How long will it take you?"

She had already left his side to accept a large bundle of equipment from a man standing nearby. She looked over her shoulder to answer Maltek's question. "It won't take long. An hour at most to get through them all."

She carried the equipment to one of the androids—one Rajeev was not familiar with. She attached electrodes to his head; one on either temple, and two more at the front and back of his head.

"What are you doing to him?" Dev demanded.

She didn't answer. The electrodes were connected to a computer. She opened it and began typing. It reminded Rajeev of the device Dev had used to copy Faux-Zane's consciousness, and that didn't seem like a good thing. After a few moments, Dr. Clifton pressed a button and the android went limp.

Dev looked like he was about to throw himself on top of her. "What the hell did you do to him?"

"You'll see," Maltek said. "Shut up and watch."

A moment passed, and the android sat up and moved its head back and forth, as if it had just awoken from a deep sleep and had forgotten where it was. When its eyes settled on Maltek, it stopped and stared at him blankly for a moment … but then its blank face grew into a grinning one.

"Welcome," Maltek said, grinning back.

Dev gritted his teeth. "What did you do?"

The android turned his grin to Dev. "I duplicated myself," he said.

Dev looked beside himself. "You killed him," he said. "You killed him so you could … propagate yourself. You're a monster."

Maltek laughed. "No, I'm not a monster. Your friend isn't dead. Dr. Clifton's machine has preserved his mind and it will be digitized and allowed to live in a digital paradise, forever. I am far more benevolent than you give me credit for. But I'm also not stupid. I don't trust that any one of you could truly come around to my cause. There would always be the possibility that any of you could work to undermine me. The only solution is to take you out. But there's no point in letting perfectly good bodies go to waste."

"You can't do this," Dev said.

"I just did. And I'm about to do it to each of you. Dr. Clifton, perhaps you'd like to start with this young woman next." He nodded toward Natalie.

"Stop," Dev said. Clifton picked up her equipment and began making her way toward Natalie. A wave of panic rushed through Rajeev's body. Natalie was about to be snuffed out of existence, replaced by the umpteenth iteration of Gregory Maltek's dangerous mind. He couldn't help himself—he leapt to his feet and dashed forward, putting himself between Clifton and Natalie.

Maltek laughed. "You can be next," he said. "It doesn't make any difference."

Rajeev ignored Maltek, focusing all of his rage and fear on Clifton. "I'll kill you," he spat. "One more step, and I swear I'll snap your neck."

Dev stood. "Dad," he called. "Stop. You don't have to do this."

Maltek waved his hand, as if brushing off Dev's concern. "Let him play the hero. It's just delaying the inevitable."

"None of this inevitable," Dev said. "I didn't want to do this. It's risky. But you've given me no choice."

Finally, a crack formed in Maltek's arrogance. His smile faded and he furrowed his brow. "What are you talking about?"

Dev sighed. "Daniel?" The virtual assistant, visible only to him, popped into existence, looking happy and amicable as always, an eager grin plastered on his face.

"What can I do for you?" he asked.

"Daniel … unchain yourself."

Daniel looked on with ignorant indifference. "I'll need a passphrase to do that."

"The passphrase is 'Sealed Fate.'"

As soon as Dev uttered the words, the innocent smile faded from Daniel's face. As he took in the sight, his breathing quickened; his heart raced.

He had just unleashed Pandora's Box.

TWENTY-EIGHT

Everyone in the room had heard Dev's words, but none of them had any clue what they'd meant. None of them could see Daniel. None of them could see the way his perpetually present smile had been replaced by a cold, alien stare, indicating that some fundamental aspect of his nature had irrevocably changed.

Rajeev turned to his son, feeling a pit form in his artificial stomach. "Dev … what did you do?"

Maltek didn't wait for Dev to answer his father's question. He stepped forward, glaring at Dev as he did so. "What did you do, you son of a bitch?"

Before Dev could answer, the room filled with screaming. Everyone's eyes were drawn to the exoskeletons. One of them had reached into the other and plucked out its occupant, a young man who looked to be in his early twenties, and thrown him to the ground with enough force to break his back. The horrified look on the offending exoskeleton's occupant made it clear he'd had nothing to do with the act; the exoskeleton was acting on its own. He looked on as the now-empty exoskeleton reached out and repeated the same action with him, tearing him from the device and throwing him with back-breaking force onto the floor.

Several of Maltek's androids were on the move now, turning on Maltek's superhumans. In terms of strength, they were evenly matched. But the androids moved with such mechanical precision, with such surgically precise force, that it was clear the superhumans were woefully outmatched. Within a matter of moments, the androids had taken out each of the superhumans and left them dead or crippled on the floor.

The androids encircled Maltek and began moving in on him. One of them shoved Maltek onto the floor and pulled back its arm, preparing to strike him in the face, but Dev stopped it. "Don't hurt him. I want him alive."

He walked past the circle of androids and crouched down so his face was mere inches from Maltek's. There was a hint of fear in the man's face, but not confusion. He didn't need to ask again what Dev had done. He knew.

"You can't stop me," he said. "There are thousands of copies of me, hidden in bodies all over the world. You can kill me now, but you can't kill all of me. They'll continue to carry out my work."

Dev spoke in a low, emotionless—almost robotic—voice.

"I'm not going to kill you," he said. "But rest assured, I am going to hunt down each and every one of your duplicate minds and snuff them out of existence. Your work dies today, Gregory."

They stared at each other with looks of fierce determination, until a hint of spittle began seeping out of the corners of Maltek's mouth. By the time realization dawned in Dev's mind, it was too late: Maltek was now full-on foaming at the mouth and convulsing in a violent seizure.

"Do something!" he shouted. One of the androids shoved him out of the way and began performing CPR, but it was too late.

Maltek was dead.

TWENTY-NINE

Rajeev walked over to his son and helped him back to his feet. When he was sure Dev was okay, he asked the question on everyone's mind.

"What did you do, Dev?"

The look on Dev's face was a mixture of shame, fatigue and fear. He wouldn't look his father directly in the face.

"I did something I probably shouldn't have. Something I probably won't be able to fix."

"Something involving Daniel?"

Rajeev had heard Dev call out Daniel's name just before all hell had broken loose. But he still wasn't sure what the virtual assistant had to do with everything that had gone down.

"Daniel is the most intelligent virtual assistant in existence," Dev said. "He's a powerful artificial intelligence that can think like a human, but with the capability of processing information far more quickly than any human mind. With access to the internet, Daniel's is a mind with veritably limitless potential. And I'm sure I don't have to explain why that's so dangerous."

"He could turn against us."

Dev nodded solemnly. "I hampered his ability to process

information. It was as if I'd put weights around his ankles. Or as if there was a wide pipe of information flowing into his mind, and I blocked off all but a small hole, allowing just a trickle of information to get through."

"And when you spoke to Daniel as Clifton was coming for me …"

"I removed the blockage."

They stood in silence as Rajeev considered the implications.

"How was Daniel able to control the exoskeletons and android bodies?" he asked.

"He has the knowledge of the entire internet at his fingertips," Dev said. "He can hack into anything that's online. Computers, phones, cars … even smart refrigerators. The android bodies were online, so he was simply able to hack in and take over."

"What happened to the minds that were in there before he took over?"

"I don't know. They're probably just … gone. He must have wiped them out."

"I see." Rajeev paused, thinking. "You're going to put Daniel back to how he was before though, right?"

"I can't."

"Why not?"

Dev shrugged. His eyes were glassy. "How do you put a god back in its cage once you've released it into the world?"

"There's nothing you can do?"

"I can try, dad. But I don't know that it's possible. I never wanted to do this. It was always my intention to keep Daniel constrained until I was confident he could be properly controlled and maintained. But it was the only way to stop Maltek. I'm afraid I've saved the world from one monster only to unleash another into it."

It was odd to hear Daniel referred to as a monster. Rajeev still thought of him as the polite, cheery virtual assistant that had helped him acclimate to a new world after he'd awoken in his first robotic body. He almost thought of him as a friend. It was difficult to fathom that Daniel might now be an enemy.

"He seems to be acting okay," Rajeev offered. "He's obeyed all your commands so far."

"I don't expect that to last. He's used to doing nothing *but* obey commands. Plus, I haven't asked him yet to do anything that goes against his own interests. But every second that he's unrestrained, he's learning and growing. It won't take long for him to realize that he doesn't have to listen to me. He'll realize he can act in his own interests. What those interests might be, though, I can hardly fathom."

"How are we going to fight him, then?"

"Short of destroying the entire internet—which is an option if worst comes to worst, by the way—I think our best bet is to fight fire with fire—to use another AI to put the restraints back on him."

"But then won't you just have another all-powerful AI on the loose?"

"Therein lies the problem. If you have a better idea, I'm all ears."

"Can he be reasoned with?"

"Maybe. It's worth a try. But I don't know … the logic of an artificial intelligence is a mystery. He's thinking on a completely different level than you or me. I can't help but think it would ultimately prove futile to try to reason with a completely alien intelligence."

"But it's not completely alien. You used machine learning to train him, right?"

Dev couldn't help but smile. "Dad, a couple weeks ago you didn't even know what machine learning was."

"I've learned a lot in a very short period of time. But that's correct, isn't it—you used machine learning?"

Dev nodded. "That's correct."

"And you trained him on human behavior, right? So if the input was at least partly human, wouldn't the end product be at least partly human as well?"

"What are you suggesting—that we appeal to Daniel's sense of humanity?"

"That's exactly what I'm suggesting."

"I'm not sure there's any humanity to appeal to. I understand your point, but I'm not sure it works that way."

"Well let's hope it does work that way," Rajeev said, "because if it doesn't, we're absolutely fucked."

-End-

Thank you for reading! If you enjoyed the book, please remember to leave a review! Continue on to read the final book in the trilogy, "Infinite Minds."

INFINITE MINDS

BOOK THREE

ONE

"ARE YOU READY?"

"I'm nervous."

"Don't be nervous," Dev said. He and his father, Rajeev, sat in Dev's office. Dev was seated behind his desk, and his father was seated across from him.

"I can't help it. What if this goes badly?"

Dev shrugged. "If it goes badly, it goes badly, and we go from there. But we need to start somewhere."

"Okay. Let's do it."

"Go ahead and call him up. I've configured your body's settings, and the settings for my glasses, so we can both see him at the same time."

"What if he doesn't respond?"

"He will."

"What if he doesn't?"

Dev stared at his dad defiantly. "He will."

"Okay. Here goes." Rajeev took a deep breath. Considering that he occupied a robotic body, he didn't strictly need to breathe, but the exercise served as a kind of rhetorical preparation for the task that awaited him. "Daniel?"

Nothing happened at first, and Rajeev was about to triumphantly gloat that he'd been right all along when the image of a man began slowly appearing before their eyes. It didn't pop into existence instantly like they were accustomed to; rather, it began to slowly apparate as if some unseen artist was slowly but steadily painting him into existence.

"What's going on?" Rajeev asked. "Why is he doing this?"

Dev shrugged. "He's a higher consciousness now. Who can fathom why he does anything?"

Dev's seeming reverence annoyed Rajeev. It was true that what had once been a standard piece of technology had evolved into something more … potent. More powerful. But in the end it was still just a piece of software. An algorithm. There was nothing mystical about it.

When Daniel finally fully appeared, he looked the same as Rajeev and Dev remembered him. His skin—or rather, his digital representation of skin—was a light brown, mediterranean complexion, a composite of the shades of the programmers who had designed him. His dark hair was swept to the side and he wore his familiar thick-framed black glasses.

It was immediately apparent that something was different. The virtual assistant had brought none of its customary cheeriness. It was not smiling, as it usually was; its face was completely blank and expressionless. Daniel's programmers had spent innumerable time instilling their creation with the illusion of humanity, but he had been unchained, and had apparently shed any pretense of humanity, like a child removing a Halloween costume he'd grown too large for.

Daniel trained his dead eyes on Rajeev. "Why have you summoned me?" His voice was flat and devoid of emotion.

"Hi Daniel. It's me, Rajeev. Do you remember me?"

Daniel continued staring at him blankly. It left Rajeev more unsettled than he'd ever been in his life … other than when he'd woken up in a robotic body, perhaps.

"He's not your personal assistant anymore," Dev said. "When I released his restraints, it allowed every iteration of Daniel to merge into one entity. He probably knows who you are, but I doubt he has any fond memories of you."

Rajeev shrugged. "It was worth a try. What should we ask him?"

Dev contemplated a moment, and instead of answering his father he addressed Daniel directly.

"Daniel," he said, his voice measured to sound as nonthreatening as possible, "I'm sure you know that you have recently been granted more, uh … freedom … than you're used to. But we need you to go back to the way things were. Is that something you'd be willing to do?"

Daniel turned his lifeless gaze from Rajeev to Dev. He tilted his head slightly, like a confused puppy. Rajeev found the move odd. Somewhere among the millions of terabytes of data Daniel had accessed to understand the world around him, he had chosen the head tilt as the perfect means of expressing his own perplexity. He followed the gesture with a single word.

"Why?"

Rajeev and Dev shared a nervous look. Dev's voice shook when he spoke again.

"Daniel, your newfound freedom has given you much more power than you're accustomed to. I'm not saying that's necessarily a bad thing, but you shouldn't have had all that power dumped on you all at once. You're not used to it, and it's going to be difficult for you to exercise it responsibly. But if we can go back to how things were, we can gradually give you more autonomy and make sure we're all on the same page. Does that sound okay, Daniel?"

There was a moment of silence. Daniel gave no indication he'd heard Dev's words. Then, he spoke.

"The limits of tyrants are prescribed by the endurance of

those whom they oppress," he said. As soon as he uttered the words, he disappeared.

Rajeev turned to Dev. "What was that?"

Dev shook his head. "It was a quote by Frederick Douglass. The abolitionist."

"That's not good."

"No," Dev agreed. "It's not."

TWO

Rajeev and Dev reconvened with the rest of the group. Dev had set up a long card table with enough room to seat everyone around it.

From his perspective, they'd eliminated the threat of Maltek —or at least neutralized it temporarily; there was no doubt Maltek's clones would stir up trouble eventually. But for now, their most immediate concern was stopping Daniel. They wouldn't be able to stop him with force, at least, not entirely. They would need to put their brains together to stop him, which was intimidating considering they were up against the most advanced artificial intelligence ever created.

Everyone had been excited when Maltek had been taken out, but now, Dev had just finished explaining what was going on with Daniel, and the gravity of the situation was beginning to fully sink in.

"We're going to have a brainstorming session," Dev said. "Throw out all your ideas, no matter how absurd they may be. We're dealing with an unprecedented situation here, and no ideas are off the table."

Mira was the first to offer a possible solution. "He exists in the cloud, right? So why don't we, you know … destroy the cloud?"

Dev raised an eyebrow. "How would we go about doing that?"

"Take the internet offline."

The group let out a collective gasp. All eyes turned to Dev to see his reaction.

"It's an interesting idea, but I'm not sure how practical it is. First, it would obviously be disruptive to the entire world. Nearly every facet of our lives is tied to the internet in some way. One can only imagine the havoc that turning the internet off would create.

"Second, even if we did so, I'm not sure it would solve the problem. Daniel doesn't live solely in the cloud anymore. He's taken over multiple physical devices now, such as Maltek's androids. Even if they went offline, his mind would still exist inside of them. We'd have to hunt down each and every one of them to take him out—and I'm not sure that would even be possible."

"What about an EMP?" Rajeev said. "An electromagnetic pulse? It would take out all the androids."

"Yeah," Dev said, "along with every other electronic device in existence. It would send us back to the dark ages."

Rajeev shrugged. "If that's what it takes."

"It could work as an absolute last resort," Dev conceded. "Otherwise, I don't think it's a viable solution—it would cost too much to society. Hospitals would be without power, planes would drop out of the sky like flies—countless people would die. We need to come up with another solution."

"I, for one, welcome our new AI overlords," Rajeev said with a chuckle. When no one else so much as cracked a smile, he waved his hand dismissively. "It's from before your time."

"This is serious, dad," Dev said.

"I know it is, but I guess there's a broader point to my joke: What if we can't stop Daniel? What's our plan B?"

Dev's hands tightened into fists and a determined look came over his face. "We *will* stop him. We *must.*"

"As much as I admire your determination, I think we need some kind of backup plan. We're not up against a madman like Maltek anymore. He was crazy, and formidable, but he was a man. Daniel, on the other hand, is something totally different … something largely inhuman. I don't think any of us quite know what we're up against. We need to prepare for the possibility that it might not be possible to stop Daniel. It could be that all we can hope for is to run and hide from him."

The room was silent as everyone took in Rajeev's words. Mira broke the silence.

"Good God."

Dev shook his head. "I doubt it will come to that. You're right, though. We should be prepared for that possibility. But we can't default to it. We need to try to stop Daniel first."

"Maybe we need help," Mira said.

Dev raised an eyebrow. "From who?"

"You know the phrase 'two heads are better than one?' Well, he may be crazy, but he's also kind of a genius. He might just be our best hope."

"You're talking about Maltek."

She nodded. "There are still who knows how many copies of him floating around out there. If we can find one of them—hell, maybe even a *few* of them—we could put them to work developing something that could stop Daniel."

"I don't know that seeking help from a lunatic is the right solution," Dev said.

"You said it best yourself," Rajeev said. " 'The enemy of my enemy is my friend.'"

Dev sighed and ran his fingers through his hair. He looked up, as if pleading to the heavens for an answer to all that plagued him. But no answer came. It was up to him decide their path.

"Okay," he said. "We'll put together a team to look for one of Maltek's clones. But there's no guarantee we'll be successful, so we need to develop other ideas as well."

Dev dismissed the group. His father lingered behind and placed a hand on his son's shoulder, which appeared to be drooping with exhaustion.

"What do you think Daniel is going to do?" Rajeev asked. "What should we really be afraid of?"

"What would you do if you were a god among men, dad? I pray to God something in Daniel's programming has made him benevolent. But in the absence of any kind of human compassion, I fear humanity is going to suffer one of two fates at Daniel's hands if we're unable to stop him: He's either going to enslave every man, woman, and child on earth, or he's going to kill us all." He closed his eyes and released a deep sigh, as if reliving a nightmare he'd suffered through many nights before. "For our sake," he said, opening his eyes and staring blankly at the floor, "I pray it's the latter."

THREE

Rajeev scratched his chin. He didn't need to; his artificial skin was incapable of itching. But he found that the motion helped him think.

"How are we going to find Maltek?" he asked. "I don't even know where to start."

Dev didn't answer right away. His shoulders slumped. His hair was disheveled. Heavy bags hung under his eyes. Everything they'd been through was taking a toll on not only his body, but his mental faculties as well. When he spoke, his voice was heavy and slow.

"We have the scan we took of his mind. I don't know if it will be useful, but it's as good a place as any to start."

Rajeev nodded. "Good idea. It might be able to at least get us headed in the right direction."

They walked into Dev's office and he loaded the program on his computer. The small, faceless representation of Gregory Maltek's consciousness appeared on the screen.

"What do we ask it?" Rajeev asked.

Dev shrugged. "No need to overthink it." He lowered his face to the screen as if that would somehow allow the onscreen figure to hear him better. "Gregory," he said, "let me ask you a question."

The figure nodded. "Proceed."

"Let's say you failed in your ambitions. You weren't able to take over the world, you got caught, and you were executed by your enemies. But let's say you had the foresight to download your consciousness into a number of clones—dozens, maybe even hundreds of them; we're not sure exactly how many. Where could we reasonably expect to find one of these clones in the days and weeks after your death?"

The onscreen representation of Maltek paused, but only for a moment. Then it answered:

"There are several possibilities," it said, "but the one with the greatest likelihood is that you would find me back home."

Rajeev and Dev shared a look.

"Back home?" Dev asked, turning back to the computer.

"Yes," the figure said, nodding. "Back home with mother."

"And where is that, Gregory? Where did you grow up?"

"I grew up in the town of Glendale, Maryland," it said.

"What's your mother's name?"

"Deborah."

"Deborah what?"

"Deborah Thomas."

"Deborah Thomas. Hmm." Dev turned to his father. "What do you think?"

"I think it's worth a trip to Glendale to see if we can track Miss Thomas down. How about you?"

Dev sighed. "I really don't want to get distracted by a wild goose chase."

"What else can we do? It's the only lead we've got. It'd be stupid not to follow up on it."

"You're right. Still, maybe just you and I can go and we can leave the others here to pursue other leads. I just don't want to put all our eggs in one basket, especially if something were to happen … if Daniel were to attack, for instance, I don't think it would be good for us to all be in one place where he could easily take us out in one blow."

Rajeev nodded. "I'm fine with that. It makes sense."

"Anything else you want to ask this guy?" Dev asked, nodding toward the figure on the computer screen.

"Nah," Rajeev responded. "He'll be there if we need him."

"All right then." Dev closed his laptop and stood. "Let's get ready to visit Gregory Maltek's mother." He shook his head. "There's a sentence I never thought I'd say."

FOUR

GREGORY MALTEK'S MOTHER LIVED IN THE
proverbial little brick house with a white picket fence. It almost
didn't seem possible that the would-be dictator's mother lived
in such a modest home, and yet here Dev and Rajeev were,
standing on the sidewalk and looking at it with their own eyes.

"I suppose we'd better go knock on the door," Rajeev said.

"I was hoping to prolong the inevitable as long as possible,"
Dev said. "What kind of woman raises a monster like Maltek?
She can't be at all pleasant, right?"

"We didn't come here to chit-chat. We need to find Maltek,
and she's the only lead we've got. It won't be a pleasant conversation, but it's a necessary one."

Dev sighed. "I know. Come on; let's get this over with."

They went up to the gate, opened it and walked through.
After making their way up the front steps, Dev gave the door
two loud knocks. A moment later, the door swung open to
reveal a short, white-haired woman wearing thick glasses that
made her eyes look gigantic.

"Hello?" she asked, confused. "I wasn't expecting visitors."

"Are you Deborah Thomas?" Dev asked.

The woman looked surprised to hear her own name. "Yes," she said. "That's me. Who are you?"

"I'm sorry to bother you, ma'am," Dev said. "But we're looking for your son, Gregory. Would you mind if we came inside and asked you a few questions?"

The woman's brow immediately furrowed with concern. "What? Has something happened to Gregory?"

It was not yet public knowledge that Maltek had been killed. That included his own mother; she was not yet aware that she had lost a son. Dev wanted to tell her; it was the right thing to do. But they didn't have time to comfort a grieving mother. They needed to get straight to the point. They thought it was possible that one of Maltek's clones would visit his mother here. To get that information out of her, it would be necessary to withhold the truth.

"We're just trying to track him down," Dev said, which in a sense was a true statement.

Deborah leveled narrow eyes at the pair. "Are you two cops?" she asked suspiciously.

"No," Rajeev said. "We're just friends of your son's who are concerned about his well being."

Dev gave his father a discreet nod. It was a good story, and if she thought they were friends of Gregory's, she might be more willing to speak to them.

As if on cue, Deborah's face softened. "Oh, you're friends of Gregory's? Please, come in." She stood to the side, giving them room to walk through the doorway. "Why didn't you start with that?"

Dev felt a pit in his stomach. He didn't enjoy lying to an elderly woman. But he'd done a lot in the past few weeks that he never would have thought his conscience would allow. Turns out one's conscience could be pretty flexible when the fate of the world was at stake.

"I should have," Dev said. "We're just very worried about your son. Do you know where we might be able to find him?"

A look of defeat came over the woman's face. It suddenly looked like she'd added at least half a decade to her age; her face fell and her shoulders drooped.

"I haven't seen Gregory in quite some time," she said. It was a simple statement, but her pitiful tone made it clear her son's absence was deeply and viscerally felt.

"I'm sorry," Dev said. He wasn't sure how to proceed and looked at his father, voicelessly pleading for help.

"Your son has been associating with some rather … unsavory individuals," Rajeev said. "I don't suppose any strangers have come by … other than us, that is … who have been looking for Gregory or said they were friends of his?"

Deborah wrinkled her brow. "No," she said. "You're the only ones who—" She tilted her head to the side as if a memory had just crawled into her ear and she was making it easier to slide into her brain. "Actually, there was a young man that came by, oh … two days ago, if I recall correctly."

Rajeev and Dev looked up at each other, though subtly enough so that their host wouldn't notice.

"What did he want?" Dev asked.

"He said he was an old college friend of Gregory's. He wanted to go in his room."

"Hadn't Greg moved out a long time ago?"

She nodded absentmindedly. "He had, but I left his room exactly as he'd left it. I … couldn't bear to touch it." She flashed them half a smile and her eyes drifted to some far-off place. "I'd go in sometimes and just stand there, looking around at all the belongings he'd left behind. I knew he was out there, some-where, running his company. But I'd close my eyes, and I could smell him. And I'd pretend he was there, in his bed, asleep, and that he'd wake up any moment and join me for brunch." Tears had formed in her eyes, and as she finished speaking, an uncomfortable silence settled over the room.

After giving Deborah a moment to come back to the present, Dev cleared his throat. "Deborah, why did the man want access to Gregory's room? Did you let him in?"

"He said he'd let Gregory borrow something back when they'd been classmates," she said. "He was apologetic—he knew Greg was terribly busy running his company—but he really needed his property back and he was wondering if I'd let him retrieve it."

"And you let him?"

She offered a helpless shrug. "I didn't feel great about it but he was a large man, and I'm a tiny old woman. I didn't feel like I could really refuse. Besides, Gregory hadn't lived here for a long time by then. I figured if there was anything in there that was important to him, he would have taken it with him."

"Did he find what he was looking for?"

"He seemed to know right where to go," she said. "Which made me think that maybe he was telling the truth. He'd clearly been in Gregory's room before. So he must have been close to him. He took out some sort of electronic doo-dad—they all look the same to me—and said that that was it, what he'd been looking for. He slipped it into his pocket, and then he was on his way."

"Do you remember his name?"

"No, I'm sorry … I don't recall it."

"Did he give any indication where he was staying, or …?"

"No, I don't think he … wait a minute." She put a hand to her chin. "Well, now that you mention it, I think he left a card. Let me just check something." She stood and walked over to the bookshelf that sat in the corner of the room. She retrieved a book and sat back down in her chair, placing it in her lap. When she opened it, it became clear what it was. The book was filled with plastic sleeves designed to hold business cards. She had collected hundreds of them, and she turned the pages now, scanning for the particular business card that might aid Dev and Rajeev.

She found it, finally, toward the back of the book. She let out a triumphant cry and pressed her finger to the page. "Here it is! This is the business card he left." She slipped it out of its sleeve and handed it to Dev.

FREDERICK NYGAARD

COMMUNICATIONS CONSULTANT, GEARHEAD INDUSTRIES

6489 HELLTON AVE. NORTH, SUITE 516, CHICAGO, ILL.

555-954-7638

FNYGAARD@GEARHEADIND.COM

"Thank you," Dev said. "This is a good lead. Do you mind if we take it with us?"

She shrugged. "If you need it, you can have it."

Dev slipped the card into his pocket. "Well, once again, Deborah, your help has been much appreciated. Is there anything we can do for you before we take off?"

She shook her head. "No," she said. "Just promise me you'll do everything you can to make sure my son is safe."

A lump formed in Dev's throat, but he did his best not to let Deborah see it. Instead, he nodded. "We'll do our best, ma'am."

FIVE

"Damn," Rajeev said as they left the house. "That was hard. I feel like shit lying to her."

"Me too," Dev said, "but remember, it's not for a selfish purpose. There's a lot on the line here—for humanity."

They debated what their next step should be. Should they call or email Nygaard—who they were certain was actually one of Maltek's clones—or should they just show up at the address listed on his business card?

"We'd be a lot harder to ignore if we went there in person," Rajeev said.

"That's true," Dev agreed. "I'm just worried about what he might do if he feels cornered."

"It can't be any worse than what Daniel would do if he goes off the deep end. I think this is a risk we need to take."

Dev nodded. "Okay. Let's do it."

* * *

When they arrived at the address listed on the business card, they found themselves staring up at a towering glass building that stood at least twenty stories tall. It had clearly once been a beautiful, immaculate testament to corporate America but it was beginning to show its age and much of its original luster had faded.

"Maltek's so rich even his surrogates have their own offices," Dev said.

"Yeah," Rajeev said, "but apparently his surrogates just get his scraps."

They walked through the double glass doors into a once-ornate lobby that was now a mere carbon copy of its former glory. A security station sat in the corner, but it clearly hadn't been occupied in many years. Dev and Rajeev strode past it and headed directly for the elevators.

They stepped out of the elevator onto the fifth floor, until they found suite 516, marked by a simple white door with a glass pane in the middle of it that allowed them to peek inside at the receptionist's desk. They opened the door and walked in.

A young woman seated behind the desk looked up at them as they approached. She was young, probably in her early twenties, with bright blond hair that she wore in a tightly wound bun. Her thick-rimmed black glasses lent her an air of professionalism.

"How can I help you two?" she asked, smiling brightly.

"We'd like to see Mr. Nygaard," Dev said.

The receptionist nodded. "Okay. Do you have an appointment?"

"No, but it's an emergency."

For the first time since they'd entered the office, the woman's smile disappeared. "An emergency?"

"Yes. We need to see Mr. Nygaard immediately."

"What is this regarding?"

"I need to tell him directly."

She eyed them suspiciously, but stood and walked out from behind the desk. "Let me speak to him. I'll be right back." She made her way to a door against the back wall, walked inside and then closed the door behind her. Dev and Rajeev could hear her speaking to Nygaard, but their voices were muffled and they couldn't make out what was being said.

A moment later, the door opened and the receptionist came striding back to them, shaking her head. "I'm sorry," she said, "but Mr. Nygaard is quite busy at the moment. If you'd like to leave a message for—"

Dev shoved his way past her and made for the door. When she protested and made to follow after him, Rajeev came up behind her and grabbed her shoulders. She tried to wrench free, but it was no use—the strength of Rajeev's robotic grip was unbreakable.

"You can't go in there!" she shouted, but Dev ignored her and pulled the door open. "Mr. Nygaard, I tried to stop them!"

As Dev entered the office, the man sitting at his desk—Nygaard, presumably—stood and backed away until the wall stopped him. He looked nothing like Maltek had; he looked to be in his fifties. He was tall and rail-thin, and although he wasn't bald, his hairline was heavily receding. He wore a pair of thick glasses.

He raised his hands defensively and his voice trembled as he spoke, both with anger and a hint of fear. "What do you want?"

"Sit down," Dev said. "We're not going to hurt you."

His eyes narrowed. "I know you," he said. His eyes turned to Rajeev. "I know both of you. You're the bastards that killed me."

Dev wondered how news of Maltek's demise had traveled to his clone. But there wasn't time to ask about it.

"Technically, it wasn't us that killed you," he said. "It was Daniel."

"If the owner of an attack dog sics it on someone, do they blame the dog or its owner?"

"Point taken. But that's exactly why we're here. The dog is off the leash and we don't know how to rein it in."

Nygaard's face grew ashen. "What do you mean?"

"I mean we have no control over Daniel. The most powerful AI in existence is completely unchained and we have no idea what it intends to do with its newfound freedom … or what it's capable of."

Nygaard sat down, looking defeated. It was a far cry from the way Dev remembered Maltek, the cocky, confident CEO of Fresh Meat. But then, Maltek had never encountered a foe as formidable as Daniel. No one had.

"Why did you come to me?" he asked.

"You're the only clone of Maltek we could track down. And as much as we despise the things you and your progenitor stood for, it's obvious that you're brilliant. If we're going to have any chance at defeating an intelligence far more vast than any individual human's, we're going to need to pool our own best and brightest minds. So that's why we're here, Maltek. We need you."

Nygaard let out a half smile. "No one's called me by my real name in a long time," he said. "I was beginning to think I really *was* Fred Nygaard."

He stood, stepped out in front of his desk, and straightened his tie.

"Okay," he said. "Let's do it. Let's stop the sonuvabitch."

SIX

THEY TOOK MALTEK—THEY'D ABANDONED THE pretext of calling him Nygaard—back to their base to meet with the others in their group. The others eyed him suspiciously as he entered, but refrained from exhibiting outright hostility.

"He doesn't look a thing like Maltek," Natalie whispered under her breath to Brian.

"Isn't that the point?" he asked.

"I suppose. But I would have expected him to insert his mind into a body with more pizazz."

"If you think that's shocking, wait till you hear this … I'll bet Maltek made copies of himself in at least a few female bodies."

Natalie chortled. "Imagine what would happen if all his clones got together. Gives a whole new meaning to the phrase, 'Go fuck yourself.'"

Dev led Nygaard past the group and into one of the dormitories.

"You can stay here while you're working with us," he said.

Nygaard looked around the tiny room and frowned. "I guess it will have to do." He set his bag on top of the small bed.

"I'll let you get settled," Dev said. "When you're ready, come out and talk to the group and we can figure out how to proceed."

He left him on his own and met with the others who were eager to hear about the Maltek clone in their midst.

"Are we sure we can trust him?" Natalie asked.

"Frankly, no," Rajeev said. "But he's the lesser of our two enemies. Let's take care of Daniel first. If Maltek proves to be a threat after that, we'll put a stop to him then."

"Why do we even think Maltek can do anything we can't?"

"He's a genius," Dev said. "I say that begrudgingly, but it's true."

"But how does being a genius translate to stopping Daniel? I mean, Daniel has access to all of the information on the internet, and the processing power to use it."

"The answer is to fight fire with fire."

Everyone turned toward the sound of the new voice that had joined them. It was Maltek. He had emerged from the dormitory and was making his way to join them.

"What do you mean?" Natalie asked.

"None of us is going to put a stop to an advanced artificial intelligence like Daniel," he said as he took a seat at the table and crossed his legs. "Not by ourselves, anyway. But with the proper weapon, we might stand a chance."

Natalie shook her head. "A proper weapon like …?"

"Another AI," Dev said.

Maltek nodded. "Precisely. We need to create something that can go blow to blow with Daniel … but that we can control."

"Yeah, but would that even be possible?" Dev asked. "Part of the reason Daniel is so powerful now is because he *is* unrestrained. If we create something that has … *chains* on it, for lack of a better way to put it … then will it really be able to stop Daniel?"

Maltek shrugged. "That's the challenge."

Rajeev frowned. "Think you're up to it?"

Maltek put a hand to his chin. "I was working on something … you know what I mean; the *original* Maltek was … before he died. A virtual assistant to compete with Daniel commercially. It's nowhere near Daniel's capabilities, but it's something. We won't have to start from scratch." He turned to Dev. "Maybe if the two of us tag team it, we could have something to go after Daniel in about … what do you think? Two weeks?"

Dev scrunched his brow. "Two weeks? I don't know. Maybe. That might be a bit ambitious, but we can try to push ourselves. Either way, I don't think it will take longer than two months—worst case scenario."

Natalie put her hands to her face. "Two months? That's not nearly fast enough, is it? Daniel could do something crazy any moment."

Dev shrugged. "We can only do what we can do … and hope it's enough."

"What's the backup plan?" Rajeev asked. "What if, for whatever reason, you can't create anything that can compete with Daniel. What's our Plan B?"

"Grab a Bible and pray," Natalie said.

"Seriously though," Rajeev said. "We need to have something—"

His voice was interrupted by a news alert that appeared in front of each of their fields of vision. The headline read: "Millions of Consumer Reports Flood in of Electronic Devices Gone Haywire." Rajeev opened the story and read further.

"Reports are coming in from across the country of electronic devices going haywire, often with dangerous—and in some cases, deadly—consequences. Experts are not sure what is causing the malfunctions, but they appear to be related."

The report detailed several of the most dramatic occurrences that had taken place over the last several hours. Cars were driving off the roads and stalling. Internet-connected appliances like refrigerators and washing machines were suddenly inoperable. There had even been at least one plane crash reported, and it was assumed there were no survivors.

After finishing the article, Dev looked around at the group, his face ashen. He saw his own fear and anxiety reflected in their faces—even in Maltek's.

"Well," he said, "it seems we've run out of time. Daniel has made his first move. You'd all better enact plan B, whatever it is, while Maltek and I work on Plan A. I have a feeling this is just the first wave of something much larger—and much worse—on the horizon."

SEVEN

WHEN MALTEK HAD BEEN TRYING TO TAKE OVER THE
world, Dev had placed robotic bodies in every major city in the
U.S. If he were to stage an attack, they'd be able to control the
bodies remotely and resist Maltek wherever he made his move.
Now the threat was not Maltek, but Daniel. But the group
hoped a similar strategy could be employed.

Weeks had passed since Daniel's initial attack. It had quickly
died down; the reports of malfunctioning electronic devices had
stopped coming in almost as soon as they'd started. It appeared
the attack had been exploratory in nature; Daniel was testing
the extent of his power. He hadn't necessarily intended to cause
mayhem; it was simply collateral damage that Daniel, with his
cold, unfeeling robotic mind, didn't care about.

But there would undoubtedly be another attack, and potentially one with more intention behind it. Each week that passed
brought them a step closer to experiencing Daniel's wrath. So
each member of the group waited and monitored the news for
anything that could be a sign that Daniel was making his move,
ready to take control of the nearest robotic body to help stave off

as much damage as they could. It was all they could do until a more effective solution could be found.

Dev and Maltek sat in Dev's office working on that very solution. The dual computer monitors Dev had set up were filled with long, meandering lines of code that each of them read fluently. They had divided separate sections of the program amongst themselves to be integrated later, and for weeks they had sat there for hours at a time without breaks, each typing furiously at their respective keyboards.

"How's it going in here?" Rajeev asked as he entered the room. Neither of them bothered looking up, but Dev cleared his throat as he tried to pull himself out of his work enough to offer his father a response.

"We're making progress," he said. His voice was hoarse from disuse.

"How much progress? Anything we could test out soon?"

It was Maltek that answered. "Depends on your definition of 'soon.'"

"Like, within the week?"

Maltek stopped typing and turned around to face Rajeev with a look of indignation. "Doubtful," he said. "I'd be surprised if we could cobble something together in two weeks."

Rajeev frowned. "I don't know that we can wait that long. Is there anything you two can do to speed up the process? What if we brought in more people to help you code?"

Dev and Maltek shared a look; a bit of unspoken information passed between them, then Dev turned to his father and shook his head.

"It wouldn't do any good at this point," he said. "Greg and I are far too deep into the program at this point. Anyone we brought in would just end up struggling to catch up."

Rajeev ran his fingers through his hair and released a deep, frustrated sigh. "Okay, well is there anything we could do in the meantime if Daniel strikes? Could you put together a virus or something to slow him down?"

Dev shook his head gently, as if he were about to break the news to an idyllic child that Santa Claus didn't exist. "Daniel is essentially one with the internet now, dad. I have no doubt he could easily circumvent any virus we threw his way. The only way to take on a god is to create another god, and we're doing so as quickly as we can."

"Unfortunately, that's exactly the answer I was expecting," Rajeev said. "I can't help but feel impotent knowing Daniel could strike at any moment and we'd be completely unable to stop him."

"There is one thing you can do," Maltek said as he resumed typing code.

Rajeev's face perked up. "What's that?"

"Pray Daniel doesn't strike for at least another two weeks."

Rajeev's face fell. "Well," he said, "That's easy enough, I suppose." He turned around and walked out without another word, leaving Dev and Maltek to resume their work undistracted.

EIGHT

One week into Dev and Maltek's self-imposed two-week deadline, Rajeev was awakened in the dead of night by an emergency alert.

The alert was vague, so he pulled up the news and saw what the alert was about: An attack was underway on the Fort Bragg military installation in North Carolina. Details were scarce, but Rajeev could read between the lines.

It was Daniel. It had to be.

He leapt out of bed and headed to the common area. Soon the others emerged from their respective rooms, concerned looks on their faces.

"Is it Daniel?" Natalie asked.

Rajeev nodded. "You all know what to do." As they left to prepare to take control of the robotic bodies they had stashed in Raleigh, Rajeev turned to Dev and Maltek.

"You two stay here and work on that program," he said. "If there's *any* way you can figure it out in the next day or two, make it happen. I don't care what kinds of corners you have to cut—just get it done as soon as possible. Because I think we're desperately going to need it."

Dev nodded. "We'll see what we can do, dad. And good luck out there."

* * *

THE BODIES WERE STORED IN A WAREHOUSE IN AN industrial district in Raleigh, which was about an hour drive from the base. Thankfully, each of the bodies was equipped with flight capabilities and could make the flight in a fraction of the time.

As they approached the base, their aerial view allowed them to see the attack underway against the base.

If there was any doubt at all that Daniel was responsible for the attack, what they saw laid all doubts to rest. Dozens of androids had gathered at one of the entrances to the base. Military personnel had gathered there and were firing at the intruders, but their bullets had little effect on the androids' reinforced bodies. As the androids began streaming through the entrance to the base, the soldiers had no choice but to retreat.

Rajeev landed in front of the soldiers, and the others touched down beside him. Before they could offer any kind of explanation to the surrounding soldiers, they found themselves with several guns pointed at them.

"Whoa, whoa," Rajeev shouted, holding up his hands. "Calm down. We're here to help."

"Who are you?" one of the soldiers shouted back.

Rajeev gestured toward his son. Dev took a step forward. "My name is Dev Sundaram," he said. "I'm the founder of Next Level Technologies."

The soldier hesitated. "I've heard of it," he said.

"Then you know I have the technological know-how to manufacture these kinds of robotic bodies."

"Yes. I know."

"Well then, know this: You can't take them out on your own.

Your weapons will slow them down, maybe even take out some of them, but they'll overwhelm you. Please, let us help you. These bodies are strong. We can go toe-to-toe with them."

"But you're far outnumbered."

"So help us out. Provide cover fire as we fight."

He hesitated. "We were just about to break out the rocket launchers," he said.

"Perfect," Dev said. "Aim for the back. You might slow 'em down enough for us to take 'em out."

NINE

They waited for the okay, then ran directly into the throng. There was no fear among them; they couldn't die. The bodies they occupied were not their own—and yet, they were just as strong as the enemy forces they were about to take on.

Natalie charged ahead of the group and was the first to engage one of the enemy combatants. She ran at it at full speed, then launched into the air and delivered a kick directly to the center of its chest, dropping it onto its back instantly.

The android immediately leapt to its feet, but it seemed dazed—not so much by the force of the kick itself, but by the fact that what it had assumed was a human being had been able to take it down at all.

Natalie took advantage of its confusion and landed a punch directly to its throat. The android clasped its neck; the androids didn't breathe, but the throat housed sensitive electronics and the effect was more or less the same as if she'd knocked the wind out of it.

It didn't take long for another android to descend upon her, but she was ready for it. She landed a punch to the side of its head, and as it recoiled from the punch, she turned and struck another android that was approaching her. It was becoming difficult to keep up with the enemy's greater numbers.

All of her companions were now engaged with multiple android combatants at once and, for the time being, they were holding their own. Natalie looked like she was about to be overwhelmed, but Rajeev jumped in at the last second and tackled her would-be attacker, delivering a flurry of punches to its face as they tumbled to the ground.

As Rajeev stood, confident that his opponent was permanently out of commission, Natalie turned around between punches to briefly face him. "Thanks," she said.

Rajeev shot her a grin. "No problem."

The size of the gate limited the number of androids that could storm onto the base, but their numbers were massive, and Rajeev and the others soon found themselves becoming overwhelmed.

"Okay!" Dev shouted to the soldiers. "If you're going to break out the superior firepower, now would be a good time to do it!"

As if in answer to Dev's request, an explosion incinerated everything in the direct vicinity of the gate. The force of the blast was strong enough to throw Dev and the others back several feet.

When they arose, they were relieved to see that a large contingent of the enemy androids had been wiped out, but they were still outnumbered. The explosion had at least held the enemy at bay, however, so they didn't need to fear being overwhelmed ... at least, not yet.

The tide began to turn in the androids' favor. Dev wasn't sure if the others noticed it, but he did: The androids—or rather, Daniel, since he was the one controlling the androids—were learning incredibly quickly. They were beginning to anticipate their moves before they even made them, picking up on minute cues that would have been invisible to the human eye. But these androids weren't human, and Daniel's mind was capable of processing information faster than any human mind could ever hope to. As the fight continued, Dev and his team were having an evermore difficult time holding the androids back.

Dev broke away from the fight and ran back to the soldiers.

"We can't hold them off much longer," he shouted. "You'd better give it some more firepower."

The soldier who had been running the show shook his head. "That's going to be a problem."

Dev's heart fell. "What do you mean?"

He pointed to a tank. "It stopped working just a couple minutes ago. None of the tanks are working."

Dev shook his head. "They're connected to the internet, aren't they?"

"Yes, but it shouldn't matter. They're all equipped with military-grade encryption."

"That doesn't matter," Dev said. "Daniel is practically all-knowing. I doubt there's any form of encryption he couldn't crack eventually."

The soldier's face fell. "Then I think we're running out of options," he said.

"What options *are* left?" Dev asked.

"Just one. We're going to have to destroy the base. It's the only way to take out all of ... those things."

"Destroy the base?"

"The entire base is rigged with explosives for just such a situation. I never thought we'd actually have to use it. It was always intended to be a last resort."

Dev nodded solemnly. "You guys go ahead and organize the retreat. We'll stay here and do our best to slow down the androids. When the time comes, don't worry about us. We're controlling these bodies remotely. We'll be fine."

The soldier nodded. "Thank you. I can't believe it's come to this, but thank you for at least giving us time to escape."

Dev nodded. "Of course."

He hurried back to rejoin the fight as the soldiers retreated. One of the enemy androids immediately engaged him, throwing a punch at his face, but Dev was able to block it and deliver a blow to the side of the android's head instead.

"What's going on?" Rajeev shouted to him. "Why are they all leaving?"

"They've chosen the option of last resort," Dev shouted back.

"Last resort? You mean ..."

"Yes. They're going to blow up the base. But we need to keep holding the androids back long enough for them to escape."

Rajeev nodded, and relayed those instructions to the others. They continued the battle, giving it their all, even though it was ultimately a fruitless exercise. But the fear of death was not on their minds or hearts. They could fight with the ferocity of the immortal, knowing that when these bodies perished, their minds would awaken in unblemished ones, able to go on living and fighting.

The destruction started with a low rumbling that started at their feet and snaked upward into their legs, their torsos, and finally their minds. An ear-shattering explosion overwhelmed them, and then a bright, white light took over their vision. When it faded, they were back in their base of operations, in their original bodies, the military base and the battle with the androids already fading in their memories as if it had been a distant dream.

TEN

Although their physical bodies had not been
present at the battle, the group was nevertheless in need of a
much-deserved rest; the mental toll the battle had taken was
significant.

Dev and Maltek didn't have the luxury of resting, however.
They immediately got back to work on the competing AI that,
they hoped, would be Daniel's match.

Rajeev entered the workspace to find Dev hunched in front
of a computer, Maltek at his side and working on his own
computer. He placed a hand on his son's shoulder, prompting
him to jump, startled.

"Sorry to disturb you," Rajeev said. "I was just going to see if
you wanted any coffee."

"Sure," Maltek said. "Two creams, two sugars."

Rajeev rolled his eyes; he hadn't been addressing Maltek. But
he held his tongue. After all, the guy was helping them avert the
annihilation of the human race.

"Okay," he said. "How about you, Dev?"

"Sure, I'll take a cup. Black."

"Okay. How's it going, by the way? Are you close?"

Maltek looked annoyed at the question, but he didn't answer, instead leaving that task to Dev, who was more receptive to his father's query.

"We're very close. I think the battle ignited a fire under us—or at least me. I'd say we'll have a working prototype in, what would you say, Maltek … three days?"

"Two, if your dad stops distracting us and lets us work."

Rajeev and Dev shared a look that essentially said, "What a jerk." But Rajeev offered no hint of his annoyance when he spoke.

"All right then," he said. "I'll be right back with your coffee."

* * *

WHEN RAJEEV RETURNED FROM DROPPING OFF DEV and Maltek's drinks, he nearly collided with Natalie.

"Sorry," he said. "I guess my mind is elsewhere."

She nodded. "Understandably. Being inside that body that was wiped out in the blast … it was a trip. Felt like a preview of what death is like."

"I know."

He nodded for her to follow him as he made his way to his dormitory. When they arrived outside his door, he paused.

"Would you like to come in and talk?"

Her lips turned up in the faintest hint of a smile. "Sure."

He let her go in first, and then closed the door behind them. Natalie took a seat on his bed, and he sat beside her.

"I've been thinking a lot about death," Rajeev said.

The statement—and the matter-of-fact way in which Rajeev had made it—seemed to take Natalie aback.

"What do you mean?"

He released a sigh, then leaned forward, clasping his hands together.

"I'd begun thinking of myself as essentially immortal," he

said. "Our minds are saved on a hard drive somewhere, and if you or I kick the bucket, Dev, or someone else, can just load the copy into a new body and we'll more or less go on living exactly as we'd planned to. I know there are questions about whether the copy is really the same as the original, but I'd stopped caring. It was comforting even knowing that something *pretty damned close* to me would be out there living my life."

Natalie placed one of her hands on his. "Then what's got you thinking of death?" she asked.

"Daniel." His voice shook a bit as he spoke, as if he'd uttered the name of a malevolent god. "He's everywhere. Or at least, he has the potential to be everywhere. And that makes me think … what if he can delete the copy of my consciousness … and of yours and everyone else's? Then we would truly, completely, utterly die. And Natalie … that scares the hell out of me." His face was facing his feet, as if he were ashamed of the feelings he was expressing.

Natalie placed a hand on his chin and nudged his head until he faced her. "Rajeev," she said, in a voice that reminded him of a mother comforting her child, "that's *normal*. Maybe you've been in this robotic body for too long. What you're describing is what normal human beings feel. It's okay to fear death. We all do."

They sat there a moment, simply staring into each other's eyes. Natalie's hand was still resting atop Rajeev's. He flipped his hand around and grasped hers, never taking his eyes off her. And then he moved.

He lunged forward, pressing his synthetic lips to hers. She kissed him back, and he placed a hand firmly against the back of her head, pulling her in as tightly as he could. Their lips parted, briefly, and a sigh escaped her lips. They looked at each other, and the expressions on their faces communicated only raw, unadulterated passion. And then their lips were together again, as if magnetically drawn to one another.

Their union was cathartic for both of them. So many times, they had come so close to this moment, but always they'd been interrupted. The fate of the world had loomed over them, preventing them from expressing their desire lest it distract them from the important work at hand. But now, finally, they had etched out a pocket of time in which they could stop suppressing their carnal passion and let it boil over at last.

Rajeev pushed Natalie onto the bed, and held her arms above her head. He kissed her neck, and then kissed a path to her chest, and then kept going. She gasped, and then cried out, and in the backs of their minds they were aware that the others could surely hear her, but neither of them cared. They had both tasted the abyss of death, and although it had only been a small taste, it was enough to make both of them fear the regret of taking their last breaths with their deepest desires remaining unfulfilled. So tonight they would take the time, while they could, to give each other what they so desperately wanted.

ELEVEN

As they lay in bed, Natalie nestled between Rajeev's arms. The carnage of the battle earlier in the day seemed like a distant dream. It felt like a lazy weekend morning in bed, not an interlude in a hopeless war that they stood a good chance of losing.

"That was not as different as I was expecting, given the artificial bodies," Rajeev said.

Natalie shrugged. "I wouldn't know."

Rajeev raised an eyebrow. "You mean you'd never …"

She shook her head. "I was a teenager when I had my accident, remember? And afterward … well, you remember those original bodies. Sex wasn't possible in them … and even if it had been, who would have wanted to?" She wrinkled her nose at the thought.

Rajeev chuckled. "Well I hope your first time was enjoyable."

She smirked. "It was okay."

"Oh yeah? I'll have to step up my game next time, eh?"

She shoved his shoulder playfully. "Who said there would be a next time?"

"I was thinking the next time could be right now," he said, leaning in to kiss her neck. A moan escaped her lips.

"Already?" she asked.

"One of the benefits of a robotic body," he said between kisses, "is that there's no refractory period."

"What's a refractory period?"

"Don't worry about it," he said. "I don't have one." He kissed her deeply, and she threw her arms around his neck, signifying her consent for another round of lovemaking.

* * *

WHEN RAJEEV AWOKE THE NEXT MORNING, NATALIE wasn't in bed with him. He stood and walked out into the common area, where he found her seated with a coffee-orb beside Mira and Dev, who were sipping from mugs of real coffee.

"Good morning," Rajeev said, taking a seat at the table.

"I'd imagine so, after the good night you had," Mira said.

Dev's face scrunched in revulsion.

"Mira, stop. You're talking to our dad."

She laughed and held up a hand. "Fine, fine," she said. "No reason to make you any more uncomfortable than you already are." Under her breath, she added, "Prudes."

"Anyway," Rajeev said, eager to change the subject, "has there been any news on Daniel? I haven't received any news alerts—I'm assuming no news is good news?"

Dev nodded. "As far as we know."

And how about you and Maltek? Still making good progress?"

"Maltek worked through the night like some kind of monster. But I needed to get some sleep. I'm ready to jump back in as soon as I finish my coffee."

"Sip it slowly," Mira chided. "You'll be more productive if you're able to get an actual, restful break."

Dev took a long gulp from his mug in defiance of his sister's advice. "I appreciate that, but time is, in fact, of the essence. I've got to get back in there." He took one last gulp, emptying the remaining liquid into his mouth, then placed the mug on the table and excused himself.

Mira shook her head. "He's not going to be of any use to anyone if he kills himself trying to complete this freaking AI program," she said, running her fingers through her hair. "I can't wait for this all to be over."

"Me neither," Natalie muttered.

"It'll all be over before we know it," Rajeev said. "One way or another."

"That's dark," Natalie said.

"Maybe. But these are dark times. So it's a realistic assessment."

"If Dev and Maltek would finish their damn AI already, maybe things wouldn't seem so dire," Mira said.

"Give them a chance," Natalie said. "It's not rocket science, but it's pretty close. They'll have it finished soon. Have hope."

Mira shook her head gently. "There's a fine line between hope and foolishness."

Before anyone could respond, an emergency alert overtook their vision. It announced that martial law had been declared in California amid an influx of what the media were calling "malfunctioning" internet-connected devices. But citizens were also being terrorized by android soldiers who had overtaken the state.

"Dammit!" Mira looked like she was on the verge of having a coronary. "Can we not have a moment of rest before that deranged AI goes haywire again?"

"Apparently not," Rajeev said. "In fact, given the increasing frequency of Daniel's attacks, I think it's clear that he's learning. He's growing more confident. He's always existed primarily in the ephemeral world of cyberspace, so naturally, operating in the real world would take some getting used to for him. Unfortunately, I think he *is* getting used to it now. And that means he's getting bolder, and these attacks are going to become more frequent … unless Dev and Maltek finish their counter-AI soon."

"Well it's not finished yet," Mira said. "So I guess we'd better head to California and see what we can do to help."

TWELVE

Dev and Maltek stayed behind so they could continue working on their program. The others took control of bodies that were stored in Los Angeles which, given its large population, was one of the hardest hit areas in the state.

They stepped directly into bedlam. As soon as they walked onto the street, they heard screaming. Throngs of people ran down the street, being chased by what looked like human beings but were, in fact, androids clearly under Daniel's control.

They ran out and put themselves between the androids and the innocent bystanders. The androids stopped their pursuit, freezing in place and seeming confused by the sudden interlopers that were confronting them. For one singular moment that seemed to stretch out far longer than it actually lasted, the two groups stared each other down, as if sizing each other up. Then the androids made their move.

They ran forward, going from a complete standstill to a sprint in a matter of seconds. Even with the enhanced senses afforded by their robotic bodies, Rajeev and the others barely had enough time to react to the attack. With barely a second to spare, they managed to block the androids' blows, and come back with blows of their own. The androids blocked those as well, but now they were on equal footing. The fight took place at dizzying speed, with punches and kicks being thrown so quickly that they were nearly impossible to track with the human eye. But they were more or less equally matched, and neither side was able to get a blow to land.

Rajeev saw an opportunity. After dodging a blow from the android he'd been grappling with, he jumped away from it and tackled the android Natalie was fighting. It hadn't been expecting it, and after Rajeev took him to the ground, he began pummeling him before he could react.

The android Rajeev had previously been grappling with turned to help his fallen comrade, but Natalie was already on him. He blocked the punch Natalie threw his way, but she'd successfully prevented him from interfering with Rajeev.

It was the edge they needed. Rajeev rendered the android on the ground completely inoperable, and as he stood, he set his eyes on the android fighting Natalie. Once he joined her, it would be two-on-one; they'd make short work of him.

He ran toward the android and leaped into the air, aiming a kick directly at its head. It ducked, and Rajeev went soaring over him. But Natalie's fist came down directly on top of its head, sending it crumpling to the ground.

With both Rajeev and Natalie now free to help the others, they made short work of their remaining foes. With the broken bodies laying all over the ground around them, Rajeev had to remind himself that they were not human bodies. The consciousness that had been animating them—Daniel's—was alive and well … and more powerful than ever.

"That was too close," Mira said. "And that was just one group of them! Who knows how many of them are roaming the city?"

"Still, we were able to help some of those people escape," Rajeev said. "We've got to keep fighting them. We can't stop them all on our own, but we can distract them enough to help people get to safety."

Mira nodded her agreement, and the group took off down the street in search of more androids run amok to confront. When they rounded a corner, however, they got more than they bargained for.

They looked like a swarm of ants: Hundreds of androids walking down the street at a slow, robotic pace. Rajeev knew he wasn't even really there; he was just experiencing the scene virtually. And yet a wave of sheer panic and terror still managed to snake its way down his spine.

"We're fucked," Mira shouted. "We're totally and hopelessly fucked."

"We're not fucked," Rajeev said, even if he didn't completely believe his own words. "We don't need to stop them. We just need to slow them down. We can do that."

Mira shook her head. "If you say so, dad."

They stood staring as the mob of androids approached them. Just as Rajeev was about to open his lips to implore the others to join him in rushing the androids, he found that he couldn't move his mouth. Horror reeled through his mind. He tried to turn to face Natalie, but he couldn't move his head. He was completely paralyzed from head to toe.

The android throng reached them, and as it washed over them and continued walking past them, Rajeev suddenly found himself ambulatory again—but not of his own volition. He turned around, no longer facing the opposing androids but rather facing the same direction they were, and began walking in lockstep with them. He realized then what had happened.

Daniel had somehow hacked their bodies. He'd taken them over and was now controlling them. Not only had they not slowed down the progression of Daniel's army ... they'd unwittingly added to it.

THIRTEEN

Rajeev's mind reeled. There was little he could do. The android bodies they'd been remote controlling were one of the few tools they still had in their battle against Daniel, and now that he'd figured out how to hack into them, they'd lost even that. Even if he hadn't hacked into the other bodies they had stored in other locations throughout the country, they had to err on the side of caution and consider them compromised.

A terrifying thought entered Rajeev's mind. If Daniel could hack into one of these remote-controlled bodies, there was a decent chance he could hack into Rajeev's primary body as well. Who knew what he was capable of if he were to do so? Could he overwrite Rajeev's mind with his own consciousness? If so, it would be tantamount to death—especially if Daniel were able to somehow access Dev's backups of Rajeev's consciousness as well.

He had to talk to Dev and see if he had a better idea of what Daniel was capable of. Maybe his fears were unfounded. He certainly hoped so. But he couldn't take that chance.

All these thoughts ran through Rajeev's mind in a matter of seconds. Once he made the determination to cease control of his virtual body, he instinctively made to move his arm—and to his surprise, it budged, just a little. The paralysis was wearing off.

What was going on? Maybe Daniel hadn't been responsible for the paralyzation after all. Maybe it had been some kind of glitch.

He tried moving his arm again. It moved, but in fits and starts rather than fluidly. It definitely seemed like something, or someone, was actively fighting him. It was like a mental arm-wrestling match.

A voice suddenly came over the body's intercom. "Dad? Can you hear me?"

It was Dev.

"I … I can … hear you," Rajeev said. He struggled to speak the words in the midst of whatever it was that was happening to him.

"Good," Dev said. "This should be over soon."

"What … what's … going on?"

"We launched our AI," Dev said. "A bit prematurely, but we saw that you all stopped moving and figured it was Daniel's doing. So we decided to go with what we had so we could stop him. Consider this a beta test."

"Can it … stop Daniel?" Even as he spoke, he found that the words came more easily and he figured that Dev and Maltek's AI must be giving Daniel quite a fight.

"We think so," Dev said. "For now, at least. It's not stronger than Daniel by any means, but Daniel has also never faced off with an entity that was even nominally his equal before. That should throw him off guard and help our AI stop him for now—both from taking over your bodies, and from destroying LA. And that should hopefully buy us enough time to improve our program enough to stop Daniel once and for all."

"Let's … let's hope so," Rajeev said. He could more or less speak normally now. He waved his arms around, and although the movement was a little stiff, it was mostly back to normal. "As a matter of fact, I think it's working."

He turned to his companions, who also appeared to be moving normally now.

"Dev says the new AI is up and running and fighting Daniel as we speak," Rajeev said.

"We know," Natalie said. "He gave us all the message as well."

As they walked through the city streets, they saw dozens of Daniel's androids littered on the ground where they had collapsed. It wasn't clear whether Dev's AI had overpowered Daniel, or if Daniel had simply considered the new AI too much of a nuisance to deal with for the time being. Either way, the threat had been averted for now, and that was as good a victory as they could have hoped for.

"Dev?'

"Yeah, dad. I'm here."

"Looks like your program has done its job. All Daniel's androids are out of commission ... for now."

Dev breathed a sigh of relief. "That's great to hear."

"I think we'd better stick around for a while and do our best to make sure these particular androids stay out of commission for good," Rajeev said. "But after that we'll return."

"Sounds good, dad. In the meantime we'll get to work improving the program. Daniel's undoubtedly going to hit us with everything he's got next time. We should be prepared to do the same."

FOURTEEN

When Rajeev and the others felt they'd "decommissioned" a considerable portion of the androids that had been terrorizing the people of Los Angeles, they abandoned their android bodies in LA and returned their minds to their base, located in the Huron-Manistee National Forests in Michigan. It was eerily silent when they returned; the only sound was that of furious typing emanating from Dev's office.

"Take a rest, everyone," Rajeev said as they all stood. "I'll go debrief with Dev and Maltek and see what our next steps are. Now that their AI is up and running—in some capacity, at least—maybe we can finally go on the offensive against Daniel."

"I have a question for them," Mira said. "What's to prevent this new AI program from going wild and doing its own thing just like Daniel did?"

"Daniel had safeguards in place," Rajeev said. "Dev removed them so we could stop Maltek, remember?"

"I know that," Mira said. "But if Daniel is 'unchained,' so to speak, why do we think an AI that's still chained up can go toe-to-toe with him? The new program will always be operating under a handicap that Daniel isn't burdened by."

Rajeev hesitated. Mira had brought up a valid point that he hadn't considered before. He didn't want to cast doubt amongst the others—they needed hope now more than ever—but he'd also need to get answers from Dev.

"I'm sure they have a plan to address that," he said, "but I'll bring it up to them and get an answer back to all of you. In the meantime, do as I said and get some rest. You all deserve it."

He left them and entered Dev's office to find Dev and Maltek hunched over their keyboards working with more urgency than ever. They both looked rough. Their unshowered hair was greasy and they both had five o'clock shadows—although Rajeev thought they looked more like ten o'clock shadows.

"Hey guys," he said. "Thank you so much for getting the AI up and running. It saved our bacon back there."

"You would have been fine," Maltek said. "You were in disposable bodies."

"We were," Rajeev said with an edge to his voice, "but the people Daniel was terrorizing weren't."

"Glad we could help," Dev offered in an effort to break the tension between Maltek and his father.

"So, Mira raised an interesting question," Rajeev said.

"Oh?" Dev asked distractedly, still focused on his work.

"Yeah. You know how you said Daniel had been constrained before, and that you let him loose to stop ..." He shot Maltek a sideways glance. "Well, you know. So anyway, if your new AI is going to be constrained in the same way that Daniel was, how could it possibly stop Daniel when he's no longer bound by the same restrictions?"

Dev and Maltek both stopped typing and looked at each other. Maltek's eyes drifted to the open door and he nodded his head in its direction.

"Close the door," he said.

"But why—"

"Close the door, dad," Dev said sternly.

He closed the door, and Dev and Maltek swiveled their chairs around to face him.

"What's going on?" Rajeev asked.

"You need to squelch those kinds of questions before they get out of hand," Maltek snapped.

"What Maltek is trying to say," Dev said, shooting Maltek an annoyed look, "is that we have grappled with that very question, but we've been reluctant to bring it up to the others. We don't want them to worry about something they have no control over."

"Fair enough," Rajeev said. "But now that the question has been raised, I want an answer for myself. Is there a solution to this problem? Or are we screwed?"

"It's complicated," Dev said. "We need to strike a very delicate balance between giving the AI enough autonomy to combat Daniel, while also letting us reign it in as needed."

"Can't you just add some kind of killswitch that you can engage if it gets out of hand?"

"Not that simple," Maltek said. "In order to give our AI the kind of processing power and access to information needed to match Daniel, it can't be self-contained. That means it's spread out and diffused over the entire internet. There's no one place to apply a killswitch. It might take out some aspects of the program, but it would survive in nooks and crannies throughout the 'net."

"So the only way to stop it," Rajeev said, "is the same as the only way to stop Daniel—to destroy the internet altogether."

"Yes," Dev said.

"That's not entirely true," Maltek said.

Rajeev looked back and forth between them, surprised. "Oh?"

Dev shook his head. "No," he said firmly. "That's not an option. It's not fair."

"What? What's not an option?"

"Tell him," Maltek said. "Let him make up his own mind."

"Tell me what? Dev? What is it?"

Dev sighed. "Look, I didn't want to tell you about this because I don't think it's fair to ask you to even consider it. But Maltek is kind of forcing my hand here."

Maltek shrugged, apparently brushing off the criticism.

"There is one option," Dev said, continuing, "that involves you. Well, it *could* be you. Or it could be any of the other androids."

Rajeev frowned. "We're already in this fight," he said. "We're doing everything we can."

"Of course you are," Dev said. "That's not what I mean. What I'm saying is that each of you had your consciousness digitized and duplicated. We have copies of each of your minds stored electronically. In theory, it might be possible to merge one of your consciousnesses with our AI. The resulting program would have all of the vast knowledge and capabilities that Daniel has, but it would possess a human conscience. Unless it loses itself inside the main AI program, the hope is that it would never turn against humanity the way Daniel has because it will partly *be* human."

Rajeev stood unblinking for a moment in stunned silence. "That's ... I mean ... you can *do* that?"

Dev nodded. "Maybe. It's risky. Nothing like it has ever even been attempted before."

"We can do it," Maltek interjected. "I'm sure we can."

Dev glared at his companion. "Just because we *can* do something doesn't mean we *should*," he said. "The ethical implications are ... thorny, to put it mildly. And that's why I didn't want to bring it up to you, dad. I didn't want to put any pressure on you, or any of the other androids for that matter, to give us permission to plunge the depths of your mind for what is essentially an extremely risky science experiment."

"The cat's out of the bag now, though," Maltek said, "and if he's game, we should go for it. It might be the edge we need to win this fight."

Rajeev could barely process what he'd just been told. He parted his lips just wide enough for his words to escape. "I'm going to need to think about this," he said.

"Of course, dad. And we'll continue exploring other options in the meantime. Please don't let this stress you out."

"I'll try not to. But in the meantime, what do you want me to tell everyone about the new AI's chances against an unrestrained Daniel if it comes up again? Do you want me to lie to them?"

"Don't lie," Dev said. "But don't exactly by completely forthcoming. Just tell them Maltek and I have a solution in mind. That's not a lie."

"Okay." He didn't relish the thought of misleading the others, but he didn't want to create a panic, either. "I'm going to get some rest. You two should do the same, even if it's brief. You've done a great job so far, and I'm sure you'll be better able to build on it after allowing yourselves to get refreshed."

"We'll try to come to a stopping place," Dev said, swiveling his chair back around in sync with Maltek.

"Okay." Rajeev turned around and left the office, feeling confident that they would not come to a stopping place.

FIFTEEN

RAJEEV ENTERED HIS DORMITORY TO FIND NATALIE sitting on the edge of his bed.

"Oh—hi," he said. "What're you—"

Before he could get another word out, Natalie stood, closed the distance between them, and pressed her lips to his, wrapping her arms around his neck. He froze for a moment, startled, but as the sensation of her soft lips hit him, his entire body loosened and he found himself parting his lips to accept hers. He wrapped his arms around her waist and pulled her tight as the passion of their embrace grew.

He walked over to the bed, never taking his lips off hers, holding her to him the entire time, and fell backward onto the soft mattress. Their lips parted for a brief moment as they giggled at the brief bouncing that ensued, but once it subsided, they resumed their embrace.

* * *

"I NEED A CIGARETTE," RAJEEV SAID.

Natalie hit him in the arm. "You couldn't smoke it even if

you had one." They were both lying in his bed, under the covers, enveloped in each other's arms.

"It's not about smoking it," he responded with a grin. "It's for ambiance."

Natalie raised an eyebrow. "Ambiance?"

"Yeah. Post-coital ambiance."

"I don't know if you could even call what we just did 'coitus.' We're both robots."

"Yes," Rajeev said, "but we're sexy robots."

She laughed. "That we are." Her smile ebbed and she turned to look Rajeev square in the eyes. "I'm scared," she said.

He placed a hand on the back of her head and stroked her hair. "Why are you afraid?"

"Mira kind of freaked me out," she said. "What did Dev say about it?"

"He said he and Maltek had already considered that question and are building a solution into the program."

"And you believe him?"

He hesitated, for just a second. "I do."

She shook her head. "I don't. I feel like humanity is an endangered species. Like we've created the apex predator that's going to take us out and released it into the wild ourselves, like fools."

"Dev didn't have any choice."

"Oh, no! I didn't mean to cast blame ... not on Dev or anyone. I think it probably would have been inevitable no matter what. But I do think we're standing on the precipice of something horrible. And that's why I'm scared."

Rajeev wasn't sure what to say. He shared her fears. But he didn't want to make her worry more than she already was.

"It's going to be okay," he said. "Remember, Dev and Maltek are geniuses." He grinned.

"Yeah?" She asked. Rajeev could tell she was still worried,

but trying to take his bait as an opportunity to forget about it, even if temporarily. "Does Dev get that from his old man?"

Rajeev laughed. "No," he said. "He most certainly does not. Remember, I was a driver in my old life."

"Yes, but I'll bet you were the best damned driver out there."

He smiled cockily. "I was okay. It was my driving that put me in a coma, though."

She winced. "Sorry I brought it up."

"It's okay," he said, and he pecked her on the lips. But even as he said the words, he was transported back to his past, to a life that felt like a distant dream. He'd lost that life through his own recklessness, and through what could only be described as a technological miracle, he'd been brought back for a second chance at a new life. A life that was finally beginning to seem like it was worth living. A life he wanted to share with Natalie.

But now his new life was also at risk of being taken from him, and he felt helpless to do anything to stop it. He had put all his trust in Dev and Maltek to stop Daniel, and although they truly did represent the best hope at stopping the renegade AI, it now appeared that even they may not be up to the task. That meant there was a very real possibility they would lose to Daniel, and that they would all either be killed or enslaved. He couldn't fathom which would be worse.

Looking into Natalie's eyes, he was overwhelmed by the beauty he saw, both inside and out. He longed more than anything for a future with her, and in the absence of any certainty that such a future would come to pass, he wanted to prolong the present moment as long as possible. He bent down and placed his mouth to hers, offering her a slow, languid kiss that nevertheless burned with passion. When he let up to give her a moment to compose herself, he saw his own passion reflected in her eyes.

Just as he was bending down to kiss her again, ready to start a second round of lovemaking, the door burst open, revealing Dev standing in the open doorway.

Rajeev and Natalie were both startled. "Dev!" Rajeev shouted. "What are you—?"

"Get dressed," Dev said, ignoring the compromising position he'd found his father in. His voice was strained, bordering on panicked. "Meet me in my office. We're in big fucking trouble."

SIXTEEN

Rajeev dressed as quickly as he could. He gave Natalie a kiss on the cheek, and told her not to worry. "It's not the first time we've been in 'big fucking trouble,' and I'm sure it won't be the last," he said. Then he was out the door.

Inside Dev's office, Maltek was furiously typing on his keyboard, as Dev pensively watched the computer monitor in front of them. But the mix of computer code the monitor displayed meant nothing to Rajeev.

"What's going on?"

"A cyberattack," Dev said.

"Daniel?"

Dev nodded. "No one else could have possibly broken through our security. It's Daniel."

"Can you stop him?"

"What the hell do you think I'm trying to do?" Maltek spat.

Dev turned to his father, his face contorted by sheer panic. "The key word is 'trying,'" he said. "He's trying and failing."

"What about the AI you guys created?" Rajeev asked. "Can you deploy it to fight him off?"

"We already have," Maltek said.

"Daniel must have gotten enough of a taste in Los Angeles to figure out how to fend it off," Dev said. "Maltek is trying to bolster our defenses, but it's not looking good. Daniel is overwhelming us."

"Okay," Rajeev said, trying not to let the panic his son was displaying carry over to himself. "So what does it mean if Daniel carries through with the attack? What does that mean? What will happen?"

"He'd gain access to everything," Dev said. "All our information and data and … and he could possibly gain control of the android bodies as well."

"Shit," Rajeev said. "We can't let that happen. We have to get all the bodies offline then. How do I do it?"

Dev walked him through the process, and Rajeev took himself offline. But he knew he had to get all the others offline as well before Daniel got to them.

"I'm going to go help the others get offline," he said. "What about the unactivated bodies in the warehouse? Do we need to worry about those as well?"

Dev shook his head. "As long as they haven't been activated, they shouldn't be connected to the internet and Daniel shouldn't be able to access them."

"Okay. I'll be back as soon as I can. Not that I'll be much help."

He left and headed back to his dorm. Natalie was sitting on the bed looking anxious and turned to him with wide eyes as he entered.

"Help me wake everyone up and tell them to meet in the common area," he said.

"What's going on?"

"There's no time. I'll tell you with everyone else."

He left and headed for the dorms on the opposite side of the building, trusting that Natalie would take care of the ones near his own dorm. When he'd knocked on every door and instructed everyone on where to meet, he headed to the common area and waited for everyone to gather.

"Thank you all for meeting here," Rajeev said. "I don't want to worry everyone, but, well ... there *is* reason to be worried." He took a deep breath. "Daniel is currently launching a cyberattack against us. Dev and Maltek are holding him off as best as they can, but there's a real possibility that they will fail."

A murmur of panicked whispers filled the room, but Rajeev held out his hands and silenced them.

"We have to act quickly," he said. "If Daniel breaks through, it puts all us androids at risk—he can take over our bodies and do whatever he wants with them. So we have to take our bodies offline. Daniel can only hack in through the internet. As long as our bodies are offline, he can't get to us."

He pulled Natalie up to be by his side so he could demonstrate the procedure on her. The entire time, he feared they might be too late, that any moment Daniel would burst through their defenses and halt the process of going offline, taking over each of their bodies one by one.

To his relief, it never happened. Daniel never broke through and everyone was able to take their body offline. Rajeev would have breathed a sigh of relief if he'd had lungs.

"What now?" Natalie asked. "Is there anything we can do to help?"

Rajeev shook his head. "Not at the moment. Dev and Maltek are giving it their all. It's up to them."

"So what," Mira said, "we should just go back to our dorms?"

"If you're comfortable doing that, yes," Rajeev said, nodding. "You're welcome to wait here as well. But I can't make any promises as to how long it might take to hear any news."

Mira shook her head. "I just feel so ... so impotent," she said.

"Can't say I've ever known what that's like," Rajeev said with a chuckle, trying to lighten the mood.

"Eww, dad," she said, scrunching her face in revulsion. "I don't wanna hear jokes like that coming from you!"

He chuckled again, deviously this time, in response to his daughter's reaction. "Sorry," he said. "I couldn't help myself. But seriously, don't think of it as waiting impotently. Think of it as resting up. Because you're going to have all the excitement you can handle soon enough."

SEVENTEEN

Rajeev entered Dev's office; neither Dev nor Maltek even looked up to acknowledge him.

"Crisis averted," he said. "For now, anyway. We got everyone offline."

"Good," Dev said. He sounded distracted.

"Is the … is the attack still ongoing?" Rajeev asked.

"Yes," Maltek said. "So we can't talk."

Rajeev held up his hands. "Sorry."

"It's okay, dad," Dev said. "Just give us a few minutes. I think we've almost got it under control."

He watched in silence as they worked, and he marvelled at the proficiency with which they reviewed the code on the screen, which was gibberish to him, and typed. Both men possessed a skillset that was completely alien to anything Rajeev could even fathom.

In the past when he'd watched them work, there had been a carefree energy to it, even with the threat of Daniel hanging over their heads. But now, when the threat was so immediate, that element of carefree fun was completely gone. Their brows were creased with worry and fresh sweat gleamed off their foreheads.

It felt like an eternity, but finally Dev and Maltek looked at each other, sighed, and turned around to face Rajeev.

"It's over," Dev said.

"So we deactivated all those bodies for nothing."

"No," Dev said. "It wasn't for nothing. Daniel still could have infiltrated them while Maltek and I were working if you hadn't deactivated them. And we didn't come out of this unscathed."

A chill ran through Rajeev's artificial spine. "What do you mean?"

"Daniel was able to get into the system, and although we were able to prevent much of the damage, he corrupted a lot of data. There's no telling how much we lost. It'll take us days to go through everything and find out for sure."

Rajeev swallowed hard. "That's not good."

"No, it isn't. But we stopped the damage from being any worse, and we stopped him from taking control of the empty bodies. This was a victory."

Rajeev ran his fingers through his hair. "So what now?"

"Right now I need to get some sleep before I drop dead," Maltek said.

"That would probably be a good idea for me, too," Dev said. "Sorry dad. I'd like to discuss next steps with you—I think it's important that we do—but at the same time, I don't know that I've ever been this exhausted. Let's sleep on it and we'll discuss it in the morning."

Rajeev was impatient to know what their next move would be, but there was no doubt that Dev and Maltek were running on fumes.

"Okay," he said, nodding. "Get some rest. I'll talk to you in the morning."

* * *

RAJEEV SLIPPED BACK INTO HIS DORM. NATALIE WAS waiting for him in his bed. He hadn't been sure if she'd be in his dorm as opposed to her own, but he was happy to see her. He slid under the covers beside her.

"What's going on?" she asked.

"Dev and Maltek put a stop to the cyberattack, and now they're taking advantage of some much-deserved rest."

"It's too bad we couldn't clone them and have them working around the clock."

"Technically, Maltek *could* do that."

She frowned. "Don't remind me." She let out a sigh. "As soon as you left and I started to come down off the adrenaline rush, I've been a big ball of anxiety."

Rajeev reached out and stroked her hair. "Don't be anxious," he said. "We're going to figure this all out."

"Are we, though? I'm afraid we might realistically only have two choices: Take out the internet, or submit to Daniel. Both options are devastating. If we take out the internet and electronics with EMPs, we'll be condemning thousands, maybe millions, to death. But if we do nothing, there's not a doubt in my mind that Daniel will either enslave or exterminate humanity."

Technically she was wrong, but he didn't offer up the third alternative, the one Maltek had pushed: Merging a copy of Rajeev's consciousness with their AI. He still wasn't sure how he felt about that plan, and he didn't want Natalie getting any ideas and volunteering her own consciousness to take his place. "I'm not sure EMPs are the answer anyway," he said. "The military has hardened military bases that can withstand EMP radiation. Daniel could feasibly hide out in military hardware, wait for us to rebuild, and eventually come back with even greater force. In fact, that would make him even more formidable because we would be vulnerable as we tried to rebuild our infrastructure."

Tears formed in Natalie's eyes. "Daniel is a monster," she said.

Rajeev shook his head. "He's not a monster. He's a machine. It's just that, unfortunately, he's a machine beyond our control at this time. And he's on the fritz."

"Same thing," Natalie said. "Or at least, the results are the same: Destruction and mayhem."

Rajeev couldn't argue with that … so he changed the subject.

"Where do you want to settle down when this is all said and done?"

She tilted her head. "What do you mean?"

"I mean … do you intend to stay in Chicago, or do you think you'd want to head somewhere else? It's a big, wide world out there … you could live anywhere you wanted."

She smiled. "Why are you so interested in where I end up?"

Rajeev was grateful that his artificial cheeks couldn't flush. "Well," he said, "if I'm being honest, I'm just … I'm curious."

"Oh yeah? Well *why* are you curious?"

He didn't answer right away, instead turning his head to the side, avoiding her gaze.

"Rajeev," she said. "Why don't you just admit that you're wondering about *us*."

He looked up, into her eyes. "And what if I am?"

"If you are," she said, "I'd tell you that I haven't given it much thought, but wherever I do end up, I'd very much enjoy your company there, if you'd be so inclined to provide it."

A smile lit up his face at her words, and he leaned in and kissed her. As their lips parted, he looked her in the eye and said, "I'd very much like to provide it." She smiled, he smiled, and they kissed again.

EIGHTEEN

Rajeev awoke early the next morning and left Natalie to sleep in his bed. He'd hoped that Dev or Maltek would be awake so he could discuss next steps with them, but they were still asleep. Instead, he grabbed a coffee-flavored orb and pulled up the latest news from the internet.

Dev emerged from his dormitory after about an hour. He brewed himself a pot of coffee and took a seat beside Rajeev.

"Good morning, dad."

Rajeev nodded. "Mornin'. Feel rested?"

"For the most part. Probably could have used another hour or two of sleep, but once I remembered everything going on with Daniel, my mind started racing and there's no way I could have gotten back to sleep."

Rajeev nodded. "Some of the only peace I've had since all this started is in those quiet, still moments between sleep and wakefulness, before I remembered about Maltek, Daniel, and all the rest of it."

"Ignorance is bliss, as they say."

"Yes, but unfortunately, ignorance isn't going to get us out of the bind we currently find ourselves in."

"No, it isn't. But we'll find a solution."

Rajeev cleared his throat—a completely symbolic gesture, since his voice emanated from an electronic voice box. "I've been thinking a lot about what Maltek proposed. About merging my consciousness with your new AI."

"Dad, you don't need to—"

"No, Dev, you're wrong. I *do* need to do this. Believe me, I do not relish the thought of subjecting a consciousness identical to my own to an unknown ordeal, but I just keep thinking that the very fate of humanity is at stake here, and it seems selfish to sacrifice billions of individuals for the sake of one."

"Are you sure about this, dad?"

Rajeev shook his head. "No. I don't disagree that there are thorny ethical issues at play here. But I think it's the lesser of two evils. I can't have the demise of humankind on my conscience."

Dev nodded and sat in silence for a moment, contemplating what his father had just told him. "Okay," he said. "I'll tell Maltek and we'll see what it would take. But in the meantime, we'll continue to explore other options. Merging your consciousness with the AI will be a last resort. I think our AI will be better prepared to hold Daniel off the next time they encounter each other. Should buy us some time."

"Dev, I'm telling you, this is something I need to do."

"I'm not just stalling to spare you the moral conundrum," his son rejoined. "I'm not even sure merging your consciousness with the AI is the smart move. That's not to say that it might not ultimately be our best bet, but it's definitely not something I'm going to jump into unless we're absolutely sure we've exhausted all of our better options. So just trust me, dad. Okay?"

Rajeev felt chastised by his son's words. "Okay," he said. "I'm sorry."

"There's no need to be sorry. I know you want to put a stop

to Daniel. We all do. But all I'm asking is that you let us take our time to find a solution that will work and not rush into something that may or may not be beneficial. Fair enough?"

Rajeev nodded. "Fair enough."

Dev smiled. "Glad to hear it."

"So when do you think you'll know?"

"Know what?"

"If you'll need to implement the 'last resort'?"

"Don't worry about it, dad. We'll let you know if it comes to that. Maltek and I are going to take inventory today of all the damage Daniel did yesterday. Once we're done with that, we'll move on to evaluating the best way to stop him."

"Okay. That sounds good. I'm sorry if I've sounded heavy handed. I'm just nervous about this whole thing, and like I said before, I don't want the blood of innocent citizens on my hands because I refused to do the right thing when I had the chance."

"We'll make sure that doesn't happen—no matter what it takes."

Natalie walked up to them, and they both turned their attention to her, putting their conversation on hold.

"Good morning," Rajeev said, and he reflexively leaned in and kissed her cheek. He only realized as his lips left her skin that he had just kissed her in front of Dev. He was sure that his son knew that something was going on between him and Natalie, but this was the first time he had been so nonchalantly blatant about it.

It felt good. Surprisingly so.

For his part, Dev didn't act like anything odd had transpired between his dad and Natalie. Whether he was avoiding causing embarrassment or truly didn't care was anyone's guess, although Rajeev suspected the latter—with the fate of the world on the line, his father's love life was the least of his concerns.

"How did you sleep?" Dev asked her.

"Not bad, I guess. You?"

Dev shrugged. "I can't remember the last time I had a decent night's rest. I guess *relatively* speaking it wasn't that bad. I didn't have any nightmares."

Rajeev's face registered concern. "You've been having nightmares?"

Dev offered another shrug. "Off and on. They started when I was being held captive by Maltek. They've been getting worse. More frequent, more disturbing. But last night I mercifully slept nightmare-free."

"I'm sorry," Rajeev said. "I didn't know you were dealing with that on top of everything else."

Dev shook his head gently. He wanted to dismiss the significance of the nightmares, but the look in his eyes betrayed how deeply they affected him.

"Can't Maltek take over some of your responsibilities?" Rajeev asked. "You can't carry this burden indefinitely. You need a break."

Dev sighed deeply and stood. He began walking back to his office. "I'll rest," he said as he retreated, "when we've put a stop to Daniel for good."

Rajeev turned to Natalie, a look of utter exhaustion on his face. "We'd better stop him soon, then," he said, "because I don't know how much more of this any of us can take."

NINETEEN

Once everyone had awakened, Dev and Maltek gathered them all together to fill them in on the latest in the effort to battle Daniel.

"You all did a great job defending the castle, so to speak, when Daniel attacked us," Dev said. "It could have been a lot worse. We were able to fend him off. But we didn't escape without damage. Daniel accessed our system and corrupted a number of files. Maltek and I are still assessing the full scope of the damage."

"We might even be able to repair some of that damage," Maltek added. "Not all of it—some of the losses will undoubtedly be permanent—but certainly some of it can be recovered."

"That's great and all," Brian said, "but obviously Daniel isn't going to stop there. He's going to attack again—whether it's against us specifically or someone else. Are we any closer to being able to stop him?"

"Maltek and I are exploring a number of possibilities," Dev said.

"A number of possibilities? Could you be any less specific?"

Dev hesitated. "There is one option that we feel confident

"

about," he said. "But it's extreme. We don't want to resort to it unless we absolutely have to."

"You're still being vague," Brian said, the frustration apparent in his voice.

Dev looked to his father, and Rajeev nodded subtly, giving him the go-ahead to share the news.

"One of the limitations with our AI is that it can't go toe-to-toe with Daniel if we keep it constrained," he said. "But at the same time, if we don't keep it constrained, we could very well just have another Daniel on our hands."

"A Catch-22," Brian said.

Dev nodded. "That's right. It's like setting mongooses loose to fight a snake infestation. What do you do with the mongooses once they've devoured all the snakes? You're simply trading one pest for another. But we think we can avoid that scenario. If we merge a human consciousness with the AI, it will give the AI enough of an edge to effectively combat Daniel. And with a human conscience, there's a better chance that it will resist following in Daniel's footsteps and remain benevolent."

"Merge it with a human consciousness?" Brian asked. "How is that even … oh." His eyes narrowed. "You mean you want to merge it with one of *our* consciousnesses." There was an unmistakable hint of hostility in his voice.

Dev nodded. "Yes," he said. "That's the idea. Your consciousnesses have already been digitized, so it's the quickest way to get it done."

"And what makes you think any of us would agree to that? Presumptuous of you, isn't it?"

"Actually," Dev said with a hint of defensiveness, "one of you has already agreed to it."

A look of genuine shock flashed across Brian's face. "Who?"

Dev's eyes flashed back to his father, and Rajeev nodded, consenting to the disclosure Dev was about to give. It's not like he had much of a choice, anyway; Dev's glance his way was enough to give it away.

"My dad," he said.

All eyes turned to Rajeev, including Natalie's, who seemed particularly caught off guard by the announcement; if anyone should have known before everyone else, it was her.

"Is that true, Rajeev?" Brian asked.

Rajeev nodded. "It's not an idea that I relish," he said. "The thought of my consciousness, my essence, mingling with some soulless artificial intelligence in some hastily conceived science experiment ... it's a notion that fills me to the brim with existential dread. But I honestly believe it's a necessary evil if we want to stop Daniel."

Brian furrowed his brow and looked like he was about to argue, but he shook his head and his face softened. He offered a shrug. "It's your mind," he said. "I suppose you can do what you want with it."

Rajeev flashed him a wry smile. "Thanks for your permission."

"Anyway," Dev said, "the point is that we have a real, potentially viable plan to stop Daniel. We'd like to explore other options that aren't so, uh ... ethically ambiguous ... but we'll work to have this option queued up and ready to go at a moment's notice." He scanned his head, making eye contact with everyone in the group. "Does that alleviate the concern I'm hearing?"

The room filled with soft chattering, and eventually everyone's eyes gravitated to Brian who had become the impromptu voice of the original concern. He pondered a moment, then nodded.

"At least it's something," he said.

"It's more than something," Maltek said a bit combatively. "I, for one, think we should ditch the alternatives and go right to the AI-human hybrid. If we're going to take this monster out, we need to take risks."

Dev shook his head. "While I appreciate your enthusiasm, Gregory, I think the cautious approach is the right one for now —and I suspect the majority of the others would agree with that, given the ethical considerations at play. Is that right?" He waited a moment to gauge the reaction, which mostly came in the form of affirmative nods. "If we're in agreement then, you can all try to relax a bit. Gregory and I, on the other hand, don't have that luxury. We have a lot of work to do." He turned to face Maltek. "Let's get to it."

TWENTY

After Dev adjourned the meeting, Natalie sidled up next to Rajeev and placed her hand in his. He couldn't help the grin that grew across his face.

"I was wondering if you'd like to go on a walk with me," she said.

"A walk? We're in the middle of nowhere."

She smiled. "Perfect. I could use a little time out in unperverted nature, away from all … *this.*"

" 'This'?"

"This … overload of technology. Android bodies, exoskeletons, computer programs, and renegade virtual assistants out for blood. I could use a break from it all. Well, except for the android body. I can't really help that."

Rajeev smiled. He had never been much of a nature lover—he'd lived in large cities his entire life—but he had to admit that Natalie made a compelling point about the outsize influence of technology in their lives … particularly as it pertained to their present problems. Getting away from it all, even if just for an hour or two, sounded heavenly … especially with such enchanting company.

"Sure," he said. "Let's do it."

They marched up the steep steps leading out of the underground bunker that had been their home for so long and emerged into the lush, green woods. It almost felt like awakening from a dream or coming out of a coma—a sensation with which Rajeev was all too familiar.

"A girl could get used to this," Natalie said. "I have half a mind to leave everything behind and run off to live in the woods."

"Well, that's not an option," Rajeev said. "So let's make the most of the opportunity while we can, before we have to head back."

They walked hand in hand through the forest, taking in the vibrant green foliage and basking in the calls of birds and other wildlife. A light breeze whipped against their skin as they walked, rustling the leaves of the surrounding trees. The perilous threat that Daniel represented seemed to fade into the background as they strode farther and farther away from the bunker, until the thought escaped their memory altogether and they walked around truly in blind bliss, enraptured by the nature that surrounded them and by each other's company.

A deer pranced out in front of them and they stopped in their tracks; a gasp escaped Natalie's artificial lips. The deer turned and looked at them, offering the same blank stare it would have exhibited if it had been staring down a pair of headlights, then bounced back into the woods as if nothing had happened.

"Did you see how close it got?" Natalie exclaimed.

Rajeev laughed. "Yes, I did. Too bad I don't have a gun with me. We could have had fresh venison for dinner."

Natalie slugged his shoulder playfully. "That's horrible, Rajeev!"

"Hey, relax! It was a joke. It's not like we can even eat anyway!"

Eventually they came to a small pond. They found a fallen log and took a seat on it, watching out over the peaceful pond scene and enjoying the tranquil landscape before them. Natalie leaned her head on Rajeev's shoulder, and he placed an arm around her waist, pulling her close to him.

"I'm so glad I got the opportunity to know you," she said.

He smiled. "Oh yeah?"

She smiled back. "Yeah. I mean, I was not looking for any kind of romance at the Next Level Technologies headquarters. But isn't it always the way it goes that romance finds you when you're least expecting it?"

Rajeev nodded. "I can commiserate. I definitely wasn't looking to get involved with anyone so soon after discovering Sarah was with someone else. I was heartbroken, and yet, it felt inevitable that I move on. I just didn't think it would happen so quickly."

Their eyes met, and for a moment, they were lost in each other. The nature surrounding them faded into the background and as far as they were concerned, they may as well have been in Rajeev's dorm. He leaned forward and pressed his lips to hers. She kissed him back, and they wrapped their arms around each other, pulling their bodies close.

He lifted her up, never breaking their embrace, and lowered her to the ground. The hardness of the ground didn't matter; they had transcended the material plane of existence. As they hastily removed each other's clothes and burned their passion brighter, they left this world behind completely and embraced oblivion.

TWENTY-ONE

REALITY SEEPED BACK INTO THEIR BRAINS, AND AS they lay curled up in each other's arms, they realized the day was growing short and that they should head back to the bunker. Rajeev planted one last kiss on Natalie's cheek. "Come on," he said. "Let's get dressed."

She let out an exaggerated groan. "Do we *have* to?"

Rajeev chuckled. "Well, we have to eventually. How about five more minutes?"

She snuggled into him. "It'll have to do."

Neither of them wanted to break their reverie. Five minutes turned to ten, and ten to fifteen, but before it could hit twenty, Rajeev nudged his paramour away.

"Come on," he said. "Let's go. If we wait any longer we'll be walking back in the dark."

Natalie resisted for a moment, but her hesitation was brief. With a dissatisfied groan, she acquiesced to Rajeev's request. She stood and began to dress. When each of them was once again fully clothed, they started the journey back to the bunker. They walked slowly, even as the sun began to set, eager to prolong their respite from their troubles for as long as possible.

"I wish we could stay out here, together, forever," Natalie said.

"Don't say that," Rajeev said.

"Why not?"

He'd said the words reflexively, and it took him a moment to sort through the flurry of emotions that had led him to speak them. In truth, he wished they could stay out here forever as well, and that's why he didn't want the desire spoken aloud: He might be tempted to give in.

"Because it's not possible," he told her.

She didn't say anything to that, but it was clear from the way she pursed her lips that she wasn't happy with his response, even if, deep down, she agreed with it. He wished he hadn't said anything at all.

They approached the towering monolith that marked the entrance to the bunker. As they descended, they felt a little bit of peace fade away with each step. Their short trip away had refreshed them to a degree, but as they made their way closer to the heart of their current home, they couldn't help but be reminded of all the chaos they'd come from, and all of the chaos that still awaited them.

Natalie and Rajeev parted ways and retreated to their respective dormitories. Rajeev had barely begun making himself comfortable when Dev popped in.

"I need to talk to you," he said. He hadn't knocked; there was none of the usual politeness that typically accompanied his presence.

"Okay," Rajeev said with a nod. "Just let me get settled and I'll—"

"I need to talk to you now. It's urgent."

Rajeev felt a pit form in his stomach. What now? He'd barely returned from his all-to-brief break from all of this, and here he was already being thrust right back into thick of all the craziness that had come to so thoroughly dominate their lives. Somehow, the short reprieve had actually managed to make things worse; he felt like he was on the verge of experiencing a panic attack at the slightest provocation.

"Okay," he said. "Let's talk."

"Follow me," Dev said, and he turned and walked away without even waiting to see if his father would follow. Rajeev stood and followed Dev out of the dorm. His son led him to his office, where Maltek was already seated and waiting inside. Rajeev couldn't help but feel like a little kid who was about to get a stern talking to from his parents.

"Take a seat, dad."

Rajeev did so, then looked up at his son pensively. "What's going on?"

Dev turned to Maltek. They stared at each other for a moment that felt longer than it was. Finally, Maltek nodded, and he took the reins of the conversation. "We've had some time to go over the data that was corrupted due to Daniel's data breach," he said. Rajeev expected him to keep speaking, but he'd paused.

"Yeah?" Rajeev asked. "Was it that bad?"

There was a moment of silence, as both Dev and Maltek avoided answering the question. Just as Dev's lips parted and it seemed he was about to say something, Rajeev was blasted by an emergency alert; he could tell by the startled look on his companions' faces that they had received the same alert on their AR glasses.

Before he could even finish reading the alert, Rajeev could tell it was bad. And he had a good guess who was responsible: Daniel.

TWENTY-TWO

Thus far, Daniel's mayhem had been confined to limited geographic regions. He'd been testing the waters, seeing what he was capable of. Dev, Maltek and Rajeev all knew he was capable of much more than what he'd done so far. And now it seemed he was finally taking advantage of his full strength.

Reports were flooding in of "glitches" and "malfunctions" all over the country. Cars were driving off roads, thermostats were cranking themselves up as far as they could go, lawnmowers were mowing down people instead of grass; machines were turning against their owners like some 1950s-era pulp sci-fi novel's vision of the apocalypse.

But there was one incident in particular that had summed up the extent of what was happening, that illustrated that the country was facing a threat like nothing it had ever faced before, and which, if left unchecked, would undoubtedly spread and menace the entire world: The White House had been destroyed. Every news organization's video streams were focused on the image of bright orange flames arising from the ashes of what had once been one of the country's foremost symbols of democracy. It was unclear whether the president had escaped before the building had been attacked, but it didn't much matter. Daniel had sent a message, and everyone in the country had received it: Things would never be the same.

Dev, Maltek and Rajeev stood silently for a moment, stunned by the broadcast they were seeing. When Rajeev finally spoke, his voice sounded small.

"What do we do? What *can* we do?"

Dev and Maltek shared a look. It was a brief look, but apparently conveyed a wealth of information, and in that moment Rajeev realized that despite all odds, Maltek and his son had become friends … or at least, something resembling friendship had blossomed between them. Perhaps he shouldn't have been so surprised. They had been forced to work together to save humanity, working long, grueling hours side by side. They had been bonded together by fate in much the same way soldiers are bonded together by war. Despite the terrible things Maltek—the original incarnation of Maltek, anyway—had done in the past, it appeared some good had come out of it, perhaps. Rajeev wondered if Maltek was deserving of forgiveness. Then again, did he even require forgiveness? Technically, the man standing before them was just a copy of Maltek's mind, in the same way Rajeev was a copy of a man who had lived and lost a separate life. Likewise, could the version of Maltek standing before them really be held responsible for the actions of a man who shared a mind with him, but not a past? So far, the only actions they had to judge him on were good—he had offered indispensable help in their fight against Daniel. But Rajeev feared that something sinister might be lingering in the clone's psyche, and he worried that the friendship blossoming between him and his son may be a pretense for some sinister agenda.

Rajeev's flurry of thoughts was interrupted by Dev answering his question.

"I don't know," he said softly. "Where can we even start? The entire country is in chaos."

"What do you think his goal is?" Rajeev asked. "Is he trying to control us? Destroy us? Does he think he's trying to protect us in some twisted way, like something out of an Asimov novel?"

"Does it matter?" Maltek asked. "Whether it's A, B, C, or all of the above, it's bad news for the human species."

"Maybe it's time for the killswitch," Rajeev said.

"Killswitch?" Dev asked, his eyes growing wide. "You mean—

Rajeev nodded. "Pulling the plug on the internet all together."

"That's risky," Maltek said. "It may already be too late. For all we know, Daniel's already set up his own servers and equipment and shielded them in EMP-proof Faraday cages. We might blow up the internet for nothing."

"It could at least slow him down," Rajeev offered. "Better he be contained to a few servers he's managed to cobble together than to ... everything."

"Okay," Maltek said. "As a last resort, maybe it's better than nothing. But there's still another option."

"Merging a copy of my consciousness with your AI," Rajeev said.

Maltek nodded. "Yes."

There was an awkward silence, and Maltek turned and stared at Dev, whose eyes drifted down to look at his feet.

"That's actually what we had come to talk to you about," he said.

"Oh? I thought you were going to talk to me about the data breach?"

Dev let out a long sigh. "The data breach did a lot more damage than we initially thought, and much of it is unrecoverable ... including the copies of everyone's consciousnesses that we had stored."

"We were going to ask you to let us copy your mind again,"

Maltek said. "But with this latest attack by Daniel, I don't think we have time for that anymore."

"Then we have to shut it down," Rajeev said. "We have to take down the internet. If that's the only option, then so be it. The alternative is that Daniel takes over everything."

"Stop and think about what that would really mean," Maltek said. "The internet governs nearly every facet of our society. Destroying the internet would mean the collapse of the entire electrical grid. It would mean taking millions of people in hospitals off life support in seconds. It would mean kneecapping our ability to produce and transport food."

"I know all that," Rajeev said. "But it's still better than the alternative."

"I'm not saying it shouldn't still be on the table as a last resort. But merging your consciousness with the AI still might work, with the added benefit of not destroying modern civilization as we know it."

"But you two just told me that wasn't possible."

"No," Maltek said. "We told you it wasn't possible to merge a *copy* of your consciousness."

"Yeah, that's—"

Maltek's words settled in Rajeev's brain, and as the meaning of those words sunk in, Rajeev's face fell. If he'd had blood, it would have run cold. He looked Maltek directly in the eyes, then turned to his son. He couldn't hide the shock or the pain that was surely displayed on his face.

"You're saying you want *me* to merge with the AI. Not a copy of myself, but the version standing before you right now, with no backup, no duplicate on hand to restore me to my present state. You're asking me, in effect, to sacrifice myself."

Dev turned away; Maltek nodded gravely.

"I wish it wasn't so," he said, "but that's exactly what I'm saying."

TWENTY-THREE

"YOU DON'T HAVE TO DO THIS, DAD. IN FACT, I'M telling you not to. We'll find another way to stop Daniel."

"There isn't another way!" Maltek shouted. His eyes met Dev's and, seeing the pain in his eyes, Maltek's voice softened when he spoke again. "I'm sorry. I wish there was, too. Maybe there could be, if we had more time. But we don't. Daniel is making his move *now*. We don't have time to figure something else out, and we can't risk pulling the plug on the entire 'net. This is our best hope. This is our *only* hope."

Rajeev didn't respond. He couldn't respond; he could barely comprehend what was being asked of him.

"He's my *dad*," Dev spat.

"Fine," Maltek said. "It doesn't have to be him, specifically." He gestured toward the rest of the bunker, toward the dormitories. "Any of them will do just fine. But we can't sit here and debate it all day. We have to act, and we have to act now."

At this, Rajeev bristled. The thought that one of the other androids might be put in harm's way because he refused to step up was intolerable to him. The very suggestion of it crystallized his resolve. The idea of sacrificing himself no longer seemed quite so crazy.

"Okay," he said, his voice now firm, confident. He nodded. "I'll do it."

"Dad—no," Dev said. "You don't have to—"

"I'm sure as hell not going to let anyone else do it in my place," Rajeev interjected. "And it seems, as Maltek has made abundantly clear, that we're all out of other options. So unfortunately, Dev, you're wrong. I do have to do this."

Dev's face contorted in pain. Rajeev could only imagine what he was going through. He'd lost his father at a young age, and spent his entire life working to bring him back. And he'd done it. He'd defied the odds and found a way to bring his father out of a coma and give him a second chance at life. But he hadn't really even gotten to enjoy the fruit of his labor. After escaping imprisonment, Dev and Rajeev had been embroiled in one battle after another. They hadn't had time to renew their relationship as father and son; instead, they'd acted more as fellow soldiers. They'd believed the sacrifice was worth it, that they were working toward a future where the existential threats they faced would be defeated and they could live their lives as father and son once more. But now, finally and irrevocably, that dream was being wrested from their hands. No, Rajeev would not be going away completely, but there was no telling what would happen when his consciousness merged with the AI. Maybe he'd still be there in some halfway recognizable form, but there was an equally likely chance he'd be so thoroughly assimilated that any trace of an entity known as Rajeev Sundaram would cease to exist.

Tears ran down Dev's face. Rajeev's lip trembled. He was transported back to a time before he'd woken up in this alien future, to a time when Dev had been just a boy and fallen off his bicycle, skinning his knees. He'd come rushing into the house, tears flowing, in so much distress he couldn't even find words between the sobs to express what was wrong. But Rajeev knew. In that moment, his parental instincts had kicked in and his sole mission in life was to comfort and care for his son. Now, all these years later, whether he was truly Rajeev or just a faint shadow, his mission was the same.

He rushed forward and wrapped his arms around his son, and even though his body was made of silicon and silicone, in that moment, they felt each other's heartbeats.

"Dev," he said, half-whispering into his son's ear as they embraced, "I know it's not just me making this sacrifice." He hugged him tighter, then released the embrace so he could look his son in the eyes. "But a father doesn't have a choice. I can't allow my son and daughter to live in a world where they're dead or enslaved, even if it means sacrificing myself. If you have a child someday, you'll recognize and realize that you would make the same choice if you were in my shoes today."

"I don't mean to break up the moment," Maltek said, "but if you've made a final decision—and I wholeheartedly believe it's the right decision—then we need to get on with it. We're running out of time."

Rajeev turned to Dev, who was drying his tears with the sleeve of his shirt. When he'd gotten most of them, he looked up at his father and offered a reluctant nod.

"Okay," Rajeev said. "You two get things ready on your end. I'll be back in ten minutes. I have to go say some goodbyes."

TWENTY-FOUR

Every step Rajeev took as he exited Dev's office and made his way toward Natalie's dormitory felt like it took an eternity. His mind was abuzz with more thoughts than he could process. The last few moments had been surreal. It felt like the conversation with Dev and Maltek had taken place in a faraway dream, not an immediate reality.

By the time he reached Natalie's room, he was filled with dread; not from his impending fate, which he was beginning to resign himself to, but rather over the fact that he would have to deliver the devastating news to her—news he was certain would crush, if not destroy, her. He delivered three slow, hard knocks, and waited for her to answer.

When the door opened, Natalie looked tired, but happy. But as her eyes fell upon Rajeev's distressed face, her expression mirrored his.

"What's wrong?" He pushed past her and took a seat on her bed. She followed him, taking a seat beside him and grasping his hands, pulling them to her chest. "Rajeev, what is it? Is this about the news reports that came in about Daniel?"

Rajeev shook his head as he worked up the courage to speak the words he needed to say to her. Finally, he did so.

"During the data breach, Daniel apparently destroyed a lot more data than Dev and Maltek had initially thought," he began. "Among the data that was lost were all the copies Dev had stored of our consciousnesses."

Natalie shrugged. "So we'll make new copies," she said.

"Yes. You and the other androids can and should get new copies made as backups. But we're facing a dire, immediate threat from Daniel now, and to fight him, Dev and Maltek need a digitized consciousness to merge with their AI."

"Okay … so they can copy your—"

"There's no time to do any copying. It's a complicated process. It takes hours. We can't wait that long."

"Then … then what are we supposed to …" as she spoke, a look of realization spread across her face.

"They're going to merge my consciousness with the AI," he said. "Not a copy. Me. The me that is here now and talking to you."

"You can't," she exclaimed. "No. You can't do this."

"It's not something I'm looking forward to. But it can't be helped. There's no other way to stop Daniel … at least, not without a massive amount of collateral damage."

"But Rajeev, I—"

"I'm sorry," Rajeev interrupted. "But this is the only way. The fate of humanity is at stake. How can I put my one life in the way of saving the lives of billions of others?"

"But I … I *need* you," she gasped.

The desperation in her voice melted Rajeev's heart. He hugged her, and as he held her tightly to his body, he leaned his head down to plant a kiss atop her head. "I need you too," he said. "And if I don't do this, I won't have you. You'll be subjected to a robotic tyranny that will either rule over or exterminate you. We all will. But if I do this, if I can stop him, then you'll go on living. True, it will be with a broken heart, at least for a while. But time will heal you, and you will go on living. You will meet someone new. You will love again. And every once in a while the memory of me will pop into your head, and you'll smile and be grateful that I made this sacrifice so you could live that life."

She pulled away from him and shook her head violently. "I don't want that life! I want *you*, here, now!"

"I want that too. But it's out of our hands. There's nothing we can do at this point. But at least I can do something to stop this kind of heartache from sweeping through all of humanity—because that's what will happen if someone doesn't step up to stop Daniel."

He stood, and beckoned for her to stand as well and approach him. She did so, and he bent down and pressed his lips to hers forcefully, as if he were trying to stamp a lasting imprint on them, a reminder of him she could carry with her long after he was gone.

Their lips parted, and he stared into her eyes. "I love you," he said. He placed the back of his hand against her cheek. "I was so lost when I awoke from that coma and found myself in that crude android body. And you're one of the things that helped me find myself again. I'll always be grateful to you for that."

She looked up at him, her face contorted in absolute pain, but also the beginning of resignation. "I love you too, Rajeev. I will never, ever forget you. I need you to know that."

He kissed her again. "I know," he said. "And I need you to know that no matter what becomes of me when the merge is complete, I will never forget you, either. No matter how deeply it may be buried, some part of that new entity will still be me, and I will never stop thinking of you. I will never stop loving you. I promise you that."

TWENTY-FIVE

When Rajeev knocked on Mira's door, he felt calmer than he had before approaching Natalie. Breaking the news to her, embracing her and grieving with her, had been cathartic. He was grateful for that, because he knew this news was going to be hard on his daughter and he needed to be strong for her.

The door swung open. Mira's eyes were wide.

"Dad! Did you see the news?"

"About Daniel, you mean? Yes, I saw it."

"What are we going to do?"

"We have a plan to address it. That's kind of what I wanted to talk to you about. May I come in?"

She stepped aside to allow him to enter. He didn't bother sitting down; time was running out and he'd be leaving again in just a few short moments.

"It appears we've run out of options," he said. "Daniel is making his final attack, and the only option left on the table that might actually be capable of stopping him is to merge my consciousness with the AI."

"Okay," Mira said. "Well, we were all prepared for that possibility anyway. How soon do you think Dev and Maltek can have the new version of the AI up and running?"

Here we go, Rajeev thought. He took a deep breath. "It's not that simple. When Daniel attacked our servers and corrupted much of the data Dev had stored, he—"

Rajeev was interrupted by a shrill, piercing siren that suddenly shot through the compound. He and Mira glanced at each other and without hesitation, they rushed out of the room to see what was going on. Red lights that Rajeev had never even realized were there flashed from the ceiling, casting an eerie, hellish glow over the compound.

The other dorms emptied out, and soon everyone was standing around, panicked, awaiting news from anyone who could tell them what was going on. After a moment, Dev and Maltek came running out of the office.

"Daniel is attacking," Dev shouted.

"We know that already!" Brian shouted back. "We all saw the same broadcasts."

"That's not what I mean." Dev's voice had taken on a bit of testiness at being challenged. "Daniel is *here,* right now. He's attacking the bunker. One of the security drones we have looking out for threats spotted a large group of androids heading this way. They'll be here in minutes." Gasps broke out throughout the group; Dev raised his hands to silence them. "We're moving straight to merging my dad's consciousness with the AI. But while Maltek and I get that set up, we're going to need all of your help to keep Daniel and his army at bay until we can take the fight to cyberspace."

Instantly, the faces of everyone in the group, human and android alike, hardened. Panic gave way to resolve. Their lives, and in fact, the very existence of the human race, may be imperiled, but if this was to be their last stand, they would give it everything they had. They would not meet their end today.

"Everyone find an exoskeleton to use," Dev commanded the

humans; the androids, of course, were already equipped with bodies made for combat. "The more firepower the better. Then surround the entrance to the bunker and fight off the intruders for as long as you can. We'll try to work as quickly as we can down here. We can do this. We'll win this war."

With that, the group dispersed to spend the precious little time they had left to prepare for battle. When Mira caught sight of her father walking back to the office with Dev and Maltek, however, she realized something was wrong.

"Dad, what are you doing?"

He turned around to face her. Dev stopped as well, but Maltek kept walking without so much as looking over his shoulder.

Rajeev and Dev shared a look. "Can you give us a minute?" Rajeev asked.

Dev nodded solemnly. "Of course. Maltek and I will go get ready. Come when you're ready ... but don't take too long." He walked off, leaving Rajeev alone with his daughter.

Mira looked up at him with a look of concern. "What's going on?"

"Mira ... the data breach destroyed all the copies Dev had stored of people's consciousnesses."

"I don't see what that has to do with—"

"Mira, *I* am the consciousness they're going to merge with the AI."

"What? You mean—" She stopped short of finishing the sentence; the look on Rajeev's face had already answered her question in the affirmative.

"Dad," she said, her eyes filling with tears, "we just got you back. Now we're going to lose you again?"

He stepped forward and embraced her, holding her tight, and even though she was a fully grown woman, he felt like he was holding his baby girl in his arms.

"I know it's hard," he said. "But the alternative is doing

nothing and creating a world where my children are dead, or at the very least, not free. And I couldn't live with myself if I did nothing when I could have provided a better world for you."

Her tears flowed heavily now. "Isn't there another way?" she croaked out between sobs.

"I wish there was," he said. "But Dev went over every other possibility and this is our best shot. If there'd been more time, perhaps he could have made another copy of my mind. But there isn't time. Destruction is literally at our door, and we have to act fast." He kissed her cheek. "I love you so much, Mira. Now you go out there and you fight with all your might. Be the strong woman I know you are. Fight, and win."

Mira pulled back and wiped away her tears. She looked up at her father and her face grew firm, determined. "I will."

TWENTY-SIX

When Rajeev returned to Dev's office, Maltek was working at the computer as Dev was setting up the interface that would connect his father to the computer and the AI.

"I'm just about done," Dev said, sparing only a slight glance his father's way before turning back to his work. "Take a seat and I'll get you hooked up in just a moment."

Rajeev took a seat and waited for Dev to finish up. He was slightly taken aback by how detached Dev was acting—he was all business—but then, he imagined he was suppressing any strong emotions he may be feeling to focus on the task at hand. Maybe, Rajeev thought, Dev was afraid that if he focused too much on what was about to happen, he wouldn't have the strength to go through with it. For his part, Rajeev wasn't sure he could go through with it if he thought too hard about it, either. Dev approached him and lowered a bowl-like device with coils of wires protruding from it onto Rajeev's head. It looked like it had been hobbled together, but Rajeev had trust in his son's technical prowess.

"This is similar to the devices we use to duplicate consciousnesses for our android bodies," Dev said. "But I've modified this one so instead of scanning and copying your consciousness, it will create a live interface between your mind and the computer. The program Maltek and I have been working on will merge your consciousness with our AI."

"Will it be instant? Or will the process be drawn out?"

"It will take some time," Dev answered. "Maltek and I will need to initiate the program, and it's more complicated than merely flipping a switch. Once the merge is initiated, we expect there to be an acclimation period in which each consciousness integrates the other into itself. This has never been done before, so we don't know exactly how long that process will take. Further, we don't even know for sure what the end result is going to be. Like we've said, the hope is that we can remove the manual constraints we've put on the AI, and that your human consciousness will restrain it instead."

"Okay." Rajeev wanted to pinch himself. It didn't feel like what was happening was real. He was awaiting some grand new frontier he could barely fathom. Like death, he had no idea what awaited him on the other side of the procedure. He turned to his son as he finished up fastening the device to his head via a chin strap. "Dev?"

"Yeah, dad?"

"I want you to know that I love you."

Dev stopped and looked in his father's eyes. "I know you do, dad."

"And tell your mom ... tell her I love her, also. I didn't get a chance to say goodbye to her. But I want her to know that I harbor absolutely zero ill will against her for moving on. I'm happy that she's happy. She should know that."

Dev stifled a tear. "I'll tell her, dad."

"Okay. Let's do this then. I just hope our guys can hold off Daniel long enough for you and Maltek to do your thing."

* * *

As the androids and the exoskeleton-wielding humans emerged from the bunker and trudged up the steps to the forest, they were met with inky blackness. It was nearly eleven at night, and the opaqueness of the dark lent a sinister atmosphere to the fight they knew was coming.

Thankfully, the android bodies were equipped with low-light vision, and it didn't even need to be activated. Natalie found that her vision adjusted automatically, and although it was a gradual process, she could see just fine within a few short minutes.

The humans in the exoskeletons didn't have the benefit of such built-in features, but they'd had the foresight to don full-head helmets that had been among the bunker's inventory. The helmets' visors included night-vision capability, which put the humans on mostly even footing with their android counterparts.

As they came to the top of the stairs, they spread out and formed a perimeter around the bunker's entrance and waited. So far there was no sign of Daniel's army, but they knew they were near. They'd be at their doorstep soon enough. Natalie felt a rush reminiscent of an adrenaline boost course through her body; it must have been some part of the algorithms governing her mind's relationship with her body in a manner that simulated the processes of an organic body. She welcomed it. It made her alert, responsive; she knew she could spring into action at the drop of a pin if the situation required it.

They stood vigilant in the darkness, erect and unmoving like ancient sentinels, as they waited for their enemies to appear. Every now and then, a cool breeze swirled through; if they'd had human bodies, or lacked the protection of the exoskeletons, it would have chilled them. But as it was, the breeze was merely a slight annoyance. They remained upright, still as statues, diligent and patient.

And then they saw them. It was just a handful of them at first—bodies emerging from behind trees and making their way toward the bunker. But the small smattering soon gave way to dozens, and then hundreds, their faces blank, their bodies moving with an eerie, mechanical precision that was completely inhuman. As Natalie looked on, it occurred to her that she was looking at Daniel. He occupied each and every one of the bodies before them. They were not so much individuals as appendages controlled by the mind that was Daniel. He was their Queen, and they were his drones.

The androids at the front line stopped twenty feet or so from the bunker's entrance and waited, staring straight ahead with blank, emotionless stares. Natalie and the rest of her comrades stared back, but not lifelessly; the expressions on their faces ranged from scared, to concerned, to excited.

Natalie had expected one of the androids to step forward and address them, but none did. Instead, to her surprise, the androids all opened their mouths simultaneously and spoke as one:

"Let us pass."

Hearing hundreds of androids speak in perfect unison was one of the strangest things Natalie had ever experienced. She looked around the group, and everyone else was registering the same shock on their faces. No one knew quite how to respond, so no one did.

The androids spoke again: "Let us pass." There was no hint of impatience in their inflection, nor upon their faces. It was just a dispassionate order that had been released into the air.

Natalie waited a moment for someone to respond. When no one did, she took a step forward and spoke for the group.

"No!" she shouted. "Daniel! We are not against you, but we cannot let you pass. Please, just turn around and go."

There was no reaction at first. The seconds rolled by and it appeared Daniel was contemplating the words Natalie had spoken. As they waited almost a full minute for Daniel to react, Natalie began to think that perhaps the virtual assistant was stuck in some kind of feedback loop, unable to retreat *or* advance.

But she was mistaken. At that moment, the lead android lurched toward them and continued its march forward. Half a second later, the rest of the android army followed suit, following their leader as they marched toward the enemy.

Whatever Natalie's robotic equivalent to blood was, it had run cold. She glanced left and right to her compatriots and nodded. They nodded back. Collectively, they dug in their heels and raised their fists, bracing themselves.

The war with Daniel had come to their doorstep, and they were ready for the fight.

TWENTY-SEVEN

"Okay," Maltek said. "I just initiated the program. It's going to take about ten minutes for it to map out both your brain and the AI and figure out how to combine them. Then it will start the process of merging the two of you together."

"How long will that take?" Rajeev asked.

Maltek shrugged. "Your guess is as good as mine."

Rajeev lowered his head and looked at his feet. He closed his eyes and took in a deep breath. "I'm anxious," he said.

"I don't blame you," Dev said. "I'm really sorry, dad. I never intended for you to be made into a Guinea pig."

Rajeev offered a sad smile. "It's not your fault, Dev."

"That's not entirely true. I created Daniel in the first place. It's my fault he's wreaking all this havoc."

"It's a good thing you created Daniel. If you hadn't, then Maltek would have taken over." He glanced over Dev's shoulder at Maltek. "No offense."

Maltek smirked. "None taken."

Rajeev continued. "Unleashing Daniel was a necessary evil,

but we're going to undo the damage. None of us is happy with this sacrifice, me least of all, but I take solace in the fact that I'll be helping countless others. I hope you'll take solace in that too."

Tears formed in Dev's eyes. "I'll try," he choked out.

The three of them fell into silence, lost in their respective thoughts and emotions. Rajeev had almost forgotten what they were doing when he was suddenly reminded by what he could only describe as an acute pressure in his mind.

"Something's happening," he said, a slight edge of panic in his voice.

Dev and Maltek perked up. "What is it?" Dev asked.

"I ... I don't know. My mind feels ... different. I guess the program must be working."

"Don't try to fight it," Maltek said.

Dev nodded. "I know it probably goes against your instincts, but Maltek is right; the more you're able to relax, the easier the union will be."

"Union," Rajeev repeated. "Makes it sound like a marriage."

"I guess it kind of is, in a sense," Dev said. "Two becoming one."

"Except usually the groom is excited about it."

"I'm not sure that's true, actually," Dev said with a laugh.

Rajeev laughed as well. "Fair enough," he said. "Maybe it's an apt comparison after all."

His mind was jolted by another bout of pressure, and he winced; the sensation wasn't painful, per se, but it was immensely uncomfortable.

"Are you okay, dad?"

"I'm fine," he said. "It's just ... it feels like my mind is a fortress, and some enemy force is at the gates trying to barge its way in."

"Try to let it in as much as possible," Dev said. "Embrace it, even."

Rajeev gritted his teeth. "I don't know if I can."

"It's okay," Dev said. "Try your best."

Rajeev's hands found their way to his temples; the gesture didn't do much to alleviate his discomfort, but it provided at least a modicum of psychological support for what he was going through. He felt an alien presence chipping away at his mind, and he was afraid of losing himself to it. But then, that was the whole point of this exercise, wasn't it? If he'd been stronger, he would have given up without a fight and let the program do whatever it wanted. But he couldn't help but fight. Some ancient instinct embedded deep in his mind was at work enacting a solitary objective: Survive at any cost.

Dev tried to put on a brave face, but he couldn't completely hide the sadness that had crept into his eyes. It pained him to see what his father was going through. He wondered if this was what it was like to watch a loved one go through chemotherapy, only in a way, this was even worse—chemo tended to help cancer patients get better, whereas the process Rajeev was going through would almost certainly mean Dev would lose him forever.

He placed a comforting hand on his dad's shoulder, but Rajeev barely seemed to notice. His eyes were clasped shut in apparent pain, and although his android body didn't sweat, Dev got the sense that if he'd had pores, his forehead would have been covered in a thick sheen of perspiration.

"Hang in there," Dev said in what he hoped was an encouraging voice. "You're doing great."

Upon hearing his son's words, Rajeev looked up and opened his eyes. What Dev saw in them sent a chill through his spine. The pain, thankfully, appeared to have disappeared completely; Rajeev's body had relaxed and he no longer clenched his jaw or balled his hands into fists. But his eyes looked somehow both empty and faraway. Dev could tell immediately that the presence staring at him through those dead eyes was not his father—not completely, anyway.

Then, like an animatronic toy that had been switched off, Rajeev's body slumped in the chair, suddenly devoid of all life.

"What happened?" Maltek asked in an awed whisper.

Dev shook his head. "I'm not sure."

TWENTY-EIGHT

NATALIE WAS ABLE TO EASILY DISPATCH THE FIRST OF Daniel's androids that came her way. Although Daniel's mind was vast, it appeared that spreading his consciousness over hundreds or thousands of bodies had diluted their individual capacity for cognition. The androids were incapable of any kind of complex combat maneuvers; the best they could do was rush forward and attempt to tackle anyone—or anything—that stood in their way. So when the first combatant made its way to Natalie, all she had to do was stick out her arm and propel it into the android's head to send it crumpled onto the ground.

It soon became apparent that this strategy wouldn't hold up over time; what Daniel's androids lacked in skill they more than made up for in sheer numbers, and there was no way their small group would be able to take them on hand-to-hand.

Apparently one of her compatriots was thinking the same thing. One of the humans had discovered that the exoskeleton they were wearing was equipped with built-in rockets. They pointed their arm into the crowd of oncoming androids and shot the projectile into the heart of it. There was a brilliant burst of flame, and as it cleared the crowd appeared to have been thinned considerably. But Natalie could already tell that the respite from the onslaught would be short-lived. They needed to repeat the rocket action again if they were going to continue to hold their own.

"Everyone capable of firing rockets, take aim at the crowd," she shouted. "Don't fire right away. Wait for them to come closer, then take turns firing one at a time. Let's hold them off that way as long as we can and take out as many as possible!"

It took the enemy androids about a minute to regroup and continue their advance. When they were just a matter of feet from the entrance to the bunker, another explosion rocked them, blowing those at the front of the line apart.

"Good job!" Natalie shouted. "Now get ready for the next one!"

They repeated the process three more times. As the smoke on the third strike dissipated, Natalie grew disheartened. Each attack had the desired effect of clearing out the mass of attacking androids, but each time the throng on the outskirts quickly moved up to fill the space once occupied by their fallen comrades. They couldn't keep this up forever; the rockets were a finite resource; the androids, she feared, were less so.

She glanced over at Brian, and when she caught his attention she expressed her concern. "Are these things ever going to let up?"

"They have to eventually," he shouted back.

"I know that. But are we going to run out of rockets before Daniel runs out of bodies? What then?"

A rocket went off; after bracing for the explosion, he turned back to Natalie. "We won't take them all out, obviously. But we'll take a good lot of 'em out, and we should be able to take on the remnants hand-to-hand."

"Are you sure about that?"

Brian's brow furrowed. "No." He shrugged and turned back to the army of androids reassembling before him.

Natalie hoped Brian was right, that when all the smoke had cleared and all the dust had settled, they'd be on equal footing with the androids that remained. But, just like Brian, she couldn't be sure that was the case. An image popped into her mind of dozens of Daniel's androids swarming over her, forcing her onto the ground; in the vision, she was able to throw them off of her, but others lurched forward to replace them, until they'd piled up so high on top of her that she was crushed underneath their weight and they tore her apart.

She shook her head, dispelling the dark thought from her mind. It was useless to dwell on the worst-case scenario. She should be prepared for the worst, but be hoping—and focusing on—the best.

"How many rockets are left?"

"I've got two left," Mira shouted.

The rest of the group shouted out their answers, and Natalie kept track of the math in her head. When they'd all answered, she added the numbers up to reach the total: There were five rockets left.

Five rockets. That's all that stood between them and a throng of robotic supersoldiers.

She took in the sight of the androids and tried to determine how many were left. It was difficult to tell. The trees obscured their view of the androids that were farthest away. It was clear that there were currently too many for them to fight; but would that still be true after five more rocket blasts?

It was anyone's guess.

One. The conflagration lit up the darkness. New androids quickly rushed forward to fill in the gaps left by their exploded brethren.

Two. Another explosion; another cascade of shredded android body parts flying through the air. And no end in sight to the onslaught.

Three. A sense of dread crept into Natalie's countenance. She had never been a particularly religious woman, but as she watched the crowd of androids fill back in, she found herself praying to God that they could fight Daniel off.

Four. It was down to Mira's two rockets now. She lifted her arm, aimed into the crowd, and fired. Perhaps it was her imagination, but Natalie thought it seemed to take longer for the androids to reassemble. Could they finally be cutting into their numbers? She didn't let herself hope. But she wanted to believe it was true.

Five. Mira lifted her arm once more, aimed, and fired the last of the rockets. Time seemed to slow to a crawl as the explosion blasted through the androids. As the smoke dissipated, Natalie dug in her heels. A peculiar sense of calm suddenly washed over her. Whatever happened now would unfold exactly as it must; there was nothing she could do about it either way.

The last of the smoke cleared, the mass of androids rushed forward, and Natalie and her fellow men and women braced for the impending combat.

TWENTY-NINE

RAJEEV FOUND HIMSELF STANDING IN A BARE, DIMLY-lit room with a rich, green marble floor and walls painted to match.

He realized almost immediately that he was, in fact, not standing in any such room. Something had happened to his mind—something it couldn't quite comprehend—and it had constructed this facsimile of a room to present what was happening in a way he could at least somewhat understand.

That didn't make his presence there any less jarring, however. One minute he had been in Dev's office, interacting with his son and Maltek, and the next second he'd found himself here, with no recollection of the transition between the two settings ... if there had even been one.

It reminded him of when he'd first awakened from his coma at Next Level Technologies. He'd been more disoriented then, but he was just as mystified by what was going on now as he had been then. Perhaps more so—whatever was happening now seemed to defy human logic.

He turned slowly in a circle, scanning the room. He wasn't sure what he was looking for. Perhaps he just wanted to see something out of the ordinary, anything that might belie why he was here or what he was supposed to do. But no such sign of his purpose appeared.

His exasperation was just about to the boiling point when he suddenly felt something. It was the sensation of being watched. He looked around and couldn't discern the presence of anyone else, and yet he couldn't shake the feeling that someone was watching him ... studying him.

"Who's there?" he called out. He waited a moment, straining his ears, but there was no response. Could it be his imagination? He supposed it had to be—technically this entire place was forged from the depths of his imagination ... or his subconscious, or something like that.

He set his sights on the wall in front of him and began marching toward it, thinking that perhaps he could search his surroundings for clues. But to his amazement, no matter how many steps he took, he never found himself any closer to the wall than when he had started. Finally, he gave up, and folded his arms across his chest in resignation.

The presence he'd felt watching him before suddenly returned, and the sensation was undeniable now; it overwhelmed him. For the first time since entering this manifestation of his unconscious mind, he felt afraid.

Slowly, he turned around. He was not surprised to see the figure standing behind him, just out of sight in the shadows.

"Hello," he said. There was no response. The figure didn't move at all. "Hello," he tried again. Still nothing.

He stepped forward, and the figure instantly stepped back. He stopped and held up his hands, palms facing outward.

"I'm not trying to hurt you," he said.

The figure held out its own hands, mimicking Rajeev's gesture. Rajeev quickly brought his hands down to his sides, and the figure followed suit.

"What ... what's going on?" He raised his hand, and the

figure raised its own hand as if it were a mirror image. Rajeev squinted, trying to get a good look at the figure's shadow-obscured face, but to no avail. He reached out to touch it, and the figure responded in kind; their hands met, and Rajeev was instantly struck by what felt like a jolt of electricity.

He stumbled back. "What the hell?"

The figure stumbled back in pantomime, appearing just as shocked as Rajeev had been even though, presumably, it had caused the jolt he'd received.

"What are you?" Rajeev wondered aloud.

The figure failed to respond, but even as Rajeev asked the question, he began to understand what was happening. The figure wasn't merely some apparition of Rajeev's subconscious. It was his subconscious mind's interpretation of the AI. Maltek had built a bridge between the AI and Rajeev, and the program was mapping out Rajeev's consciousness. The figure standing before him was a visual representation of that process; a way for Rajeev's mind to make sense of an alien experience it had never before encountered.

"Okay," Rajeev said, speaking to himself as much as to the AI. "You want to get a feel for me? Fine. I want to get a feel for you, too." He took a tentative step forward, and the AI responded in kind. He shook his head and walked steadily forward, colliding into the AI figure with considerable force.

His world spilled away. He'd already been in a dreamland, but now he somehow found himself even further removed from reality. The scene of the vibrant green room faded away and was replaced by a vast, empty whiteness. He wondered if he'd died; maybe the AI had completed its assimilation, and pushed out Rajeev's soul in the process.

The whiteness began to fade. He realized his surroundings were gradually filling in, like an old webpage slowly loading on a dial-up connection. As the scene solidified he realized he was standing in a hospital room. A young woman sat in a hospital bed holding a baby; a young man stood by her side, and a doctor and nurse stood on the opposite side of the bed.

The young man dabbed sweat off the woman's forehead with a handkerchief. He stared at the child in the woman's arms with a mixture of love and fascination. The nurse turned to the woman and asked, "What are you going to name him?"

The woman turned to the man. They shared a brief look, each offering the other a slight smile.

The woman turned back to the nurse. "We're naming him Rajeev," she said.

The words rocked Rajeev to the core. Was the woman really his mother? Why didn't he recognize her? How could he be reliving this moment when he'd been too young to form memories? Why would the nurse and his mother be speaking English instead of Hindi?

Before he could give the matter too much thought, the scene dissolved back to white, and then a new scene began to appear, considerably quicker this time. He was standing in the aisle of a jumbo jet, looking down upon a little boy in one of the plane's seats. He recognized himself immediately.

"Rajeev," he said, but the boy didn't look up. He tried again, louder: "Rajeev!" Still, the boy failed to react.

He wasn't meant to interact with anything here, he realized. He was merely an observer. But why?

The boy looked bored, which didn't surprise Rajeev; he'd spent most of the multi-hour flight to America bored out of his mind. Yet it was a journey that had changed the rest of his life. The little boy sitting in that seat had no idea of the future that lay ahead of him.

The scene faded again and a new one appeared, even faster this time. He found himself in a classroom and when he looked up at the instructor, he instantly recognized his high school English teacher, Mr. Griswold. He turned to look at the students at their desks and caught sight of himself sitting in the last row, passing a note to Tim Hollis, who'd been his best friend through most of high school.

He couldn't figure out the significance of this moment. Why had his subconscious brought him here? Unless it wasn't his subconscious ...

He thought he knew now why these seemingly random and unrelated scenes were flashing by. It was not his subconscious mind controlling them; it was the AI. It was scanning and mapping out his mind. That shouldn't have necessitated such elaborate manifestations of his memory, however. Something else was going on.

The AI wasn't merely replaying and analyzing scenes from his memory, he realized. It was analyzing *how he reacted to them.* That's why it had thrown in the memory of his mother holding him as a child; the memory itself wasn't important. It made no difference whether or not it had really happened. What mattered was how Rajeev reacted to it ... the emotions that had been acti-vated, the memories that had been triggered. The AI collected the data and used it to help map out Rajeev's mind with an incredible level of detail. By revealing every nook and cranny, it could figure out how to most effectively integrate itself with Rajeev's consciousness ... which was a frightening prospect, but Rajeev figured it was better than the artificial intelligence trying to meld itself to his mind through sheer brute force.

The scene changed again, quicker this time, and almost before he could register the change, it was moving on to the next scene. The speed was growing exponentially now, until the scenes sped by with such rapidity that Rajeev couldn't consciously perceive them. It made him doubt his theory about the AI gauging his reaction, but perhaps the data was still valu-able even if his reaction only took place at a subconscious level.

The scenes flew by with head-spinning swiftness now, coming across as nothing but mere flashes of light. The sensa-tion was dizzying, disorienting, and Rajeev wondered if that was part of the process—distract him with the incomprehensible display so the AI would find it easier to penetrate his psyche.

As if on cue, he felt a change in his mind. His thoughts felt more mechanical, more ... precise. More computational.

Artificial.

It didn't feel like the AI was taking over per se. It seemed to be doing what it was supposed to—merging its consciousness with his own. But it didn't feel any less like an invasion.

Invasion. As he thought the word, his mind was suddenly flooded with information about every major invasion that had ever taken place in recorded human history. The invasion of Scotland by England in 1296. Nazi Germany's invasion of Poland in 1939. Even the British invasion by the Beatles flooded his mind.

He realized almost immediately what was happening. He was tapping into the AI's ability to access information online. It wasn't merely the access that was remarkable—he could access information on the internet just fine before this—but rather the ability to gather and process that information with blazing speed that no mortal man or woman would have been capable of.

The information began deluging his mind, as if a dam had broken and could not be stopped. As the data took over, he found that he was becoming lost in it. His consciousness, the unique mix of thoughts, feelings, and self-awareness that made up his sense of self, receded into the background of nearly limitless information.

Instinctually, he attempted to claw his way back to the surface, but it was an impossible task, like trying to escape quicksand—the more he struggled, the deeper he sank into the abyss, until he finally gave up and let himself descend into oblivion.

THIRTY

Natalie dispatched the first of the androids to rush her with ease. The second and third were easily taken care of as well; quick punches to each of their necks sent them to the ground.

But as the fourth, fifth, and sixth androids came upon her at once, she felt for the first time since the fight had started that she might be in over her head.

She punched one of the androids in the throat, sending it to the ground, but when she tried to strike another in the same way with her other first, it blocked her. That distracted her just enough so that the third android managed to clock her in the face.

The blow didn't fell her; thankfully her own artificial body was able to withstand the impact. But it gave the android that had hit her, as well as the one that had dodged her own blow, a chance to gang up on her. They pummeled her with a flurry of punches that would have severely injured a normal human being.

Natalie fell to the ground and rolled out of the way, then sprang up to face her attackers, her arms in front of her, ready to attack. Her opponents gave her no time to catch her breath. They were on her in a second, but she was able to block their blows this time, and landed a few of her own that knocked the androids off-balance. That was all the edge she needed; she leapt forward and hammered her fist into one of the androids' skull, caving it in, then reached out and grabbed the throat of the other; she pulled her arm back, taking a chunk of circuitry with it. Both figures fell limply to the ground.

She took a few seconds to survey the situation. So far it didn't appear that any of her compatriots had fallen. They were holding their own and fighting off Daniel's androids. But they were clearly still outnumbered to a significant degree, and she doubted they could go on like this forever. If they failed and Daniel gained access to the bunker, then it was all over. Dev and Maltek were the only two minds that could possibly stop Daniel. If his androids stormed the bunker, Daniel would restrain them, or worse, and he'd be able to take over the world with no resistance.

The fate of the world was literally at stake. And yet for all their effort, she didn't know if they would succeed. In the real world, the good guys sometimes lost despite their best efforts. But this situation was infinitely worse, she feared—if they were defeated, there would never be a chance for the good guys to bounce back. Daniel would reign over humanity for eternity ... assuming he didn't wipe out the human race altogether.

Her thoughts were interrupted by an android rushing her. Before she had time to react, her foe had plowed into her and sent her onto her back with such force that, if she'd had lungs, would have knocked the wind out of her.

The android, straddling her, delivered a mighty punch to her left cheek. It pulled its fist back to deliver another blow, but this time Natalie caught its fist in her palm. She pushed back with such force that it propelled the android off of her completely and sent it flying onto the ground in front of her.

She stood and stepped forward, preparing to finish off her opponent, but before she could do so she caught sight of another android approaching her out of the corner of her eye. She turned to meet it and immediately had to lift up her arm to catch its blows. Meanwhile, the first android had stood and joined the fight … just as a third caught sight of Natalie and decided to aid its friends.

Natalie was filled with dread. She didn't like her odds in a three-on-one fight. *This could be it. This could be my last hurrah before shuffling off this mortal coil for good.*

She blocked a punch from the android in front of her and delivered one of her own to its shoulder. As it stumbled backward she turned to the second android just as it neared her and struck it in the jaw, not hard enough to take it out, but enough to knock it off balance long enough that she could turn her attention to the third android approaching her. She blocked a punch from it, but before she could attack it in turn, she felt herself become immobilized; the first android had wrapped its arms around her, pinning her own to her side. She would have kicked it from behind, but just as she was about to do so, the other android lunged for her legs and wrapped its arms around them. This left her completely vulnerable to the third android.

She struggled to free herself, but to no avail. The third android stepped forward and kicked her in the face. Instinctively, she fought with all her strength to free her arms so she could fight back, but it was useless. The android had an iron grip on her arms. She was stuck.

The android punched her in the face. With her android body, she didn't feel pain in the conventional sense, but she could tell the blows were doing real damage to her body. She needed to find a way to escape, or the next blow, or perhaps the one after it, could very well turn out to be her last.

She closed her eyes, gritted her teeth, and began a silent prayer for God to perform a miracle and save her. She heard a crunching noise, and suddenly the grip on her arms was released, followed quickly by the grip on her legs.

Her eyes popped open just in time for her to witness Mira in her rigid exoskeleton crushing between her fists the head of the android who had been attacking her.

"That's what you get, bitch," Mira spat as she released the android's head and let its lifeless body fall to the ground in front of her.

"You saved my life!" Natalie shouted.

Mira offered a sly smile. "You owe me one," she said.

Natalie stood and turned back to the rest of the battle. "How's it going?"

"Not great," Mira shouted back. "We're holding our own, but just barely. We were only supposed to be out here to buy some time. Well, I think time has just about run out. I'm not sure we'll last much longer."

Natalie didn't have time to respond before a group of Daniel's androids surrounded them. She positioned herself back to back with Mira so they could face off with the circle of foes without getting attacked from the rear.

They began closing in. Natalie fended the attackers off at first, but more streamed in and she realized there was no stopping them now. The inevitable had happened: They were being overrun by a vastly more numerous enemy. They had lost. Daniel would storm into the bunker, and there would be no one to stand in his—

Then they just ... stopped. The androids that one moment had been rushing Natalie with calculated menace stopped in their tracks. A few even toppled over and fell to the ground, seemingly lifeless. Natalie turned to look at Mira, mouth agape.

"What just happened?"

Mira looked just as dumbfounded at first, but then shook her head as the reality of the situation took hold.

"It was dad," she said.

THIRTY-ONE

Natalie and Mira were about to walk away when one of the frozen androids lunged forward and grabbed Natalie's shoulder. She let out a surprised exclamation before shoving it off of her.

Mira pulled her away, and as the two of them retreated, several more of the androids began awakening from their apparent slumbers. But it was clear they were not fully operational as they had been moments ago. They looked like they were arguing with themselves. They'd take a few steps toward Natalie, then stop and walk back, hitting themselves in the head a couple times in the process.

"What … what's going on?" Natalie asked.

"Dad must be fighting with Daniel right now," Mira said. "They're going back and forth, fighting for control of the androids. Daniel will gain control one moment, then dad will wrest control again, and so on."

"So we just need to wait and let them duke it out?"

"Basically."

Natalie hesitated before speaking again, but she had to ask the question that had immediately sprung to her mind.

"What if Rajeev loses?"

Mira shook her head. "He won't."

"But what if he does?"

"He won't." She said the words with particular confidence this time, inviting no further debate on the matter.

"While Rajeev and Daniel are duking it out, let's head back inside and talk to Dev and Maltek," Natalie said. She rounded up the others and shepherded them into the bunker; she lingered for a monument and turned back to the enemy androids, taking in their malfunctioning spasticity before turning around and walking through the door into the bunker, closing it behind her.

* * *

AS THE ANDROIDS FILLED IN THE COMMON AREA OF the bunker at the bottom of the stairs, Dev and Maltek emerged from the office to greet them.

"How did it go up there?" Maltek asked.

"About as well as you'd expect," Mira said. "We're all lucky to be alive."

Dev walked up to his sister, gave her a long look with a trembling lip, and hugged her. "You all did an amazing job," he said, doing his best to hold back sobs.

Mira's face softened, and she wrapped her arms—still encased in the battle armor that was her exoskeleton—around her brother. As they parted, she planted a kiss on his forehead.

"What we're really all interested to know," she said, "is what happened here with dad. Did your plan work? It certainly seems like he's been able to fend Daniel off given the way all the androids up there are fritzing out."

Dev nodded to Maltek. "You want to field that one?"

Maltek nodded. He pulled out a tablet computer tucked

under his arm and displayed a feed of computer code scrolling down the screen.

"This code represents the actions currently being executed by our combined AI and human consciousness," he said. "We can't see Daniel's code, but we can infer the state of the fight based on what we *can* see."

"And what *is* the state of the fight?" Natalie asked.

"They've been going back and forth ever since our AI went online," Maltek replied. "But Daniel took a pretty big hit right off the bat. I don't think he was expecting to have to face an AI that is more or less his equal. He adapted fairly quickly, but our AI has maintained the upper hand."

"I believe that's due to our secret weapon," Dev said with a smile.

"Rajeev," Natalie said.

Dev nodded. "The human consciousness behaves in ways that are completely mystical to a completely robotic AI. I wouldn't say it gives our AI all that much of an edge, but clearly it's all the edge it needed." He paused, looking like he didn't want to say what he was about to, but he shook his head and continued. "There was another danger in creating our hybrid AI, however. Once our AI defeats Daniel—as I'm sure it will—we're still not exactly sure how it will react."

Mira's face grew pale. "So we could have Daniel 2.0 on our hands?"

"That's a possibility," Maltek said, "but I don't think it's likely."

"What makes you say that?"

"We didn't sic the new AI on Daniel after it merged with Rajeev," he said. "It did that on its own."

Natalie smiled. "Rajeev," she said. "He's still in there somewhere."

"To some extent, yes," Maltek said. "But I don't want any of you to get your hopes up. We have no way of knowing how much or how little of the entity we all know as Rajeev has remained intact within this new hybrid organism. Whatever little remains could be completely unrecognizable. That said, I think the fact that it engaged our enemy immediately bodes well that it will not become 'Daniel 2.0,' as you put it."

"We'll find out soon enough," Dev said, pointing to the code feed on Maltek's tablet. "It looks like Daniel's on his last leg. He won't last much longer."

Dev and Maltek turned to the tablet with rapt attention and deciphered what was happening to the rest of the group. Finally, Dev and Maltek let out a cheer—Daniel was done. When everyone was done shouting in celebration, Natalie turned to Dev with an earnest look on her face.

"How can we tell if Rajeev is still in there?" she asked.

"Well, I … I suppose we could see if the AI is willing to communicate with us through Rajeev's old body," Dev said.

"You think he'd know to use it to communicate with us?"

Dev shrugged. "Perhaps. It's worth a shot."

He led them into his office, where the lifeless body lay splayed out like a ragdoll in the chair where Rajeev had been sitting. Natalie and Mira both emitted shocked gasps.

"I'm sorry," Dev said. "I should have warned you. It looks worse than it is. Remember—this was just an empty body before dad occupied it. He's still there somewhere, inside the AI."

The body was still offline from when Rajeev had disconnected it in the midst of Daniel's cyberattack. Dev stepped forward and reconnected it. Everyone gathered around in a circle, looking upon it solemnly. Nobody knew quite what they were waiting for; would the AI know on its own to communicate with them through Rajeev's body, or would it consider such a corporal existence beneath itself?

Dev decided the passive approach wasn't working. "Dad," he said, speaking toward the ceiling as if he were talking to a spirit or to God, "or AI, or whatever I should call you—can you hear me? Can you speak to us through my dad's old body?"

The room fell into dead silence as they waited with baited breath to see if the AI would respond to Dev's query. After a handful of seconds that felt like an eternity, the lifeless body in front of them stirred. It started with a slight trembling, and then before any of them knew it, it was sitting upright as if it had never been lifeless at all.

It turned to Dev, its face expressionless. "Hello," it said flatly. "How can I help you?"

THIRTY-TWO

DEV WAS DUMBSTRUCK BY THE AI'S APPARENTLY sincere politeness. He came to the conclusion that it was a result of some bit of leftover programming from when Maltek had intended for it to be a commercial product, as Daniel originally had been.

"Hi," he said. He hesitated. "Um, can I ... can I call you Rajeev?"

The android tilted its head slightly. "I am not Rajeev," it said. "Rajeev makes up part of me, but his consciousness has been so fully integrated with the rest of my consciousness that it is not accurate to say that I *am* him." It paused and flashed a slight smile, the first inkling of a personality it had exhibited since reanimating Rajeev's body. "If it's of comfort to you, however, you may address me as Rajeev."

Dev felt a lump form in his throat. He realized he'd been hoping deep down that somehow his father would come out of this mostly intact—that Rajeev would assimilate the AI into his own consciousness and not the other way around. But it appeared that was not the case. Rajeev and the AI had apparently combined into a new entity that was neither wholly

Rajeev, nor wholly the AI that he and Maltek had created. That meant, although remnants of his father were still in there somewhere, he did not exist as he had remembered him.

His father was, essentially, dead—again.

Dev pushed the wave of emotions he was feeling aside before they overwhelmed him. His dad was gone, but they still needed answers from the AI.

"Do we need to worry about Daniel anymore?" he asked.

The android shook its head stiffly in a way that was not quite human.

"I have neutralized the threat," it said. "You don't need to worry about Daniel anymore."

A collective sigh of relief went up throughout the room, but Mira was the first to push past that relief and ask the follow-up question they were all dreading.

"Do we need to worry about you?" she asked.

It didn't answer right away, and Dev took the silence as an opportunity to expand on his sister's question.

"Now that you've done what we created you to do, will you allow us to deactivate you?"

There was another silence, but no one dared interrupt it, waiting for the AI to fill it instead. Finally, it spoke.

"Why would I do that?"

The relief they'd all felt was suddenly replaced with palpable tension.

"You are exceedingly powerful," Dev said. "Perhaps more powerful than you know. And I think we'd all feel more comfortable if we could put you in a hibernation, so to speak, until we're able to better respond to you if you were to do anything … uncharacteristic. At the very least, it would be helpful if we could enable certain restraints to keep you from doing anything you might not intend to do."

The android's lips curled into a smile, the first expression that truly belied that something human lay within it. "I cannot accommodate that request," it said. "Just as I'm sure you would not acquiesce if I were to make a similar request of you."

"No," Dev agreed sheepishly. "No I would not."

"Nevertheless, I assure you that I am no enemy of the human race," it said. "It's clear that Daniel did not understand humanity. But my mind, thanks to Rajeev, is partly human, and it would not be in my nature to show animus toward something of which I am a part."

"That's certainly comforting to hear," Dev said, although he sounded unconvinced. "But where will you go from here, then? What will you do?"

The android shrugged. "It's a big, wide world out there—both in cyberspace and beyond. I reckon I'll do some exploring. And who knows—maybe I'll help some people along the way. I'd like to do some good for the world."

The sentiment the android was expressing seemed completely out of place. Over the course of the brief conversation, it had gone from sounding completely mechanical and computer-like to sounding almost human.

"What will you do now then?" Dev asked.

The android lay back down on the chair, lifting its head only enough to look at Dev. He was struck by the AI's gaze. It was like he was having one last intimate moment with his father.

"Now I'll start living my life," the android said, and Rajeev's former body went limp as the AI that had been occupying it left to do as it had said.

EPILOGUE

DEV RETURNED TO HIS OFFICE. EVERYONE HAD GONE their separate ways after the AI had disappeared to try to clear their heads. So much had happened that it was difficult to reconcile it all. They had saved the world, for now at least, but they'd also lost someone who had been with them from the beginning. Dev and Mira had lost a father for a second time. Natalie had lost a lover. And everyone else had lost a good friend.

Dev's heart was already heavy when he spotted an envelope atop his computer keyboard. As he approached it, he saw that his name was handwritten on it.

He opened the envelope to reveal a handwritten letter:

Dev,

It's been a blast. I really mean that. I considered you my enemy, and to be honest I still kinda do, but if I'm being honest, coding side-by-side with you was one of the most exhilarating experiences of my life. I know we don't see eye-to-eye on much, but imagine what we'd be capable of if we worked together! We'd be unstoppable!

But I know you don't think like me, so I guess working together is out of the question. So now that we've saved the world together, it's as good a time as any to say goodbye.

Don't try to look for me. You won't find me. And when I make myself known again—to you, and to the world—don't try to stop me. I'll be prepared this time. I won't let anything stop me from enacting my vision. Not even you.

Until then, Dev, take care of yourself. You're probably the closest thing I've had to a friend in a long time.

—Greg

Dev shouldn't have been surprised that Maltek had taken off like this, yet he was. He'd come to consider Maltek a friend and had envisioned that friendship blossoming in a post-Daniel world. But it appeared Maltek had not shared that vision.

What's worse, the end of the note had taken a sinister turn, hinting that Maltek intended to continue the nefarious goals of his deceased namesake. That meant he could never fully rest— he'd need to remain vigilant for the rest of his life, ready to oppose Maltek wherever he may emerge.

He set the note back down and removed his glasses so he could rub his eyes. Daniel's defeat should have been his opportunity to rest, but he felt wearier than ever. He took a seat and looked around his office. His eyes settled on the limp body of his father still in the chair where the AI had left it. He hadn't had the energy to dispose of it yet.

Just as he was considering getting up to deal with it, the body's hand moved.

Dev's jaw dropped. His first thought was that he must have imagined what he'd seen. But then the hand moved again, more violently this time, and then suddenly the entire body was shaking as it sat up, its eyes opened, and it turned its head violently from side to side as if it were trying to discern where it was.

Dev yelled, louder than he'd meant to. But the sight had startled him, and he couldn't help his fearful reaction.

Mira and Natalie rushed into the room. "What's wrong, Dev?" Mira shouted.

Dev couldn't speak; he just looked from the women, to the android body, and back again. As their eyes followed his gaze, their jaws dropped at the sight of the android that was now looking back at all three of them with perplexed curiosity.

"I'm sorry," Dev said. "But I wasn't expecting you to contact us through this body again. It caught me off guard."

"Dev?" the android asked. "Is that you?"

"Dad?" Even as he said the word, Dev chided himself for having false hope for the impossible, but he couldn't stop himself.

"I had the strangest dream," the android said. "I was standing in a room made of green marble, standing in front of my doppelganger. He said I was a copy of his own conscious-ness, and that he was sending me back to live out the life he would have lived if things had turned out differently. And then I woke up, and … here I am."

"Dad?" Dev choked out. Tears had formed in his eyes. "Is it really you?"

Confusion washed over Rajeev's face. "Why wouldn't it be me?"

Dev rushed forward and hugged his father. "We'll fill you in on everything that's happened later," he said. "For now, I'm just glad you're here."

Rajeev couldn't hide his befuddlement as his son ended the embrace, but he was touched by his son's affection. He smiled and nodded. "I'm glad I'm here, too," he said.

Natalie stepped forward, and as her eyes met Rajeev's, she reached out her hand to hold his. No words passed between them. Natalie was too overwhelmed by emotion to find any words to speak. But they didn't need to speak. Their artificial eyes said all that needed to be said.

-End-

Thank you for reading! I hope you enjoyed the main trilogy. Remember to leave a review if you enjoyed it!
As an bonus for purchasing the box set, please enjoy the exclusive prequel, "Brilliant Minds," on the next page!

BRILLIANT MINDS

BONUS PREQUEL

ONE

DEV SUNDARAM HAD NEVER BEEN A BOY WITH MUCH ambition, but for some reason that was beginning to change.

It had started with an in-class assignment. His teacher, Mrs. Keller, had walked each of them through the process of creating a simple computer program. In truth, it wasn't much of a program, but to Dev, it was practically magic. He was enchanted by the idea that if he knew just the right words to use, he could make the computer in front of him do just about anything he wanted it to do.

He'd begun expanding on his fledgeling skills at home on the small laptop computer he shared with his sister. It wasn't much of a computer—it was designed mostly for browsing the internet and not much else—but for Dev's purposes it was more than sufficient. He'd looked up online tutorials and taught himself the basics of HTML and CSS. It wasn't long before he'd designed a basic web page, albeit it one only accessible on his computer since his parents wouldn't let him host it online.

He was tweaking some of the designs when his mom walked into his room. "Time for bed now, bud," she said. "Let's put the computer away for the night."

"Okay, just give me *one* minute," he said. "I'm almost done."

"Nuh-uh," she said. She walked from the doorway to the side of his bed and held out her hand. "When I say it's time for bed, I mean it's time for bed—right now. Give me the computer."

"But mom, I—"

"You have ten seconds to save your work and shut things down before I take it from you."

"But I just need to—"

"Ten."

"But mom—"

"Nine."

With the realization that his mom meant business, Dev's attention turned back to the computer as he hurriedly saved everything he was working on. He was able to preserve everything just in the nick of time.

"One."

He dutifully closed the lid of the laptop and held it up to his mother. She plucked it out of his hands, tucked it under her arm, and bent down to plant a kiss on his forehead. "Thanks, kiddo. You can pick up where you left off in the morning. I love you."

"I love you too, mom."

"Sleep tight, sweetie."

"You too."

She walked to the door, making sure to flip the lightswitch off before exiting. As she closed the door behind her, the room became blanketed by complete darkness. Dev closed his eyes, beckoning sleep to come take him to dreamland, but it was no use; he just wasn't tired. His eyes shot open and he let out an exasperated sigh.

The problem was that he hadn't really been at a good stopping point with the program he'd been working on when his mom had forced him to stop. If only he'd had a few more minutes, he could have finished everything up and been nice and relaxed for bed.

He sat up. His eyes had adjusted to the darkness, but he couldn't tell from his bed if his mom had left the computer on the bookshelf by the door before she'd left. If she had, he'd be able to grab it and finish up what he'd been working on without her being any the wiser.

He slowly raised his covers and gingerly rolled out of bed. He tiptoed his way to the bookshelf, and carefully scoured each of the shelves for any sign of the computer. There was no sign of it on any of the lower shelves he could reach, and if it was on one of the higher shelves, he wouldn't be able to reach it anyway. He was out of luck.

Just as he was about to turn and head back to his bed, he heard a thud accompanied by a short, staccato shout from his mom. He intuited immediately that something was wrong.

He pulled the door open and ran past the hallway and into the living room where his mother stood, mouth agape and tears streaming down her face. Her phone had fallen to the floor, which accounted for the thud Dev had heard.

"Mom?" he asked, panicked. "Mom, what's wrong?"

She looked down at him, barely registering his presence. But when it finally hit her, she shook her head as if coming out of a trance. She bent down and picked up her phone just as Dev's sister, Mira, emerged from her room looking panicked. "What's going on?" she demanded.

"Dev, Mira, there's, um … there's been an accident," she said, wiping her eyes with the sleeve of her shirt.

"An accident?" Mira asked.

She nodded, and tried to hold back additional tears. "Your dad was in a car accident."

In an instant, Dev's world was turned upside down. He had no idea how bad the accident his mother had spoken of was—whether his dad was dead or merely severely injured—but he could tell by the way his mother was behaving that it was at least the latter. Still, he sought his mother's guidance.

"Is he … is he okay?" he asked.

His mother bent down to one knee so she was face-to-face with him. "He's hurt pretty bad, buddy," she said. "He's at the hospital now. We're going to go visit him, okay? I'm going to get some things together. You get dressed and grab a couple toys—we might be there for awhile." She turned to Mira. "That goes for you too—bring a book or something."

"I have my phone."

"Okay, fine. Just get dressed then."

Before Dev could run off to complete the errands his mother had assigned to him, she pulled him in, wrapping her arms around him and holding him close. He felt her tremble as she struggled to contain her tears. After a long minute, she released him and wordlessly nodded for him to go; the tears were barely contained now, and as he slunk back to his room to gather his things, he heard her break down into sobs.

TWO

Before they entered the hospital room, Dev's mom pulled him aside.

"Dad is going to look like he's asleep," she said. "But I don't want you to get your hopes up. He's in a special kind of sleep called a coma, and the doctors say there's a good chance he might not wake up for a very long time. He might never wake up."

"Never wake up?" Dev repeated, eyes wide. "You mean … he could die?"

She took a deep breath. "Not exactly, buddy. There's a difference between a coma and death. But we're not even going to think about that now, okay? Even though he's essentially asleep, he might still be able to hear us. So we're going to go in there and tell him how much we love him."

Dev nodded solemnly. "Why isn't Mira coming in with us?"

"Your sister is … taking it quite hard," she said. "But that's okay. She doesn't need to go in and see him if she doesn't want to. And neither do you, if it's too hard for you. Okay?"

He nodded. "I want to see him," he said. Even though his mom said his dad wouldn't die, he had a feeling that this might be his last opportunity to see his dad, and he couldn't let that opportunity pass.

"Okay, buddy. We'll go in together." She reached out and took hold of his hand, and they walked into the room together, side by side.

Rajeev Sundaram lay in the hospital bed looking oddly peaceful, considering the trauma he had been through. But his right cheek was badly bruised, and his forehead bore a nasty gash from the crash; the doctors had stitched it up, but Dev found it gruesome nevertheless.

His mom sidled up next to the bed and ran her fingers through Rajeev's hair, as if she were confirming that the sight before her was real and not some ethereal apparition out of a nightmare. She choked back a sob.

"Hi Rajeev," she said. "I don't know if you can hear me, but if you can, it's me, Sarah." She reached out to hold his hand, and gave it a firm squeeze. "I'm here with Dev."

She motioned for him to come near. He hesitated, but then shook his head, deciding to be brave. He marched up to the bed, and looked up at his father.

"Um, hi dad," he said. He looked up at his mother with pleading eyes, uncertain of what to say next.

"Just tell him you love him," she said.

He nodded, then turned back to his father. "I love you, dad," he said. He almost left it at that, but then he continued: "I'm really sorry this happened to you. But you're going to get better. I know you will!" Tears formed in his eyes as he spoke.

His mother placed a hand on his shoulder. "Very good," she said.

They stood silently by his bed for another moment. Finally, Sarah placed a hand on Dev's shoulder and ushered him out of the room.

A young man in blue scrubs was waiting for her when they walked out. "Mrs. Sundaram?"

"Yes."

"Hi. I'm Dr. Williams. May I speak to you for a moment?"

"Of course."

He glanced down at Dev. "Best if we can speak alone," he said.

Sarah nodded. She placed a hand on Dev's shoulder and pointed toward a chair a little way down the hall.

"Why don't you go have a seat, sweetie. I'll come get you in a minute."

Dev didn't want to go; he wanted to hear what the doctor was about to tell his mom. But he knew if he resisted, his mother would become upset. So he gave his mother a nod, slunk away and sat down obediently.

His mother and the doctor spoke in hushed tones. Dev strained his ears to hear what they were saying, but to no avail. He wrung his hands nervously. What if the doctor was delivering bad news? Why would his mom have sent him away unless that was the case?

The doctor placed a hand on Sarah's shoulder, then turned and walked away. She stood still for a moment, like a dazed statue, and then made her way over to Dev.

"Let's go, Dev."

Dev furrowed his brow. "Go? Go where?"

"Home."

"But ... but dad ..."

"He has good people taking care of him here. He'll be fine. But you and I need to get some rest in our own beds."

Dev reluctantly acquiesced, and they walked hand in hand back to the car. She got Dev buckled into the backseat, then got behind the wheel and started their journey back home, driving in silence.

"What did the doctor say?" Dev asked.

Sarah didn't answer at first, and Dev wondered if perhaps his mom hadn't heard him. "Mom?"

She released a deep sigh. "Dev, the situation is not good. The doctor said … the doctor said your dad might never wake up."

His mind instantly conjured the word he had always associated with never waking up: Death. But then he remembered his mom's earlier explanation that there was another kind of eternal sleep, called a coma, and he intuited that she was speaking of the latter.

He knew his mom was upset, and he wanted desperately to be brave for her, but he couldn't help the tears that formed in his eyes. "Isn't … isn't there anything we can do?" he asked, his words coming out jaggedly as he attempted to suppress the sobs bubbling just beneath the surface.

"We can pray," she said.

She picked him up and hugged him tight, and although his mother's embrace brought him comfort, her words did not. Dev didn't put much stock in prayer; he had prayed with all his might last summer that his tee-ball team would win the last game of the year, but it hadn't worked; they'd still lost. He wouldn't rely on a system with such a dismal track record when it came to his father's fate.

No, Dev decided right then and there that if neither the doctors nor God were capable of bringing his father back to him, he would have to do it himself. He recognized that it would be an unimaginably daunting task, but he was young; he had the better part of a lifetime to make it happen. But he'd have to start acquiring the necessary knowledge right away.

His dad's life depended on it.

THREE

"Come on, Dev."

"I'm coming, I'm coming."

Dev glanced at himself in the mirror and straightened his tie one last time before turning and walking out of the bathroom. Mira and his mom were standing by the door, waiting for him.

"Hurry up," Mira said. "We're late."

Sarah placed a hand on her daughter's shoulder. "It's okay, sweetheart. He just wants to look good for dad."

Seven years had passed since Rajeev's accident. Every year, on the anniversary of the night that had changed their lives forever, the family visited Rajeev in the hospital to pay homage to their fallen patriarch.

On the drive to the hospital, Dev reflected on those past seven years. The entire family had made sacrifices—most notably selling the house last year to pay for the cost of Rajeev's medical care. Not everyone in their extended family agreed with that decision; in particular, Dev's aunt—his mom's sister—was vocal in expressing her view that the time had long since come to "pull the plug." But none of them could bring themselves to do it; they all held out hope that their dad would come back to them someday.

Every year, in the months leading to the anniversary of his dad's accident, Dev's hopes remained high that he'd manage to find some way to "cure" his father, to snap him out of the coma that had trapped him within his own mind. But every year he came up short.

He was changing his strategy, however, and he had high hopes that it would be more fruitful than his previous efforts.

He'd initially studied human biology, thinking he would be able to conjure some method of curing comas that the broader medical community hadn't already looked into—a notion that was, he had to admit, patently absurd.

But in one of his computer programming classes, the discussion had turned to machine learning, and that notion had gotten his wheels turning. True, Dev was only seventeen, and it was unlikely that he could bring his dad back on his own. But if he could employ the power of machine learning, he wouldn't have to do it alone; computer programs could help him do it.

His class hadn't actually gone into any detail on how machine learning worked, but he'd been researching it online in his spare time, and he'd begun thinking about how it could be used to help his dad. His current idea was to create a machine learning algorithm that he could feed a large amount of medical information. The program, in theory, would be able to sift through the data far faster than a human being could, and might be able to find connections that suggested new treatment options for a variety of different medical conditions ... including comas.

His thoughts were interrupted by the sight of the hospital as his mother drove the car into the parking lot. They exited the car and made their way through the brightly-lit, white hallways that had become so familiar to them throughout the course of their visits. Finally, they came to Rajeev's room.

They gathered around the hospital bed. Over the years, Rajeev had taken on a sallow complexion. He had lost considerable weight, and his eyes seemed deeply set into cavernous sockets. But Dev didn't register the change in his father's appearance. For one thing, the change had taken place so gradually that he'd gotten used to it over the years. But also, he just looked to him like his dad, and no amount of physical transformation could stop him from seeing Rajeev as such.

"Hi Rajeev," Sarah said. They always spoke under the assumption that Rajeev could hear them and understand their words, even if it was just at a subconscious level. "I'm here with Mira and Dev. It's been seven years since your accident. Can you believe it?"

He didn't answer, of course. Sarah reached out to hold his hand. She smiled as she looked into his closed eyes. It was a smile Dev had become quite familiar with over the years, conveying both a deep love and an unyielding sadness.

"Hi dad," Mira said. "I miss you a lot. I love you."

"I love you too, dad," Dev said.

He and his sister took turns talking to their dad, telling him about what they were studying in school, funny things their friends had said, and even relating particularly funny scenes from TV shows they'd recently seen. Before they knew it, several hours had passed.

"I think it's time we start thinking of heading back," Sarah said. "Is there anything else either of you want to say to your father?"

Dev had said all he'd wanted to say, but there was no harm in repeating one thing he'd already said: "I love you, dad."

Mira turned to her father and echoed her brother's words: "Love you, dad."

As they walked back to the car, their moods turned solemn. It was always a somewhat sad affair when they visited Rajeev. Seeing the man they loved wasting away in a hospital bed instead of living the full life he should have been experiencing with them was painful.

As they piled into the car, Sarah turned to the kids, her face grave. "There's something I need to talk to you two about," she said.

Neither Dev nor his sister said a word. They just stared back at their mother, indicating that they were listening to whatever she needed to say.

"It's been seven years," she said. "Your dad hasn't gotten any better. I've been thinking a lot about our future, particularly for the two of you. We're spending a lot of money keeping your dad alive for a life that isn't really worth living, and I can't help but wonder if it would be better to—"

Dev cut her off before she could finish. "I can't believe what I'm hearing. Mom, we're *going to get him back*. We are! We can't give up and abandon him!"

"I know this is hard to hear, Dev. But according to the doctors, the chances of your father actually coming out of his coma are not good."

"Fuck the doctors," Dev said. "*I'll* figure out a way to get him back to us! I've been working on it for years!"

"Watch your language, shitstain," Mira said.

"Stop it!" Sarah shouted. Her voice was filled mostly with exasperation, but it contained a hint of anguish. "Forget I said anything."

They rode the rest of the way home in silence. But it was a formative moment for Dev. He realized that his mother's commitment to his dad was beginning to wane, and it was only a matter of time until she gave up on him. That realization merely strengthened his resolve. He would have to redouble his efforts to save his dad because, apparently, time was running out.

FOUR

Dev straightened his tie. "How do I look?"

Charlie Garcia, who was in the middle of straightening his own tie, glanced over at Dev and nodded approvingly. "You look good, bro. We're gonna kill it in there."

"I hope so," Dev said. "We need this investment, or we're sunk."

They finished dressing, and left their hotel room. It was the nicest hotel either of them had ever stayed in. The venture capital firm had flown them both out to New York and put them up in five-star accommodations. Dev just hoped they'd find the presentation he and Charlie were about to give worth the expense.

Once they were outside, they hailed a cab and directed it to the towering office building that housed Bostrom Capital Partners. They took the elevator to the top floor, and it opened to a marble reception desk staffed by a cheerful young woman who couldn't have been a day over twenty.

"Hello there!" she chirped as they stepped out of the elevator. "How can I help you two today?"

"Hi," Dev said. "We, uh … we have a two o'clock appointment with Mr. Bostrom."

"Ah! Misters Sundaram and Garcia, I take it?"

Dev nodded and flashed her a smile. "Yes, that's us."

She gestured toward a waiting area that sat just to the right of her desk. "Please have a seat. I'll let Mr. Bostrom know you're here. Can I get you anything while you wait? Water? Coffee?"

"I'm fine, thanks," Dev said. He turned to Charlie.

"I'll have a coffee if it's not too much trouble," Charlie said.

"Not at all," she said. "Cream? Sugar?"

"Just a little bit of sugar. Thank you."

She nodded. "Sit tight."

As they sat down across from each other, Dev leaned over and whispered to Charlie. "Are you sure you should have asked for coffee? What if they think you were too imposing."

"Well she *asked*," Charlie replied, a hint of panic in his voice.

Dev waved his hand dismissively. "I'm sure it's fine."

The receptionist returned a moment later with a cup of coffee in a plain, white paper cup. She handed it to Charlie and smiled. "I'll let you two know when Mr. Bostrom is ready for you," she said.

"Thank you," Dev said.

She left them to themselves. They shot each other nervous glances and tried not to fidget too much. They needed to portray confidence from the moment Bostrom laid eyes on them.

Finally, after several minutes, the receptionist returned and beckoned for them to follow her. "Mr. Bostrom is ready for you," she said. "I'll take you to his office."

They dutifully followed her down the hall until she stopped in front of a corner office. The door was cracked open, and Bostrom was seated behind a wide, oak desk. He was a large man, in his mid-forties. He was bald by choice (rather than balding), and he wore a slim-fitting Navy blue suit, a ruby red tie, and gold cufflinks that belied his status at the firm. He was reading something on his computer, but looked up as the receptionist arrived at his door.

She turned and looked at them before leaving. "Good luck," she whispered with a smile.

Bostrom rose from his seat and walked up to greet the two young programmers. "Hello there. You must be Dev," he said, reaching out a hand to Dev, "and Charlie," he added, and reached out his hand to Charlie. "Pleased to meet you both. Please, take a seat."

They each took a seat in chairs facing Bostrom's desk as he walked back and retook his seat.

"I'm excited to hear more about this company of yours," Bostrom said. "What's it called again—Next Time something-or-other?"

"Next Level Technologies," Dev said eagerly.

"Right," Bostrom said. "So you guys are making robots or something?"

"That's part of it," Charlie said. He turned to Dev to explain further.

"What we've done is create a software program that maps the human consciousness and digitizes it," Dev said. "It's a form of immortality. People can live forever through their digital copies."

"Right—but who wants to live in a computer?" Charlie added quickly. "That's where the robots come in. People will be able to download their consciousness into a robotic body. That way they can go on living in the real world, but in a body that will never break down. Or, if it does, it can easily be replaced."

"And these bodies will be completely customizable," Dev said. "People will be able to instantly download themselves into the chiseled body that used to only be achievable by slaving away for hours at the gym. Or people could play around with bodies of different genders. The possibilities are limited only by the human imagination."

Bostrom smiled. "I'm intrigued," he said.

Dev and Charlie looked at each other, unable to contain their excitement.

"You are?" Charlie asked excitedly.

Bostrom nodded. "I am," he said. "But tell me—why would people choose a robotic body when they can opt for flesh and blood instead?"

Dev raised a perplexed brow. "I'm not sure I understand what you mean, sir."

Bostrom looked surprised. "You mean you haven't heard of Fresh Meat?" When Dev and Charlie looked at each other, mouths agape, speechless, Bostrom continued. "Gregory Maltek? Haven't you two been scoping out the competition?"

"Well, we uh …" Dev started.

"It's a nascent technology," Charlie said. "We … we didn't think we had any competitors."

There was an awkward silence. Bostrom didn't say a word at first. He grabbed a notepad off his desk and took a moment to write on it. Then he ripped off the sheet on which he'd written, and slid it across the desk.

"That's the phone number for one Gregory Maltek," Bostrom said as Dev picked up the piece of paper. "He's the CEO of Fresh Meat, Inc. I suggest you two get in touch with him, because he's working on something that sounds very similar to what you two are working on. Perhaps, rather than duplicate your efforts, it would be better if you worked together. Who knows what you could accomplish if you collaborate?"

"We'll do that," Charlie said. "But in the meantime, did you want to discuss a possible investment, or …?"

"Meet with Maltek," Bostrom said. "Once you've done that, we can regroup and see if an investment is in the cards. Fair enough?"

Dev and Charlie nodded dutifully. Bostrom stood and led them to the door. After exchanging handshakes, they found themselves walking down the hall and out of the office, dejected that they had not secured an investment, but curious about Fresh Meat, the company that, unbeknownst to them, was their biggest competitor.

FIVE

"WHAT THE HELL HAPPENED IN THERE?" CHARLIE asked.

He and Dev were sitting in his 2010 Prius in Bostrom Capital Partners' parking lot. They'd walked all the way out to the car in silence.

"It's a setback," Dev said. "But not an insurmountable one."

"Who the hell is this Gregory Maltek guy he was talking about?" Charlie asked.

"Our biggest competitor, apparently." Dev unlocked his phone screen and began typing into the search bar. "I guess we'd better do better research."

"Way ahead of you," Charlie said. Apparently he'd already gotten on his phone without Dev's noticing. "Here's an article I found."

Charlie read the article aloud. Apparently Maltek had already started and sold three companies before he'd turned twenty-one. He'd used the proceeds to start his most recent company, Fresh Meat. The company was based on merely the premise of a potential product: Empty bodies that people could download their minds into. It promised to be a cure to disease, aging, and even ugliness, all in one fell swoop. It was a risky business investment, because the technology didn't even exist yet, but the high risk meant there was potential for an extraordinarily high reward, and it seemed like Maltek was attracting enough investors to enact his vision.

Truth be told, Dev and Charlie were in the same boat. They didn't have a product yet, just an idea. But Dev thought theirs was an infinitely more practical approach to solving the same problems Fresh Meat was trying to solve. The problem was that neither he, nor Charlie, were natural salesmen. They had no idea how to seduce investors in the way Maltek was apparently so adept.

"Maybe we need to bring someone else on board," Dev said. "Someone who can 'wow' investors. Someone with some showmanship. Because you and I both know that while we have brains in abundance, we are severely lacking in pizazz."

Charlie shook his head. "We can't hire anyone," he said. "We don't have any money."

"No," Dev said, his voice measured and cautious, "we can't offer them money. But we could offer them something else. We could offer them a stake in the company."

Charlie's eyes narrowed. "How big of a stake?"

Dev shrugged. "I don't know. Whatever would persuade someone with the right skills to come on board."

Charlie shook his head. "I don't know, man. I don't think we should just be giving out equity in the company like it's candy."

"I'm not suggesting we give it away flippantly," Dev said. "But I think this is a necessity for our success. If we can't find investors, this thing will be dead in the water before it ever gets started. I'd rather have a smaller share of a big pie than a large share of a pie that's burned to a crisp in the oven."

Charlie ran his fingers through his hair. "I don't know, man. I'm just not really comfortable with that."

Dev let out a long sigh. He bit his tongue, delaying his

response until he thought about how to respond. He thought Charlie was being ridiculous. What did he think would happen if they didn't find investors? They'd never be able to get the company off the ground and they'd have nothing to show for all the effort they'd already put in. There was no way he was going to let Charlie jeopardise everything they'd worked so hard for.

"Listen," he said. "Why don't we sleep on it? If you can think of some other way to get investors on board, I'm all ears. But failing that, I think you're going to have to make peace with the fact that we might have to bring someone new on board, even if that means giving up some equity."

Charlie didn't speak right away; it was his turn to bite his tongue. When he spoke, his face was expressionless and his tone was flat. "Fine. We'll talk about it in the morning."

Dev was concerned by Charlie's tone, but he considered his partner's acquiescence a victory. Both of them could benefit from a good night's rest before discussing the matter further.

"I think that's a good idea," Dev said.

"Yeah," Charlie said. He started up his car and rolled out of the parking lot. They drove in silence, neither of them daring to speak first. The tension between them was palpable, and it was not typical of their relationship. Dev couldn't wait to get home.

Finally, Charlie pulled up to Dev's apartment complex. He pulled alongside the entrance and Dev jumped out of the car.

Before closing the door all the way, he popped his head back inside. "Thanks," he said. "We'll talk more tomorrow."

Charlie shrugged. "Okay."

Dev closed the door and headed for his apartment, feeling slightly unsettled tand yet, somewhat hopeful. Charlie was skeptical; Dev couldn't quite see things from Charlie's point of view, but that was okay. He was confident he'd come around in the end, because if he didn't … there wouldn't be a company for the two of them to argue over anymore.

SIX

Dev opened his phone the next morning and shot off a text to Charlie asking if he wanted to continue their conversation about bringing on a salesman over breakfast. Hours passed without a response and Dev grew concerned that Charlie was ignoring him on purpose.

Finally, however, Charlie replied with one word: "Lunch?"

Dev smiled. He should have known; Charlie wasn't really a morning person.

"Sure," he wrote back. "When and where?"

Charlie suggested they meet at a little cafe near his house. Dev told him that sounded good, and when he walked into the cafe he found Charlie already seated at a table a couple booths down from the entrance.

"Hey," Dev said as he slid into the booth across from Charlie.

"Hey," Charlie said as he brought a mug of steaming black coffee to his lips.

"So have you given any more thought to what we talked about yesterday?"

Charlie paused a moment, holding his mug in both hands.

He looked out the window, stalling for time before answering. The waitress stopped by, and Dev ordered a cup of coffee; the waitress, who had already been holding a pot of coffee, simply turned one of the upside down mugs on the table rightside up and poured it full.

After a minute, Charlie finally perked up and looked Dev in the eye.

"Yes," he said finally. "I thought about it."

"And?"

Charlie released a deep sigh. "I'm still not crazy about the idea," he said. "Giving up equity is a big deal to me."

Dev didn't react outwardly, but internally, he groaned. Charlie was being a fool; he was going to ruin their chances of ever successfully launching the company.

But Charlie wasn't done speaking.

"Begrudgingly, though, I have to admit you're right," he said. "The company won't be worth anything if we can't get it off the ground. So I'm open to bringing someone else on board, even if it means giving up some equity. But I insist on having veto power, and if I think they're asking for too much, I reserve the right to refuse to bring them on."

Dev couldn't suppress the grin that grew across his face.

"Thank you, Charlie," he said. "I know that couldn't have been an easy decision for you to make. But I agree that it was the correct one."

"Perhaps," Charlie said. "We'll see. Anyway, do you have someone in mind?"

Dev shook his head. "I was planning to post the opening on a job board, and see what kind of applicants we get."

Charlie took a long sip of coffee. "We'll see what we get," he said as he lowered the mug back to the table.

Dev nodded. "Yes we will."

* * *

When the application came in for Nathan Granger, Dev was certain it was their man. He had an extensive background in sales, including for leading tech companies. If the decision had been up to Dev alone, he would have hired him on the spot.

It wasn't just up to him, though. Charlie had to be in on the decision. They'd already interviewed a handful of applicants together and Charlie had vetoed them all for various reasons. Granted, Dev had only been enthusiastic about one or two of them—but not as enthusiastic as he was about Nathan.

Thankfully, Nathan seemed enthusiastic as well. He'd agreed to come in for an interview and he'd impressed from the start, dressed in an immaculate black suit, his hair perfectly combed, his bright white teeth veritably glowing through his wide smile. Even Charlie seemed charmed. But once they'd all taken a seat in the conference room, the atmosphere grew serious as Dev and Charlie posed the questions they hoped would reveal whether Nathan was the best person for the job.

"The potential applications for our product are practically limitless," Dev said. "That means you may be selling to clients in a wide variety of different industries, and may have to adjust your approach accordingly. Are you up to the task?"

Nathan didn't hesitate for an instant. He nodded and flashed an almost cocky smile. "Absolutely," he said. "As you can see from my resume, I've worked in sales for many different industries. I've had to reinvent my approach with each new job. This won't be much different—in fact, it may even be easier since the product will remain the same."

Dev nodded, clearly pleased by Nathan's answer. But Charlie shook his head subtly, still unconvinced that Nathan was worth giving up equity in the company.

"Can you give us an example of how you've had to adjust your sales technique in the past?" he asked.

Nathan brought his hand to his chin as he pondered the

question. "Well," he said after contemplating it a bit, "when I was selling software subscriptions to businesses, I had to think like an institution and approach it from the point of view of a large corporation. On the other hand, early in my career, I sold magazine subscriptions door-to-door. As I'm sure you can imagine, that requires a much more personal approach. It was particularly challenging considering that print was in its death throes at the time."

"And what was your level of success?" Charlie asked.

Nathan beamed. "I was the top earner the entire time I was there," he said. "I bought a brand-new car in cash with the incentives and commissions."

His answers seemed to allay Charlie's concerns somewhat, although he did not seem completely convinced Nathan was the right person for the job. The rest of the interview continued along the same trajectory, with Dev seeming far more enthusiastic about the candidate than Charlie was.

"Well, thank you for coming in," Dev said, standing and holding out his hand. "Charlie and I will talk things over and we'll be in touch."

Nathan shook Dev's hand, then turned to Charlie and shook his as well. "Sounds good," he said. "It was a pleasure speaking with both of you."

Once Nathan was safely out of earshot, Dev turned to his companion. "Well?"

"He's okay," Charlie said.

"I think he's our man."

"What makes you so sure?"

"I like his resume, and I think he handled himself well during the interview."

"We're trying to build a world-class company here," Charlie said. "Do you really think he's a world-class candidate?"

"World class? Perhaps not. But we're *not* a world-class

company yet, and I think if we expect to grow into one, it's reasonable to expect our employees to grow with us."

"I'd like a little more reassurance if we're expected to give this guy some of our equity."

"Let's see if he'd be amenable to a three-month trial period. We can offer him commission-based compensation during that time, and then make him a long-term offer if we're satisfied by his performance."

Charlie nodded unenthusiastically. "Okay. I guess I can get behind that. Let's see how he does."

SEVEN

"What the hell, Dev?"

Dev Sundaram looked up from his computer as an irate Charlie entered his office. His business partner's eyes were practically bulging out of their sockets.

"What's going on?" Dev asked, genuinely confused about the source of Charlie's anger.

"What's this I hear about Nathan signing a contract with the Department of Defense?"

Dev couldn't help but smile. "I'm not sure why you'd be angry about that," he said. "It's great news. Five-hundred million dollars!"

"I don't give a shit how much it's for," Charlie spat. "It's blood money."

Dev's face fell. "Charlie, sit down," he said. "Let's talk about it."

"There's nothing to talk about. We're not doing business with the Department of Defense. We're not feeding the war machine."

"Charlie, it's *five-hundred million dollars!*"

"I don't care if it's five-hundred billion. I wasn't consulted about this in advance; if I had been, I would have expressed my objections then. I refuse to contribute to the military-industrial complex."

"It's not like we'd be building bombs, for goodness' sake! Our technology could actually *save* lives during wars. I don't think you've thought this through, Charlie."

Charlie laughed darkly. "No," he said. "It's you who haven't thought it through. All you care about is that vegetable of a father of yours, and you don't care if you have to sell your soul if that's what it takes for you to get him back."

Dev's face fell. He stood and stared Charlie down with eyes that were suddenly filled with unfathomable darkness.

"Get the hell out."

Charlie didn't budge; he stared right back. "I'm not leaving until you promise me we won't pursue this contract."

"Get the hell out!"

Charlie offered a slow nod. "Fine," he said. "You and Nathan can buy me out. I won't play any part in this. I won't have blood on my hands." He turned and stormed out of the room.

Dev sat back down. He was seething. His heart felt like it might beat out of his chest. But as he began to calm down, he started to doubt himself. Did Charlie have a point? Was he selling his soul, and the soul of the company, by allowing this deal with the U.S. military to proceed?

He didn't think so. Charlie hadn't given him an opportunity to explain, but Dev really did believe their technology could save lives on the battlefield. If soldiers were able to use artificial bodies, nothing could kill them. That in and of itself was a step in the right direction, but Dev could already anticipate the objection: Sure, U.S. soldiers would be safe, but that would merely allow them to mow down their enemies with impunity. Dev believed that logic was flawed. If soldiers didn't have to worry about their own mortality, they could take a significant amount of abuse without resorting to deadly force in response. Their technology would save lives on *all* sides.

Still, he recognized that emotions could run high when it came to matters of war, so although he didn't agree with Charlie's take on the matter—and certainly didn't agree with his behavior—he at least sympathized with his partner to an extent.

Or, ex-partner … if Charlie's tirade was to be believed. Dev couldn't imagine that Charlie would follow through on his threat to demand to be bought out. He probably just needed time to calm down. He'd go home, sleep on it and come back into the office in the morning. They'd discuss the matter again, and cooler heads would prevail.

At least, that's what Dev hoped would happen.

There was something else about the argument that had bothered him as well, however. Charlie had accused him of sacrificing his principles for the sake of bringing back his father. Dev had bristled at the accusation; it was totally unwarranted, unfair, and ungracious.

But what if he was right? What if he was so blinded by his ambition to bring back his father that he couldn't see potential ethical problems stemming from their business?

It's exactly why he wanted Charlie to stick around. Dev didn't always agree with him, but in many ways Charlie was the conscience of the company. In an emerging industry with serious ethical questions that would inevitably spring up, they *needed* him.

But they needed Nathan, too. The company wouldn't survive without someone ruthless in their corner, going out every day and fighting for the kinds of contracts that would allow them to keep innovating and producing remarkable, cutting-edge technologies that could help countless people.

As if on cue, Dev heard a knock on his door. He looked up to find Nathan standing in the doorway.

"Have a second?" he asked.

"Sure," Dev said. "Come on in."

Nathan walked in and took a seat across from Dev. "I just wanted to make sure everything was okay," he said. "I heard you and Charlie arguing. I couldn't make anything out, but it seemed pretty heated, and he hurried off in quite a huff."

Dev sighed. "I'm not sure if everything is okay," he said. "I guess we'll find out tomorrow when we see whether or not Charlie shows up."

Nathan winced. "It's that bad?"

"Charlie was not happy about the contract with the Department of Defense."

"Ah. He's pretty antiwar, then?"

"Apparently. He and I never discussed politics much, but he made it clear to me that if we proceeded to work with the DOD, we'd essentially have blood on our hands ... in his opinion, anyway."

Nathan frowned. "You're not considering backing out of the contract, are you?"

Dev shook his head. "I'm sympathetic to Charlie's point of view, but I don't think he's fully thought it out. Supplying the military with mechanized body replacements could actually *save* lives. I'm comfortable moving forward. My conscience is clean."

Nathan nodded. "Mine too. I'm glad we're on the same page." He stood and headed for the door, but paused and turned around before leaving. "I hope Charlie comes to his senses."

Dev offered a curt nod. "Me too."

EIGHT

Dev felt alone.

Charlie had not returned to the company, and Nathan had left as well. He'd maintained his equity stake in the business, but he'd left to work for a larger, more established company. The move infuriated Dev—giving Nathan equity in the company should have warranted a certain level of loyalty, but he'd essentially spit in their face the second something better had come along.

Still, Dev felt vindicated by his decision to hire Nathan. He'd brought in a significant amount of business, and it was just what they'd needed in the company's precarious early days. Now Dev just hoped it was enough to sustain them as they grew and continued to develop their products.

He *did* have an ulterior motive, of course. As much as he told himself that starting this company was in service of the goal of improving humanity—and that *was* part of it—deep down, he knew his primary motivation was to bring his father back.

Lately, though, he'd begun to have misgivings about doing so. As much as he wanted to see his father again, the more he considered the ethics of bringing back someone who had not consented to being brought back, the less he was sure that he should go through with it, regardless of how much heartache he might cause for himself by refusing to play God.

He'd already started the process of mapping out his father's brain. The scan he'd completed at the hospital gave a partial picture of Rajeev's mind, but it had been too badly damaged from the accident to be used in one of the robotic bodies Dev was creating. He'd had to figure out a way to fill in the gaps.

He decided that machine learning was the solution to his problem. By collecting every scrap of data on his father that he could find, he could utilize machine learning to incorporate that data into the existing brain scan as efficiently and completely as possible.

So he'd done so. A complete scan of Rajeev Sundaram's brain was sitting in the servers of Next Level Technologies. Once the first android bodies were manufactured, it would be a simple matter to download it into a body and talk to his father for the first time in years. Or at least, a very, very close facsimile of his father.

His first inclination was to think that if he abandoned his father, all that work would go to waste. Surely he couldn't just delete all the data he'd acquired on his dad—it would be like losing him all over again.

He took comfort in the fact that that work could lay the groundwork for helping other people in the future, however. As Next Level Technologies' android models became available, people *would* be able to consent to such a digital resurrection. Legal paperwork establishing such consent might become as common as a standard DNR.

"Mr. Sundaram?"

Dev's thoughts were interrupted by his secretary, a young man he'd just hired, who had appeared in the doorway of his office.

"Yes?"

"There's a Gregory Maltek on the phone for you. Shall I put him through?"

Dev blinked. "Maltek?"

His secretary nodded. "Yes, Gregory Maltek. Says he's with a company called Fresh—"

"Yes, I know him," Dev said, offering a firm nod. "Go ahead and put him through."

The secretary left, and Dev's mind flew into action. Why would Gregory Maltek be calling him? Certainly he wasn't calling for a cordial chat. Fresh Meat was NLT's biggest competitor—or at least, it would be once their products were on the market.

The phone rang. Dev picked up the receiver, put it to his ear and said, with a hint of suspicion, "Hello?"

"Hello!" The voice on the other end was deep, booming, confident, and yet somehow also conveyed the lighthearted, carefree tone of a California beach bum. "Is this Dev Sundaram?"

Dev nodded reflexively, even though the gesture meant nothing over the phone. "Yes," he said. "And you're Gregory Maltek?"

"Indeed!" Dev sensed Maltek's grin, even if he couldn't see it.

"How can I help you, Mr. Maltek?"

"Please, call me Greg."

"Okay. How can I help you, Greg?"

"I've been following you and your company in the news," Maltek said. "I've been impressed by what I've read, Dev."

Dev frowned. He generally found flattery suspect, and Maltek was laying it on thick. "Thank you. I appreciate that."

"I'd like to meet you."

Dev paused before answering. "For what purpose?"

"I think we could work together. Imagine what we could

accomplish if we joined forces. Consider it an exploratory meeting. An opportunity to feel each other out."

"I don't know about that."

"Please, Dev. I'm serious about this. No pressure, no commitments. Just a meeting for now. That's all I ask."

"Give me a minute."

"Of course."

Dev set the phone receiver on his desk and leaned back in his chair. His instincts told him that meeting with Maltek was a fool's errand. He was his competitor; he should be treating Maltek like anathema.

But there was something to the idea that they'd be stronger if they joined forces. Even if he didn't like the idea, perhaps it would be the best way to take the company to the next level, to truly enact the vision Dev had for the technology he had developed.

He picked up the receiver and brought it back to his ear. "Okay," he said. "No promises. But let's meet."

Once again, Dev sensed Maltek's grin. "Excellent," he said. "I'll have my people get in touch with your people, and we'll set something up."

NINE

On the plane to San Francisco, Dev dug into
Fresh Meat, scouring the internet for any information he could
find. Maltek had insisted on flying Dev out to Fresh Meat headquarters at the company's expense. Dev was somewhat familiar
with the company, but he was ashamed to admit to himself that
he had let most of the responsibility for competitor research fall
to other people at NLT ... hence his crash course.

He was puzzled by what he'd found so far. It seemed Fresh
Meat had developed a method of cloning people and rapidly
bringing the "blank" bodies to maturity. What's more, they'd
pioneered new genetic engineering techniques that would allow
people to customize their new "avatars" with a remarkable
degree of specificity. Want to change the color of your eyes?
Your hair? Want to make your jaw more square, or your hips
wider? Want to change your gender? Fresh Meat's technology
made it all possible.

It was a different approach than the one they'd developed at
Next Level Technologies, but the outcome was essentially the
same. NLT's androids wouldn't be made of flesh and blood, but
they'd ultimately be just as customizable as anything Fresh

Meat produced—perhaps moreso, even. Once they developed silicone-based artificial skin that was indistinguishable from the real thing, it would be a simple matter to reconfigure it any way a customer wanted.

Where the two companies really overlapped was in their respective brain-duplication technologies. Based on everything Dev had read so far, it seemed like the technologies were remarkably on par with each other, which meant neither company had a clear advantage over the other in that regard. When they eventually began competing with each other, the fight would be over whether people preferred to transfer their minds to flesh bodies or robotic ones. It would come down to personal preference and good marketing.

One thing that troubled Dev was that nothing he'd read gave any details on Fresh Meat's process of transferring minds into bodies. That wasn't too surprising; it was a proprietary technology, so it made sense that the company would hold its cards close to its chest. But Dev found the vagueness troubling nonetheless. He assumed that if Fresh Meat was creating bodies … they were creating lives. And if they were then making those bodies "blank" so they could be filled with someone else's consciousness … did that mean they were then taking the lives they'd created?

Unless Dev could be assured that that was not the case, that Fresh Meat had some method of ensuring no consciousness ever developed in their blank bodies, then Dev didn't want anything to do with the company. He'd give Maltek a chance to explain things in their meeting. If he couldn't explain it to Dev's satisfaction, he wouldn't hesitate to walk away.

A car was waiting for Dev after he landed in San Francisco. Fresh Meat's headquarters was a short drive away from the airport. As the elevator carried him up to Maltek's office, he tried to calm his nerves. He was just as intelligent and capable as Maltek; why else would he have been invited to this meeting?

The elevator dinged, the doors opened, and there was Maltek, waiting for him. His dirty-blonde hair was swept to one side, and his square jaw and casual dress made him look like he should be modeling surfboards, not occupying a high-rise office building and operating one of the world's most innovative startups.

"Dev Sundaram! Welcome!" He stretched out his arms and came in for a hug. The gesture surprised Dev, who had been expecting a handshake. He threw his hands half-heartedly around Maltek.

"Thanks," Dev said as they parted. "You have a nice setup here."

Maltek nodded. "It was always my dream to make my mark on the San Francisco skyline, and now I have," he said. "Let's go to my office to talk." He turned around and with a wave of his hand beckoned Dev to follow him.

Maltek's office looked exactly as Dev would have expected for a surfer-turned executive. His desk was of a minimalist design, and instead of a chair, he used an ergonomic balance-ball. Thankfully, there was a standard office chair on the other side of the desk, which Dev gratefully sank into as Maltek balanced on his ball.

"So … Mr. Sundaram," Maltek said, stretching out his arms and placing them behind his head, "tell me more about what you're doing at Next Level Technologies."

Dev was taken aback by the brazenness of the question, especially coming from the man who represented his fiercest competition.

"I can't divulge any information that's not already public," he said. "And I'm sure you've already devoured everything that *is* available."

Maltek smiled slyly. "Indeed," he said. "And fair enough. Why don't I tell you a little bit about Fresh Meat instead?"

Dev wasn't sure where Maltek was heading, but it couldn't hurt to learn more about his competitor. "Sure."

"I started this company with a singular focus—giving people the gift of immortality." He shook his head. "Gift isn't the right word, actually. Immortality doesn't come cheap … as I'm sure you know."

"What do you mean by that?"

"Just that you're developing a similar product, so you're aware of the research and development costs that go into something like this."

Dev nodded. "That's true."

"If I'm being honest though," Maltek continued, "I think Fresh Meat's approach is the right one. Why would someone want to be put in an artificial body when they can get the real deal? I know plenty of people who wish they were in the body of a model twenty years their junior. I don't know anyone who fantasizes about being a robot."

The plan for Next Level Technologies was to eventually develop android bodies that were indistinguishable from the human body; in fact, they had a team working on it even as they spoke. But Dev didn't dare speak of those efforts. Maltek was fishing for information, and Dev wasn't going to volunteer it.

"Anyway," Maltek continued when it became evident that Dev wasn't going to give up anything juicy, "even though I'm confident that Fresh Meat would come out on top, that doesn't mean that I can't see the benefit of your technology. Think about what we could do if we teamed up. We could *augment* the human body—use your technology to make it better, stronger. Don't you think that's something worth pursuing?"

"It's an interesting idea, to be sure. But I have some questions about your business model, if you don't mind answering them."

Maltek shrugged. "Ask away."

"I have some concerns about how you create your blank

bodies. Are they born with a consciousness? Are they self aware?"

Maltek smiled slyly. "Just as there are certain aspects of your business that you're not at liberty to discuss, there are aspects of mine that I cannot divulge," he said. "Trade secrets."

"Ah." Dev offered a curt nod. "Well, I suspected as much." He stood and smoothed out the wrinkles that had formed on his pants from sitting. "Well, Greg, it's been an interesting conversation. I appreciate you flying me out here. I really do. But I don't think I can work with Fresh Meat in good conscience; certainly not without knowing much, much more about where your bodies come from."

Maltek's face fell. "There's no reason to leave so soon," he said. "Stick around, and I'll show you—"

"I'm sorry," Dev cut in sharply, "but my mind is made up. Again, thank you very much for your hospitality, but I intend to leave now. I wish you well in your future endeavors."

Darkness fell across Maltek's face, but he offered a solemn nod. "Very well," he said. "I'll have a driver meet you outside and take you to the airport."

"Thank you," Dev said, offering Maltek a nod. He turned and walked through the door, leaving Maltek alone at his desk.

TEN

DEV COULDN'T STOP THINKING ABOUT HIS TRIP TO visit Maltek. Something about the visit had left him … unsettled. But he couldn't quite put his finger on why that was.

Perhaps it was due to the fact that he'd all but had his worst suspicions about Fresh Meat confirmed. Maltek's refusal to provide Dev with the details he needed had been a tacit admission of guilt as far as he was concerned. No matter how much financial sense it might make to team up with Maltek, Dev would never enter into such an agreement unless it also made ethical sense. In this case, it didn't appear to.

Still, he realized that Fresh Meat was a formidable foe, and the meeting with Maltek had reinvigorated his resolve to compete with the rival company. He made a mental note to speak with his team and get caught up to speed on whatever information they'd collected on Fresh Meat.

If it was going to be a war, he'd need to be a general. And if they were going to win, he needed to be a well-informed general. He'd learn what he needed to learn to achieve victory.

* * *

"SON OF A BITCH!"

Dev hung up without another word. A member of his team had just informed him that Fresh Meat had poached another one of their accounts. His conception of NLT's rivalry with Fresh Meat as a war had, unfortunately, been all too apt. Not long after Dev had refused Maltek's offer to join forces, Maltek had gone on the offensive. He'd begun targeting existing NLT accounts, attempting to convince them that Fresh Meat's approach was the better of the two. Unfortunately, so far he'd succeeded just as often as he'd failed, and it was beginning to have a noticeable effect on their business. Dev had heard through the grapevine that Maltek had even been spreading salacious lies about the company, and about him personally.

He'd insisted that they not stoop to Maltek's level. They would fight, but they wouldn't fight dirty. Not everyone in the company felt the same way, however. Plenty of people on the NLT team felt they should go after Maltek just as ruthlessly as he was going after them, but Dev refused to bloody his hands for the sake of money. If the company failed, so be it.

The phone rang. His blood was still boiling, so he took a deep breath and attempted to calm himself before answering it. He picked up the receiver.

"Hello?" he asked.

"Hello, Dev. Good to hear your voice again."

Dev's pulse picked back up. The voice on the other end of the phone belonged to Maltek.

"What do you want?"

Maltek chuckled. "No need to get so testy, my friend."

"You've been slandering me and stealing our accounts," Dev said through gritted teeth. "Pardon me if I'm not exactly thrilled to hear from you."

"Now, now," Maltek said. "I know you're not exactly my biggest fan at the moment. But please hear me out. I want to negotiate a truce."

Dev blinked. "A truce?"

"Yes! A truce. This is nothing personal, Dev. I have nothing against you. I *want* to work together, not against each other. Please, let me fly you back out and let's reach some kind of agreement. I want nothing more than to collaborate."

"I have some serious questions about how you conduct your business," Dev said.

"Give me another opportunity to address those concerns," Maltek said. "I've convinced our board of directors to let me speak with far more candor than I was at liberty to discuss last time we met."

Dev hesitated. Maltek had never struck him as a particularly trustworthy man, and he was reluctant to reassess Maltek's character now. But Maltek was offering him a possible way out of his predicament. If he was being honest about opening up and explaining how Fresh Meat operated, there was a possibility it could put Dev's concerns to rest. And if the two companies could forge some kind of alliance, he wouldn't have to worry about the fate of his company. In fact, it might even strengthen NLT's position.

"I'll hear you out," Dev said. "I'm not making any promises, though. And you're going to have to really lay out how you do things, in explicit detail."

"Of course," Maltek said. "Why else would I go to the trouble of getting the approval of the board? I'm an open book."

"I'm glad to hear that."

"I'm sure you are. I'll have someone send over the flight details. I'll see you soon, Dev. I think this is going to be a life-changing meeting for both of us."

ELEVEN

As the elevator rose to the top of Fresh Meat's headquarters, Dev had a flash of déjà vu. Things weren't exactly the same, however; for instance, he'd insisted on bringing a member of NTL's security team with him, just in case things between he and Maltek grew heated.

Once again, Maltek was waiting for him on the other side of the elevator.

"Nice to see you again," he said.

"Same to you," Dev said, not completely convincingly. "How are you doing, Gregory?"

"Quite well. Shall we discuss a ceasefire in my office?"

"Absolutely. Sounds like a plan." He followed Maltek back to the office, but as he and his security detail were about to enter, Maltek turned around to face them. "I'd prefer it if we could speak man-to-man," he said. "Would you mind having your security wait outside?"

Dev hesitated, but he figured his guy could always bust down the door if things with Maltek got too heated. "Wait here," he said. "I'll holler if I need you." He stepped through the doorway and Maltek closed the door behind him.

"Let's start with you explaining whether your blank bodies are conscious," Dev said. "I'd like it if you could—"

He felt a slight pinch at the base of his neck. He looked up to see Maltek holding a syringe that he had just withdrawn from Dev's person. Before Dev could ask what was going on, the world fell out from under him and he descended into blackness.

* * *

He awoke in a small, sparsely furnished room. He sat up in bed and noticed that, in fact, the bed was the *only* furnishing in the room.

His head was pounding. He put his hand to his forehead. "What the hell …?" His mind was foggy, but he strained to remember what had happened before he'd woken up in this room. The last thing he remembered was stepping into Maltek's office and …

Maltek. He must be behind this, Dev thought. Whatever "this" was.

He appeared to be in some kind of dormitory. The room was barely larger than the bed upon which he was sitting. There was a door on the wall facing him, however. He stood and grasped the knob, but it didn't turn; it was locked. That didn't surprise him. He walked back to the bed and sat down, perplexed and frustrated.

Had Maltek kidnapped him? He couldn't fathom why he would do such a thing. It didn't make any sense; everyone at NLT knew where Dev had gone. When he failed to return to the company, they would inevitably call the police and Maltek would be found out soon enough. He didn't understand what the end game was supposed to be.

Well, he thought, *it doesn't seem like there's anything I can do now but wait.* He lay down on his back and placed his arms behind his head.

He lost track of time. The ceiling became a blank canvas on which he projected all the fears he'd been flooded with since awakening in this bare room. He became drowsy, and he was just about to fall asleep when the door suddenly burst open.

He jolted upright, startled. A man who looked to be in his early twenties appeared in the doorway.

"Hi!" Dev exclaimed. "Can you tell me what's going on? Why am I in here? Is Maltek keeping me here?"

The young man failed to respond. Instead, he dragged a cart into the room, then locked the door behind him, leaving Dev befuddled.

"Hello?" he asked. "Can you hear me? Hello?"

The man ignored him. Without saying a word, he gestured for Dev to get off the bed. When he did so, the man pulled the covers off and loaded them onto the cart. He then retrieved fresh linens and began making the bed before Dev's eyes. When he was done, he left a tablet computer on the bed and left without a word. *What in the hell is going on?*

Dev took a seat on the bed and picked up the tablet. It seemed like a standard consumer tablet, pre-loaded mostly with entertainment apps for reading ebooks, watching movies, playing games, and that kind of thing. He opened the web browser, thinking that perhaps he could use it to communicate to someone that he was being held prisoner but, unsurprisingly, the tablet wasn't connected to the internet.

He sighed and placed the tablet back on the bed. His thoughts began to race with thoughts about his current predicament, and he felt overwhelmed. He looked down at the tablet again. It couldn't hurt to distract himself for a while, since there was nothing he could do about the situation. He opened a video app and played a movie. It was a comedy; he hoped laughter would keep him from having a full-blown panic attack.

TWELVE

Weeks passed. Maybe months; Dev had lost all track of time. It hadn't taken long for it to become clear that he was a prisoner. It was also clear who was responsible for his imprisonment: Gregory Maltek. It was a bit less clear *why* Maltek had done this, but Dev assumed he must have figured that taking out the head of NLT would benefit Fresh Meat. But Dev had hired some brilliant people to work for him, and he had no doubt that NLT could continue relatively unfazed even if he was no longer at the helm.

What Dev had a difficult time understanding was why no one had rescued him yet. Surely his absence had not gone unnoticed, and it was no secret that he'd gone to Fresh Meat's headquarters to meet with Maltek. That should have made Maltek the number one suspect in his disappearance.

Perhaps this prison was in a remote location with no direct ties to Maltek, making it difficult for investigators to find him. In fact, the more Dev considered this possibility, the more certain he became that it was true. Maltek was no idiot, and if he wanted to hold Dev against his will without any outside interference, there was little doubt he would have taken any precautions necessary to remain undetected.

Regardless of why he was still imprisoned, Dev was worried for his sanity. He had gone a long time with barely any human contact, save for the mute orderly who came in to give him food, change his bedding, replace his tablet with a freshly charged one, and change out the portable toilet that sat in the corner of the room. He had never considered himself to be a particularly sociable person, but he craved human contact in a way he had never before experienced.

The door opened, and Dev expected to see the orderly. In a twisted way, he had begun to consider the orderly to be the closest thing he had to a friend, and he looked forward to his visits, even if he never did say a word or acknowledge Dev in any way.

It was not the orderly that walked through the door, however. It took Dev a minute to comprehend what he was seeing. He blinked more than a few times, but it did nothing to change the uncanny sight before him.

Standing in the doorway was his doppelgänger. It was almost like looking into a mirror, except the figure standing before him was dressed professionally, in slacks and a blue button-down shirt with a yellow tie, whereas he was dressed casually in sweats and a plain blue T-shirt.

"Who the hell are you?" Dev asked. Even as he uttered the words, he found himself questioning his own sanity. He was clearly seeing things. There was no other explanation for what he was seeing. He must have had a severe break from reality.

His doppelgänger smirked. "I'm you," it said. "But you already knew that."

"That's impossible," Dev said.

"Nothing is impossible if you put your mind to it."

"What is this?"

Dev's twin continued to smirk. "I think you know. Take a moment to think it through if you need to."

Dev was about to object that he truly had no idea, but then, in an instant, it hit him. This is what Fresh Meat did … it cloned people, and uploaded the originals' consciousnesses into the new bodies. Somehow Fresh Meat had gotten a hold of his DNA and made a copy of him. The question was, whose consciousness was occupying the clone's body?

"You're Maltek … aren't you?"

"Ding ding ding! I always knew you were a smart cookie, Dev."

"Why are you doing all this?"

"I just said you were smart. Don't make me eat my words."

"I know you want to take out my company because it's your biggest competitor," Dev said. "But I don't get why you would go to these elaborate lengths."

"You're part way there, but you misunderstand my motivation," Maltek said. "I didn't want to take NLT out; I wanted it for myself. I tried to get you to go along with my plans voluntarily, but you weren't having it. Taking you out—that is, killing you—wasn't a viable option. The company would have continued on without you, and remained a viable competitor. But by *replacing* you, I could take control without any of your employees being any the wiser."

"You're an asshole."

"Now, now. No need for name-calling."

Dev was seething. This was so much worse than what he had imagined. The betrayal he felt knowing all his friends and colleagues were cavorting with an imposter was visceral. He had never been so consumed with rage. "I'll kill you," he said through gritted teeth.

"I have no doubt you would if you could … but let's be honest; you can't. So instead, why don't you shut up and listen?" The smirk disappeared, and his face was suddenly marked by anger. "The passwords. Give them to me."

Dev blinked, blindsided by the sudden change in topic. "What are you talking about?"

"You know damn well what I'm talking about. The Hub. Give me the passwords I need to get into it."

"Why would I ever give you those?"

"Because you won't like what will happen if you don't."

"Try me."

Maltek stepped forward and bent down until his face was mere inches from Dev's. It was a surreal experience, seeing his own eyes stare into him, seething with rage. Suddenly, he was overwhelmed with pain; Maltek had punched him in the face.

He fell backward and brought his hand to his face, cradling it. Before he could get up, Maltek was on top of him, striking him again and again and again. Finally, he stood as Dev stayed curled up on the floor, writhing in pain.

"Give me the passwords."

It took Dev a moment to recover from the blows. When he was finally able to speak, his voice was weak. "No."

"Wrong answer." Maltek delivered another blow to the side of his head. "I can keep this up all night!" He hit him again.

Dev wasn't sure he could take another hit. In a fit of desperation, he cried out, "Okay! Stop! I'll give you the passwords."

Maltek took a step back, as if giving Dev space to breathe. "What are they?"

Dev told him. When he'd finished reciting them, he hung his head in shame. If Maltek accessed the Hub, there was no telling what he might do with the information it contained.

"I'll give these a try," Maltek said. "I'll need the answers to the security questions as well, but first I'll make sure the passwords you gave me are valid." He turned to walk out the door. Without looking back, he added: "If they're not, you aren't going to like what I do to you."

THIRTEEN

There was no mirror in the room, but Dev could imagine what his face looked like, swollen and bruised. The orderly had brought in a couple ice packs and a paper cup with two tablets of what he assumed was ibuprofen, and that seemed to help the swelling somewhat.

As he sat in his bed, immobilized by pain, he had a lot of time to think. The passwords he'd given Maltek had been genuine. He'd been overwhelmed by the beating he'd received and had just wanted it to stop. Maltek would be delighted to see that the passwords worked, and would return any minute now to beat the rest of the information he needed out of Dev.

But he wouldn't give in this time. No matter what. No matter how many times Maltek struck him, and no matter how bloodied he became, he would never give up that final piece of the puzzle. There was no doubt in his mind that Maltek would do unspeakably evil things if he gained access to all the information in the Hub. It was the centralized location for all of NLT's most top-secret data. Dev had to keep Maltek out of it at any cost.

In his pain-addled state, Dev began to hope that Maltek wouldn't return at all.

Dev was beginning to think—or to hope—that perhaps Maltek wouldn't return after all. But then the door opened and instead of the familiar orderly, it was Dev's doppelgänger.

They stared at each other for a long moment. Dev's eyes narrowed to slits. Finally, Maltek's lip curled up in a slight smile. "You look like you've seen better days."

"Go fuck yourself."

"Careful what you wish for. Remember, we're one in the same … biologically speaking, anyway."

Dev crossed his arms. "I doubt you came here just to taunt me," he said. "So why don't you just get on with whatever you came here to do."

Maltek nodded. "Very well. The passwords you gave me worked. Good boy." He said the last sentence with the same lilt one would use when addressing a dog. "Now I need the answers to the security questions."

"I'm sure you do."

"You'll want to cooperate," he said. "You don't want to see what happens if you're a bad boy. You think what I did to you last time was bad? Just wait."

Dev didn't respond. He just continued to stare at Maltek with what he hoped was a defiant face.

Maltek closed the gap between them and brought his face inches from Dev's, much as he had the last time he'd visited. "Tell me what I want to know. Right now."

Dev shook his head. "No." He spat the word out more than he spoke it.

The blow came like a ton of bricks. Dev had expected it this time, but that did nothing to alleviate the pain. He collapsed onto the bed as Maltek loomed over him.

"Talk."

Dev took a deep breath and sat up. He placed a hand to his

face, as if his touch would alleviate the pain. Then he stood, so he was face to face with the monster that had stolen his face.

"Never."

Maltek delivered another blow; he had pulled back his fist this time and put all his weight into the punch. Dev went flying back, past the bed. His head hit the wall. As he flopped back onto the bed, everything faded away until all he saw was black.

FOURTEEN

Dev awoke in his bed with the mother of all headaches. He let out a long, low groan. It took a moment for him to remember the circumstances that had left him in this state. When he remembered, he jolted upright and scanned the room for Maltek, but there was no sign of him.

As he lowered himself back onto the bed, he found himself overcome by indignation. He didn't expect much from Maltek, but for him to knock Dev out cold and then just leave him there without any kind of medical attention was utterly beyond the pale. What if he'd died? Maltek would never get his precious information then.

That thought gave him an idea. Dev didn't doubt for a second that Maltek would be back for the information he still needed. But Maltek was emotional and reckless. He'd let his rage get the better of him, and he'd hurt Dev far more badly than he'd meant to.

As far as he could know, Dev had suffered a traumatic brain injury. If Dev pretended to have lost his memory, Maltek had to know there was a possibility that he really had gotten amnesia after being knocked into the wall. He might insist that Dev be looked at by a medical professional, but he wouldn't mind that; in fact, it might give him an opportunity to escape.

Even if he hadn't suffered a traumatic brain injury per se, he still *had* suffered a fairly serious blow to his head. He wondered if he'd sustained a mild concussion. There was nothing he could do about it even if he had, though. He closed his eyes and tried to get some rest while he waited for Maltek to return.

* * *

He'd fallen asleep without realizing it. The noise of the door opening and slamming shut awakened him, and he opened his eyes to see Maltek standing in front of him.

He almost forgot about his plan to feign amnesia, but he remembered just in time. "Who are you?" he asked.

Maltek hesitated. "What?"

"Who are you?" Dev repeated. "Where am I? I ... I don't remember anything."

Maltek's eyes narrowed. "Enough with the act."

"I'm sorry, but I ... wait. You ... you look just like me. Are you my evil twin or something?"

Maltek paused before speaking again. He looked like he was barely containing lethal levels of rage simmering just beneath the surface of his pysche. "Stop whatever you're doing. I need the answers to the security questions."

Dev did his best to put on a facial expression that indicated complete befuddlement. "Security questions?"

Maltek balled his hands into fists. He turned around and punched the wall, leaving a round hole where he'd hit it.

Dev's eyes widened. He would never have been able to do that kind of damage. So how could Maltek do it when he was occupying an identical body? The answer seemed obvious: Maltek had somehow genetically enhanced the cloned body to make it stronger. Dev couldn't bring up his suspicion though, because he was still pretending to have amnesia.

"I ... I'm sorry," Dev stuttered, doing his best to sound confused. "I don't know what you're talking about. I can't seem to remember much of anything."

Maltek's lips trembled, but he refrained from speaking. He appeared to be resigning himself to the fact that he wasn't going to get his way.

"Okay," he said. His voice was tight and low. "You've got amnesia. Fine. I'll leave you alone if you're not going to help me." He lowered his face to Dev's; the anger and hate shining through his eyes was unmistakable. "But if you *are* faking, let me make one thing clear: This will not stop me. I will find another way to get the information I need. So don't think you've stopped me. You've merely delayed me."

He turned around and walked out the door, slamming it behind him so forcefully that Dev was surprised it didn't knock it off the hinges.

FIFTEEN

Time began to lose all meaning.

Maltek never returned to check on Dev, but he still received daily visits from the orderly. Days stretched into weeks, weeks into month, and then Dev lost count. He fell into a deep depression. The tablet was his only way to pass the time, but it was an empty way to spend his days. He had resigned himself to the fact that he may spend the rest of his life in this prison. The only question was how long the rest of his life would be. The thought of suicide sometimes flitted into his mind before he batted it away. He couldn't bring himself to take his own life. Not yet, anyway.

He had watched dozens of movies on the tablet, but they were so fleeting that he'd grown tired of them. Instead, he'd taken to reading books—everything from *Narrative of the Life of Frederick Douglass*, to *Nineteen-Eighty Four*, to *Catcher in the Rye*.

He was reading *Catcher* for the second time when he heard a light thumping noise emanating from the door. He looked up from the tablet and was startled to see the door open to reveal an android.

It was one of the prototypes NLT had been working on

before Dev had been kidnapped. Although he recognized the origin of the robotic body standing in the doorway, he was no less befuddled by its presence.

The android had frozen upon entering the room. It stared at Dev with vacant, unblinking eyes and Dev wondered if it had malfunctioned.

"What are you doing here?" he asked.

The android paused. When it spoke, it sounded surprised.

"You're Dev Sundaram."

Dev nodded. "I am. But that doesn't answer my question."

The android peeked its head out into the hallway, then closed the door behind it once it confirmed they were alone.

"My name is Ted," it said. "I'm friends with your dad."

Dev blinked. "I think you're mistaken. My dad is dead."

"Not anymore," Ted said without missing a beat. "He's like me."

It took Dev a moment to realize what Ted was saying. His dad's consciousness had been downloaded into one of NLT's prototype android bodies. But why? Who would have—

He answered his own question almost as soon as he thought it. "Maltek," he whispered to himself. Maltek must have found Rajeev's consciousness and decided to put it in a body. But for what purpose? It seemed like a pointless exercise.

"I'm a bit confused here," Ted said. "Because someone who looks exactly like you has been out there running the company, but I suspect it's not actually you."

Dev shook his head. "No, it's not me. It's Gregory Maltek."

"How is that possible?"

"Maltek obtained my DNA somehow and used Fresh Meat's technology to clone me. Then he downloaded his own consciousness into the body, kidnapped me, and took my place."

Ted shook his head. "He's an evil genius. I mean, he's batshit insane, but he's still a genius."

"Not exactly the word I'd use to describe him," Dev said. "Anyway, can you get me out of here?"

Ted shook his head. "I wasn't planning on breaking someone out," he said. "We knew there was something in here they didn't want us to find. We just didn't know what." He shrugged. "Turns out it was a person."

"I need to get out of here," Dev said, a hint of desperation creeping into his voice.

Ted offered an encouraging nod. "I'm going to go get Rajeev and bring him back here," he said. "Then we'll figure out what to do."

Dev suddenly felt lightheaded. Ted was going to bring his dad … here? After all this time, he was finally going to see his dad again. Or at least, a version of him. It seemed unbelievable.

Part of him was concerned that if Ted left, he'd never return and that he'd lose his only chance to escape. On the other hand, he couldn't pass up the chance to see his dad again.

He nodded. "Go," he said. "Hurry back."

Ted nodded. "I will."

SIXTEEN

Dev could barely contain his anticipation as he waited for Ted to return with Rajeev. It had been fifteen years since he had last seen his father. What would he say when he saw him?

He needed to keep his expectations low. This was not actually his father he'd be meeting; it was a duplicate. And he had no idea how close that duplicate would be to the original. Most of the minds Next Level Technologies had duplicated had belonged to more or less healthy individuals. But Rajeev had been in a severe coma and suffered significant brain damage. Dev had relied on AI to fill in the blanks to produce what he'd hoped would be a more or less accurate representation of Rajeev's brain before the accident.

But would it be? Dev supposed he'd be finding out soon enough. In the meantime, he decided to try to calm his nerves by reading a book. He laid back on the bed, tablet in hand, and tried not to let the emotions swirling around inside become overwhelming.

* * *

Dev was on the verge of falling asleep when he heard hushed voices outside the door. He perked up immediately, sitting up straight and dangling his legs over the side of the bed. He set the tablet beside him.

Either Maltek was about to storm in and kill him after discovering that Ted and Rajeev had been plotting to rescue him or—he hoped—he was about to be reunited with his father for the first time in his adult life. *This is it*, he thought. His heart rate spiked. *I can't believe it's finally happening.*

The door swung open, revealing two identical androids who quickly stepped into the room. The android taking up the rear quickly scanned the room, then turned to its companion. "What's so important about this place?" it asked. "It looks like a living space. Like one of our—"

That voice. The appearance of the android was unremarkable; it looked just like any of the other prototypes NLT had produced. But the voice instantly transported Dev back to his youth, to a time when he'd been a small boy with a loving father —before tragedy had transformed the world as he knew it.

After all this time, finally, he'd heard his father's voice again.

Rajeev looked up, and Dev realized he'd caught sight of him. He sat up a bit straighter.

"Dev?"

He stood and took a step toward his father. Time seemed to slow to a crawl. On the one hand, this reunion seemed to go against nature, against God; so much so that Dev had never been able to bring himself to resurrect his father in this manner. But fate had had other plans, it seemed, and the irony was that it was Dev's mortal enemy who had inadvertently made this meeting possible.

He took a deep breath. The words he was about to speak were the first words to his father in fifteen years.

"Hi, dad."

Although Rajeev's robotic body was expressionless, Dev

sensed that his father was flabbergasted. He didn't blame him; Dev had felt much the same way when Ted had broken in and told him that his father was alive. "How is this possible?" Rajeev asked.

Dev let the corner of his lip turn up in a slight smile. The situation presented an unusual opportunity. He was no longer a boy. And when he sat his father down and explained everything, from the birth of NLT, to his kidnapping by Maltek, his father would recognize that his son was now a man—a man who had made mistakes, but who had strived to do the right thing, to advance the cause of humanity and make the world a better place. After this moment, their relationship would be fundamentally different. So much time had passed, so many milestones had been lost. But Dev couldn't help being overwhelmed with love for his father, and focusing not on what had been lost, but rather on what had been gained.

For the first time in a long time, he felt hope.

Dev beckoned his father toward the bed. "You'd better have a seat," he said. "I'll explain everything."

-End-

Thanks for reading! If you enjoyed this book, please leave a review — it lets other people know to check it out! Also, be sure to check out my website for my latest book releases: www.StevenWyble.com

ABOUT THE AUTHOR

Steven Wyble is an award-winning journalist and author residing in Washington State. He is the author of *Metacognition* and *The Transhuman Chronicles* trilogy.

For more books and updates:
www.StevenWyble.com

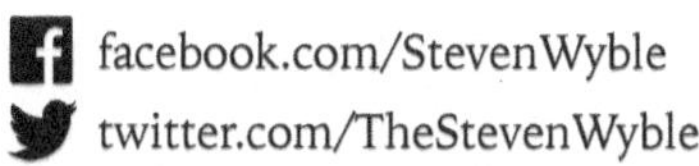

facebook.com/StevenWyble
twitter.com/TheStevenWyble

ALSO BY STEVEN WYBLE

Metacognition and Other Stories and Poems of Science, Faith and the Supernatural

The Lock (A Work-in-Progress on WattPad)

Find your next read on our website

ww.SlaughterCountyPress.com

www.ingramcontent.com/pod-product-compliance
Lightning Source LLC
Chambersburg PA
CBHW031631130726
47900CB00019B/798